Rob J. Hayes

CITY OF KINGS

by

ROB J. HAYES

*For Vicki, who must have
very broad shoulders indeed.*

Author Preface

City of Kings is the sixth book in my First Earth Saga, which started with **The Ties that Bind** trilogy, and continued with the **Best Laid Plans** duology. Though it is the sixth book, it is designed to work as a stand alone novel with no previous knowledge of the world or any of the characters or places that inhabit it.

For those readers who have already discovered my piratical series, Best Laid Plans, City of Kings takes place at roughly the same time as the latter half of **The Fifth Empire of Man**, and shows a different side of the world, and the struggles of the characters in it.

As an addition, there is an event mentioned within these pages called the Siege of Reingard. This event takes place between the prologue and the first chapter. While that little side story does not really fit within the narrative for City of Kings, I have included it at the end of the ebook version for anyone who wishes to read it. It is also available on my website. That short story is called **Pre-emptive Revenge** and was originally published by Grimdark Magazine.

You can also find a few other short stories on my website, maps of First Earth, and more information about the timeline (www.robjhayes.co.uk).

Thank you for reading,

Rob

Rob J. Hayes

PROLOGUE – 9 MONTHS AGO

Rose

It dawned on Rose that forcing a parley in a town named Shallowgrave was perhaps not the most auspicious of omens, but that was where they were. Neutral ground between her territory and whatever the blooded had left. A ghost town, devoid of life and drowning in dust. There were places just like it all over the Wilds, abandoned settlements turned to ruin. It was hard to make any sort of living out on the plains when outlaws and tax collectors took everything you owned, and then came back for more three days later.

Soldiers lined up either side of the main street. Some stood out in the open and others worked their way through buildings, setting up in windows with bows at the ready. Rose spotted men and women wearing Crucible blacks and knew at least one of the blooded lords had turned up. Niles Brekovich rarely left his impregnable city for anything. Perhaps that meant he was worried.

Betrim leaned against a signpost nearby. It had the town's name written on it, not that the Black Thorn seemed to care. Chances were he couldn't read it anyway. Still, Rose felt better having her husband nearby. They were in this situation together and up to their necks.

Rose fought the urge to check the pockets of her riding leathers for her knives. They were there, always close by in case she needed them. It was reassuring to know, even though she knew she couldn't use them. Any sort of bloodshed now and Shallowgrave would soon turn into a bloody open grave. Soldiers on both sides of the street killing each other.

Two figures appeared out of an old tavern from across the street. One was Niles Brekovich without a doubt, his waxed moustache and intense stare gave him away. Dressed in chain armour and armed with a long sword he looked every bit the warrior the stories claimed him to be. Beside him stood a tall man wearing robes the colour of bleached bone.

Rose didn't recognise him, but his yellow eyes had an unnerving quality to them.

With arrows and sharp steel on both sides of the conflict, all it would take now was a twitchy finger and the whole thing would end in bloodshed. Neither side wanted that. No one would make it out alive.

Niles Brekovich stepped off the wooden walkway outside the tavern and into the dust. He crossed into the centre of the street and waited. Rose closed the distance between them.

"What do you want, Black Thorn?" Niles Brekovich said, ignoring Rose and staring towards her husband. He didn't raise his voice but it carried all the same.

"I'm the one who summoned you here, Lord Brekovich," Rose said with a vicious smile.

"Whore!" Niles Brekovich spat the word and spared Rose only a glance before turning his attention back to Betrim. "You've carved yourself out a portion of land from those you've killed. Well done. A city under your rule and a few villages maybe, nothing of any real value. But it will take more than a couple of blooded families in the ground for you to hold onto your prize. You'll never be anything more than savage warlord without the backing of myself and the other families. So, what is it you want? A legitimate claim on the city of Chade? A title?"

Rose let out a chuckle. "He really doesn't care. The Black Thorn is only here in case he gets to put his axe in something. You're dealing with me."

Again Niles Brekovich turned a dismissive stare on Rose. "A woman's place is on her back or on her knees."

Rose bit back an insult and forced her words out through clenched teeth. She promised herself she'd use diplomacy this time. "I'm here to discuss terms of your surrender, Lord Brekovich. My armies are already larger than yours', and I now own more land than any one blooded family. Maybe you should be begging me for legitimacy."

"Be silent, woman!" Niles Brekovich hissed. "You insult me, Black Thorn. I have come here on good faith, against the advice of some, to talk terms of bringing you into a position of real power. I am prepared to offer you something you cannot gain with the swing of an axe. Now stop hiding behind your bitch and treat with me like a man."

Betrim rasped out a laugh and shook his head. Rose let out a sigh. "Lord Brekovich, my husband knows where the power lies here..."

Niles Brekovich turned furious eyes her way. "Must I teach you your place myself?"

"My place," Rose hissed, her patience snapping. "Is on a throne, ruling over the Wilds, and your blood staining the ground behind me."

Niles Brekovich scoffed. "See how quickly negotiations turn to threats when a woman is involved. This is your last chance, Black Thorn."

"Negotiations are nothing but demands with threats to back them up," Rose said, taking a step forward and fixing Niles Brekovich with a stony glare. "And here are my demands. Leave. Exile. Every member of every surviving blooded family. I'll even ship you out myself. Your regime is over. The Wilds belong to me."

The blooded lord turned his intense stare on Rose once more. "Whore! Bring whatever pitiful armies you can muster. Bring your cutthroats and sellswords. Turn coats and traitors who should know their true masters. The blooded stand united against you. We will crush you as we have so many others before. And as your husband is fitted for a noose, I will teach you your place. And then you will die with my cock in your mouth like the whore you were born to be!" With that, Niles Brekovich turned and started away.

Rose ground her teeth together, patience and frustration warring within. "This is your last chance, Lord Brekovich. I offer you exile. A peaceful way out of this. A last chance to save your family and your line. Please, don't be stupid. Take the deal I'm offering, because I won't offer it again. Walk away now and it can only end in blood."

Niles Brekovich stopped and glanced over his shoulder, but he was not looking at Rose. "What a waste. You are a coward, Black Thorn. You should have negotiated with me like a man, not sent a woman to beg for you." With that he walked away, the man in the white robe joining him.

Betrim sauntered up from behind and spat into the dust of the street. "War then, is it?"

Rose nodded. She'd known it would end this way, but she'd had to try. At least now no one could say she hadn't tried to do things differently.

Betrim sniffed and scratched at the burned side of his face. "Up ta you, love. You say march an' we do. Say kill an' we ask who. We're all behind ya. Whole Wilds is, I reckon."

Rose grinned at that and turned savage, hungry eyes on her husband.

Day 1 – The Siege

The Black Thorn

Betrim wished he had something to lean against. Always felt a lot safer with something solid against his back, less likely to find a knife there of a sudden. Unfortunately, there was never a chance of leaning on anything when sat on a horse. "Don't remember 'em lookin' so big last time we was here," he said.

"The walls? Or the cocks walkin' 'em?" Henry asked. Betrim glanced down at the little murderess with his one eye to see a sharp grin underneath the cavalier hat. He couldn't see her eyes, but he'd wager they were pretty fixed on the city in front of them.

Betrim shrugged. "Both?" It had all been a bit of a blur last time they came to Crucible. Betrim remembered chains for a certainty, rattling about his wrists and chafing the skin raw. There had also been a fair bit of unconsciousness and the matter of his execution. Now he thought about it, he couldn't remember much at all about the place - other than a brief stay in the darkness of a cell, and walls so thick and high anyone would be beyond cracked trying to assault them. And yet here he was, at the head of an army set on an assault.

He squinted towards the walls, shading his one eye with a three-fingered left hand. "What's that hangin' from the walls? Ain't what I think it is, is it?"

Henry spat and sucked at her teeth. Betrim didn't need to look at her to know the snarl she was wearing. "Bodies. A fuck load of 'em."

"Anyone we know?"

Henry snorted. "There's always someone we know, Thorn."

Betrim nodded at that and started fumbling in his saddlebags. His eye never left the bodies. He'd never been able to count much past his own dwindling digits, but Betrim guessed at hundreds and knew that was a large number. They were all hanging on long ropes, halfway down the walls. Rotting bodies wearing his colours. They were his soldiers. Men and women following the Black Thorn into war. Betrim pulled out a wineskin from his bag and held it up to the wall. "Drink to the fallen." He sucked down a mouthful of cheap wine and passed the skin to Henry.

"We'll be joining them soon." Henry finished the toast and winced at the taste of the wine before passing the skin back.

General Kurt Verit arrived - his stallion larger than most and needed to carry the giant man in his armour - and set about directing the troops and setting up the war camp far enough from the walls to be out of range of the bows. The day was long past its zenith, and it wouldn't be long before the light started fading. The Untamed Wilds were a cold grey expanse so far north even with a hot sun beating down on them, at night the place seemed even worse, almost lifeless. Nothing but rocks and shrubs and the occasional goat staring at the army as it passed. Well, that and the cries of the laughing dogs, shadowing them every step of the way. Betrim hated the north, and he hated the cold; he sourly wished the blooded bastards could have made their last stand somewhere a bit warmer.

"At least there'll be somethin' going on 'fore the lady's carriage arrives," Betrim said as he scratched at the burned side of his face. "Might put her in a better mood than usual."

Henry cackled.

"Don't you start," Betrim warned her. "Bloody woman is a nightmare in her state."

"You put her in that state," Henry said, turning her head and tilting her hat to give Thorn a mischievous stare ringed by the scars the demons had given her.

"Weren't exactly the plan at the time."

General Verit chuckled and wheeled his horse around before bellowing orders to the troops muddying up the ground behind them. The sounds made by thousands upon thousands of soldiers all plodding along and churning up the ground was never something Betrim would get used to. Even worse that the sound had been behind him for the entire journey. Something about having to lead his troops, Rose said. Still, Betrim had to admit, he preferred having twenty thousand folk at his back to spending

12

another hour in the carriage.

Betrim slid from his horse and hit the ground awkwardly. He took a good few bow-legged steps and rubbed furiously at his stones. He had never quite got the hang of horse riding.

It didn't take long for the sounds of troops marching to become the sounds of troops setting up tents and digging trenches. Lumber was unloaded from some of the carts and pointed logs were driven into the ground. A good deterrent for any sort of mounted counter-attack, he reckoned. Kurt Verit knew his job for a certainty, and that job was general of Rose's substantial armies.

Betrim took a stroll towards the front of the camp as it was setting up and stared up at the walls of Crucible, getting as close a look as he dared. They looked a mighty challenge and then some. Last time he was here it had been as a prisoner. Trussed up and delivered to that blooded arse, Niles Brekovich. Even back then, Betrim had spied the battlements and decided any sort of siege would be something close to suicide. Now here he was fixing to throw himself right up against those same battlements.

"Don't look good," Betrim said, more to himself than anyone else. His eye once more drawn to the corpses decorating the walls. He remembered another body hanging from a wall. Six-Cities Ben had been a friend for longer than any save Henry, and a part of the Black Thorn's crew to boot. None of that had stopped the Jogarens from hanging him.

"Tell *her* that," Henry replied. "Maybe she'll do the smart thing for once an' turn us around, march on home."

"Don't seem likely. 'Specially not once she sees the welcome." Betrim turned away from the scene, disgust putting a snarl on his face and making ugly that much uglier.

"Lord Thorn," said a young man's high-pitched voice. Pug was barely big enough to know how to stick his cock in a woman, but Rose insisted he was an excellent servant, and a man in Betrim's position needed an excellent servant. Didn't mean Betrim liked being called a lord though.

"Know why they call it a duster, Pug?" Betrim asked as he turned to the lad, pointing to his long overcoat.

13

"Uh, no. Sir?"

Betrim grinned, stepped close to the lad and took hold of his coat's collar. He gave the duster a hard tug and dislodged all the road dust it had collected over the past eight hours. Pug stepped back, coughing and spluttering. Betrim chuckled, and clapped the lad on the shoulder.

"Few years ago, I'd have said boys like you don't last long in the game," Betrim said. "But then Rose is busy changing the game, and I reckon boys like you are the ones who'll last longest."

"Sir?" Pug asked.

The lad was busy patting himself down, trying to remove all the dust that settled onto his tabard. Seemed right strange to Betrim that the boy's tabard, much like all the soldier's breastplates, was wearing his sigil. Seemed even stranger that *he had* a sigil. A black rose with an enlarged black thorn. Fitting, he called it.

"She want something?" Betrim asked.

"Lady Rose requests your presence, sir."

"Requests?" Henry asked and followed it up with a bark of laughter. "Bloody woman don't make requests. That right there is a demand an' no mistake."

"Henry," Betrim said in his very best warning tone.

"What? I already do what I'm told. Don't mean I have ta like the fuckin' bitch too."

Betrim nodded at that. There was no sense arguing with her over it. He turned and started back through the noise and clamour of the camp being set up. Hundreds of soldiers passed this way and that - some in their uniforms and dusty armour, others having stripped down to continue their labours with a bit less weight on them. More than a few of those soldiers nodded to Betrim as he passed, and he saw something approaching respect in their faces. Weren't too long ago those faces would have been showing anger or fear. Truth was, Betrim wasn't sure which he'd prefer.

Up in the northern tip of the Wilds, there was ever a bit of a chill in the air, and Betrim had never taken too well with the cold. He'd keep his leathers and his duster on no matter how sweaty it might get underneath. He spent years on the plains of the Wilds running one job or another, racing from one end of the continent to the other. Sometimes he was chased by lawfolk; sometimes he was chased by other folk playing the game, wanting to make a name off ending his. Weren't until recently that he started washing regularly, and now that he did he found he missed the relaxing soak of a hot bath. Soft. That's what it was. He was turning soft.

He found his horse pretty much where he'd left it. The soldiers knew the beast was his and knew not to touch the bad-tempered mare unless he said so. Never knew when he might need to mount up and make a quick journey or something, and the last thing he needed was to be wandering around camp asking after his own damned horse.

"Gotta get back on," Betrim said, stopping next to the beast. The horse turned its head and gave him a baleful stare. "I know. Neither of us wants it. But I gotta go see the woman, an' she'll be a journey back down that way. Don't reckon she'll be pleased with either of us if I decide ta make her wait while I walk it."

The horse swung its big head away, and Betrim took that to mean she accepted his piss-poor excuse. He stepped a foot into the stirrup and swung his other leg up and over the saddle. With Henry and Pug climbing up onto their own beasts, Betrim kicked his mare into motion and started down the column of arriving soldiers.

The carriage was just a couple of miles back down the column, and the mare made a short journey of it. Soldiers stretched both in front and behind as far as the eye could see, and it gave Betrim a shock every time he saw it. So many folk all fighting for him. Seemed like half the Wilds had united under his banner, or maybe they just wanted rid of the blooded so bad they'd even take a name as dark as the Black Thorn as their saviour.

It was a big carriage and no mistake, easily able to seat eight normal folk. Also, just about able to seat one aggravated Rose. The driver looked a sorry state with a kerchief over his mouth and nose and squinting against the dust kicked up by so many folk all marching in a line. He gave a long-suffering nod to Betrim as he approached.

Betrim swung down from his horse for the second time in not too long and again rubbed at his stones. The driver didn't stop the carriage, and Betrim kept easy pace walking along beside it, trying to work up the courage to open the door. The thorn and rose of his symbol painted on the carriage door seemed to stare at him accusingly.

"I can see you out there, Betrim." Rose's voice was not sharp, nor angry. The woman had the patience of lion waiting for hours in the bushes while the herd passed, biding her time until she could pounce on a weak one. Betrim didn't really consider himself a weak one by any stretch, but there was no denying Rose had her claws in him.

Henry slipped down from her horse and decided to walk alongside it. Betrim could see her grinning underneath the rim of her hat, her chin a criss-cross of faint scars. The demons had left their mark on them all, but none more so than Henry.

"Wish me luck," Betrim said.

"I can hear you as well, my love." Good ears Rose had, like one of those black creatures that flitted through the sky on...

The carriage door swung open revealing Rose as she leaned back with a wince against the cushioned seat. She had a look on her face. A look that said Betrim better do as was told before her lioness-like patience ran out.

Betrim took a deep breath and let it out as a sigh as he climbed into the carriage, pulling the door shut behind him. First thing he noticed was the heat. Heavy curtains hung across the windows, and they seemed to be doing a right good job of keeping the heat in the cabin. Betrim thought he'd been a bit sweaty before on the road; in here he felt as though he were melting.

Rose glanced down at the floor of the carriage, and Betrim followed her gaze with his one eye. He'd trailed a fair portion of the road in with him. He shrugged and that was about all the apology she was likely to get.

"We've arrived?" Rose asked. Her voice was like sweet honey dripping over his ears. Her hands were folded across her straining belly, and her dress did nothing to hide it. Rose had always been one for skin-hugging silk even after she started showing. Betrim didn't mind it really. Something about the woman carrying his child got him excited, made him want her even more.

"Aye," Betrim said with a nod. He scratched at the burned side of his face with his three-fingered hand and poked underneath the eyepatch a little. Seemed some dust had worked its way up there and was irritating the melted flesh. "Kurt is setting everythin' up. Useful bastard ta have around, I reckon."

"Well, we're paying him enough to be." That there was it. For the past couple of moons, Rose had been as civil as always, and her voice never betrayed a hint of it, but there was something in the things she said and the way she said them. Made her a right terror to be around. Betrim couldn't wait for her to push the child out. He was struggling to remember a time when she wasn't pregnant.

The carriage gave a jolt as one of the wheels hit a dip and Rose winced and cradled her belly. Betrim saw her jaw clench under the skin, but her voice was calm when she spoke.

"I can't wait to be out of this carriage and on my own two feet again."

"Should ya be walkin' in your, uh, state?"

"I'm carrying your daughter, Betrim. I'm not a cripple."

Betrim nodded. "Right." It seemed odd to him that she claimed to know the child was a girl. Didn't seem like any folk could know until the child popped out, but mothers were strange creatures where their kids were concerned.

It was passing cloying in the carriage, and Betrim decided he needed some air. He pulled open one of the heavy curtains and found Henry sneering at him from outside.

"You'll let the dust in," Rose said in a calm voice.

"Aye," Betrim agreed and pulled the curtain closed again. "Pug said ya wanted ta see me."

"I want them all dead, Betrim." Rose's voice didn't change, but there was a cold glint to her beautiful blue eyes. "Every last one."

"That's why we're here, ain't it?"

"I want D'roan and Brekovich's heads on spikes. I want to be able to announce to the whole of the Wilds that I have finally rid them of the blooded leeches. I want to be able to put a crown on my head and call myself queen. And I want to do it before our daughter is born."

Betrim scratched at his burn again. It was times like this he really wanted to spit, but the carriage was a bit fancy, and he doubted Rose would much appreciate it.

"Cuttin' it a bit close, I reckon, but we'll make a good go of it."

"I'm saying this needs doing quickly, Betrim."

"Aye." Betrim nodded. "Reckon ya called in the wrong lad. Should have asked for the general. I don't know the first fuckin' thing 'bout warfare. Just tend ta stand beside him an' make agreeable noises as he gives out the orders. Seems ta make the troops happy enough. Lookin' at me like I got all the answers ta see 'em through it."

"Kurt Verit is not my husband, and he won't be the one sitting beside me on the throne."

"Throne for two?" Betrim grinned at Rose. She was one of the few folk who didn't mind it when he smiled, most seemed to think the way it tugged his burned flesh made him look half a monster. "Sounds interesting."

"Yes. It does." Rose winked at him, and it got his blood stirring. He could smell her perfume, earthy and sweet all at once, and he knew full well her breasts had swelled with the pregnancy. "But we'll never be able to do anything on it if we don't remove the last of the blooded from Crucible." She sighed. "Unless we crush them here and now they will fester inside my kingdom like a wound gone bad."

"Aye. I get ya. Faster is better."

Betrim leaned forward in the carriage and placed his five-fingered hand on Rose's swollen belly. She smiled at him, took hold of his hand, and moved it a bit further down and to the left. He waited a while and then felt something move beneath the skin. Seemed right strange thinking about there being a small person inside of her. Seemed even stranger knowing he'd put it there.

"Won't be long," Rose said and smiled at Betrim. He couldn't help but smile back. "I want our daughter to know peace. Free of the damned game that made us all what we are."

"Aye, love. We'll..."

"Thorn!" Henry's voice was sharp and followed by a hard rapping at the carriage door. Betrim let the smile drop from his face and pulled his hand back. He opened the door to find Henry with her hat tipped back and a hard look on her scarred face.

"What is it?" Betrim asked.

"Sorry 'bout this," Henry said and nodded once to Rose. Henry had never really liked Betrim's wife, probably something to do with the atrocities her brother had once committed, but there was undoubtedly respect between them. "Word came in from down the line. Pern needs us."

Pug was standing behind Henry, looking nervous with one hand resting on his sword hilt.

"Aye?" Betrim asked.

Henry nodded, and there was a hint of the old murderess she had once been hiding in those hard angles. She damned near growled as she said the next words. "The Haarin have found him."

The Black Thorn

They found Pern Suzku fairly near the end of the column of moving steel, flesh, and dust. Some of the soldiers were studiously ignoring the big warrior, while others had crowded around him to ask their questions. A woman lay at his feet leaking bright red into the dust of the road. She wore a bronze chain shirt underneath a white leather poncho and a conical straw hat.

Suzku looked up as they approached, and there was a sad look on his face. This was not the first Haarin from his clan he had killed, and it would not be the last. They would keep coming until they killed him and sent him to the afterlife to protect the charge he failed to in life. It was the Haarin way. Bloody stupid way, when Betrim thought about it.

"Well that was fairly anticlimactic," Betrim said as he steered his horse near. The soldiers scattered, remaining nearby but not getting too close. Slipping from the saddle, he winced as he limped the rest of the way over to Suzku.

"Woman this time," Henry said. She pushed past Betrim to stare at the red blood leaking from the Haarin's neck.

"Her name was Feyl," said Suzku. "She was Haarin."

Betrim nodded. "They're all bloody Haarin. Far as I see it, ya the only Honin in the whole damned Wilds. It's why they keep throwin' themselves at ya." He stopped at the body and squatted down to get a proper look at the corpse.

Betrim was the first to admit that he'd been an ugly bastard even before the fourth witch hunter had set his face on fire, but this woman made him look like one of the pretty boys that whore houses kept for the lasses and weirds. Her nose was a bulbous tumour on her face, her skin was milky white with brown patches, and her eyebrows connected into one solid line of dark brown hair. He could see why she chose to wear a hat to obscure that face. Not that it mattered now, he reckoned. Everybody looked like shit when they were dead. Smelled just about as bad as well.

Pushing back to standing, Betrim ignored the popping of his knees. He reached up with his five-fingered right hand and grabbed hold of the axe slung across his back. It was designed more for chopping firewood than fighting with, but that didn't really matter. Betrim had long since discovered he struggled to use the thing in combat, something to do with it needing two hands and him only having the three fingers on his left. Still, he looked right fearsome carrying it, and the thing made chopping through necks a fair bit easier.

Suzku held up a hand in front of Betrim, his face a picture of sorrow. "She is Haarin." It was about as much argument as Betrim was used to from the Honin.

There was a time when Betrim would have shoved the big warrior aside and just done as he pleased, but things had changed in the last few years. That and he knew first hand that, if it came down to a fight, Suzku would put Betrim on his arse ten times of ten. The big bastard had an indomitable strength and the skill to put it to right good use. They'd fought once before, back when Suzku was still Haarin, back when it was his job to protect Rose's evil shit of a brother. Suzku had made the fight look easy, and not once had he even drawn his sword.

"I don't really care if she's the God Emperor of Sarth. We ain't really got time for a pyre an' you know as well as me that we're livin' in dark times. Ain't about ta risk a Haarin comin' back with a mind for vengeance. One way I know for sure ta stop that from happenin'." Betrim hefted his axe and pointed it at the corpse's neck.

The Five Kingdoms was a journey away and no mistake, with plenty of saltwater in that journey, but over there they had to deal every day with the problem of the dead coming back. Betrim had spent just a few moons in that cursed land, and it had been more than enough to convince him that it was always best to make sure. And the best way to make sure was to chop the head off. Burning also seemed to work, but Betrim wasn't the biggest fan of fire for good reason; the skin on the left side of his face remembered the taste of flames even decades after the fact.

Suzku lowered his head, let out a weary sigh, and then removed his hand and stepped aside.

Betrim might have asked if Suzku wanted to do the deed himself, but his friend had already made the corpse, and Betrim got the distinct impression he had known this Haarin well. There were times when it was a boss' job to look after his crew, and this was one of them.

"Ya wouldn't like what comes back," Betrim said, as much to himself as to Suzku.

Betrim swung his axe up over his head and brought it down hard. The blade bit through flesh and bone and buried itself in the bloody mud underneath. The head of the Haarin rolled free.

There's a sound someone makes when they retch up everything they've eaten in the past day, and it was one that had never been pleasant to Betrim's ears. He glanced over his shoulder to see Pug on his knees and a puddle of sick spreading out below him. He half expected to hear Henry laugh at the lad's misfortune, a couple of the nearby veterans certainly did, but the little murderess was staring up at Suzku with a savage intensity.

"What ain't you sayin', Pern?" Henry asked over the sounds of Pug's retching.

Suzku lowered his eyes. "She isn't alone. Only a scout. It appears my clan have grown tired of me killing them one by one. They have all come this time."

"Eh?" Betrim grunted. "The whole clan have upped an' travelled the length of the Wilds just ta find ya?"

"To find and kill me," Suzku corrected. "I was charged with protecting a client, and instead I allowed him to die. Even worse than that, I refused to take my own life to protect the client for eternity in death. The dishonour I visited upon the clan has apparently convinced them to forego some of the other traditions."

"Like comin' at ya one at a time?"

"As you say," Suzku agreed with a nod.

Some of the soldiers moved away, joining back into the column. Eight stood around waiting for orders, and another one tended to Pug, having led the lad away from the decapitated body.

"Say it," Henry growled. She was standing close to Suzku, her hat tilted back and her fierce eyes staring up into his face. It weren't often

Betrim had seen Suzku back down from a fight, but the big Honin couldn't seem to meet Henry's gaze.

"I must face them alone."

"No!" Henry didn't shout, but her voice carried all the fury of a dragon attack. She pushed Suzku hard in the chest, and he stumbled back a step. Betrim had seen the Honin stand immovable against men three times Henry's size, but against her, Suzku retreated, and Henry did not stop with one push.

"Ya got this fuckin' dumb shit idea of honour, Pern. Fuckin' Haarin. Ya ain't a Haarin no more. Ya Honin. Say it yaself enough times. An' what is a Honin? Just like one of 'em Haarin but without no fuckin' honour." She kept pushing him again and again, and Suzku retreated again and again.

There were some fights Betrim reckoned weren't his to fight, and this seemed like one of them. He was never really sure just what was going on between the two of them, but at the very least they had a friendship that ran deeper than most. Deeper even than his own though without the history he and Henry shared.

"Ya might have taken this one without too much issue, but I've seen ya fight others an' there ain't no way ya can take the whole clan on ya own." Henry gave Suzku a final push, and the column of soldiers had to move around them.

"What little honour I have left demands..."

"Ya ain't got no honour left, ya stupid fuckin' sun kisser. Ya been crewin' with murderers, thieves, an' whores for the past three years. Ain't any of us got a scrap of honour left. The only thing we got left is us. You, me, Anders, that dumb fuck." She thumbed over her shoulder towards Betrim. "We're all any of us have got left."

Wasn't the first time Betrim had seen Henry angry, and it wasn't the first time he'd seen her intimidate a man twice her size. It was, however, the first time he'd seen it and been certain she wasn't likely to get all stabby over the issue. Betrim didn't reckon there were many folk Henry refused to stab. He'd tasted her blades himself on more than one occasion.

Suzku was silent for a few moments, still not meeting Henry's gaze, while nearby soldiers marched around them, trying not get involved.

Pug moved up beside Betrim. The lad was still wiping vomit from his mouth. Betrim held up a hand to stop him from saying anything and stared on at the confrontation through his one eye.

"I couldn't ask..." Suzku started.

"Ain't no askin'," Henry interrupted, some of the anger leaving her voice yet none of the steel. "Ya part of the crew, what little is left. We look out for each other. Right?"

"Aye," Betrim said. "Fight these fuckers together, I reckon."

Suzku looked at Betrim. "These aren't just some mercenaries or brigands. There will be Haarin trained from birth to fight. Some maybe even my equal. There will be women and children, the old and infirm..."

"Whole clan, is it? Littleuns too?" Betrim asked. It was nasty business killing children. One he'd never really taken to no matter how many times it might have been required.

"Yes," Suzku said, grief already in his eyes. "Maybe ten Haarin. Four or five times as many others. All will not stop until I am dead, even the children. It is a matter of honour for them. The whole clan will die before they suffer me to continue living."

Betrim took a few steps closer. The column of soldiers was almost at an end now. He could see the last of them and the second army of carts and camp followers that trailed in the wake.

"An' you're still of a mind ta survive?" Betrim asked Suzku. "No matter the cost ta other lives."

Suzku nodded. "I will not die for Swift. If there truly is an afterlife, he should walk it alone without my protection." He glanced down at Henry. "He deserves that fate and worse."

"Much worse," Henry hissed through clenched teeth.

"Well then." Betrim cracked a grin. "Good job I got a whole fuckin' army backin' me up, eh? Anyone here in charge?" Betrim raised his voice to a shout.

"Thought you were," one of the soldiers shouted back, and Betrim had himself a good chuckle at that.

"I got command of a unit or two," said a tall, rakishly thin man with horseshoe moustache and piercing eyes.

"Captain Allestrue," Pug said quietly enough that only Betrim could hear.

"Allestrue?" Betrim said with a horrific smile. "Allestrue the Lost?"

The captain nodded. "Used to be. Found myself a place in your army."

Betrim closed the distance between them and gave the captain a good one-eyed stare. "Reckon I remember a bounty notice with your name on it just a year or so back."

Captain Allestrue let loose a mountainous shrug. "I remember seeing one with your name on a while back, Thorn. Biggest number of bits I ever seen offered for a head."

Betrim laughed. "Aye. Sounds about right."

He had, in fact, had the largest bounty on his head the Wilds had ever seen, but that was long gone now. Now, Betrim wasn't a criminal. Now, folk called him the Guardian of the Wilds, whatever that meant.

"Gather ya men, Captain Lost," Betrim said with a nod and the man scurried off to do just that. "Ya know where we can find this clan of yours, Suzku?"

"I have an idea."

"Well then. Let's go put an end ta these Haarin fuckers once an' for all."

Rose

For a woman used to moving with an easy, fluid grace, pregnancy was a little frustrating for Rose. Waddling would not be an inaccurate description for how she sometimes felt forced to move, and now appeared to be one of those times. It didn't help that she was trailed by her guards and they watched her every movement.

Rose had known pregnant women in the past– it was impossible not to given that she had lived and worked in a brothel for most of her life. Some women seemed to cope with their pregnancy as if it wasn't even there, while some women suffered from all manner of maladies. Rose found herself caught somewhere in between. The largest problem she had was with the size of the child nestled inside of her - it seemed to have inherited that trait from Betrim. Rose only hoped the child would not inherit her looks from her father also.

"Where are we at, General Verit?" Rose asked.

Kurt Verit turned and looked shocked for a moment. He was standing with a number of high-ranking soldiers from Rose's army, and they looked to be debating the walls of Crucible. They were very high walls, perhaps even taller than those of her own city of Chade.

"We're busy setting up the camp and the blockade at the moment, my lady," Kurt said as he split away from the soldiers and moved to stand at Rose's side. "I have scout parties circling the city, but we've yet to hear back from them."

Kurt Verit was a big man, even taller and broader than Betrim and thick with muscle. He wore his hair short and his beard full and seemed to have no idea how to properly deal with the fact that a woman was in charge. He had been a prince of the Five Kingdoms once, but their complicated right of succession led to him being exiled as soon as the new king took office. One empire's loss was her gain. Kurt Verit was one of the most seasoned military commanders in the known world, and it hadn't taken much past the promise of a decent wage and a decent war to get him to agree to lead her armies.

"How much do we know about their defences?" Rose asked. She shifted her weight to her other foot and waved away the servant who rushed forward to help her.

Her general shrugged. "Big fucking walls. Archers on top. Reinforced gate. We don't know much, and I wouldn't want to throw any men up against it unless we have a better idea what we're dealing with."

"In time, General," Rose said with a sly smile at the big man. "I have an ace in the hole on the way. For now, we need to make certain no one enters or leaves. The last blooded families in the Wilds are holed up in that city, and I will see them all dead if I have to burn the place to the ground."

Kurt nodded slowly. "You can name them blooded, or you can name them nobles. In my experience, people die the same at the point of a sword no matter how high their birth. Come tomorrow I'll have a better idea of exactly how to go about it."

Rose nodded and pointed towards the walls. "Are those bodies?"

The general nodded, and Rose noticed his jaw clenching. "Soldiers wearing your colours and emblem. They must be the advance units we sent. We never heard back from some of them. Gruesome way to make a statement."

"It's the only kind the blooded know how to make, General. This is how they've kept us below their heels for generations, with brutality in one hand, and clipped bits in the other. Paying us to kill each other over and over again.

"What about in front of the walls?" Rose squinted. "More of my soldiers staked out?"

Kurt Verit shook his head, a noise like a growl hissing from his throat. "No. They look like good-folk. Farmers most likely. Those who would have supported you and your army. They kill them here as a message to others, and so they have fewer mouths to feed. The tactics of war are never kind, my lady."

Rose leaned forward, still squinting. "Are some of them still moving?"

"Yes, my lady. Many of them are still alive. There is a way to drive a stake through a person's body that will leave them alive for days. There is nothing we can do for them. To venture that close would put us in range of their bows." The general looked away and shook his head.

Rose winced as the child inside of her moved. Her hands went to her belly, and she slumped a little. Pains, she was told, were absolutely normal at this stage of the pregnancy. That didn't mean they were pleasant.

Kurt Verit cast his eyes down, and she saw some colour flood to his cheeks. The man was more than happy to fuck a camp follower in the presence of his men, but a little discomfort from a pregnant woman had him blushing like a boy seeing tits for the first time.

Her servant rushed forward and took hold of Rose's arm to steady her.

"Enough, Lucille," Rose snapped. Her calm composure returned almost as quickly as she had lost it. "I will call for you if you are needed, and I do not need a midwife at every niggle and pain."

Kurt was still standing nearby, paying particular attention to the walls again, a grim set to his jaw. Other soldiers were wandering past, all with jobs to do. Some of them made certain not to look at the pregnant woman in the expensive dress who seemed so out of place amidst a camped army; others stared at her with little or no recognition.

For the past two years, Rose had been using her ever-growing armies to cut through the Wilds, removing the blooded like the necrotic tissue they were. But she had never been at the front of those armies. Most of her soldiers had never seen her face. They followed the Black Thorn, and most of them probably didn't know that he was her tool. That she made all the decisions and simply moved Thorn where she needed him most.

It was time for all that to change. It was time for her troops to see her instead of the man who would one day sit beside her. It was time for them all to realise who was really in charge.

"I want a tour, General," Rose said. She reached up and tied her long black hair into a tight tail. Trailing her red silk dress through the mud and dust wouldn't be ideal, but she didn't have time to change and didn't have any leathers that would fit over her bulging belly.

Kurt Verit turned to her and grinned through his beard. "Of course, my lady."

"I'm not sure that's wise in your condition..."

"Lucille," Rose said in a voice as hard as iron. She turned and fixed the midwife with a stare that could have frozen lava. "If you argue with me again I will take one of the knives I have strapped beneath my dress, you know they're there because you helped put them there, and I will drive it into your eye."

Kurt Verit let out a chuckle, probably thinking it an idle threat.

"General," Rose said, turning away and putting on a beaming smile. "A tour. The whole camp."

Rose sent a glance up at the walls of Crucible, tearing her eyes from the bodies hanging there. Niles Brekovich and Alistair D'roan were up there somewhere with the last members of their blooded families. Rose hoped they were watching. She hoped they could see her, a red beacon in an ocean of brown and black and grey. She hoped they were scared.

The Black Thorn

Allestrue the Lost, or Captain Lost as they had decided to call him, brought thirty-six men with him. That put them at a small force of forty-one if Betrim trusted Pug's counting. Of course, the lad was counting himself and Betrim was far from certain he could use the blade hanging at his hip. Given that Suzku estimated a maximum of ten true Haarin and a bunch of folk more used to washing pots and baking bread, Betrim reckoned they had a good chance of killing the bastards and getting out of it with their lives thoroughly intact.

The sun hung low behind them, casting long shadows on the swaying ocean of grass. There wasn't much lying to the west but flat, featureless plains before the land gave way to the sea. Made the afternoons stretch out for somewhere close to forever so far north in the Wilds.

To the south lay the slow-moving, murky waters of the Greywash. Some folk said the Greywash was deep enough and long enough that every person in the Wilds could fit underneath the languid waters. Betrim wasn't really sure why those folk would even consider such a thing, couldn't decide if he cared if it was true or not.

He once knew a man who swam in the Greywash, though not nearly so far west. Ten Thumbs the Swimmer, they called him, and the bastard sure knew how to swim. Used to dive down and stay there for minutes upon minutes, so long Betrim was sure he had drowned, and then he'd pop back up with some sort of deep water plant or a long-lost artefact he claimed was likely a thousand years old. He had some sort of glass contraption that he strapped to his face in order to see and wouldn't let anyone anywhere near it. The Swimmer made a sort of living from selling whatever junk he found beneath the waters. Betrim wondered if the man was still jumping into the Greywash, still drudging up things best left drowned.

The Greywash always held a peculiar smell. Betrim didn't reckon water could rot, but it sure smelled like it. There was another smell on the wind as well, cooking flesh. Seemed it might be coming from the little village up ahead.

Might have seemed odd, a makeshift village popping up just a few hours from the walls of Crucible, but it wasn't unusual for villages to spring up in the Wilds. Some folk didn't feel like paying taxes, and those folk either joined the game or moved into the wilderness. Betrim couldn't decide which choice meant you had more stones. Players of the game, outlaws by any civilised name, didn't tend to live long, and all that awaited most of them was cold steel, hot fire, or stretched necks. On the other hand, villages without protection were prime targets for folk playing the game, and the Wilds was never short on bands of outlaws.

"It's them," Suzku said, his voice thick with something like choked tears.

Betrim had himself a quick a glance, which meant turning his head pretty far because the Honin was on his left side, the one without the eye. Suzku had a strange look on his face. Betrim might have called it fear on another man, but he'd never known his friend to fear anything.

"Ya sure?" The huts did seem a tad flimsy in design, easy to pack and move. The Haarin were nomadic folk for the most part.

"I would know those huts anywhere. I grew up in them. I helped build some of them."

Betrim pulled on his reins, and the horse stopped and gave an annoyed *whinny*. Pug and Henry were at his side in a moment, and Captain Lost wasn't far back, his men stopping behind.

"What d'ya think? Ride on in and charge 'em down with the horses?" Betrim said, sucking at his teeth.

"Know how ta fight on horseback, do ya?" Henry asked.

Betrim had a think about it and reckoned she might be right. He was barely competent enough to sit in a saddle for a few hours, swinging an axe at the same time might be a little dangerous to all those around him, himself included.

Suzku was the first to slip from his saddle, and he stepped forward past the line of soldiers. Already Betrim could see a group of folk stepping out of the circle of tents and walking towards them. More and more folk actually, until he reckoned they matched Betrim's crew for numbers. Some of them even looked small - midgets or children most likely.

"Ya know how ta fight, Pug?" Betrim asked as he joined the others on the ground, stamping down the grass beneath him. It sprang back up in petty defiance.

"I've taken a few lessons, sir."

"Lessons?" Betrim said, shooting the boy a cocked eyebrow. "Reckon I'll take that as a no then. Just stick close ta me an' try not ta stab me in the back, eh?"

Betrim squinted towards the folk opposite them. They didn't seem to be in any sort of hurry. A casual walk was about as fast as he'd be willing to call it. Something about it seemed a little off. Suzku waited with Henry at his side, staring straight ahead.

"Shall I form up the troops, Thorn?" asked Captain Lost.

Betrim nodded, more to cover up his own failing at battle tactics than anything else. He knew how to win fights, and rarely by what folk would call fair means, but real battles were beyond him. The closest he'd come was in Absolution a couple of years back, but even that hadn't been a real battle. The demons they'd fought had no idea about tactics. They were savage creatures who tore at Betrim's crew with teeth and claws. They were strange and dark times Betrim walked in, and he couldn't help but feel an itch between his shoulder blades that meant things were sure to get stranger and darker yet.

Some of the soldiers had spears and others had swords and shields. It looked like not a one of them had thought to bring a bow. Betrim had a good grumble at that. Archers were dangerous folk and no mistake.

"I have a bow," Pug said quietly, almost like he was reading Betrim's mind.

"Ya do? Ya any good?"

"I used to hunt deer and pheasants before I came to Chade to serve you."

Betrim shook his head at that. "Where the fuck did she find you?"

"Acanthia, sir. I'm the fourth son of the Bel'zane family. My father believed it would be a great honour for me to squire for the future king of the Wilds. I'm not sure he realised what it's actually like over here. Or maybe he did, and that was the point. I don't really fit in, but I am..."

"I didn't ask for ya life story, lad. Go get ya bow an' when the fightin' starts try ta feather a few of the fuckers."

Pug ran back to his horse, and Betrim shook his head. Hunting deer and hunting men were two different things. For a start, deer rarely fought back. The soldiers started forming up behind Betrim, and at Captain Lost's command, they formed into a loose shield wall with the spearmen behind. If there were two things Betrim hated it was shields and spears. Tended to turn any fight into a test of patience and luck.

"Thorn," Henry called, glancing over her shoulder and nodding towards him. Her daggers weren't yet drawn, but she had that severe look she sometimes got when she was scared and trying to hide it.

"Something is wrong," Suzku said without turning, his eyes fixed on his clan.

Betrim stepped up beside them and squinted. His vision hadn't been quite so good since that thrice-damned witch hunter, Arbiter Kessick, had torn out his left eye. The folk of Suzku's clan were still a good distance away and moving slowly. A long line of them stumbling forwards, but Betrim couldn't make out much more than that.

"They look drunk ta you?" Betrim asked. He'd seen drunkards up close, and he'd seen them from a fair distance, and they tended to have a way of moving about them, a sort of stumbling lurch.

"Something is wrong," Suzku repeated, his voice shaking with whatever he was holding back.

Henry pulled her cavalier hat from her head. It wasn't often she let that hat go. Betrim reckoned she liked it to hide the scars these days. She had a bunch of criss-crossing claw marks all over her face and arms, not mention one very missing left ear. She'd been through some shitty times, had Henry, her and Betrim both together. They both had faces to prove it.

"That smell on the air," Henry said with a sniff. "It have a familiar scent ta you, Thorn?"

Betrim nodded. Didn't feel like saying it though. Cooking flesh had one sort of smell to it. Human flesh seemed to give it an altogether different one, almost like pig but sweeter, more rotten. It made the inside of his nose itch.

"They have no auras," Suzku said. He turned then to look at Betrim, and there were tears in his eyes. Weren't often Betrim had seen men cry, and it tended to make him feel a little awkward. "Even demons have auras. Everything living has an aura."

Betrim let out a groan. He'd crewed with Suzku long enough not to question his odd ability to see what he called auras. He squinted again at the approaching clan of Haarin, moving closer every moment. Suddenly he recognised that lurching stumble and it wasn't because they were drunk. It was because they were dead.

Betrim may not have spent long in the Five Kingdoms, but he'd been there long enough to see the dead rise and walk. Rotting flesh peeling from the bone. Held together by sinew and magic. He'd seen it, and he'd fought it. And he'd hoped never to do either again.

"Fuck," he cursed and somehow it didn't quite seem to cover it. For a moment he wished Anders was there, the blooded bastard always seemed to know some long, fancy words to make a curse feel a right mouthful, and this one could do with being chewed over.

"Stay loose!" Betrim shouted over his shoulder to the troops behind him. "Bunching up ain't gonna help no one but them. Watch out for each other, work together, and make sure they stop moving before you go after the next."

"What is it, Thorn?" Henry asked. Worry made her features long and sharp, pulled on her scars to make her seem half a monster herself.

Suzku was staring at him. The bastard already knew, Betrim was sure, but he needed someone else to say it.

"They ain't alive." Betrim spat. Suzku's dead clan were getting closer and closer now, almost close enough to see the pallid flesh and empty eyes. Some of them looked like they still carried weapons, maybe never had a chance to draw them. What sort of evil could sneak up on a bunch of Haarin wasn't something Betrim wanted to contemplate.

"I've never seen the dead walk," Pug said. Betrim hadn't noticed the boy sneak up beside him.

"You're seein' it right now, lad. Stay behind me."

Suzku drew his sword. Three feet of curved, razor-sharp death. The tears weren't just in his eyes any more, they were on his cheeks, dripping from his chin. The Honin took a step forwards, and then another, and he didn't look like he was about to stop.

Henry didn't wait for orders, she followed after Suzku, giving him space but backing him up, knives restless in her scarred hands.

"Orders?" Captain Lost had a touch of fear in his voice and Betrim couldn't blame him. Folk in the Wilds didn't deal with the dead - they'd never needed to. The dead only got up and walked about in the Five Kingdoms and they were a whole ocean away from that cursed land.

"Back 'em up," Betrim growled and started after his friends. Why everyone always seemed to look to him for orders when shit started getting creepy, he'd never know.

It didn't take more than a dozen paces before the smell got stronger; burning flesh and rot mixing in the air with an unhealthy stench of shit. Betrim could see them better too and they were dead alright. Clothes torn and shredded, faces bruised and bloody, and skin sloughing off the bone. Men, women, children, elders. The dead never seemed to care for age or gender; all were just meat and bones as far as necromantic magic was concerned.

He heard some curses uttered from behind and Pug gagged, but the boy managed to keep his stomach this time. Lad didn't realise it yet, but things would look far worse before all this was over.

"Aim for the head, lad. Eyes, eh?" Betrim growled and doubled his pace to catch up with Henry and Suzku.

Betrim had just enough time to see the empty look in dozens of dead eyes, and then they were on him.

Suzku moved into the throng of the dead, his sword whipping one way and then the other as limbs dropped to the dust. Henry wasn't far behind, watching the Honin's back and stabbing into the press of dead whenever she could. Then she was gone, swallowed up by the horde.

Betrim brought his hatchet down onto the skull of an old man, grey in hair and bent in back. He had a full set of white teeth gnashing at Betrim even with an axe embedded in his skull. Then Captain Lost was there beside Betrim, shoving his sword into the dead thing's face.

Lost's soldiers joined the battle just as a wave of dead things washed forwards to engulf them. All around, Betrim could hear moans and shuffling feet and the snap of teeth clamping down. All around, Betrim could hear the shouts of soldiers, cursing at an enemy they neither understood, nor cared to. There was no clash of steel on steel, only meaty thuds of flesh being pulverised and rent.

Betrim and Lost were enveloped by the loose wall of shields. It was a bit of chore to have to reach over other folk to hammer down on the dead with his axe, but he supposed it was better than being surrounded by them on all sides and all of them wanting to taste the Black Thorn. It didn't take long for the screaming to start. Didn't take long for the first of the living to fall.

The Black Thorn

Another scream ripped through the air. Betrim couldn't see where the poor bastard had fallen, but he knew the sound well. Only dying folk made sounds like that.

He was shoulder to shoulder with Lost and another fellow, pushing up against the men in front as they held their shields high and tried to hold as the tide of dead crashed against them. Grunts and growls punctuated a close, frenzied fight as Betrim chopped down, again and again, sometimes feeling his axe bite, other times not. He could barely see the creatures he was swinging at. This right here was why he hated battles. A good fight was one thing, but this was a chaotic grinder of folk just trying to survive. Flashes of silver steel, splatters of blood and filth, and terrified faces screaming rage to cover the fear.

Some fool soldiers were still trying to use their spears for the good it did them. Betrim saw a man skewer one of the dead only for the nightmare to drag itself along the shaft, over the shield of the man in front, and bite down on the fingers of the spearman. The dead thing was quickly shoved away, but it took a couple of digits with it. That right there seemed a good reason to wear gloves, Betrim reckoned, and decided he might have to find himself a pair.

"I said ta fight loose!" Betrim roared, sick of all the shoving and tight quarters. "Fuck the spears. Spread out an' let the bastards come onto us. They ain't smart. Split 'em up an' gang up on the fuckers. An' anyone with an axe start choppin' heads off!"

Took a few moments, but the press eased a bit and the soldiers started backing off, spreading out and teaming into twos or threes as the dead shambled on towards them mindlessly. They left a good few of their number behind on the ground, some already gone, others screaming in the dust. The dead leapt on those still alive, biting through flesh and spilling rivers of blood to soak into the dirt of the Wilds.

One of the dead, a tall man with a pinched face like all his features were drawn towards his nose, was quicker than the others. It lurched into something like a run and chased Betrim down. He swung his axe at the thing as it came close, and it swayed out of the way so the metal bit into its collarbone. Teeth closed around Betrim's right arm and bit down hard.

"Fuck!" Betrim screamed, stumbling backwards, dragging the dead thing with him. The pressure on his arm grew with the pain as the thing bit down, its hands clawing at his face.

Betrim punched at the dead man attached to his arm, hitting it hard in the face with his three-fingered left hand with no response other than more pain.

"Hold still!" And Betrim did. He stopped moving and tried to hold his arm up as high as possible.

Swords bit down into the dead man's skull as Captain Lost and another soldier took turns hacking at it. Bits of blood and skull and brain spattered Betrim's face, and still the thing bit into his arm. Eventually, its arms stopped clawing at him, and Captain Lost reached in and pried what was left of the dead man's jaws apart until it fell away.

Betrim found two teeth buried in the sleeve of his duster. The thing had bit down hard, but cured leather was tough stuff, and his arm was intact. Hurt like all the hells though, and Betrim would put money on him having a nasty bruise coming up sometime soon. He picked the teeth out of his duster and threw them down into the dust next to the owner.

There were small skirmishes happening all around. Betrim leaped to the aid of one soldier who had wrestled a lanky woman to the ground and was attempting to avoid the thrashing arms while another soldier held back a dead child with his shield.

Betrim pulled his two-handed axe from its holster on his back, swung it up high, and then brought it down on the lanky woman's face as she wriggled and clawed. The body went limp, and the soldier who had been sat astride the woman rolled away to heave into the dust. Betrim wrenched his axe from the mess, turned and swung the steel at the child. He missed, and the momentum carried the axe around to bury itself in the second soldier's shield.

The dead child leapt at him, and Betrim had to admit the thing was stronger than it looked. He wrestled with it for a moment before the soldier with the shield grabbed hold of its legs and pulled it away groaning and snapping. The child tried to turn on the soldier, but he raised his shield and brought it down on the child's head once, twice, and a third time. The soldier was panting, sweat running down his face, and his eyes were as wild as the laughing dogs that roamed the plains. The child's body gave a twitch, and the soldier crashed his shield into its broken skull once more.

Betrim plucked his axe from the ground and slapped the shield bearer on the shoulder with a three-fingered hand, then started towards another soldier who looked in a bad way. His leg was bloody, and he was trying to crawl away, but one of the dead things was biting down on his mid-section. Betrim ran up and brought his axe down on the dead woman's spine before pulling her off the soldier. With three big boots to the back of the skull, Betrim stopped the woman from moving, but he reckoned it was long past too late. The soldier was bleeding like a river running red, and gagging on his own vomit.

After a few moments of staring down at the bleeding, dying soldier Betrim decided it was an act of mercy to put the poor bastard out of his misery. The soldier's eyes went wide just as Betrim's axe severed his head from his body with one big chop.

By the time they finished putting down the dead for a second time Betrim was weary, smeared in gore, hurting from a dozen different places, and sick to his stomach. It was one thing to kill a man, another thing to kill a child, but killing the dead... They had a habit of not laying down no matter how many wounds you gave them, and hacking up bodies was messy work.

They lost fully half of the soldiers Captain Lost had brought with them, some dead, others dying. Most of those who survived looked like they maybe would have preferred not to. Harrowed looks and plenty of empty stomachs. Dirty work.

"Make sure none of them that's dyin' come back." Betrim's voice sounded raw to his ears. Seems he'd done a bit of shouting, maybe a bit of screaming, though he couldn't remember any words.

Captain Lost nodded. The old outlaw had a vacant look about him, almost like with the things he'd just seen and done it was easier to switch off, not think about it. Betrim reckoned he might be a smart man for choosing that way. Especially with the things that still needed doing. Men they had fought with needed seeing to before they became things to fight against.

It took a bit of searching once the fighting was done, but it soon became clear to Betrim that Henry and Suzku were among neither the living or the dead. Last he'd seen of the two they'd been swallowed up by the horde of corpses, Suzku cutting a swathe, and Henry backing him up. Her loyalty to the Honin might well be the death of her one day, but Betrim wasn't one to talk. Plenty of times he'd been looking at the sharp end of steel for sticking up for someone, and often enough it was Henry herself.

Betrim struck off towards the little village of huts. His two crew members had to be somewhere, and if they weren't at the site of the battle, there was only one other place they were likely to be. He had to believe they were there. The alternative wasn't worth considering.

Pug caught up at a jog, slowing only after he reached Betrim, and looking like he had a few ghosts chasing him. The lad looked no worse for wear, certainly better than most of the soldiers. He had his bow with him and a quiver counting just two arrows. Betrim reckoned that meant he had loosed a few, maybe even feathered a few of the walking dead.

"Put any of the fuckers down?" Betrim asked as they walked. He pulled his duster a bit closer. Might be the aftermath of the fight, or maybe the time of year, but seemed it was getting a touch chilly. Winter finally setting in, he reckoned.

"I, uh... I think I slowed a few down," Pug offered. The lad looked to have aged a decade since the morning. No doubt his first real taste of life in the Wilds. Boys like him didn't tend to last too long, least not without the protection of someone like the Black Thorn.

"How's that?"

"I shot a few of them in the leg, sir."

"The leg?" Betrim rasped out a harsh laugh. "Those things ain't people, lad. Don't feel pain, nor get dizzy from a bit of lost blood. Those things are dead. Gotta treat 'em just like. Slowed 'em down. Waste of bloody wood is all it was."

"Yes, sir."

"Stop callin' me sir."

"No, sir."

"Eh?" Betrim stopped and stared hard with his one eye. It was fair to say Pug was already looking quite pale, what with the recent set of events, but the lad somehow managed to go whiter than a wraith - and Betrim had some experience with those monsters too.

"You are Lord Thorn," Pug stammered. "Soon to be king, if all goes well. I am your squire. It is only right I call you sir. Sir."

Betrim chuckled. "You picked a fine fuckin' issue ta stand up on. At least ya got some stones down there."

He turned and started walking again. The very idea of the Black Thorn, the biggest outlaw the Wilds had ever known, sitting on some throne while folk pandered and offered fealty and such. Betrim reckoned the world was playing some sort of joke on them all and he was the punchline. Either way, it was only because of Rose, and only because she had chosen him to sit beside her. Without her, Betrim reckoned he'd still be running jobs and fleeing bounty notices. Down in the gutter where he belonged.

From a distance, the huts looked to be spaced haphazardly, but up close Betrim could see they formed a loose ring, probably with the more important folk towards the centre. He counted twelve tents before he stopped trying.

"How many ya reckon, Pug?"

"I would say maybe thirty tents in all, sir."

"Aye. Thirty." Betrim nodded, mostly to cover up his own innumeracy. "Sounds 'bout right."

The first tent they came to was taller than any man Betrim had ever seen, and he'd seen a few giants in his time. It had a circular base and all manner of animals painted on the outside of it.

"A nomadic people, living off the land," Pug said as he hurried up to the tent and gave it some scrutiny. Betrim reckoned he'd need to get any looking done now as the light was fading fast now the sun was setting, and he wanted to be away from the site before full dark set in.

They found Suzku and Henry sitting outside one of the smaller tents. Suzku was kneeling in the dust, an ancient body more wrinkle than man lying dead at his feet. Henry squatted nearby, her hat long since gone and her face looking ghoulish in the waning light. Neither of the two looked to be saying much.

Betrim had seen Suzku half dead with the other half sporting a pronounced lean before. Now he saw the man looking broken. Collapsed in the dust of the Wilds with his shoulders slumped and his precious sword, usually his first priority after any battle, lying forgotten a good few paces away.

Pug made to run towards the two, but Betrim stopped him with a three-fingered hand on the boy's collar. He pulled the lad back in line and stopped them both from approaching.

"You two injured?" Betrim asked with a raised voice.

Henry looked up at them, a grim set to her mouth and her scars making it seem even worse. She gave her head a shake and turned back to Suzku.

Betrim skirted the two, and he pulled Pug with him. Some matters were private, best left to those who were wanted, and he doubted Suzku wanted anyone but Henry to see his grief.

"Where are we going, sir?" Pug asked.

"Centre of the camp." Betrim spat into the dust. "This ain't the Five Kingdoms, dead don't just get up an' walk in the Wilds, lad. Something got 'em up. Same thing that killed 'em most like. Reckon we should probably have a look, see if we can't figure out what."

"Is that safe?" Pug asked as he trailed along behind.

Betrim thought about that for a moment. It almost certainly wasn't safe, but he was committed now, and the Black Thorn wasn't the sort of man to second guess himself or show fear, least of all to some noble-born, nameless Acanthian brat.

As they passed alongside the tents and came towards the centre of the camp, Betrim could see it opened out into a small clearing. The smell of burnt flesh was stronger, and he could see Pug was struggling with it.

"Smells a bit like pig, eh?" Betrim said with a rasp. "Gotta wonder if it tastes the same."

Pug gagged and Betrim grinned, forging on into the clearing. What he saw there near made him gag as well, and he heard Pug set to retching all over again.

Bodies were lined up in the centre of the clearing, burned and blackened from being set on fire. Strange thing was they didn't look to be piled. It was clear even from a distance that the corpses were laid out in some sort of pattern. There didn't look to be much blood either. The dust of the Wilds was ever thirsty and did a good job of soaking it up, but a body held a lot of blood, and it tended to seep out even after death. The ground looked to be stained a little red near the corpses, but that was it.

There didn't seem to be anyone else around, no more moving dead things, and no signs of who caused the whole mess. Betrim edged closer to the bodies and swivelled his head. He'd long ago come to terms with the problem of only having the one eye, didn't have much of a choice, but that didn't mean it wasn't a real annoyance sometimes.

"What do ya make of it, lad?" Betrim asked.

Pug retched in response.

The light was dying now the sun had almost finished dipping below the horizon. There wasn't much of a moon to speak of and squinting only got a man so far.

"It's a blood rune," Pug said once he had the gagging under control.

"Eh?" Betrim had never heard of it before, but he knew the Arbiters of the Inquisition used runes in their magic.

"We've seen them in Acanthia, sir. The last few years they've been turning up here and there, always near big cities and..." The boy paused, closing his eyes and holding his breath against a wave of nausea. "Whole villages killed, the people... uh, the bodies arranged in such a pattern."

Betrim squinted against the dying light and stepped closer to the grisly scene. Now that Pug mentioned it there did seem to be some sort of design to the placing of the bodies. "It have something to do with the dead getting up an' walkin'?" The creepy shit always seemed to follow Betrim no matter where he went.

"I don't know, sir. But some people say the blood runes started about the same time as the Shamblers appeared. A new gang of thieves in Acanthia who dig up the dead. There's a saying, sir. Bury them deep, six feet at least. Bury them with salt, to ward off the spirits. Don't mark the grave, don't make it easy for them to find."

Betrim sniffed loudly, grimacing at the smell and then spat. "Spirits don't give a shit about salt, lad. Run back ta Captain Lost," Betrim ordered Pug. "Tell him ta bring some torches an' some stones."

"Stones, sir?"

"Aye," Betrim turned a horrific grin on Pug. "The type that's needed ta look at shit like this an' not waste ya lunch." He had a feeling things were going to get far worse before the walls of Crucible fell.

ℛose

Rose's first siege was not going quite like she expected. Actually, she wasn't entirely sure what she expected, but there seemed to be very little in the way of activity.

Night had well and truly fallen, and the moon was little but a sliver. Torches were staked out all along the camp lines, and similar torches lit the walls of Crucible. Cook fires provided both heat and the smell of food, and the soldiers exchanged stories with each other around the flames. Every now and then she heard a loud grunt, the sort of exclamation that could only come from sex, and Rose knew the camp followers would be earning more than a little coin.

The brief accounts she had read on the matter of sieges tended to depict far more battles and far less sitting around drinking up the supplies of alcohol. She had heard of grand siege engines designed to smash through walls and gates, of catapults able to fling entire cows into the enemy garrison. She had read of mass infantry charges and climbing ladders and all sorts of accounts. It seemed if any of those things were coming, they were not coming until the morning at the least. The last thing she was about to do was expose her naivety on the matter by accosting her general. Kurt said everything was according to schedule and she would believe him. For now, at least.

Lucille flitted about attending to Rose's needs - not that she had many at all. There was very little to do at this juncture - and sitting inside her tent reading seemed to be the most of it. Rose bathed in lukewarm water and dressed in the sturdiest attire she could find that would fit her.

Tomorrow she intended to stand out on the front line of her army where Brekovich, D'roan, and the other blooded could see her. She would watch their last city fall and smile as they died. Most folk thought her quest was as simple as wanting to conquer the Wilds, unite its people, and see an end to the blooded. For the most part that was true. But there was something else, a far more personal reason to hate the blooded folk. One she had nurtured since childhood.

45

Rose heard a loud cough from outside the tent. She gave her eyes a furious rolling then schooled her features into a mask of calm omnipotence.

"Come in, Pug," Rose said as she leaned back in her chair and placed the book on the nearby table.

The Acanthian squire waited a moment before pulling open the tent flap and marching in, his eyes down. He always held his eyes to the floor around her, and she wagered it was because he couldn't look at her without staring at her belly.

"My husband?" Rose prompted after the squire was quiet for a few seconds too long.

"Just got back, my lady," Pug said. The boy was covered in dust and looked as pale as the sliver of moon up in the sky. "He's having a drink with the troops. I thought I should come and announce his imminent arrival."

Rose narrowed her eyes just as the boy glanced up. He quickly found the floor more interesting, though the rug was actually anything but.

"What aren't you telling me, Pug?"

"There was... We found... I don't know, my lady. I think it best Lord Thorn explain."

Rose levered herself to her feet and took two menacing steps forward. She was of a height with Pug and not quite so broad, but the boy took a step back all the same.

"Then you should probably go and fetch Lord Thorn because I don't like mysteries."

Pug nodded and vanished out of the tent.

Rose waddled back to her chair and lowered herself into it. Lucille stood nearby looking worried and saying nothing.

The problem with being so heavily pregnant was that Rose did not entirely feel herself. Her patience was approaching non-existence, and the noise of others enjoying themselves outside of her tent frustrated her.

It wasn't too long ago she would have joined in, drinking half the soldiers into a stupor and flirting the rest into a lusty panic. It wasn't too long ago the Black Thorn had walked into her mother's whorehouse, and

46

Rose had led the man up to a room by his cock. Now they were married, she was on the verge of uniting the Wilds, and the child he had put inside of her kept wriggling yet refused to make an appearance. It took after its father in that regard; Betrim always liked to linger inside of her– not that she minded.

It was a while before Betrim made an appearance. So long, in fact, that Rose was stifling a yawn as he ducked through the tent flap without ceremony. Far from the wild grin and rosy cheeks that she had expected to see after a few drinks, Betrim looked stony-faced and grim. His duster bore fresh blood stains, and he was wearing a new pair of gloves despite only filling three of the five fingers on his left hand. The middle and ring fingers of the glove flopped about impotently. She'd pin them once he was asleep.

Betrim slumped down into one of the waiting chairs and let out a loud sigh. His one eye flicked up to Rose and then away. The ghost of a smile breezed across his lips, and he nodded.

"I'm late," Betrim agreed before Rose had chance to accuse.

"Out," Rose ordered Lucille, and the woman knew the tone well enough not to argue.

As soon Lucille was gone Rose stood awkwardly and crossed the distance between her and her husband. She lowered herself into the other chair and took hold of Betrim's hand, staring up into his eye.

"What happened? Did you find Pern's clan?"

"Aye," Betrim said with a sigh. "Weren't the first to, though. By the time we got there... Someone or something already killed 'em all. Bodies lined up like some sort of Arbiter rune or something, blood drainin' down into the earth. Burned backs an' guts opened up."

"You think the Inquisition did it?" Rose asked. The last thing she wanted was that organisation intruding on her plans.

Betrim shook his head. "Witch hunters don't go around raisin' the dead. This was... What do they call it? Necromancy. The boy called it a blood rune, and Kurt agreed. They've been seein' 'em pop up all over Five Kingdoms an' Acanthia. Somethin' about drawing power from the Land of the Dead."

"The dead?" Rose let out a sigh and gave her husband's hand a squeeze before pushing to her feet and fetching a pitcher of wine. "Perhaps you should tell me the whole story."

Betrim took one of the cups of wine and held it up high. "Drink ta the fallen, love."

Rose gave him a compassionate smile and raised her own cup. "We'll be joining them soon."

Once Betrim was finished with his telling, they drank another toast to the fallen. It seemed they had lost a few soldiers and, though Betrim wasn't close to any of them, he was fiercely loyal and that extended to anyone he deemed part of his crew.

"I'll give Kurt orders to double the guard duty," Rose said with a nod.

"Ya think whatever the fuck killed Suzku's clan will be comin' for us? For this army?"

"I can't say for sure. But I would rather have an early warning if it does. It wouldn't surprise me if this is some sort of trick being played by Niles Brekovich. We need to take that city and soon, Betrim."

"Ya seen those walls, love? There ain't no takin' Crucible quick."

Betrim pulled one boot off and then the other, mindless of the mud he was depositing in the tent. He leaned back in the chair and crossed his arms. A few moments later his eye was closed, and a few after that he was snoring softly. Rose watched him for a while. For such a long time Thorn wouldn't sleep without a wall at his back. Now he trusted her to watch it for him.

Rose crossed to the tent flap and pulled it open. The sight of a thousand torches atop Crucible's high walls greeted her. The mountains at the city's back made it seem small, yet it was anything but.

Pug waited outside along with Lucille. Rose held the tent flap open and nodded at her servant and midwife, and the woman hurried inside.

"Find me my general, Pug," Rose said in a cold voice. "I don't care if he's cock-deep in a brothel of whores. Find him and bring him to me now."

DAY 2 – THE PARLEY

The Black Thorn

The sun rose and with it came good news. Rose would be happy for the information Anders brought. Betrim was just happy to see his friend again. The drunkard's dual loyalties might put a strain on their relationship from time to time, but they'd been through half the hells together, and that made up for all the shit Anders put them through.

The news of his arrival preceded Anders by a fair stretch. Scouts rushing into camp with tales of a large column of soldiers arriving from the west with a drunkard wearing a green suit at the head. Didn't take a lot of deducing to figure out who that might be, but the scouts had done their jobs and asked.

Betrim sipped his ale, grinned, and disappeared back inside the tent to wake Rose. The woman wasn't the light sleeper she used to be. Ever since she started to swell, she'd been a devil to wake and snored like a broken trumpet.

Betrim had only known one man to ever have a worse snore, truth be told, and the fellow had regretted it. It was a different time back then, and Betrim was a different man. Levi Half-foot they called on him on account of having only half of his left foot. Man snored loud enough to sound like thunder across the plains of the Wilds. Whole crew had put up with it for ten days before Ron the Brown Tongue took a knife to Half-foot's nose. The resulting fight had broken up the crew and left two names bleeding their last in the dust, one of them by Betrim's own axe.

He sat down on the edge of Rose's cot and gave her a gentle shake. Nothing. He gave her a bit of a push, and she murmured. Eventually, Betrim gave Rose a hard shake of the shoulders and found bared steel kissing his throat.

"Every time, love," Betrim said. He wasn't about to show fear, even to his own wife, yet he really hated the way she slept with a knife in her hand.

Rose pushed herself up on one hand, keeping the knife at Betrim's throat, and leaned in for a kiss. Her eyes were dark and more dangerous than a storm at sea, and her hair was tousled from sleep. Betrim felt his blood start to rise.

"Can never be too careful," Rose said huskily, and there was a yawn in her voice. "Has Crucible fallen yet?"

The knife vanished, and Rose winced as she struggled to sit up properly. Betrim retreated from the bed and poured her a mug of weak ale. She never looked more beautiful than when she had just awoken. Before she put on her powder and armour. The Rose everyone else knew was just a show, but he knew the real woman and wouldn't trade the two for an instant.

"Walls are still standing. Blooded twats are still holed up behind them." Betrim grinned. "Good news is Anders will be here before noon. Got himself a small army too, though can't say where it's come from."

Rose yawned and arched her back, giving Betrim a good eyeful of both breasts and belly. She was watching him all the while too, letting him know it was as much for his benefit as hers. He handed her the mug of ale, and she sipped at it, her armour already starting to appear on her face.

"Any more incidents with the dead rising?"

Betrim shook his head. "Suzku still ain't right, neither. Lad is always quiet, but this... Haunted, I reckon. Reckon Henry might bring him out of it eventually. I spoke ta Kurt, seems ta think there might be a weak section of wall on the north. Needs ta check it out himself though. Spoke ta Lost too..."

"Who?"

"Captain Allestrue."

Rose just shook her head and frowned at her hair.

"Right. Well. He's, uh, one of our captains, I guess. Asked him ta be my personal guard, I reckon."

Rose smiled. "Well, it's about time you agreed to be guarded."

"Ain't never needed guardin' before. Not more than can be done with Henry an' Suzku anyway."

"How many men?"

Betrim shrugged. "Ten or so. All that made it through the dead shit last night."

Rose nodded and stretched again, but this time it wasn't for Betrim's benefit. The sun was starting to shine in through the tent flap, and Betrim reckoned it was going to be a bright day. Bright but cold.

"Let's hope Anders has some good news," Rose said and levered herself off the bed. She gave Betrim another kiss, then set about making herself look the queen she was soon to be.

Betrim watched Anders' column approach and settled into a good lean. He'd found himself an empty cart set up near the road and placed his back against it. It was probably the happiest he'd been since they left their home back in Chade. There was nothing quite like having a good solid wall of wood or stone at your back.

Some folk would have ridden ahead of their troops and hurried to meet up with the main army. Not Anders though. The blooded drunk rode along slowly, chatting with a black-skinned southerner nearly twice his size. Betrim reckoned Anders was doing most of the chatting, and he also reckoned the southerner probably wanted him to shut up.

The column of troops came to a halt as they approached the outskirts of the extensive camp. Anders grinned down from his saddle.

"See. I told you I knew him. I told him I know you, boss," Anders said as he swayed out his saddle. "Kur... kun. Am I pronouncing that right?"

"Kuren," the big southerner said in a quiet voice.

"That's it," Anders beamed. "Kuren here said the Black Thorn would have no need to know a sot like me. Well, I told him he was wrong, of course, but he insisted I was a liar. Which isn't altogether untrue, though I was..."

Betrim lurched away from the cart and gave Anders a hard clap on the shoulder, shutting him up. He looked up at the big southerner on his horse and nodded.

"Don't reckon I know you."

The southerner slipped from his saddle and approached. He was a good inch or two taller than Betrim, and that put him close to a giant. He was built like he knew his way around a fight too.

"You freed me. You freed Solantis."

"Ahh," Betrim smiled though no one wanted to see the horror it made of his face. "That."

He'd given up telling people that it was Henry who started the freeing and the slaves themselves who did most of the real work. Rose had spread the rumour it had all been Betrim, and now he had a reputation for putting slavers to death and breaking chains. He was fairly certain he'd done neither of those things.

"The free folk of Solantis fight for you now," Kuren said and gestured back towards the column of soldiers behind him. It was a fair number, Betrim reckoned, and he wondered if all of them were ex-slaves.

"Ain't a small force you're bringing, mate. Ya welcome ta join. Keep your lot here for now. I'll have the general send someone ta sort out who's goin' where."

Kuren nodded and held out a hand. Betrim looked down at it for a moment and then met it with his own five-fingered one. Not many folk shook hands in the Wilds - it was a dangerous prospect as folk were known to take the opportunity to commit murder. A sign of trust, Betrim reckoned, and, though it was against his nature, he had to show it.

"Come on, Anders," Betrim said, turning away from Kuren and his army. "If I don't get ya ta Rose soon she'll have both our stones."

"Not even time for a drink first?" Anders pleaded. The drunk did look a little too sober for Betrim's liking, and he was completely intolerable in such a state.

"We'll get a bottle of somethin' on the way."

Rose had already assembled her war council by the time Betrim and Anders ducked through the tent flap. The largest tent in the entire camp and it was mostly given over to a large table and several rickety chairs. A single cot sat in one corner, and the furs covering it were rumpled from use. Betrim would put money on Kurt Verit being the user, and he doubted very much that the big general had been alone. Man seemed to take it as some sort of challenge to try out every whore the army had following it and in every cot he could find.

They'd picked up a bottle of rum and Betrim had stolen a few swigs before Anders had proceeded to neck half the bottle. It was ever a surprise just how much booze the blooded drunkard could put away. Even more of a surprise that his body hadn't given up yet. Betrim had seen drunkards go terminal before. It wasn't pretty.

"Oh dear," Anders said with a grin. "Were you all waiting for me?"

"You are a little late, dear," Rose replied in a carefully calm voice. Betrim knew that voice well, and the woman beneath it was not nearly so calm as she claimed.

"Him?" Kurt said with a snort. "This drunk is your ace in the hole?"

Anders took a swig from the bottle and straightened up to his full height. "I have been called many things in my life, and I have earned most of those with gusto, but that may well be the least insulting of them all."

Kurt shook his head and let out a growl. His two captains behind him were silent but seemed to share their general's distaste.

There were seven of them in the tent now; Kurt and his two captains, men he had brought with him from the Five Kingdoms, were in charge of most of the army. Betrim and Rose were the two who had brought the whole thing together and made all the important decisions. Henry was there because she refused to be left out and had earned her place by the Black Thorn's side a hundred times over. And Anders was there because he had knowledge they needed. Always felt like there was a couple of them missing since Ben got himself hanged at Reingarde, and Rilly shipped out with Rose's boats to help Elaina Black fight for the Pirate Isles.

"Anders has first-hand knowledge of Crucible's defences, General Verit," Rose said. She was standing, and it was clearly uncomfortable, but she didn't look likely to sit even if Betrim insisted. "The benefits of being a Brekovich, I suppose."

"Ah." Anders held up a single finger. "Not any more. My father disinherited me... And tried to have me executed. Twice now actually.

Our relationship is somewhat strained, and I sincerely doubt of anything approaching a reconciliation."

"I don't care what your last name is," Kurt growled. "You have information regarding the city's defences? Tell me."

"How very brusque," Anders said with a smile. "Are you sure you wouldn't like a drink first?" He held out the bottle to the general who looked in no mind to take it.

"Anders." Betrim decided it was wise to inject some authority into the situation. "Get ta the tellin' or I'll set Henry on ya."

Henry grinned. Anders winked back.

"Right you are, boss. I assume you've had the foresight to wander around and see the whole city, hmm? Rather large, no? Well, those very high walls go all the way around. Unbroken. Unbreached."

"Ever?" Henry asked.

"Ever," Anders confirmed. "The city of Crucible has never been breached. D'oro, the very first ruler of the Wilds and the bloodline from which all the blooded are descended, built Crucible to stand against any and all invaders. Of course, he then invited all would be invaders into his City of Kings and proceeded to murder and or kidnap, threaten, and coerce them all into following him. Then he had nine sons who each wanted a piece of the pie and broke the Wilds apart, hmm?"

"I know the history of the blooded families, Anders," Rose said patiently. "Between the Black Thorn and myself we have put an end to six of those families, and only three are left, all of them holed up in Crucible. So, tell me how to get to them."

"Yes, well... At first glance, I'd say you can't, my lady. Crucible is ringed by two sets of walls. The first is a hundred feet of solid stone. The second is even higher, designed just so defenders on that second wall can rain arrows down on anyone who does manage to take the first.

"You might have seen the shallow moat ringing the outside wall? Well, there's another, even deeper, between the walls. Each wall has a single gate made of ironwood and bound with more iron. The inner gate has a portcullis behind it, so heavy it takes half a dozen men pushing a wheel to raise it. There are enough murder holes to wipe out the great herd, and it wouldn't surprise me if my father has ordered some oil to be

54

kept on the boil just in case. Honestly, the only good news here is that the two gates are aligned."

"An oversight," Kurt said with a nod. "They should have put them at opposite ends of the city, so any invading force would have to skirt the inner wall to assault the second gate."

Anders tapped his nose and pointed at the big Five Kingdomer. "My father will have stocked enough arrows to feather every man, woman, child, dog, and rat in this camp ten times over. He probably has the archers to do it too. Have we got a semi-accurate account of his numbers?"

"We estimate about four thousand," Rose said.

"Roughly a fifth of our own. I'd be happier with twice as many men before assaulting a city like this," Kurt said, looking as grim as the porridge Betrim had for breakfast.

Betrim left the debating of numbers up to wiser folk. He couldn't count for shit, and the words they were spewing at each other meant little to nothing to him. He stared down at the map of the region. It was staked out on the table and showed Crucible and much of the surrounding area including the mountains to the north, the Greywash a good way to the south, and the Boneyard to the east. The last was a place Betrim would happily forget. Wasn't too long ago Niles Brekovich had Betrim, Henry, and Anders staked out in the middle of the Boneyard and left for the laughing dogs to reduce to bones and bad memories.

Henry didn't look to be too interested in the numbers either. She was staring out the tent flap with her hat lowered to obscure her face. Betrim couldn't blame her. The last siege they'd been part of ended with a sewer and the little murderess killing babes. That was always a horrible job. Shame it needed to be done from time to time.

"Assaulting the city is suicide," Kurt argued. "We'd lose ten men for every one of theirs, and we don't have those sorts of numbers."

"What about firing them out?" Rose asked.

Anders gave his head a solemn shaking. "Even if we could get a fire going inside somehow, there are four deep wells in the city fed by flooded underground caverns and more than enough people to fight a few blazes."

"What do you suggest then, General Verit?" Rose asked, her voice the very definition of welcoming.

"Our siege is set up. They have one way in and out, and no one is using that without going through our army. We should settle in, starve them out. In the meantime, we build trebuchets and launch a steady stream of rocks at their walls. Eventually, they will crumble."

Anders sighed. "Yes. Why don't we launch some rotting carcases into their midst as well, ey? Start spreading the disease."

Kurt nodded.

Betrim shook his head. "Walls are what? Twenty paces thick at least. Didn't get a good chance ta measure last time I was marched through the gates, bein' in chains an all, but they weren't small. Two sets of them as well, separated by another fifty paces. Then another fifty inside the second wall cleared of anythin' ta create a killing zone with no cover should the walls ever actually be breached. Can't see any machine you could build throwin' a corpse that far."

That brought on a measure of quiet.

"He's right," Kurt said. "Our best chance is of a protracted siege. Starve them out."

"Indeed," Anders agreed. "Shame my father keeps food stores to feed all his people for about a year. Might be the pirates have built an entire kingdom out of water by the time we succeed."

"No," Rose said quietly. She was using the tone that commanded obedience. Didn't need to speak loudly, just dangerously and folk started to listen. "I don't want this done in months or years. I want that city taken in days."

Another dose of quiet fell over the group, long enough that even Henry turned around to see what was happening.

"That can't be done, my lady," said Kurt.

"It can. And it will, General Verit. I hired you, despite the animosity it has earned me from the Five Kingdoms, to use my soldiers to bring an end to this war. Are you saying you can't do it?"

All eyes turned to the big Five Kingdomer. He opened his mouth then shut it again, choosing his words carefully. "I'm saying you may not be able to afford the soldiers it will cost you to take the city, my lady. We have taken everywhere else. The Wilds belongs to you. This city and the remaining blooded are a formality. My advice is go back home and sit on your throne. Have that child growing in your womb. And let your army wait this one out. Eventually, Crucible will fall."

"No. It won't," Rose drew in a deep breath and Thorn knew she was steeling herself to share one of those secrets she liked to keep so well guarded. "Order your captains to leave, General."

The big man nodded, and his two captains ducked out of the tent with a shrug. Still Rose hesitated, chewing over what she needed to say. There was no sense in rushing her; Betrim knew that much at least. She'd tell them in her own time or not at all.

"You consider only the way to win this battle," Rose said in a tight voice. "I, however, am trying to win the war. Not just from a military standpoint, but from an economic standing also. We are running out of resources, General Verit. Anders..."

The drunk looked a little shocked to be called upon and paused with the bottle half way to his lips. "Oh, you want me to..."

"Well, you could lie to me and tell me you don't have our coffers memorised somewhere in that booze-addled brain of yours." Rose shrugged. "Or you could just make it easy on us for once."

Anders nodded. "Right. Well... You're broke. Between the renovations on Chade, the levying of this rather impressive army, supplying said army, waging the war against the blooded, and outfitting the pirates of the isles with both ships and crew... Oh, and the cost of setting up new trade routes throughout the world. You're pretty much down to pocket lint, my lady. Not to worry though, my father is nothing if not a frugal bastard. There's a fortune hidden somewhere in that city. I saw it once..." Anders trailed off, staring into the corner of the tent.

Rose placed two hands on the map table to steady herself, and Betrim wanted nothing more than to go to her and convince her to sit down, but she wasn't the type of woman to show that kind of weakness to others, and that was one more thing he loved about her.

"You've no doubt inspected our supplies yourself, General," Rose continued. "We have enough for a week or two at most, and no more is coming. Brekovich didn't just execute farmers outside of his city walls, he burned their fields and butchered every edible beast within a hundred miles. We cannot hold this siege for as long as you might think.

"And the blooded have allies." That seemed the last straw, and Rose's shoulders slumped a little. Her powder hid it well, but there was a deep weariness written in the lines on her face and distance in her eyes, Betrim could see it even if the others couldn't. "Sarth and your own Five Kingdoms have been supporting the blooded for decades. Weapons and troops and the bits to pay them. They want to keep us fighting amongst ourselves. They want to keep us from forming into a true kingdom. They believe themselves to be the peacekeepers of the world and do it by crushing any attempts to rival them. Right now, they see the pirates as the bigger threat. That's exactly why I supplied Elaina Black with her ships, to keep the attention on them. But it hasn't worked as well as I would have liked. Anders."

"Me again? Right you are. Capital spy and all that."

"Anders..." There was a warning in Rose's tone.

"You may have underestimated the depth of the resources the Five Kingdoms are able to bring to bear. A little." Anders through up his hands at the glare sent his way. "Don't look at me like that. He's the Five Kingdomer." He pointed at the general. "You'd think a prince would know things like that."

General Verit let out a sound like a growl.

"Down, you monster. Sit. Now roll over."

"Anders!" Betrim waded in before the general could take too much offence.

"What? If he sounds like a beast and smells like a beast, he's probably a beast."

"He's a prince."

Anders shook his head. "He was, a while ago. Not so much now, I fear."

General Verit took a menacing step towards Anders, rolling the muscles in his shoulders. "I'll make you fear."

Rose's voice cut through the argument. "You're delaying, Anders. If you're willing to provoke Kurt here, there really must be something you don't want to tell us."

Anders let out a loud sigh followed by an accompanying shrug and tapped the general on the arm. "All in good sport really. She's quite savvy, our queen here. Saw right through me. The Five Kingdoms have allied with Sarth to raise a fleet that they intend to throw at the pirates."

"Just as I planned."

"Indeed. Unfortunately, that's far from the true depth of their resources. Word has it they're sending fresh troops here to reinforce the blooded. And..." Anders trailed off, mumbling.

"Say it!" Rose hissed.

Anders upended the bottle into his mouth only to find it empty, and then sent a wistful look towards the cabinet where more bottles were held. "I've heard rumours they may have people here already. Working in Solantis and Korral and Chade, and all our other cities. Trying to drum up fresh support of the blooded. Or... more accurately... fresh support against yourself."

Betrim sighed. "Fuckin' bastards."

Anders shrugged. "Honestly, I think you should take it as a compliment. You have them quite scared."

"So, we're running out of resources." Rose said, her eyes pinned to the map table. "The blooded have fresh support on the way. And there are spies in my cities trying to undermine everything I have built!"

Anders shrugged on his way to the booze cabinet. "A fair, if a little unwelcome, summation. Just remember, the messenger is not to blame."

Rose sighed. "We don't have months for a lengthy siege, General. We have days, weeks at best. I intend to meet these reinforcements with a unified Wilds, but my kingdom will not be complete while even one blooded lord still draws breath. I will see them all dead before I claim a crown. I'd like to see them all dead before my child opens her eyes for the first time, General. Get it done."

Kurt drew in a deep breath and let it out as a sigh. Looked like he was about to argue. Betrim might have spoken up then, pointed out that there was no point to bitching and moaning and Rose was in charge. But he didn't need to. If there was one woman who could make that point all on her own, it was Rose herself.

"Give me a day, my lady," Kurt said. "My scouts have reported some caves north of the city. They need further exploration. And we need to find the necromancer who made that blood rune in the earth."

"Necromancer?" Anders' voice broke a little. "Blood rune? I feel I've missed something quite important."

Betrim grabbed the bottle from Anders and sniffed at it. "The last of Suzku's old clan caught up to us. Only somethin' got to them first, turned them into the dead."

"Wonderful." Anders sighed. "And the blood rune?"

"Necromancers use them to curse the land," Kurt said. "It takes three blood runes, carved into the earth with bodies and blood. If they're positioned right, along... ah, what do the Arbiters call it? Lines of power or something. If they're positioned right all the land between those runes becomes cursed. Connected to the Land of the Dead."

Rose shook her head. "We've never had necromancers before, General. This is almost certainly some trick of Brekovich's."

Betrim glanced at Anders. The blooded drunk looked like he had something to say, but was holding back.

"What if it isn't, my lady?" Kurt pressed. "If a necromancer is carving blood runes into the earth, the last thing we should be doing is fighting a war. The dead will rise. I've seen it. Give me time to scout properly. Explore the caves and find this necromancer, or at the very least destroy any other blood runes."

Rose held the general's gaze for a few moments before nodding her head. "One day, General. Tomorrow I want those walls to belong to me."

Kurt nodded and made a noise somewhere between a laugh and a sigh. He turned to go.

"Take Suzku," Betrim said.

"Eh? Your bodyguard?"

"He ain't... He needs time," Henry said.

"He spent all last night doin' a right good impression of Anders," Betrim said, fixing Henry with his stare. "An' one of the fuckers is more than enough."

Anders looked about to argue but nodded and kept his mouth shut.

"I'm goin' too," Henry declared.

"No. Ya ain't." Betrim needed Suzku right, and it seemed the best way to do that was to put him out in the world without his usual backup. "You'll be stayin' right here with me an' Anders. Kurt, you find Suzku an' take him with you. Give him somethin' ta fuckin' do. Don't let him wallow."

The big Five Kingdomer shrugged and ducked out of the tent. He looked more than happy to have a reason to be away from Rose and her demand. Seemed most everyone thought it was close to insanity, but it wasn't like they had much of a choice.

"Go find yaself some food, Anders," Betrim ordered. "Henry, go sharpen ya knives. Reckon me an' Rose got some talkin' ta do."

Suzku

The sun was too bright, the camp was too loud, and the sun was definitely too bright. Pern rolled over and found something hard digging into his chest. He was fairly certain his eyes were closed, but the sun was still there, lighting up his eyelids an odd red colour. He tried to shift the hard thing digging into his chest and found it was attached to him. Felt a lot like the hilt of his sword.

"The general is lookin' for ya." Henry's voice, hard and sharp. Pern had seen people cringe away from that voice before, but he never had.

Pern tried to open his eyes, and the effort was too much. Instead, he drew in a deep breath and puffed it out as a sigh. Dust tickled his nose. He wondered why there would be dust in his cot.

"Fuck's sake," Henry snapped. "Get up."

Pern felt a kick to his ribs, softened by the chainmail and not very hard to begin with. Henry wouldn't hold back for most people. That thought should have made him happy, but it was hard to be happy with the pit of despair that was settled in his gut.

The previous day's events came back to Pern and with them came scattered memories of the night, of indulging in alcohol. He was Honin, trained as a Haarin. Trained to resist temptations, to always be alert and on guard. Pern was trained to be one of the best bodyguards in the known world. Yet he had made a true fool of himself during the night, stupid actions fuelled by a substance he had never before imbibed in any real volume.

Pern let out a groan and made an earnest effort to pry his eyes open. Light flooded in, and the world was too bright and too loud all over again. A wave of nausea rolled over him, and he drowned in the tide. Bile rose up, and he vomited into the dust.

Henry scoffed.

Pern had made a fool of himself drinking with the soldiers the night before, but now he was losing Henry's respect, and that hurt him even more. He knew he should shape up, sober up, be the Honin everyone expected him to be. But he couldn't find the effort. His clan were dead. Not just dead but desecrated. Their souls wouldn't be reborn into the next generation of Haarin. They had no client to serve in the afterlife, no way of being reborn. They were lost souls now. In time they would become wraiths, cursed to plague the living for eternity. And it was all his fault.

He retched again into the dust, his stomach was empty, and his mouth tasted foul. Pern wanted nothing more than to drop back into the oblivion of sleep.

"Get up, ya dumb fuck," Henry cursed. She ducked down and heaved on Pern's arm, pulling him upright, then put it over her shoulders and lifted him. Pern thought about resisting, he was twice Henry's size and could easily stop her, even pull her down into the dust with him, but he had already made enough of a fool of himself. He had already lost enough of her respect.

With help from Henry, Pern managed to deposit himself on a nearby stool. It was mid-morning, judging by the sun, and he was in the remains of a camp. A small fire had burned during the night but was now nothing but ashes and bitter memories. He couldn't remember how he had got there, how much he had drunk, or even who he had drunk with. Pern wondered if this was how Anders lived his entire life. He couldn't imagine being so scattered all the time.

"I think I may have passed out," Pern said slowly. His speech sounded slow and laboured to his ears.

Henry let out a harsh laugh as she stared down at him. "First time drinkin'. Ain't really a hobby worth takin' up."

Pern shook his head slowly and fought another wave of nausea.

"Them folk are dead, Pern." Henry gave up standing over him and sat down next to him. "Ain't a consolation. But they're dead. An' you're not. Ain't worth joinin' 'em over a little guilt."

"A little?" Pern winced against the sunlight and wished the bustling camp of soldiers would quiet.

"Maybe a lot. Still ain't worth dyin' over. Anders might tell ya ta find some sort of peace at the bottom of a bottle. Problem is Anders don't know shit. Only thing ya ever find at the bottom of a bottle is a reason ta look for a full one.

"Folk die. Sometimes it's your fault, sometimes not. Only thing ta do is drink ta the fallen an' then keep on goin'. One day ya might have ta drink ta me. Or maybe I gotta drink ta you. Don't reckon either would be a cause for the other ta stop though. World keeps bein'. An' so do we."

Henry fell silent then. The little woman just sitting with him. He glanced down to find her staring at the sky. Some men cringed away from the scars on Henry's face, but not Pern. He found them as fascinating as Henry herself.

"Ya gonna keep starin' at me, or go an' find the general?"

Pern levered himself onto unsteady legs. Henry watched him.

"Thank you," Pern said with a nod.

Henry's cheeks turned a slight shade of red, and she snorted, tilting her head so her hat blocked Pern's view.

There didn't seem much else to say. Or maybe there was, and Pern just didn't know the words. Henry certainly didn't seem about to volunteer any. Pern stumbled away, fighting the urge to vomit and the pounding in his skull.

Pern found General Verit loading supplies into his saddlebags while his scout force did the same. They were close to fifty soldiers, and all had followed the general from the Five Kingdoms after his exile. There was no doubt they would follow him to the Hells and back if he asked it of them. Pern respected that sort of loyalty, and he respected that it came from somewhere. If his soldiers would die for him, it was likely because he would die for his soldiers.

The sun was high, but the day was chilly. Usually, that wouldn't have bothered Pern, but he was strangely on edge, as though his patience was worn to nothing. It wasn't helped by the gnawing pit that was his stomach. He was chewing on his fourth strip of dried beef, yet he still felt empty inside.

The general looked up as Pern approached, and a smile broke across his wide face. The general was a big man with strong features and piercing eyes. He wore his hair short and his beard wild. His aura was the purest royal blue, the colour of control. Pern respected anyone with such an aura.

"You have the look of a man who is regretting a good night, Honin Suzku," General Verit said, the grin not slipping even for a moment.

"I cannot remember if it was good. I think not though. I think I may have dishonoured myself."

General Verit waved away the comment. "Not a soldier here hasn't been in your position. I once woke up in my brother's bed with four women, and I couldn't name a one of them." He shrugged, and a frown crinkled his brow though the smile never left his lips. "I'm told one of them was his betrothed, but... Uh, well I suppose it didn't go to term after that. Strangest thing, the snively little shit blamed her and not me."

Pern said nothing. He had never woken up with a woman, drunkenly or otherwise, so he felt he had little to add to the conversation.

After a few moments of awkward silence, the general nodded. "Where's your horse?"

Pern frowned. "I was told you were looking for me?"

"Well, yes. Did Thorn not tell you?" He shook his head and frowned. "Piss poor excuse for leadership. We're riding north of the city to have a look at some caves. It'll do me some good to get away from that damned woman and her drunken blooded pet. The Black Thorn volunteered you to come along."

"I'm no scout. I am Honin."

General Verit nodded. "So I hear. All the same. Orders are orders, Honin Suzku, and you're to come with us."

Pern nodded. He wondered if he'd be able to ride without either throwing up or falling out of the saddle.

"Looks like the air might do you some good. Never seen a man with your colouring go so green before." The general gave Pern a slap on the shoulder. "Get your horse. We're leaving... well... now."

Anders

By midday, Anders had truly settled into the siege. He hadn't been to many, and one of those had been on the other side of the wall, but he knew how most of these sorts of things went. There would be an awful lot of sitting around and even more drinking. It was impossible to hold any sort of prolonged siege without ample booze supplies for the troops and, though Anders wasn't one of the soldiers, he was more than happy to partake in those supplies. Actually, the sitting around and drinking was a large part of why he had decided to come. He'd need to nip off back to the Pirate Isles soon enough, but for now, he had a little time and spending it camped outside his family home, drinking to their poor health, seemed a fair way to spend it.

"Does anyone have any sort of musical, um, ability?" Anders slurred. The best thing about large armies was there always some soldiers off duty, and that meant there were always folk to get drunk with.

"I can play the lute," said a woman with a pretty face and a body hard with muscle. Anders had a type when it came to women, and the more dangerous they were, the more they interested him. And this woman looked like danger heaped on top of peril.

"Oh, but I was hoping to steal a dance from you, my dear," Anders slurred and gave her a lurid wink. She smiled back, and he was happy to see she knew the game and looked a willing player.

"Black Thorn wants you, Lord Anders," said a young and irritating voice.

"So how about it?" Anders ignored the voice and concentrated on the muscular woman who claimed some ability with a lute. The best thing about soldiers, other than their love of a good drink, was their love of a good fuck.

"Now, my lord."

Anders swivelled his head to see the young squire, Pug, standing to rigid attention nearby. The lad didn't look in the least bit put off by Anders' clear lack of enthusiasm.

"I'm no lord. Actually, I have no title whatsoever. Technically speaking, little Pug, you outrank me." Anders grinned at the lad.

"Then we'll call it my order as well as Lord Thorn's."

A few of the soldiers Anders was drinking with took to laughing, including the woman whom Anders was fairly intent on exploring.

"You may outrank me, boy. But I don't have to follow your orders. I'm not part of this army. I'm not part of any army. I'm what's known, in many circles, as a free agent. I don't have to do anything you say." He finished by giving the lad his most patronising of grins and turned away.

Pug was silent for a few moments, and Anders took that as a victory. He was just about to redouble his efforts to find out how muscular the woman with the lute really was under all that armour.

"I am squire to the Black Thorn," Pug announced. The lad stepped up beside Anders and pointed at both the muscular woman and a man with a head the shape of a rock. "You two, please pick this man up and follow me."

"Now wait just a minute," Anders started, but it was too late. Within moments he found himself grabbed by the arms and dragged through the camp behind the young squire.

"In there please."

Anders was dumped rather unceremoniously through the tent flap and the soldiers quickly turned and hurried away. Pug followed in and stood by the entrance. Anders surged to his feet and rounded on the lad, more than a little annoyed that they were both of a height and of a build. It was quite possible the squire would be a rather big man once he had stopped growing.

"Now listen here, boy. I don't take kindly to being manhandled."

In the lad's defence, he didn't back down, and Anders had to give him some credit for that. He had seen much larger men quail in the face of a verbal onslaught, but Pug stood his ground.

"As you just pointed out, Anders," Pug said, neither grinning nor showing a drop of fear, "I am still a boy, and one of those soldiers was a woman. I'm not sure you could really call that being manhandled."

Anders opened his mouth to reply and realised he couldn't think of witty quip. In times like this, he had long ago discovered it usually best to admit defeat.

"I reckon he has ya, Anders," Thorn said from further inside the tent.

"I believe you might be right, boss." Anders grinned and gave Pug's hair a ruffle. "Quite the little thug you're mentoring."

Thorn nodded. He was leaning against the central tent pole and looking quite severe. Rose was there too, seated by the table and looking radiant despite her bulging belly. Anders was never one to find pregnancy an attractive situation for a woman to be in, but Rose wore it well, and she was quite easily the most dangerous woman he had ever met. And that was saying something.

"My lady," Anders said with a deep bow. "You are more beautiful than the sun after a year of night."

Rose cocked an eyebrow and smiled. "You're not getting out of it, Anders."

Anders had no idea what it was he was trying to get out of, but he was most certain that he wanted out of it. Thorn's plans had a habit of getting him beaten up, and Rose's plans had almost killed him on no less than two separate occasions.

"Worth a try, I suppose. Exactly what am I not getting out of? And please don't say parley."

"Parley," Thorn said with a grin.

"Do you ever get the feeling you've just dug your own grave, boss?"

Thorn nodded. "Pretty much every time I talk ta my wife."

Anders took to shaking his head. "Boss, I can't see this going well. No one wants to parley with you after what happened at Reingarde."

"Part of why we're sendin' you."

"What happened at Reingarde?" Pug asked.

They all took a moment to stare at the young squire, and Pug took a moment to look thoroughly embarrassed to be the centre of such attention.

"Murder," Thorn said and had the stones not to look guilty. "Bloody murder an' more than enough of it. The blooded lost an entire family an' we lost a good friend."

"That price doesn't sound so much for the taking of an entire city." Again, Pug became the centre of attention.

"Ya weren't there, lad, an' ya didn't know Ben, so I'm gonna let that slide." Thorn spat onto the rug at their feet, and Rose winced, but she didn't say anything. "Losing Six Cities Ben was too steep a price for what went down there."

There were a good few moments of silence. "Regardless," Anders continued after it looked like Thorn was well and truly done. "Word spread. You killed the Hammer under a parley..."

"Seem ta remember it were a duel... Of sorts."

"Well whatever you're calling it, boss, does not exactly mean my father sees it the same way."

"Ahh, but there it is, Anders." Rose joining the conversation probably spelled the end for any sort of opposition Anders could give, but he was damned well going to try anyway. "Niles Brekovich is your father."

"Well that doesn't mean a bloody thing. Have I mentioned how many times he's tried to have me executed?"

Rose gave him a patient smile. Some folk might think it gracious, but Anders knew patronising when he saw it, partially because he was so fond of using it himself.

"If myself or Betrim were to approach those walls we would be covered in arrows before speaking a word. You, on the other hand..."

"Me?" Anders scoffed and turned to Thorn. "You, at least, must remember the time my father tried to have us killed? I lost a finger!"

"I remember you sayin' he didn't try too hard on account of maybe not wantin' you so dead after all."

Anders let out a bark of laughter. "When it comes to attempted murder, not trying too hard is not the same as not trying at all. Send Pug over there. He's nobody. No one cares if he lives. My father is unlikely to kill someone of so little importance."

"Pug doesn't have the experience necessary to treat with your father, Anders," Rose said calmly and took a sip of something that looked suspiciously like fruit wine. Anders felt his mouth start to water. "Nor does he have the required knowledge to treat on my behalf."

Anders tore his eyes away from the wine and shook his head. "It doesn't matter what he says or doesn't, my lady. Could I maybe get a cup of wine?"

Rose sipped again and stared at him.

"Right. Well, my lady. The thing is. After Reingarde, none of the remaining blooded will believe a word coming from Thorn or yourself."

"All of the remaining blooded are holed up in that city."

"Yes. And none of them will listen to a word I say because it's obviously coming from you."

"What I want you to say isn't for their ears, Anders."

"Oh bollocks."

Rose settled into a victorious smile.

"Can I at least get drunk first?" Anders asked.

"Ya already drunk," said Thorn.

"More drunk."

Suzku

The city of Crucible sat nestled at the foot of the greatest mountain range in the known world, the World's End Mountains. Pern doubted the world truly ended at these great peaks, but then he had no basis for a claim one way or another.

The first of the mountains rose up north of Crucible. It started off a slight incline before giving way to rockier, steeper ground. Before long, their horses proved useless, dangerous even on such unstable footing, and they were forced to dismount. Pern stared up at the mountain and shivered at the cold air. Not for the first time, he wished he had brought a cloak and cursed his scattered mind for forgetting. He vowed never to drink again.

"Impressive, no?" General Verit asked. The big Five Kingdomer was wrapped up warm and tight against the chill, and the furs made him look even more of a giant. His cheeks were red, and he wore a wild grin on his face.

Pern nodded. The mountain dwarfed Crucible. It dwarfed anything man had ever built. Made all their accomplishments seem small and insignificant. They were little more than embers in the grand scheme of things, brief flashes of existence and then gone. But the mountain went on. It had seen the rise of Crucible, and it would see the city fall as well.

"It's a baby," the general continued. "There are mountains further north that could swallow this one a hundred times over. Same in my homeland. We have some impressive peaks in the Five Kingdoms. Unfortunately, they're populated by bastards who only come down to steal our food and women."

"I hear a man could walk from the Wilds to the Five Kingdoms if he were a brave enough climber," Pern said and blew warm air into his hands.

General Verit laughed and shook his head. "The mountains do cross the whole of the Forlorn Sea north of here, it's true. But I've never heard of anyone making the trip. It would be years of travel, all up and down and the most treacherous footing in the world. Not to mention the situation of food. Snow can be melted for water, but food... The only things living in those mountains would likely see a lone man as an easy meal.

"And the cold. Your teeth are chattering now, Honin. Up there," the General pointed up past the mountain they stood at the foot of, "the air is so cold you can't breathe it. So icy your eyes would freeze in their sockets."

Pern looked up at the mountain again. It did seem a cold and desolate place. Broken rocks and steep inclines with only the odd wiry shrub as signs of life. It seemed a stark contrast to the city below it with high walls teeming with activity.

He turned to find the general grinning at him. "Don't worry, Honin. We're not climbing the beast. Not much of it anyway. The caves are just a short way up, hidden from sight, but my men assure me they are there."

"What do you hope to find, General?" Pern asked. He was still fighting the ache in his head and the urge to vomit what little he had managed to eat; the general's good humour was grating on the patience he had managed to piece together.

General Verit shrugged, his big shoulders shifting the furs on his back. "A way into the city would be nice, no?"

Pern nodded. "What do you think you'll find?"

The general smiled. "Rocks."

One of the general's men came hurrying down the slope, far faster than Pern would have guessed was safe. Even from a distance, he could see a concerned look on the man's face. A look that might have been fear.

Pern felt his stomach grumble, and his head ceased its pounding for a few moments. He drew in a deep breath, closed his eyes, and turned his head up to the sky, before blowing out a sigh. How men could live such an existence, Pern could not fathom. Day to day on the knife edge, drink to drink just to stay sane. As a Haarin, Pern had been hired to serve the vilest man he had ever known in Swift, but at least his life had purpose, direction, meaning. Perk shook his head at the self-indulgent brooding. Scattered thoughts and a sour mood were indeed the price paid for drinking so heavily. Once more he questioned how Anders could stand such an existence.

Pern turned tired eyes towards Crucible. The soldiers in the city would have seen the small force heading north. They could no doubt see them now, a hundred men and women in armour and just as many horses were a difficult sight to hide on such barren terrain. There were places they could hide though, ways in which people could move unseen against the backdrop of a mountain. It was, after all, a grand sight to distract the eye.

The soldier came skidding to a halt among the rocks and nodded to the general. Now he was closer, Pern could see the man's aura was flaring yellow. The man was scared, fear pulsing off him in waves.

"Report," the general ordered.

"Found the caves, sir. Claw marks outside, deep gouges. The entrance had a smell about it. Musky."

"Any blood? Carcases? Bones?" the general asked.

The soldier shook his head slowly.

General Verit nodded and looked around at his troops. One hundred of them all armed and armoured. It was the look a man gave when he was about to order people to their deaths, and Pern had seen it many times before. He wondered what might be up in those caves that the general would appear so hesitant. It said a lot that the general was here with them, unwilling to send his soldiers into any situation he wouldn't put himself in.

"Armour off, lads," the general said, already unbuckling his plate bracers. "Bollocks to your swords. Maces and spears only."

Pern waited and watched while all around him soldiers started stripping their plate and mail and leaving them by the horses. Many dropped their swords too.

"Okam," the general continued as one of his men helped him with the buckles on his breastplate, "take your ten and stay with the horses."

"Yes, sir."

"Are you coming, Honin?" the general asked.

His aura was still a deep blue, but wisps of purple had started to seep into it. The general was excited and a little bit nervous.

"I only have a sword."

The general shrugged out of his breastplate and caught it before it hit the rocky ground. "I suppose it will have to do. I'd ditch the mail though; it will only slow you down."

"It never has before."

General Verit laughed and shook his head. "Those things in there won't care about your armour. If they catch you, no amount of metal will save your life. Better you keep lighter, faster."

"What exactly are we going to find in there, General?" Pern asked.

The general glanced up towards the mountain, where the scout had come from. All around them the soldiers were stripping out of their armour and Pern found himself swamped by orange auras. The fear and excitement were like a miasma, so thick it nearly choked him.

"Trolls."

Suzku

The cave was south facing and as ominous as it was dark. Despite the afternoon sun shining down into the mouth, Pern could not see more than ten feet inside. It was tall and wide, easily large enough for a creature many times taller than a man. He wondered how they hadn't seen it from the trail at the foot of the mountain. He also wondered how it might have gone unnoticed by the people of Crucible for so long.

A part of Pern considered the possibility of a trap. That the cave might be some ambush laid out by the blooded to lure members of Thorn's army away to their deaths. The claw marks, huge rents dug out of the cave mouth, convinced him that ambush was the least of his worries. Pern knew of no beast that could gouge out solid rock like that.

The general was nearby with his scouts, two men and a woman who had found the cave. They were showing him signs near the cave mouth, tufts of hair and the like. The general nodded, his face grave, and peered into the darkness of the abyss. He sniffed the air and nodded again. He seemed to have some experience with the matter of trolls.

Pern gave a shiver and wished he hadn't listened to the general. Discarding his mail with the horses may make him lighter and faster in a pinch, but with the weather so cold he could have done with the extra insulation.

"Looks like trolls," said a young soldier with fiery hair and a cleft chin. Many of General Verit's soldiers were young with only a few true veterans among them.

"A pack, aye," Captain Otto agreed. "Never heard of trolls in the Wilds. Might be different to our Five Kingdoms' sort, eh?" The man looked excited, as though the prospect of encountering a new species of troll was a good thing, but his golden aura said otherwise. He was scared.

"I would expect there to be blood outside a predator's lair," Pern said, stepping closer and looking at the coarse hair the general held between his fingers. It looked a lot like a horse's hair only thicker and more wiry. "Bones maybe. Signs of..."

"You an expert on trolls?" Otto asked.

Pern shook his head. "I am Honin."

"What's that?"

"It means he doesn't know a damned thing about trolls," General Verit said and shook his head. "What do you think they eat, Honin? A pack of trolls maybe ten strong."

"Bodies? Large herbivores such as travel with the great herd. People, maybe."

The general laughed, and some of his troops joined in. Not Captain Otto though, the man shook his head in disgust and turned away.

"Shrooms. Fungus," General Verit said. "That's all they eat. Underground caverns full of the things. Some are massive, grow a good fifty feet high. The Drurr harvest them, but they got the idea from trolls. Doesn't mean a troll won't kill a man by biting him in half, though."

"Something one might want some protection from. Such as armour," Pern glanced back down the mountain. They were a good way up from the horses, and it would take quite some time to go back and get his mail.

"Oh, they can bite through metal as well, Honin. Even if they couldn't, a troll is strong enough to tear a man limb from limb. They might only stand as tall as two men stacked, but they're as strong as ten. Bloody hard to kill as well."

"So why are going to try?" Pern asked.

"To explore the caves, Honin. There might be a way into the city down there." The general paused and glanced back at the city. "I hope there's a way in."

Pern was anything but convinced, yet it was not his place to argue. He was there on the Black Thorn's orders, and it was most likely to protect the general. He was one man the army could not do without if they were to take the city by force.

"General, just inside the entrance," said another of his scouts, a woman with mousy hair and one white eye. "Trollbane."

General Verit nodded and turned back towards his troops. "Looks like there might be some Drurr in there along with the trolls. Makes sense. Perhaps they're trying to dig into Crucible. Let's hope so. Stay alert. Keep your torches lit. And don't give any the fuckers a chance to speak.

"Otto, Vanda, we'll take your lot in first. Fielder and Book, have yours follow us in at a distance. Can't say how many might be down there and if we clump up they'll tear us apart. We'll need room to manoeuvre."

Torches were handed out, one to every man or woman entering the cave and Pern accepted his gladly. Though auras often looked like bright colours to his eyes, they did nothing to provide any actual light. He felt lost. The soldiers with him were all Five Kingdomers and the general's personal troops. They had fought beside him for years, likely they had also fought trolls beside him. Pern was not one of them.

"General," he said as he fell in beside the big man. They were of a height and almost of a build, but the general was slightly bulkier. He had shed his plate and cloak but kept his leathers, and the weapon hanging by his hip was no sword. It was three feet of solid steel growing wider towards the end. Flanges ran up each of the four sides of the weapon, and many were dented or chipped from use. Even Pern would struggle to use such a weapon with any real finesse such was its weight, but the general carried it with ease.

"No one would blame you if you wanted to stay out in the light, Honin. Trolls are nothing to be taken lightly. But there is true glory in taking one down."

"What is trollbane? And what should I expect down there, General?"

The general smiled at him. "It's a weed. Doesn't grow in the light though. Trolls can't stand it; the smell, we believe. It won't stop one of the monsters from charging you, but the Drurr use it to– herd them. Keep them away from places, such as cave mouths, when they don't want their pet trolls spilling out into the night."

"The night?"

"Trolls aren't fond of light, Honin. They live most of their monstrous lives underground. Torchlight is annoying to them. Daylight is blinding.

"You can expect fifteen to twenty feet of towering, pallid flesh.

Some have hair, others not. They have squat legs and overly long arms, reaching down to their knees. Their hands are massive paws, each finger with a talon, and they spend their days digging through solid rock underground, so you can imagine how tough they are."

Pern was struggling to imagine such a creature. "How should I fight one?"

Otto laughed. "Carefully." Some of his soldiers joined in, and a few shot Pern mocking looks. He ignored them all. He was Honin. Their approval did not matter.

"He's not wrong," the general continued. "Stay in the light of the torches. Their eyes are huge, used to seeing in pitch black conditions. Big ears and nose too. They'll likely smell or hear us long before we see one.

"Try to distract one, get its attention, and then stay out of its reach. Your sword won't do much good, but they can feel pain."

"They heal fast," Otto added. "Almost as fast as you can cut them."

"Their skin does, aye," General Verit said. "Tough as scale mail and knits in minutes. But their bones don't heal so quickly. We distract them with spears, then shatter their legs with maces. Once they're down, we aim for the heads. Try to finish them off quickly. Work in a group, always. Stay close to me, Honin. You distract them, and I'll do the damage." The general patted the weapon hanging by his side and grinned, his excitement palpable.

Pern nodded. "Anything else?" he asked. They looked almost ready to enter the darkness now. The soldiers being left outside appeared relieved.

Captain Vanda stepped closer and lit Pern's torch with her own. "Stay. In. The light."

Anders

Anders approached the walls alone. They hadn't even provided him with a horse. Thorn's justification had been that they couldn't waste the beast should the blooded folk decide to fill Anders with arrows. At least that had been his bold proclamation. Anders suspected Thorn's motives were actually far subtler, and he wanted the long walk between siege lines and city walls to sober him up a bit. Anders pulled his hip flask from a hidden pocket in his faded jade green suit and sipped at the delicious whiskey within. It took about as much to remove Anders from alcohol as it did to remove the Black Thorn from sharp pointy objects.

The people up on the walls still looked very small, but then Anders supposed they were still quite far away. He stopped a good twenty feet before the moat and waited. The smell from the dead and dying farmers staked out before the moat was atrocious and Anders did his very best to ignore both it and the pleading look one of the still-clinging-to-life farmers gave him. The bridge across to the gate was a permanent feature yet he wasn't about to risk setting foot on it without permission. He planted his white flag in the dirt, taking no less than three tries before the damned thing stuck, and then waited some more.

Anders waited a good long time before he decided the city and its inhabitants weren't about to make the first move.

"I've, um, come to parley with Niles Brekovich. My father. Lord Brekovich. The one with the scary eyes. Never blinks. It's quite unnerving; you must have noticed!" Anders shouted to make certain they heard him.

No response other than the shifting of a few spears atop the wall and the unmistakeable sound of a bow being drawn. A *twang* later and an arrow lodged itself in the dirt just a step to Anders' right.

"Well that was a waste of an arrow" said a loud, brutish voice that could only belong to his brother Francis. "Good job we've got about a million more!"

Anders swallowed. He truly hoped Francis was under orders not to kill him, because his younger brother had expressed many an interest in murdering Anders, and now was about the best time he'd ever get.

"I'm here on behalf of Lady Rose and the Black Thorn," Anders shouted, "to parley with our father. Not you, Francis. Honestly, there will be a lot of big words, and I'm really not sure you'd understand them."

The air went silent between them. So quiet Anders could hear the wind. The tension was only further raised by the drawing of a bowstring. He looked up, past the hanging corpses, to the top of the wall and saw his younger brother aiming that bow straight down toward him.

The arrow whistled past Anders' left ear and *thudded* into the ground behind him. He let out a ragged breath and glanced down to make certain he hadn't pissed his trousers. He was safe on that matter for now and decided to take the opportunity of his extended living to sip from his flask again. If Anders were about to die, he would do so with a fiery taste on his lips.

"Your aim is getting worse, little brother," Anders shouted. "I assume that's why Lisha isn't pregnant yet?"

A couple of laughs, quickly cut off, floated down from the wall.

"This one goes right through your cock, Anders," Francis snarled from up above.

"Such a large target," Anders said with a shrug. "How could you miss?"

It was, perhaps, not the smartest of decisions to antagonise his little brother so, but it had always been one of Anders' favourite pastimes even when they were children. Francis was the younger, but from an early age he had always been the larger and large boys were often bullies. Francis was no exception. Anders had never been able to match him for strength, but what Francis had in brawn he lacked in wit.

Twang!

Anders winced but didn't move. He had the distinct impression he was safer if he stood as still as stone. The arrow buried itself in the dust between his feet, and Anders let out a ragged sigh.

"Missed," Francis called down. "Must be a smaller target than you think."

Anders shrugged. "Your wife never complained."

"Fuck you, Anders. You're going to die down there with your whore and her army."

"Right. Well, are we done with the unpleasantries?" Anders shouted. "I'm here to talk to our father. I suppose if he won't see me I can turn around and go back to camp. I must admit, that would be my preference. If it comes to a pinch I suppose I could talk with D'roan instead. Is Alistair up there?"

Another face appeared at the wall, just a few paces from Francis, and it did look suspiciously like Alistair D'roan, though he was wearing a smattering of stubble these days. The blooded lord looked down on Anders with a face one part disgust to two parts hatred.

"Wonderful," Anders shouted and gave D'roan a little wave. "Good to see you again, Alistair. I never really got to apologise for murdering your son, did I? Sorry about that. Bit of a mistake really. I wasn't trying to have him killed... Just... you know... buggered."

Another arrow hit the ground near Anders, and this time he didn't even flinch. "Oh, I think we can do away with that now, Francis. It's quite clear my father has ordered you not to kill me just yet. Besides, we've moved on from you, little brother."

"Your father isn't the only one in charge," Alistair D'roan called down, a sickening smile spreading across his handsome face.

"No?" Anders decided he needed another sip of courage and found his flask running horribly towards the empty side. "In his own city? Is he sharing power with you, Alistair? What's he put you in charge of? Is it the women? Say, how is your daughter, Emin? Last time I saw her my father was beating her like a mule. Riding her like one as well. He promised he'd send her back to you with a bastard inside her belly."

A truly uncomfortable silence blossomed, and Anders started to wonder how much longer he could push his luck before Francis really did put an arrow in him. This was why Rose and Thorn had sent him. Pug would never have been able to get under their skin, he was a nobody, but Anders was one of them. He was blooded, disinherited or not.

"Rumour has it she does have a little child, just a year or so old," he continued.

The silence reappeared as all those on top of the wall stared down at him.

"I look forward to seeing you burn, Anders," Alistair D'roan hissed, a voice full of venom.

Anders saw Francis drawing his bowstring back again, sighting down the arrow. Then he went rigid and released the tension, dropping the bow and bowing his head. There was only one person in all the world who could elicit such a response and Anders felt his stomach turn at the thought.

Niles Brekovich stepped up to the parapet and looked down upon his eldest son. His hair was greying and artfully tousled, his horseshoe moustache was perfectly trimmed, and his wide blue eyes were goggling as they always did. He didn't blink as he stared down at Anders. The bastard never blinked.

For a long time, no one said anything, and Anders struggled to find his own tongue. He was, it had to be said, quite cowardly at heart, and through all the things he'd seen - demons and wraiths and death itself - nothing scared Anders quite like the stern disapproval of his father. He upended his flask, found it empty, and licked at the last few drops. The liquid courage had finally run out.

"I'm..." Anders coughed and found he couldn't meet his father's unblinking stare any more. "I'm, uh, here on behalf of Lady Rose and..."

"I do not care what that whore has to say," Niles Brekovich said. He did not shout, yet his voice seemed to travel the space between them with ease. "I should have known you'd come sniffing around behind her."

Anders thought of a dozen witty replies and gave voice to none of them.

"My first-born son. You were always such a disappointment. Too much like your mother. Weak. Driven by addiction. Treacherous."

Anders might have argued with the accusations, though all were true, and he was struggling to find his voice against his father's derision.

"If only Francis had your wit and intelligence. Between the two of you, you might make a worthy successor."

Anders glanced upwards to see his younger brother looking almost as ashamed as he felt.

"Go back to the whore, Anders. Tell her I will see her army

scattered below my walls and when her husband lies dead at my feet I will cut that child out of her and feed it to the dogs."

Niles Brekovich turned to leave, and Anders realised this was likely his only chance to say what needed saying.

"Right," he started, raising his voice and cursing the fact that it didn't carry as well as his fathers. "Well, I suppose I'll say that, but they were really quite insistent that I convey their terms."

Anders cleared his throat. His father had stopped moving, his head just about visible.

"The Lady Rose offers amnesty for any willing to lay down their arms. Surrender the city..." Anders felt a lump in his throat and swallowed hard. "Niles Brekovich, Alistair D'roan, and Tanith Fanklin will be put to death, all other members of the blooded families will be allowed to live and exiled to a city of their choosing.

"Nobody needs to die here for the sake of the blooded families who have strangled the Wilds for generation upon generation. There's no..."

"ENOUGH!" Anders had never heard his father shout before; the man had never needed to. It seemed he was at least half foghorn given the volume he produced and the way his voice carried. Anders found his mouth was shut and very much refusing to open again.

"One more word, Anders, and I will give Francis permission to kill you." Niles Brekovich was serious about the threat. He returned to the parapet and looked down on his son. "Run!"

Anders blinked twice, a little confused by the seriousness of his father's order. The man really wasn't joking. He turned on leaden feet and started into a sprint as fast as his drunken coordination would allow.

Suzku

The flickering glow from twenty torches kept the dark and the cold at bay both. Pern followed the general in, staying close and keeping alert. He was Honin, trained as a bodyguard, and he felt better when he had someone to protect. Kurt Verit needed protecting. He was likely their only hope to take Crucible.

A dripping echoed through the caves. It was the only sound save for the *pop* of the torches and the scuff of boots on hard stone. No one spoke a word, and Pern was happy to mimic with the silence.

The passage started to dip down, and before long they were walking down a steep slope. A small stream ran alongside the left-hand wall, cutting a slow groove in the stone below it.

Pern glanced about at the group. Weapons were drawn, faces were grim, and the torches made everyone look slightly demonic. It was hard to see auras in such darkness, but Pern could feel the nervous fear even without his strange sight.

They came to a fork in the tunnel. One direction led off farther north, into the mountains, while the other seemed to double back on itself. The general pointed to the passage leading back towards the south, and one of his men moved forward and marked the wall for the second group. They continued on, moving farther down into the depths.

The tunnel walls were strange. They looked scraped away by something. Pern hadn't entirely believed the general when he said the trolls dug the passageways, but now he was starting to reconsider his position.

There was a smell on the stale air. Something Pern hadn't noticed before. It was an earthy musk, almost sickly sweet. General Verit saw him sniffing and smiled. Pern shot him a worried look in reply. Still no words were spoken.

They crept along as quietly as they could, taking each step carefully. Their vision only extended twenty paces, and everything beyond that was pitch black, almost unnaturally so.

The tunnel seemed to open out around them. One moment they could see the walls, torn and shredded rock, and the next it was more darkness. General Verit stopped. He held his torch in one hand and his mace-like weapon in the other. The soldiers stopped behind them. Pern heard one man sniff, and it sounded loud in the darkness. Certainly louder than the breathing.

Soft, deep breaths of air drawn in and out. Measured and even as though in sleep. It was a strange thing being able to tell a creature's size by its breathing, and this one was big.

All smiles were gone from the general now. He stood still as stone and waited, though for what Pern could not be sure. They all waited on his orders, and he waited on some unknown sign or signal - perhaps hoping they hadn't woken the beast they had obviously stumbled upon.

General Verit nodded his head left and right and the soldiers behind them started to move. Pern had no idea what orders had been given and without asking he was unlikely to find himself enlightened, so he stayed close to the general. But not too close, he didn't want to get in the way if the big Five Kingdomer started swinging.

With the light scrape of boots on the floor, Pern could no longer hear the thing's breathing. He crept alongside the general as they inched forwards in the dark.

Two round spots of light lit up in the darkness, flickering torchlight reflected off large eyes. The lights blinked out and then back once and twice, then started to move. They rose up higher and higher from the ground until Pern had to look upwards to see them. There they hung for a moment, watching the soldiers and their torches.

Another set of reflected eyes lit up behind the first and then another. Before long Pern was staring at six dots of light in the dark. No one moved. Even the general seemed paralysed. Transfixed by the darkness and the monsters hiding within it.

Pern heard a sharp intake of breath and then a roar erupted so loud it hurt his ears and almost made him drop his torch. It echoed around them, filling the world with noise and Pern saw more than one soldier collapse, torch clattering to the stone floor.

As the tumult died down the first of the creatures took a slow step into the flickering light of the torches. It held a great, clawed paw up to its face and turned its head away a little. A giant head, brutish and square with wrinkled skin that looked colourless in the dim. A huge bulbous nose twitched as the troll sniffed at them and scratched at one of its long ears.

The troll took another step towards them, and Pern saw it lit in full. It was a giant, nearly three times as tall as a man with small, thick legs and long, gangly arms reaching almost to the ground. Its body was slim, packed with muscle and scarred from the gods only knew what. Its eyes, each as big as a fist, twinkled in the light and its mouth worked up and down as though it were chewing. Pern saw big teeth in that mouth, not sharp like a predator's, but flat like a cow's.

"Spread out," the general said, all pretence at stealth useless now. "Remember the tactics. Keep your distance, distract and maim. Bring them down before going in for the kill."

A second troll stepped up behind the first. This one was smaller, and its skin looked almost green. Half its nose was missing, ending in a rough set of scars. The third beast stayed out of the light. It took Pern a moment to realise they were grunting at each other and he wondered if it was some sort of language only the trolls could understand.

The first troll took another step forward and reached out a great hand. Three fingers and a thumb each ending in a ragged claw. One of the soldiers, possibly the bravest of them all, stabbed at the paw with his spear and the metal dug into flesh. The troll withdrew its hand, drew in a breath, and roared again. It charged even before the echoes had died down.

The soldiers scattered and Pern went with them, trying to keep track of General Verit in the flickering light of the torches. The troll barrelled through them all, but it did not catch anyone. The second troll and then the third joined in, and the cave soon became chaos and shouting.

Pern caught sight of the general - his torch dropped to the ground and his strange weapon in both hands, closing in on the first troll, stepping from the darkness into flickering light. The beast was busy swatting at spears and screaming at its tormentors, and the general was approaching from behind. Pern hurried to catch up just as the troll turned and swung a huge paw at the general. He ducked underneath and backed up a couple of steps, almost disappearing into the inky darkness. The troll tried to close on him only to take a spear thrust into the armpit. It stopped its advance and grabbed the spear, snapping the wooden shaft in half with ease and swinging at the solider. The poor woman didn't get out the way fast enough, and the slap sent her flying off into the darkness, her torch rolling on the floor in her wake. Pern never saw what happened to her, whether she got back up again or died there in the gloom. The troll looked down at the torch, ignoring two men trying to pierce its hide with their spears, and reached out towards it.

Pern looked at the general, and the man seemed paralysed, watching the troll fascinated by fire. All around them men and women were fighting with the beasts, patches of barely lit combat amidst the black, and here Pern was just watching one. Mesmerised by its size and its almost childlike fascination with the flames.

The troll touched the torch and then pulled its hand back with a scream. It flailed its long arms, knocking aside spears and one unfortunate soldier and then slammed its hands down onto the torch, smothering the light and splintering the wood.

General Verit grabbed hold of Pern and pulled him to the ground as the body of a man flew out of the darkness and sailed over their heads. A moment later one of the trolls collapsed to the stone ground and let out a gurgle, a spear lodged in its throat. Its arms flailed, and within moments there were soldiers all around it, maces rising and falling and spattering them all with gore.

"Distract it!" General Verit shouted, pointing at the first troll. The beast had a man pinned against the ground now and pushed hard. The soldier didn't even have time to scream. One moment his eyes were filled with terror, staring up at the troll and the next his body collapsed with a sickening crunch and a spurt of blood squeezing out from under the troll's great hand. Dead in an instant.

Something pushed against Pern's back, and he found himself stumbling forwards toward the beast. He changed that stumble into a measured approach as the troll lifted up its hand to look at the gore dripping from it, sniffing at it as though somehow surprised by what it had done. Pern slashed, and his curved sword, a traditional Haarin shuick, connected with the troll's forearm and the blade slid across, leaving nothing more than a scrape across the creature's skin.

The troll swung at Pern, one great arm backhanding through the air. Pern ducked it and thrust as he stood, his blade sliding an inch into the troll's gut. It roared, maybe in pain or anger, or maybe just because it was a terrifying sound, and made a grab for Pern. He ducked and rolled away, a hard rock digging into his back as he did.

Pern came back to his feet just in time to see the troll start into a charge, coming towards him with two big arms stretched out wide. Against a human opponent Pern would dodge, brush aside the attack and counter with a deadly stroke. Against a beast like this he froze, unable to determine any way to survive the onslaught.

General Verit stepped into view. Rising from a crouch nearby and swinging his great flanged weapon into the troll's knee as it charged. The noise of the weapon connecting was somewhere between a fleshy *squelch* and a *crack* like a tree snapping in two. The troll squealed as it came crashing down, its momentum carrying it over and over again. Pern leapt sideways away from the mess and narrowly avoided being crushed by it.

He held his sword in one hand and his torch in the other. The light revealed soldiers closing in on the prone beast and elsewhere Pern could see the third troll being driven back into the darkness by a dozen spears. A nearby soldier leapt at the downed troll and drove the tip of a spear into the beast's left eye. The monster screamed and grabbed the poor soldier with both hands. The noise that came from the soldier's mouth was guttural, raw, and filled Pern with a greater terror than the trolls themselves. That noise was cut off as the troll snapped the man in two, covering itself in red gore and throwing both halves of the man aside.

The creature struggled to rise, flailing at soldiers with spears and maces. Its knee was shattered, and a spear was sticking from its left eye. General Verit approached from the left side, using the monster's blind spot. He brought his weapon down with a horrifying crack. The first strike stopped the troll from moving. The second and third made a mess of what had been a giant skull.

The general stood, panting from the exertion and dripping with sweat, a grin on his broad face. A bloody victory and no mistake, but at such a cost.

By the dim light of the torches, Pern could see that the final troll was on its knees, swatting at spears and issuing a mewling cry as more and more cuts opened up in its skin. The men and women with maces weren't far behind, and soon the monster was whimpering, trying to shield its face with its big hands. Pern saw a finger crack from a blow and looked away. Here was a creature of myth and legend, three of them, and here were humans slaughtering the creatures in their own home.

"I hope we find what we are looking for down here," Pern said, his voice barely more than a whisper.

"Eh?" General Verit barked. "Why so glum, Honin. This was good work. Three dead trolls and only twice as many men lost. Good work."

Pern couldn't find the energy to argue with the general, and he wasn't entirely sure the man was wrong. Now the fight was over, he felt tired. The nervous tension giving way to a weary melancholy.

"*Tsck!*" the noise was loud even over the sounds of the troll mewling as the soldiers beat it to death.

Pern turned to see another creature of legend standing over a fallen torch. The flickering light showed the Drurr's black eyes and tight skin. A grimacing mouth with too many teeth to be human. He looked ancient. Wrinkled skin and hair so white it shined in the torchlight. Pern had heard the Drurr were long-lived, some seeing years into their centuries. He wondered how old the creature that stood before him now might be.

There were lights above and behind the Drurr. Not lights, Pern soon realised, but reflected light.

"More of them," General Verit breathed. His soldiers were already forming up around him.

Pern counted at least four more trolls. He paled as the biggest one yet stepped into the light behind the Drurr. Making a mockery of the size of its brethren.

"Kill the Drurr first," General Verit growled.

The Drurr looked up at that, a wide smile on his face. With a wave of his gnarled hand, all the torches gutted out.

Suzku

The darkness was complete. Pern couldn't see his hands, couldn't even see his own nose. He heard panicked breathing rising faster and faster and the sound of heavy padded feet on the rock. Someone, somewhere was muttering curses over and over again in a terrified voice.

A scream ripped through the cavern. An ear-piercing guttural noise that sent shivers up and down Pern's spine. It was cut off abruptly with a wet *crack* followed by another and another, each one becoming more and more sickening to hear.

"Get the torches lit!" The general's voice and nearby.

Something bumped Pern on the right arm and he froze. He couldn't see it. Couldn't see anything. He couldn't tell if it was a soldier, a troll, or something else entirely. His heartbeat thumped in his ears, and he struggled to squash the feeling of panic rising inside his gut. Never before had he been so scared. He was trained as Haarin, trained to resist fear, but this was something else entirely. How could he fight an enemy he couldn't see? An enemy that could crush his bones as easily as breathing.

Another scream and another, both cut off and followed by sounds that froze Pern's blood and loosened his bowels. Still someone somewhere was cursing. Footsteps echoed all around him, some leather scuffing the stone and some heavier, louder, plodding closer.

A trail of sparks lit the darkness for a moment to Pern's right and in that moment, he saw a terrified face frantically striking at a torch and behind it a giant hand. As the darkness fell again, there was a strangled cry quickly turning to a gurgle.

"TORCHES!" the general cried again.

"RUN!" shouted another voice, high-pitched and sobbing.

Another something bumped into Pern, this time on his left side. He tensed, froze. Ready to make some sort of move but no idea what that move should be. He couldn't tell if he was safer standing still or running blind.

Pain blossomed in his left side as something sharp buried itself in his mid-section. Pern heard someone fall to the ground and cry out, but he could make no sense of the words. He looked down, but the world was still complete darkness. Dropping his unlit torch, Pern reached down and found the thing buried in his side; it was slim and long. A spear. It did not appear to have gone deep and Pern took hold of the shaft and pulled it out, wincing, and collapsing to a knee.

Without sight there was no way to know how bad the wound truly was. It hurt like he expected it should, and it certainly felt as though it were bleeding, but Pern could only hope it was not bad enough to kill him. He struggled to block out the pain.

A torch flared to life to Pern's left, and he saw Captain Vanda grinning over the little flame. He also saw the troll looming up behind her. His warning died in his throat as the captain was grabbed and then smashed into the nearby cavern wall. She had no chance to scream; her torn, bloody carcass was mashed and dragged against the wall leaving a dark wet stain in the flickering light.

Pern dashed towards the discarded torch and plucked it from the ground before the troll could finish mangling Vanda's corpse. He stepped backwards quickly, holding both his torch and sword out in front of him. They would do little good against a determined troll, but at least he would see his death coming and make it bleed for the victory.

In his small circle of light Pern could see monstrous shadows moving beyond, smaller shades flocking towards him. He heard heavy feet and soft, all moving about in the darkness and someone out there was crying, sobbing, pleading to the gods.

One of the smaller trolls, a runt at only twelve feet or so, lumbered forwards and reached out towards Pern. He was ready to slice at the monster's hands. Maybe, if he could find a joint, he could remove one of its fingers. It wouldn't stop the creature from crushing him should it fully commit, but it might make it think twice. If they thought at all.

A spear thrust over Pern's right shoulder and stabbed into the troll's armpit. The monster roared and stumbled away, batting at the spear as it disappeared into the darkness beyond the dim torchlight.

Pern didn't look back to see who had saved him. He wasn't willing to take his eyes from the threat in front. He kept backing up slowly, hoping he hadn't gotten too turned around. It was entirely possible he was backing towards most of the trolls. He'd counted four before the lights had gone out. Four monsters and a Drurr who appeared to have some magic about him.

"Good man," General Verit said as he stumbled over to Pern and held a torch out to the flames. Two sputtering torches seemed a great deal safer than one, and the combined light gave them a wider circle of vision.

Pern risked a glance to find the general bleeding from a cut on his head and looking pale in the light. He still held his giant weapon in one hand, and that gave Pern some comfort.

More soldiers were joining them now. Pern thought he heard Captain Otto's voice as a third torch was lit. A cluster of six of them, slowly backing into the darkness. They couldn't see much past a few feet, but they could hear huge feet stomping about and the cries of those left behind, too scared or injured to join those in the light. One voice was cut off abruptly and followed by a horrific tearing noise that had Pern swallowing down bile.

Six of them. Of the thirty soldiers who had entered the cave, only six remained. The trolls and the Drurr had devastated their numbers. And Pern was fairly certain they would all soon join the dead. The wound in his side was agony, and a glance told him he was still bleeding.

A loud thumping started up, something big and heavy hitting the ground over and over, faster and faster and coming closer. A troll, running forwards and swinging its arms, came lunging out of the darkness and the soldiers scattered. Pern ducked and stepped aside. The general ducked and swung his big mace, connecting with the troll's ankle. The creature collapsed, catching Otto on its way down and knocking him down, one big hand wrapped around the captain's left leg.

Otto screamed. General Verit and two other soldiers darted in and struck at the troll again and again, but the monster squeezed, and blood oozed out between its fingers. Captain Otto fell silent, his head dropping and striking the stony ground even as the troll's skull finally caved in. Pern considered trying to prise open the big hand and pull the captain free, but he couldn't see it making a difference, Otto was either dead already or too close to it to save.

"Come on!" The general pulled on Pern's arm, and they all started backing away again. Somewhere out in the darkness, they could hear a loud scraping noise, like giant claws tearing into solid rock.

"What is that?" asked one of the soldiers behind Pern.

They all listened to the noise over the sounds of their feet scuffing backwards along the ground.

"Digging," Pern said with a surety.

"They're running?"

As if to answer the soldier's question a loud *crunch* sounded in the dark followed by a grunt. A moment later a rock as large as man came sailing out of the darkness towards them. They scattered again, and the rock crashed into the ground behind them.

"We need to run!" shouted one of the soldiers.

"No," General Verit growled. He was staring off behind them. "We need to attack."

Pern heard it then. Boots thumping on the ground, lots of them. The cavern was getting lighter by the moment, torches joining from the rear. Their reinforcements had arrived.

"It's about time," the general called. "We're all but gone here. At least three trolls left and a Drurr. Some sort of sorcerer."

"A Matriarch?" Pern recognised the voice as Captain Book.

"No. Male."

"Thank Pelsing!"

A laugh sounded out in the darkness. A deep baritone that echoed around the cavern walls even over the sounds of boots scuffing the ground, torches popping and hissing, and trolls scraping the walls.

"Ahh," the general growled and stamped a big boot on the ground. "What the fuck now?"

The body of Captain Otto twitched and then looked up at them, though there was no life in its eyes.

"Necromancer," Pern said, his voice barely a whisper.

Suzku

Captain Otto's body started to claw at the ground, trying to drag itself towards them, but even in death, the troll's grip was iron. A ragged moan escaped the dead captain's lips as he struggled to reach for them all.

"Fuck!" Captain Book swore. "Thought we left the dead back in the Five Kingdoms."

Another boulder came hurtling out of the darkness and soldiers scrabbled to get out of the way. There was little to see but inky black past the light of the torches, yet they could all hear the trolls working away at the walls. They could all hear the moans and cracks as the dead started to rise.

"Stick together," the general said. "Small groups. We know how to deal with trolls, and we know how to deal with the dead, been doing both all our lives. No more cowering here in the dark. We're Five Kingdomers. We were born to beat back the dead!"

A cheer went up, and the soldiers' courage seemed to rally around them, the aura changing from a yellowy orange to a light red. It was a strange thing to see auras combine, but it always seemed to happen. When groups of people converged together, their auras became aligned, as though they were all feeling the same way. There were always some who stood out though. Some whose auras refused to mix with the others, or sometimes those who influenced the others. General Verit was one of those, a leader of men. Respected and loved. His aura enveloped those around him, and that colour soon started to spread. Even Pern found his anger rising and his courage along with it.

They started to move forwards, marching step by step together in a loose formation. Another rock hurtled out of the darkness, and one man let out a cry of pain, but they didn't stop. As they closed on the dead troll, Otto still held in its death grip, the dead captain was dealt with by a single mace blow to the back of the head. There was no delay, no sad words said for the man who had been their comrade. He was deftly sent back to the grave, and the soldiers continued on, Pern marching with them.

"We need to kill the Drurr," the general said, his voice a throaty growl. He sent a sidelong glance at Pern. "If that creature is the necromancer we need to stop it before it completes its blood runes. You with me, Honin?"

Pern nodded. It was not a stretch to realise that this Drurr was likely responsible for the death of his clan. He was responsible for men, women, and children all kept from the next life. It made sense now he thought of it. Ten Haarin were a force to be reckoned with, but they would have no idea how to fight against trolls or a Drurr sorcerer. One blood rune, carved into the earth with the bodies of his family members. If the general was right then just two more of those runes and every man, woman, and child who died in the assault on Crucible would rise again under the necromancer's control. The City of Kings would become a fortress of the damned.

The first of the dead came shambling out of the darkness, an old soldier with flesh as grey as his hair, and he wasn't alone. Four of them stumbled forwards, those killed by the trolls and still intact enough to be risen.

The Five Kingdomers showed no hesitation or remorse in cutting down their fallen comrades. Some of them had been fighting the dead for longer than Pern had been alive and it showed. They surged forwards, protecting each other from clawing hands, and caving in skulls and removing heads from necks. As the last of the dead fell dead once more, the trolls came again.

The first of the monsters to reach their lines was the largest Pern had seen yet. It charged towards them, arms flailing, and the soldiers scattered. One woman was caught by a clawed hand and fell away screaming, her arm nearly torn off at the shoulder. Someone moved in to drag her away, and others started jabbing at the troll with spears, stabbing into pallid flesh and then pulling away before the creature could react.

Another troll and then another reached them, and soon all three of the monsters were in amongst them, batting away spears and grabbing for soldiers even as metal sunk into flesh.

Pern was about to join in the battle with the giant troll when a hand fell on his shoulder. It was General Verit, and his face was grave and stony.

"You and me, Honin," the general said. "We have a Drurr to hunt."

With that the general turned and started walking into the darkness, his torch a meagre beacon of light against the inky black. Pern didn't hesitate to follow. His anger was hot and cloying. He wanted revenge against the monster who had murdered his clan.

They found the Drurr just a little farther into the cavern, making no attempt to hide. His face was pale in the flickering light of the torches, his eyes dark, and too many teeth showing in his snarling mouth. He wore a grey robe and carried only a gnarled, wooden staff. He seemed a poor match for two men both tall and broad and in their prime. Still, they approached him carefully, each with a torch held in one hand and weapons drawn into the other.

"Flank him, Honin," the general said. "And don't underestimate it. A Drurr and a necromancer. An abomination even to his own people."

The Drurr watched them both, black eyes flicking one way then the other.

"Is that why you're here, monster?" the general asked. "Chased away from your own folk because of your perversion of magic. How they must shun you for practising your necromancy, the magic that almost wiped your kind from existence. I wish it had!" The man was taunting the Drurr, drawing its attention away from Pern.

As soon as they had him pincered, the Drurr flicked out a hand towards the general, and the torch guttered out. General Verit struck, a heavy swing with his flanged mace, but the Drurr was faster, stabbing out with his staff into the general's arm.

With a cry, General Verit's swing faltered, and he all but dropped his mace. Pern darted in, using his training to predict the Drurr's movements and stabbing towards him, but the old creature was too fast. Inhumanly swift. He turned and brushed aside Pern's strike, and then made a reply of his own.

Pern felt his right arm go numb as the staff poked into his bicep. His guard dropped and before he could recover the butt of the staff whipped across his face and sent him stumbling away, spitting blood.

General Verit was there again, roaring as he raised his mace and brought it down hard upon the Drurr. The old necromancer stepped out of the way and darted in, placing a palm against the general's chest. He fell away, clutching at his belly and retching. A small tangle of eels hit the ground along with the general's vomit.

Pern moved in again, his arm still feeling numb, and rained in three swift blows. The Drurr turned each aside with his gnarled wooden staff then whispered a word in a language Pern did not recognise. The Drurr slammed his staff down on the ground, and Pern's legs went out beneath him.

He crashed to the ground, dropping the torch and barely getting his hands beneath him. As he struggled back to his knees, the Drurr darted in and stabbed his wrist with the sharp end of the staff. Pain flared to life, and Pern grabbed at his arm. An unbearable itch started deep within the flesh of his hand, and in the flickering light of the torch, it looked like something was moving underneath his skin.

The Drurr smiled down upon him, a mouth full of teeth.

The general lurched forward, bile dripping from his mouth, and grabbed hold of the Drurr's staff with both hands, trying to use his larger size to wrestle the stick away from the man. Yet the Drurr held tight, resisting the giant's strength with ease.

Pern let go of his right wrist, picked up his sword in his left hand, and thrust forwards, putting his full weight into the sloppy strike. The blade hit home, plunging deep into the Drurr's chest and tearing out through the back. The itching started to travel, moving up from Pern's wrists towards his arm. It was all he could do not to tear at his own flesh.

The Drurr stared down at him, steel lodged in its chest, and bloody spittle dripping from its lips. A gnarled hand closed around the blade of Pern's sword. "Not done yet," the creature hissed. "The land will bleed. The dead will ri..." Pern gave the sword a twist, and fell away, ripping the blade out of the Drurr, and the wrinkled monster collapsed.

"Hold your arm," the general ordered, rushing to Pern's side with the torch in one hand and a dagger in the other. "There, above the movement."

Pern did as he was told, grabbing hold of his right arm and

squeezing tight. There was definitely something moving under the skin, something wriggling through his flesh. He could feel it itching, tearing through him and he felt his blood go icy with a fear that almost smothered the pain.

General Verit stared at Pern's arm for a few moments then dropped the torch and stabbed, digging the little dagger into flesh.

Pern resisted the urge to scream. He had received worse injuries in his life, but somehow this one seemed to hurt more. He winced but refused to close his eyes, watching as the general dug into his arm and pulled out something black and as long as a finger. The thing squirmed in the general's grip for a few moments, and then he squeezed, and it popped. Black filth oozed over his hand like tar.

"What was that?" Pern asked, unable to keep the panic from his voice.

"Quiet!" the general hissed. He picked up the torch and held it to Pern's face, so close the flames licked at his skin. The general stared into Pern's eyes, the dagger just inches from his throat.

For a long time, the general stayed there. Pern could hear soldiers fighting with the trolls. He heard men and women dying. He heard trolls crashing to the ground. It seemed they should be joining the fight, helping to bring the monsters down, but the general stayed there, staring at him.

"Corpse Worm," the general said eventually, dropping the torch on the ground and relaxing. "It's how they make Wights."

"Wights?"

"Smart dead. Dead that keep their mind but lose their life and will. If that thing had reached your head... Had to make sure. If your eyes had started to change I would have put you down."

Pern nodded. He was still gripping his arm tight. Red blood, looking almost black in the light, seeped out of the wound. It wasn't his only injury either, the spear wound in his side still hurt, and he hoped that one, at least, had stopped bleeding. Now Pern thought about it, he was feeling light-headed.

A loud, fleshy thud echoed around them and was followed by a roar cut short with a sickening crunch.

"That's the last of them," the general said as he pushed back to his feet and retrieved his mace. He held out a big hand to Pern and helped the Honin to his feet. "But we still have to push on farther into the cave. We have to make sure the necromancer didn't complete another blood rune."

Rose

Anders hadn't just taken his time in reporting the results of his parley; he had gone missing as soon as returning to the camp. He vanished into the line of stakes and soldiers that faced the city, and neither Pug nor Henry had yet to find him. It seemed as though the blooded drunkard had slipped away and that did not bode well for the results.

Not that Rose had expected anything to come from the terms she had given them. The blooded would never willingly surrender. They knew it would mean their deaths. She had wanted the soldiers to hear though, she wanted them to know there was a way out if only they would turn on their masters. It now seemed as though that plan had been for naught. She shrugged. It had always been a gamble, and the only risk had been to Anders' life. She counted it a risk well worth the taking.

The sun was just beginning to set on the second day of the siege and Crucible's walls still stood. The blooded hiding within still breathed. A second day and she was no closer to finally uniting the Wilds. She did, however, feel a lot closer to popping out her child.

Every day the life inside of her seemed heavier, and every day it seemed to find a new part of her to press upon. Today the little parasite seemed to be taking great joy in pushing on her bladder, and Rose found herself pissing every few minutes. It was ceaselessly frustrating.

The witch doctors back in Chade claimed they had ways of bringing on the birth early - some mixture of herbs and shamanistic magic, Rose reckoned. Lucille had warned against it, claiming such practices killed the child as often as not, and Rose definitely didn't want a dead kid inside of her. It was bad enough having a live one.

"Anything?" Rose asked. She was standing at the entrance to her tent, staring towards the city walls. They looked so strong and indomitable. She wondered how they might look once she had torn them down. Rubble below the greatest pyre the Wilds had ever seen.

"No sign of Anders, my lady," Pug said, his eyes downcast. Betrim was sleeping inside, ever willing to grab some rest where he could take it, so Pug was at her beck and call for now. "General Verit has returned."

"Bring him to me."

"He and some of his men are being treated at the infirmary, my lady."

"Then take me to him," Rose countered in a soft voice.

"Uh..." Pug looked past Rose, clearly looking for someone else to suggest visiting the infirmary was not a wise choice for so heavily a pregnant woman. But there was no one to help him. Betrim was asleep, and Lucille was off fetching food, and neither one would have stopped her anyway.

"Now, Pug." Rose made sure to put some menace into her voice.

Pug blanched and nodded, turning away to lead her to the infirmary. Rose had long ago discovered that most men would bend to her will with either a little flirting or a little threatening. The more swollen with child she found herself, the more she relied on the threat. It seemed very few men were willing to argue with a pregnant woman.

Rose was surprised to find the infirmary quite full, and not just of the wounded Five Kingdoms soldiers General Verit had brought with him. Many of the cots were taken up with Wilds' soldiers, some moaning and clutching at their mid-sections.

A number of folk moved about tending to all manner of illnesses or injuries, many of them wearing cloth masks over their mouths and noses.

Rose paused at the threshold. She had been all for the visit before, but now she was here she paused. There was illness, she could smell it on the air, and she did not wish to pass a disease on to her child before the thing was even born.

Pug noticed her hesitation and gave her a smile. "I'll have the general brought outside, my lady."

Rose nodded and spent a further moment staring into the tent. She thought she saw Pern sitting on a bench, his chest showing a number of old scars, long healed over, and a small woman wrapping a bandage around his right arm.

Rose turned away from the tent. The infirmary was situated towards the rear of the camp on top of a slight incline. From here she could look out over her troops. There were so many of them. Thousands upon thousands. A sea of tents and faces all going about normal camp business as though an unbreakable city did not stand just a short march away. She hoped Brekovich and D'roan were watching the camp from their high walls and shitting themselves. Thousands upon thousands of soldiers was more than enough to break down those walls and slit the throats of the last of the blooded.

"My lady," the general said as he ducked out of the infirmary tent. "I was just about to come and find you."

He looked a little the worse for wear with a bandage wrapped around his head and his left arm in a sling. Pern followed the man and, though he had his white robe draped over his shoulder, she could see a number of new wounds including something in his mid-section.

Pern had always been a mystery to Rose. The man was a trained Haarin - it seemed ludicrous that he would crew with the Black Thorn, and his relationship with Henry was maddeningly curious. Rose was more than adept at seeing the signs of both love and lust, and there was clearly something between the two, though neither seemed to act upon it.

"I felt restless," Rose said, making sure a playful smile sat upon her ruby lips. The general's eyes slipped down to her mouth and from there a little lower to her cleavage. Some men were so very predictable. "Report, General. What did you find in those caves of yours?"

"Trolls, my lady, and the necromancer."

Rose frowned, she couldn't help it, her mask slipped. "Trolls?" she asked with an incredulous laugh. "Trolls are real." She glanced at Pern and found a haunted look on his usually serene face.

General Verit sighed. "You people have no idea how easy you have it here. Aye, trolls are real. The dead walking is real. Drurr are real. Those little fucking sand pygmies who wear men's faces are real. And here in the Wilds, all you have to deal with is people being arseholes to each other. Well, until now, it seems. Everything but the pygmies, and you really don't want those."

Rose smiled. "And the occasional army of folk possessed by demons. Believe me, General; we have our own set of problems. I would have liked to see these trolls."

The general shook his head.

"Did you find a way into the city?"

"I have people looking now. We had injured needed tending to. Dead that still need burning. I lost some of my best people down in those caves, my lady."

Rose nodded at that. They would all be drinking to the fallen before this siege was done and they had all lost too many friends already. Wars made victims of everyone, it seemed, and this was a war the like of which the Wilds hadn't seen since the days of D'oro hundreds of years ago.

"What did the Drurr want?"

General Verit grimaced. "Necromancers aren't well regarded by the Drurr. Actually, I've never heard of one before. My guess, the blood runes were his doing. His attempt to turn your Wilds into another Land of the Dead. What better way for a necromancer to raise an army than at a battle likely to see both sides reduced to ruin?"

"I trust you have ended his plan with his death?"

Huge shoulders let loose a weary shrug. "We killed the bastard and his trolls. Found a second blood rune down in the caves, made from soldiers wearing Crucible blacks. Both runes are broken now. We'll just have to hope the magic didn't have too long to soak into the ground. I have scouts out, searching the land nearby for the third rune. But the truth is, I just don't know, my lady."

The child kicked, and Rose placed a hand on her belly. "Regardless, I want to attack tomorrow, General. As agreed."

The general gave a nod and a sigh. "And tomorrow I'll be in a better mood to talk you out of it."

"You are welcome to try." Rose smiled at the man, and he nodded, a weary look dragging his face down and making him seem much older. "Suzku, I believe Henry will want to see you. She has been worried. In her own way."

Without waiting for an answer, Rose turned and ambled away as fast as her condition would allow. Pug hurried to catch up and fell in beside her. His hand never strayed far from the little sword at his side, as if he could protect her should someone attack. The thought made Rose smile; it was far more likely she would be the one protecting him.

"I've never seen a real battle before," Pug said as they walked.

"Me either," Rose admitted. "I can't wait to see those walls fall."

Day 3 – The Walls

The Black Thorn

"... murder. Bloody murder!" Kurt Verit all but shouted.

"Tell me, General; what is war but bloody murder?" Rose argued.

"Murder of the enemy, sure. This is murder of our own fucking men."

"And women," Henry said with a smirk. It was just like the little murderess to argue the toss when no one else seemed to care.

"Do you have a way to assault those walls without losing some of our own soldiers?" Rose continued, giving Henry a sound ignoring. "Do you have some miracle way you're not telling us about how to siege a city without killing anyone?"

Kurt growled and stamped a foot on the rug. They were all crowded into what Betrim liked to call the command tent. Rose, Kurt, Henry, Suzku, Anders, Pug, and what was left of the general's captains. The sun was only just poking above the eastern horizon, and already they were talking war. It seemed Kurt wasn't too happy about throwing men against the walls of Crucible and hoping to find a crack.

"I didn't think so," Rose said, her voice compassionate. "One way or another, General, this is going to end in blood. Rivers of it."

"Give me more time," Kurt argued. "We've only just got here. I need time to properly assess all of our options. The caves might still yield..."

"How much time, General?" Rose asked. "You've already advocated a lengthy siege, and I've already told you that can't happen. In a month from now, six months from now, will those walls have crumbled? What about the soldiers inside? All that will have happened is we will have lost the war. We are losing the war every moment we hesitate."

Kurt shook his head. "Walls aren't going anywhere. And if this useless bastard is right," he waved a hand at Anders, "they've got food enough for a year or more with good rationing. Might be illness could set in, but you can't count on it. Give me a couple of weeks."

"We don't have a couple of weeks, General. We may not have a couple of days. We are running out food and booze and the bits to pay our men to stay. Men get bored easily, General, believe me. A drawn-out siege will see our numbers dwindle while theirs... Well, they have nowhere to go. In just a week, my army will be bored, half-starved, and ready to pack it all in and go home to their families. In just a week, those bastards in Crucible will have shored up any holes in their defences.

"Even if we could hold the siege for long enough, somehow manage to outlast and starve them out, how do you think that will end? Niles Brekovich won't just allow them all to die in there. The man is a seasoned military commander, is he not?"

"Oh quite," Anders joined in. "Why my father has won countless battles. Quite the warrior too. He once brought down an elephant all on his own. Sword slashing and stabbing. It was a sight to behold for a boy of just five years."

"Shut up, Anders," Rose said.

"Better he brings his forces to us." Kurt was sounding deflated now, his argument running out of steam. Betrim pitied the man. He'd been on that end of an argument with Rose many times, and he could count the times he'd won on one three-fingered hand with digits to spare.

Rose shook her head and let out a sigh. "Time is not something I can give you, General. The blooded are reeling from their losses over the past year. They are down and almost out, but if we do not finish them now, in another year's time I fear it will be us holed up behind the walls of city, hoping for a saviour. And Chade's walls are not so impenetrable as Crucible's. You have ladders and a ram constructed?"

"Aye," Betrim said. He'd overseen the work himself. Not that he had any idea how to build a ladder, but the troops seemed to work better with someone of authority standing around trying to look important. "Bloody big things. Wouldn't want ta be climbing them myself."

"Then we attack today," Rose concluded. "So instead of arguing against me, General, try coming up with a plan."

That seemed like the end of it. Another argument decided in Rose's favour. She ambled away and collapsed into a cushioned chair, groaning and spending a good few minutes trying to find a comfy spot. The others all waved their goodbyes and went off to find something to occupy them. Anders pinched a bottle of something on the way out. Pug waited at the tent entrance for a few moments, but Betrim waved him out.

"You sure about this?" Betrim asked, staring down at the drawings of Crucible's defences. He didn't know a lot about attacking a city, but he knew a death trap when he saw one.

Rose sighed. "Please, Betrim, don't you question me as well."

Betrim turned to find his wife looking somewhere beyond weary. He reckoned he even saw a few lines on her face, near her eyes. Was passing odd to see her so tired and something she'd never allow anyone else to see.

Betrim wandered closer and put a hand on her shoulder. There was something about Rose, something he'd seen in her that very first time in the whorehouse back in Bittersprings. She was stronger than anyone else he'd ever met, smarter than most, and more ruthless than a laughing dog with wounded prey. She'd pulled herself up from nothing. Turned herself from whore, to city regent, and now she was bordering on calling herself a queen. And she'd dragged Betrim along for the whole ride. He wasn't one to throw around words like love, it seemed a foolish concept here in the Wilds, but he was damned sure he'd do anything for Rose if she asked. Including throw himself against the unbreakable walls of Crucible.

"I ain't questionin' ya. Damn sure ya the smartest one out of the two of us, an' if anyone can do the impossible, I reckon it's you. So if you say attack, we'll fuckin' attack. Just... Kurt seems ta think it ain't the best idea. Reckon he knows a thing or two 'bout war."

Rose snorted. "He knows a thing or two about battle. I'm not so sure he knows about the real war that happens around it. Half the fight is keeping everyone paid and fed and fitted with new shoes, all while trying to govern an empire so used to living by their own rules they don't know how to work together."

Betrim waited for Rose to fall silent. "We already got the Wilds. Those fuckers have one city. Holed up in there, hidin'. Ain't no one gonna argue if we leave them ta rot, head back ta Chade, an' pop out that kid of ours."

"The blooded are a blight on the Wilds. If we leave even one of them alive, they will come back and destroy everything we are trying to build. Crucible is a festering wound in that needs to be cut away. I promised the good-folk I would rid them of this plague of blooded, and I will deliver on that. I promised myself."

Betrim took a step back and leaned against the cupboard with the booze in it. It wasn't the most stable of surfaces, but it sure felt good to have something at his back. Some folk took him for a fool, decided he wasn't smart because he had no learning and looked like a bad dream, but Betrim had a sense when it came to stories, and for a while now he'd been thinking Rose hadn't told him all of hers.

He crossed his arms and gave her his best one-eyed stare. "Fancy tellin' me just what ya got against them?"

"No."

For some that would have been an end to it, but Betrim had married Rose and spent the last couple of years helping her cut a bloody path through the Wilds. He reckoned he deserved some sort of explanation, and he could be damned stubborn himself when he decided he wanted something.

"Shame that. 'Cos neither of us is leavin' this tent 'til you get ta the tellin'. An' I don't reckon Kurt is gonna order anyone into that city without you givin' him that scary stare of yours. Aye, that one."

Rose rolled her eyes at him and then smiled. "But tellin' ya is nothin' but hot air." She dropped into a Wilds' drawl and levered herself out of the chair, swaying towards him and gripping at his cock through his trousers. "Far more fun things I could do with my mouth, hmm?"

Betrim felt himself stiffening at the idea of it, but he wasn't about to let her distract him. Not this time. He put his hands on her shoulders and gently pushed. Rose resisted at first but soon gave up, rolling her eyes and sighing at him.

"Fine." She plopped back down into the chair and looked relieved to be off her feet again. "At least fetch me a drink."

Betrim poured a couple of mugs of ale as Rose started her telling.

"Did you know I'm a few years older than my brother, Swift?"

Betrim had never really thought about Rose's age, nor Swift's. Truth was, he was just glad the bastard was long since beheaded and buried. That there was one person Betrim never wanted coming back.

"I actually remember the very night he was conceived," Rose continued. "I was maybe three or four, running about my mother's brothel. You learn about fucking at a very early age in a whore house."

Betrim nodded at that. "Seen a few. Ya ma's weren't bad."

"Not at all," Rose agreed. "Quite lucrative, but then Bittersprings had a wealthy clientele, and my mother didn't allow any other whores to operate in the city. More than one enterprising lady ended up with her cunt slit for trying."

Betrim winced at that, and Rose nodded.

"One evening a blooded lord shows up. Gregor H'ost, a little drunk and flushed from a dip in Bittersprings' bitter springs. You remember that blooded fuck, I'm sure?"

Betrim shrugged. "Never met him myself. I was outside dealin' with the demons when the Arbiter pinned him ta the table with his own cutlery. Heard him screamin' though. Reckon everyone in Hostown heard that fucker scream."

Rose smiled. "It warms my heart thinking about him tortured by an Arbiter of the Inquisition. I do hope Gregor died in pain and terror."

"What did he do?" Betrim asked.

"Fucked my mother, for a start. But then I think you knew that bit already. He paid her; I have to give him that much. Fucked her, paid her, and put a little bastard in her belly. Not that Swift was all bad. He was actually quite a sweet child, spoiled though, by all the whores. It went to his head being handsome as well. Being the brat of a blooded lord made him think he was better than us all." Rose smiled, but it was savage with no humour in it.

"On the way out, afterwards, my sister was staring at him. She'd never seen a blooded lord before, neither of us had. The closest we'd seen was the town mayor and, as fancy as he liked to act, dressed in frilly finery, he was still just a commoner playing at money. H'ost was different. The way he walked, the way he smelled, the way he acted like everyone and everything belonged to him."

"Ya had a sister?" Betrim asked. Rose had never mentioned her before, seemed there was likely a reason for that.

Rose nodded. "Twin sister actually. Anemone. I remember she used to tease me about being older because I crawled out of our mother first. I can't even remember her face it was so long ago, nor her voice. I remember we were close, two peas in a seedy pod.

"H'ost didn't like the way Anni stared at him. Everyone always said he was a bit mad, but... He beat her to death right there in the brothel while everyone watched. Just snatched a tankard from a table and– hit her and kept hitting her..." Rose sniffed. A fat tear rolled down her cheek.

Betrim had seen her cry before, for a while, early on in the pregnancy, it had been fairly common. Not like this though. This was grief. In all the time he'd known her, in all the shit they'd been through, this was the most real he'd ever seen her. He crossed the distance between them and winced as he lowered himself to one knee, taking her tiny hand in a big, calloused paw and squeezing. Rose sniffed again and took a few moments to collect herself. It didn't take long before she'd forced the tears to stop.

"Gregor H'ost caved in my sister's skull with a mug of beer because she looked at him." Rose looked up at Betrim, and he could see fire in her eyes. A fire that very nearly had him scared. But the Black Thorn wasn't the type of man to be scared by a vicious look, even one from his own wife. "No one lifted a finger to stop him. Everyone just watched. Even my own mother. Anni's own mother.

"I didn't fully understand at the time. Didn't realise what was happening. I remember asking my mother about it later. She said to forget about it. To pretend that it hadn't happened. To pretend Anemone had never been. Because no one would do anything about it. No one would help. Because if they tried, H'ost would just murder them as well. We were just whores. Anni was just a child and life out in the Wilds is cheap." The rage choked her voice tight.

"That's what the people of the Wilds are to the blooded; cheap and

111

worthless. And that's what the blooded are to the people of the Wilds; dictators and despots. He murdered her, Betrim. Barely even broke his stride, just..." Fresh tears welled in her eyes again. "It's not just H'ost. All the blooded families are same. The good-folk, players of the game on both sides, we're all nothing to them. Worth less than the scraps they feed the dogs."

Betrim didn't really know what to say. Wasn't sure there was anything he could say. Rose was right, life was cheap in the Wilds, and the blooded liked to keep it that way because it meant their lives were the only ones worth a damn. A handful of years ago that probably wouldn't have mattered to the Black Thorn, but now he found it did. He wondered if that was the effect of his child, even still nestled inside its mother. Didn't seem right a child could make a man a better person. Betrim had certainly never made either of his parents better.

Rose sniffed and wiped at her eyes. "I don't want our child being born into a world where the blooded still live, Betrim. I intend to give her the Wilds, a brand new Wilds united and free. She doesn't deserve to grow up living in fear of what bastards who consider themselves her betters might do to her on a whim. I won't have her grow up like that."

Betrim shook his head and gave Rose's hand another squeeze. He wondered if their child, once fully grown, would be as deft at manipulating him as its mother.

"Reckon we best go fuck up those walls an' kill ourselves some blooded then. 'Cos you look about ready ta pop, love."

Henry

"We really doin' this?" Henry asked. She didn't like the look of the walls and liked the look of the folk standing on top of them even less. Something to do with all the bows, she reckoned. Henry never did like arrows, even before Swift. Just the thought of that bastard's name made her leg ache where he'd cut her open.

"Looks like," Thorn said as he struggled with a round shield and settled for Pug helping to attach it to his arm.

He looked about as awkward as Henry felt. She had no idea what to do with a shield and hated the helmet they'd given her too. She liked to be able to move and see, and she could barely do either of those things in the little suit of chain they'd squeezed her into.

"Got a good reason why?" Henry asked. She wasn't about to back out now, but if Thorn did, then that would be all the excuse she needed. He was the only reason she'd even considered putting herself in so much danger. Hard to watch his back from back in the camp.

"Does the troops good, I reckon. Seein' one of us down in the shit with 'em. Kurt needs ta sit back an' do the real important stuff, an' Rose ain't goin' nowhere near a fight like she is. Guess it falls ta me, eh?"

"And me. Fucked if I'm lettin' you die in here alone." Henry spat into the mud, and Betrim gave her a light shove with his shoulder and followed it up with a horrific grin. They'd been in worse situations. Been in worse and come through the other side with nothing but a few more scars to add to the list. At least that's what Henry kept telling herself. She couldn't quite shake the feeling that shit had never been quite this bad.

"First time in the crush?" a ruddy-faced soldier asked. He looked to have a bit of grey around his dark hair and fair few lines near his eyes.

"Fuck you!" Henry hissed and sneered at the man until he looked away. She was bordering on terrified and some bastard grinning at her, seeming like he was happy as a wet cunt to be down in the midst of it, was about more than she was willing to take.

"You remember bein' a heartless bastard not carin' about nothin' but yaself?" Henry asked Thorn. She was nervous and shifting relentlessly from foot to foot, and she couldn't seem to stop herself.

Thorn laughed and tried to scratch at his burn scar, almost smacked himself in the face with his own shield. "Aye, reckon I remember always carin' about you, though, ya crazy little bitch. Even after ya stabbed me." He gave her another shove, and she stumbled a step and grinned up at him.

"Aye. Ya always did have a soft spot for any woman who'd led ya stick ya cock in 'em."

"With a face like mine can ya blame me?" The words were true enough, but the banter was forced. False cheer to hide the fear.

A horn echoed out around them, almost quiet, and was soon joined by another, louder one. The atmosphere changed a bit, and Henry could feel the restlessness turned to nervousness. She felt a fair bit of both her own self, and for once was happy for being so short. It meant she couldn't see over the bastards in front of her. Meant she couldn't see death coming for her.

"We movin'?" Thorn asked. He was as new to the front lines of a battle as she was.

"Not yet," said Captain Lost. He'd happily taken the position as captain of Thorn's guard and he and his fifty men were tasked with keeping the Black Thorn safe in what was likely to be the bloodiest conflict the Wilds had ever seen.

The thought of sticky red blood did wonders to calm Henry; it always did. She loved the colour, the feel, the smell, even the taste a little bit. She'd spent many of her years stabbing a range of different folk, trying to find out how different people bled and if they all bled red. Turns out everyone was the same on the inside no matter how different they might look.

"We're support for the ram," Captain Lost continued. "Our unit will move up to protect them once the first unit starts to fall."

Thorn nodded. He had no idea what he was doing; any dumb bastard could see that. Neither of them had any place in the battle at all, let alone the front lines. They were criminals, not soldiers. Outlaws made good thanks to a pardon they didn't earn.

114

"Fuck!" Henry swore and couldn't quite keep the quiver out of her voice.

"Not too late ta back out," Thorn said.

Henry could see Pug behind them looking just as scared as she was. Someone started banging on their shield, solid steel hitting wood over and over again, soon joined in by more and more of them. Before long Henry found herself standing in the middle of a cacophony. She wasn't sure what it would be doing for the bastards up on the wall, but it sure seemed to be emboldening the soldiers around them. Henry saw a couple of lads, looked to be barely old enough to grow hair on their stones, exchanging jokes and looking excited. She reckoned they'd never seen a real fight. Reckoned they'd never seen those they care about bleeding to death in the dust. Never felt the fear of a situation so far beyond their control life and death came down to sheer luck.

"Fuck! What's goin' on?" Henry shouted over the din and punched at Thorn's arm.

He glanced down at her and then back up. "First lot of ours movin' forwards. Ladders to the walls. The big fuckin' ram of ours is trundlin' along. Reckon we'll be followin' it soon, eh?"

Another horn blared out over the sounds of folk shouting and dying, Henry heard it over the scream of a man with an extensive set of lungs.

"That's for us," Captain Lost said. "March close. Keep together. Shields up against the arrows."

"Fuck!" Henry breathed as their group started moving forward, nearly two hundred folk all with shields. She could barely see more than Thorn, Pug, and the ruddy-faced veteran who was now being careful not to catch her eye.

Henry raised her shield above her head and marched with the others. It seemed oddly dark under the canopy of wood they created. A strange peacefulness washed over her. They were marching forwards, boots squelching in the mud. Sounds of folk screaming and dying seemed a long way off. Here everything seemed easy. Keep the shield up, keep moving.

"What do we do when we get there?" Thorn shouted.

"Whatever is needed," Captain Lost shouted back. "Brace the ram, pull back the hammer, protect the others. Shields up all the time. The real fighting comes when we breach the gate."

Henry tried to catch Thorn's eye, but the bastard kept it fixed ahead, not that he could see anything over the shields. She glanced at Pug, but the boy was intent on the ground, eyes wide and bright even in the dim light. Fever bright. Fear bright. Henry had to admit the boy was perhaps smarter than he looked.

"Fuck!" She tripped and almost went down, catching herself on one of the other soldiers and continued on. A spare glance revealed bodies on the ground. Some were bleeding from arrow wounds, others from being trampled. All of them were dead, she reckoned. Didn't take much to kill a man when it came down to it, though some definitely died easier than others.

Something struck her shield with a smack and a force that made Henry wince. "Fuck!" Her voice shook. Reckoned they were close enough for arrows now, that meant they were close enough to the walls of Crucible to start dying. Wouldn't be long before there were piles of bodies outside the walls. Mountains of bodies.

It was one thing to die in a fight, another thing to die alone or surrounded by folk. It was something completely different to die just another nameless corpse amidst a few thousand of them. Henry didn't want to die, and she certainly didn't want to die like this. Made her decision to join Thorn something like madness.

More arrows rained down on them, thudding into shields, some slipping through. Henry saw the ruddy-faced veteran go down, a shaft sticking out of his collar, between his armour. Seemed a right unlucky shot to take, and a right lucky one to let loose. She quickly lost sight of the poor bastard, and another soldier moved up to her right, filling in the hole and keeping her covered. He was a thin man with a jutting chin and wire-thin strip of hair on his lip. Henry wondered if he'd be the next one to die, or maybe if it would be her.

"Fuck!" she hissed to herself and kept on marching forward.

The bodies beneath them were getting more regular now. Some piled on top of others. More and more arrows thudded down into their shields and Henry saw more men drop around her, the holes in the shield wall quickly plugged.

The man in front of her went down screaming. She didn't see what wound had got him, just stumbled a step, placed a foot on his back and stepped over him, filling into the spot he had taken. Others crowded in behind her.

Her arm was getting tired. Just a few minutes in she reckoned, though it felt like hours, and already she was struggling to keep the shield held up above her. Henry wasn't weak, but this was work she wasn't used to and only her own defiance and determination not to die was keeping her wobbling arm held above her head.

"Move! Forward! Now! Move! Up to the ram!" Henry couldn't tell who the orders came from. Couldn't tell if they were worth following. Neither did she have a choice. The press of soldiers all around her started to move more quickly, a march turning into a run.

She caught a glimpse of the walls as she was pushed forwards. They were close now and loomed so high above her. She saw men atop of those walls, leaning out and loosing arrows down towards them. So many arrows. Henry pulled in tight below her shield as another shaft thudded into it and kept on moving.

A huge log, bound in strips of iron and covered in arrow shafts, swung up above her head. She moved past men heaving on ropes, protected by their comrades. Then she found herself pressed up against the wooden structure of the ram, almost crushed against it by the weight of the folk behind her. The whole thing groaned as the hammer reached the top of its back-swing and then came thundering back down towards the city gate.

The ram shuddered. The ground beneath her shuddered. Henry shuddered and almost dropped her shield. The force of the blow rattling through felt like it shook her teeth loose and she clapped her jaws together to stop from biting off her own tongue on the next blow.

"Fuck!" Her voice was shrill even to her own ears.

All around her men and women were dying, some dropping where they were shot, others being kicked aside into the moat. All Henry could hear were screams and the thud of arrows hitting her shield as she struggled to keep it above her and leaned against the ram.

The hammer started moving again, drawn slowly backwards by the men on the ropes. Someone, somewhere nearby was crying. A sobbing sound weak and pitiful to Henry's ears. As the hammer crashed against the gates once more, she wiped the tears away from her eyes and screamed up at the bastards raining death down upon them.

Rose

The command post, as General Verit liked to call it, was a slightly raised hummock overlooking both the camp and the battlefield below. From their position, they could see the whole attack as it played out. Rose could see the ladders being raised into position against the walls and the strange contraptions at the bases to keep them locked against the wall once in position. She could see soldiers, men and women sworn to fight for her, surging up against those ladders, shields raised to protect them against the hail of arrows.

The general did not look entirely happy with how things were going, a bad sign considering the attack had only just begun. Rose had lost track of time, but she doubted it could have been going for more than a few minutes.

The ram was wedged up against the great gate of Crucible. The huge truck of it being drawn back and released to pound against the big door. She could hear the *crash* even so far away. Down there would be where Betrim was.

Rose had called him a fool when he said he be joining the front lines. It was an opinion she stuck by, though it hadn't changed his mind. There were times when Betrim truly believed in his reputation as the Black Thorn, truly believed that he was unkillable. Rose hoped today wouldn't be the time to prove him wrong. She was, after all, quite fond of her husband, and she knew the man would protect their child with everything he had, his life included. He wasn't a good man, nor even a decent one - the Black Thorn had done things most folk would see him hanged for - but he was loyal, loyal to Rose above all others, and that made him useful.

"Is it always like this?" she asked.

They could hear the clash of battle even from this distance and Rose could see men and women down in the thick of it. Sometimes she'd see one of her own drop at the rear of the lines. Sometimes she'd see one Crucible's defenders topple over the walls. Archers on both sides of the conflict. Rose loved archers. Sometimes it was good to see a man die up close, other times it was best to watch them drop from afar. A life snuffed out in such an impersonal manner.

The general let out a sigh. "I usually like it to be going better actually."

The big Five Kingdomer made for an imposing sight all decked out in his plate armour and sitting atop his horse, staring down at the battle below. There was something in the way he held himself, something in the tension on his face. Rose could tell he wanted to join the fight. Kurt Verit was a man born for war and for battle. Raised in blood and tempered by the constant wars the Five Kingdoms fought with the clans to the north and the dead to the south.

The general reached down into a bag hanging at his side and pulled out a green flag. He held it high into the air and waved it up and down a few times. It took only moments for a unit of troops on the southern side of the wall, to the right of the great gate, to start moving forwards to support the dwindling numbers of those trying to climb one of the ladders.

"We're losing too many. We haven't even made the walls yet, and we must have lost a thousand lives down there."

Rose looked from her general to the battle raging down below and smiled. "By my count that gives us twenty thousand more to lose yet, General. Numbers are the greatest weapon of mankind. Enough coins will buy you an empire. Enough hands will win you that same empire in blood. Enough ships can rule the seas. Enough farmers can feed the world. Numbers win battles. Numbers..."

General Verit let out a bitter chuckle. "That's a simplistic view, my lady. I've seen one man fight a hundred. I've seen a hundred men hold off a thousand. Numbers may win battles of coin, but they do not always win the battles of blood. We're losing ten soldiers to every one of theirs, and that's a loss we can't sustain."

"What would you have us do, General?"

"Pull back. In a few weeks, I could have towers built. Armoured against the archers and tall enough to run straight onto the outer walls. We could fully explore the caves. There was a Drurr down there; it's possible he was using the trolls to tunnel into the city in an attempt to take it themselves. We could build siege engines..."

"I'm tired of having this argument." Rose interrupted the man. "You said yourself those walls will never come down. The longer we give them, the more chance they have to counter whatever we do. And in a few weeks, half our troops will be starving to death and the other half will have deserted. We're committed now."

The general took another flag from his satchel and waved it diagonally in the air. Another unit of soldiers, this one nearly a thousand strong with three great ladders, moved up towards the north. They were now attacking the outer wall in three different places, spreading Crucible's forces thinly.

"We can always pull back, my lady. This attack does not have to be all or nothing," General Verit said quietly.

"Yes, it does," Rose said.

She shifted from foot to foot and winced at the discomfort. Rose wished she could sit a horse like the general, but it wasn't possible in her condition, and she wasn't about to have a chair brought up to their position while men and women died for her down against the walls of Crucible. She paced, back and forth, back and forth, turning every time the ram struck the great gate.

Every moment was more lives lost, some atop the walls, more down below. Doubt started to creep in as Rose stared down at the battle unfolding below them. What if the general was right? What if they simply didn't have the numbers to fight an all-out assault? Despite the general's warnings, Rose had hoped it would be going better.

"I need a drink, Lucille," Rose snapped, unable to contain the tension. Her mouth was dry, and her feet ached almost as badly as her back, and she needed to piss, but there was nowhere to do it with any privacy. Her maid ran off to fetch a cup of wine, and Rose continued her pacing.

The ram hit the gate again, and the sound signalled it was time to turn and pace the other way. Rose found the general watching her, and she stopped, schooling her features into her usual mask.

The general turned his attention back to the battle and pointed.

Rose followed the gesture, eager to see any new development.

"To the left of the gate. Some of our troops have gained the outer wall."

Rose squinted, and it did look as though men were now pouring up the ladder more quickly than before. She smiled at the little victory. The soldiers who had gained the walls were hiding behind their shields, pushing the enemy back and creating space for more of their comrades to surge up the ladder behind them. If they could push far enough out they would soon have more coming up the other ladders to help.

"See!" Rose said in triumph. "Numbers, General."

"We'll see." He waved another flag in the air, this one red. Rose did not see any new units move to join the fight, she didn't see any change at all, but she wasn't about to expose her lack of military knowledge by asking about the command. "The inner wall is a problem. The archers stationed there have the height advantage on the outer wall. Our people are being attacked on three different fronts."

Pain shot through Rose's abdomen, and she let out a strangled cry, nearly collapsing from the agony. Lucille was there in a moment, cup of wine in one hand while she supported Rose with the other.

"Are you..."

Rose shook her head, determined not to show any weakness. "I think maybe I just need to relieve myself. If you wouldn't mind helping, Lucille."

"My lady Rose," the general said. She turned to find him watching her again, a concerned look making her feel a fool for crying out when so many people were dying down at the city walls. "If you need to rest, I can look after the battle."

"A generous offer, General," she said. Sweat was springing forth on her forehead, and now she thought about it, she was beyond desperate to empty her bladder. "But someone has to be here to stop you from calling a retreat."

The general turned away again. "If the battle starts to go any worse, your presence won't stop me pulling back our forces."

"My forces, General," Rose corrected him. "My soldiers."

He shrugged.

Rose let Lucille support her, and she waddled away a few paces before squatting down and hitching up her dress. Lucille held her steady as Rose released the pressure, watering the ground.

"Damn, but this child seems to enjoy embarrassing me already."

"You shouldn't be out here so close," Lucille said, a hint of steel in her voice.

Rose smiled. Now she was finally peeing she was starting to feel herself again, starting to feel less like an invalid. "When it is time, Lucille, and this bloody child is coming. Then, I will allow you to dictate my whereabouts. Not before. Good?"

Lucille nodded and helped Rose stand.

"As you can see, I'm fine now. Where did you leave that drink?" Rose shook the woman's hand from her arm and stood as straight as her swollen belly would allow.

She looked back towards the battle. Her troops were still surging up the ladder to the north. To the south, they were still dying by the score. And at the gate, the thumping of the ram was starting to sound more like splintering.

The Black Thorn

Pug stumbled and fell as a rock battered his shield from above. The heavy bit of stone hit the ground a moment before the lad followed it. One of Captain Lost's soldiers tried to move in to fill the gap, stepping on the squire, but Betrim gave the man a solid push and reached down, pulling Pug back to his feet and shielding him until he could get his arm back up.

"Thanks," Pug shouted over all the noise and Betrim grunted in reply.

They were squashed up tight against the ram with bodies cluttering the ground and all manner of shit, both sharp and blunt, being dropped down on them from above. Truth was Betrim had been in a good range of crappy situations, and none of them really compared to the mess he found himself in now.

He'd lost sight of Henry during the initial push and hadn't found a chance to look for her since. There was a good bet she'd be buried underneath the bodies around them, but Betrim hoped otherwise. He didn't much like the idea of not having the little murderess by his side. Couldn't even imagine life without her, truth be told.

A fresh wave of arrows peppered the ram, the ground, and their shields. Another couple of men went down with a scream, but Betrim couldn't see them in the crush of bodies.

Captain Lost pushed through the heave of sweat and flesh and steel and blood, ducking underneath the hammer as it was slowly drawn back for another swing. He stumbled, tripping over something, and came up with a second shield in hand.

"Here!" Lost shouted, shoving the shield at Pug. "Yours is a twig." He wasn't wrong. The constant rain of arrows and rocks had shattered Pug's shield and reduced it to little more than kindling strapped to the lad's arm. Betrim thought it half a miracle the boy hadn't been punctured yet.

Pug made to drop his battered shield, but Captain Lost put an arm on his hand and shook his head.

"Drop the sword first, lad. Second shield will do you more good."

The captain's cheeks were flushed, and his eyes were bright. If anything, Betrim would have said the crazed fool was enjoying being on the knife edge and surrounded by death and chaos. Some folk were far beyond his understanding. Betrim might have volunteered to be on the front lines with the troops, but he'd pay good money to be pretty much anywhere else.

"BRACE!" The shout went up, and Betrim threw himself against the rear support beam of the ram. He wasn't even sure it needed bracing any more. The wheels were half buried in thick, bloody mud.

The hammer swung down and crashed against the wooden gate, and Betrim heard something splinter. He risked looking up to check if the ram was falling apart and his spirits soared to see the gate was starting to buckle.

"We're almost through!" Betrim screamed, his voice feeling raw. Something smacked against his shield and reminded him how close he was to death; his enthusiasm dropping with the realisation that even once they were through, they would have a bloody fight to gain the outer wall and even that was only half the battle. Maybe even less than half now that he thought about it.

Captain Lost nodded to some of his men, and soon there were a bunch of them all pushed up against the ram. The hammer started drawing back again, as folk began pulling on the ropes. Betrim couldn't say how long they'd been at it, couldn't say how long the battle had been going on. Felt somewhere close to forever though. At least, here in the crush, with bodies all around and everyone's blood all sorts of up, he didn't feel a chill. Here at the heart of the assault, he felt almost too warm.

The captain ordered a few of his lads to push in front of Betrim and took up his own position just behind.

"When that gate goes," Captain Lost shouted, his shield held high against the shit dropping on them. "It's gonna be a bloody melee. Lots of stabbing, no real thought to what gets the pointy end. You stay behind us. Let us protect you like we're meant to."

Betrim frowned at that but nodded. He wasn't used to folk wanting to protect him. Used to be most of them wanted to be the ones trying to stab him, folk wanting to make their name off killing the Black Thorn. Odd how things changed. Now he had folk willing to put themselves in harm's way to keep him out of it just because he was fucking the woman in charge of things.

"BRACE!"

Betrim put his shoulder against the ram again and tensed as the hammer came swinging down to another splintering *crunch*. For a moment he thought he saw Henry's face on the other side, spotted with blood and grimacing against the shuttering machine of war, but that glimpse was soon lost amidst the crush of soldiers.

"A few more!" Captain Lost shouted.

They were almost through now. The gate was splintered and cracked, a hole showing where the ram had punched through. If Lost was right then just a couple more swings and the gate might pop its hinges allowing them to surge through and the real fighting could begin, not this crappy feathering each other with arrows.

The hammer was drawing back again. The crush got tighter. More and more soldiers piled in, ready to burst through the gate once it came down for good and all. Betrim was barely able to move, barely able to tell which bit was him and which was someone else. He certainly couldn't decide which of the shields above his head belonged to him.

"BRACE!"

The shock of the impact ran through Betrim again. Felt like his teeth were rattling around in his head. Felt like his eyeball was rattling too and for once he was glad he only had the one of them.

"AGAIN!" Lost shouted.

Betrim looked around for Pug, but the lad was nowhere to be seen. The crush was as tight as a virgin arsehole, and he could barely see the face next to him. Lost's soldiers, those set to guard Betrim, were the closest to him now. Lots of grizzled faces, lots of veterans. They all knew the game, and they would likely be better use than Pug when the fighting started. Still, it seemed a shame if the boy had died already, Betrim wasn't particularly sentimental, but he liked Pug. It was something to do with the innocence, he reckoned.

"BRACE!"

This time when the hammer struck home the gate gave a tortured groan and slumped open. The bar was finally broken. Soldiers surged forwards, pushing against the gate, using the weight of themselves and those behind them to force it open further and further.

Spears waited for them on the other side.

Henry

Henry was on the front lines, pretty much as front and centre as she could be. It wasn't by choice. Folk in front of her kept dying, picked off by archers leaning out over the parapets, and she kept getting pushed further and further forwards by the bastards behind her. She might have screamed at them to stop, but her throat was already so raw from screaming that it hurt to breathe. Even muttering a word at this point seemed out of any sort of question.

With one final hammer blow, the gate caved in as the brace on the other side snapped in two. The soldiers behind her pushed, and she found herself crushed up against the gate, struggling to draw a breath and wishing the damned thing would open quicker.

When it did start to swing open Henry found herself being pushed forwards faster than she'd like, faster than her feet were ready for. Fear and anticipation mixed into a sort of cocktail that flushed any thought from Henry's head. Spears thrust out at her from the city side, and she let out a squeak of alarm. It was too late though. The men behind her weren't stopping, and neither was she. One spear hit her side, tangling in her baggy suit of mail, and another slipped under her armpit to skewer the man behind.

Henry went down, her momentum arrested by the spear snagged in her mail. The shaft snapped, and she leapt into a roll before the soldiers behind could trample her. The world slipped by in a blur and then she was crouching in between two soldiers who looked almost as surprised as she was. A moment later the wall of Rose's soldiers crashed into them, and Henry found herself on the wrong side of a bloody melee.

There was something to be said for being lodged in the enemy lines. Henry slipped her hand from her shield and dropped the sword they'd given her too. Her daggers were never far from her hands, and she excelled at the close kill. The closer the better. Henry liked to feel the blood wash over her hands as she murdered, and this right here was nothing but bloody murder.

She didn't have a lot of space, wedged between one living soldier and one quite clearly dead, and her face was just a few inches from another of Crucible's defenders, snarling at her but completely unable to move in the crush. Henry slipped one of her hands up and out of the mess. She saw the soldier's eyes go wide with fear just a moment before she put one of her daggers in one of those eyes. He screamed, raw and pitiful, but he couldn't move he was pressed so tight. Henry stabbed again, putting out his second eye and then again into his throat. Blood sprayed over her, coating her face red and she stabbed down at someone else.

Henry liked to be close, but this was something else. She liked to be able to move, to use her speed and slight size to their greatest advantage. Here she was just another target. One more body in a grinding press of reeking death. She stabbed down again and again, hoping that no one managed to cut through the dead body in front of her acting as a shield. Hoping that none of her own folk behind her got the wrong idea and stabbed her by accident. She might not be wearing Crucible blacks, but in such close quarters, it was nearly impossible to tell.

She wasn't sure how long that first crash of battle lasted. Spears thrust back and forth, and every time Henry saw one coming, her heart missed a beat, and she was certain she was about to die. She stabbed down at every soldier she could reach and felt the desperate panic rise within her. She'd felt it before, the tightness in her throat, the blurring of her vision down to a focused little tunnel.

The crush started to lessen as the Crucible soldiers beat a retreat, and the dead bodies kept up by the weight of those behind them dropped to the bloody ground. An arrow slammed into a dead woman at Henry's feet. The head buried itself into her neck with a meaty *thwack* and nothing else. No scream. No shout. The woman was already long dead. Henry had no idea whether the deed had been done by her own daggers or by someone else's spear. It didn't really matter after the fact; dead was dead no matter which hand wielded the cause.

There were corpses all around her. Bodies of those from both sides of the conflict. Crucible's soldiers were backing further and further towards the safety of the inner gate. Spears held ready in case the attackers made another rush.

Henry just stood there for a moment, panting out her exhaustion and feeling light-headed. She was covered in blood. So often she found herself coated in the stuff. She couldn't tell how much of it was hers, certainly some. Rose's soldiers surged up around her, jostling her as they pushed inwards towards the inner wall. More arrows started to fall. More and more as the defenders atop the inner wall loosed a hail of them towards the attackers.

The panic consumed her, binding her limbs, and drawing fresh tears from her eyes. Just like in Hostown when the demons attacked, the fear crowded all other thoughts away. This was no fight. Henry had no control over whether she lived or died here. They were all going to die. She knew it with a sudden certainty, a painfully crystal clarity.

"SHIELDS UP!" Henry couldn't tell who or where the shout had come from. She looked around for her shield. There were plenty lying around on the ground, but none of them looked like hers. She couldn't remember what her shield looked like now she thought about it.

The soldiers enveloped Henry, and she found herself once again under a canopy of dead wood held high, pressed closed to the men next to her. The stink of sweat and blood enveloping everything. Rays of light broke through the meagre gaps, and the *thump* of arrows impacting into their protection became a constant thing. Sound with no rhythm or pattern. So impersonal. Slaughter on a mass scale. Names lost to the world without even the contemplation of what it might mean.

Henry looked down at her hands. Her right hand was coated in blood, some dry, some still wet and dripping. Her left hand had a few spots, small wounds where the skin had rubbed away but was otherwise clean. She started wiping her right hand on her tunic underneath the mail, but that too was soaked in red.

"We're the bulwark for the others to come in behind us now," said someone, a man's voice she didn't recognise. "Get a shield and get it up."

Someone pushed her left shoulder, and Henry acted on instinct, spinning around and shoving one of her daggers up into the man's back, underneath his armour.

The soldier looked at her, his mouth gaping and his eyes shocked and fearful. Henry felt hot blood wash her left hand as well, all the way up to her wrist. The man stared at her a moment more before his eyes rolled back in his head and he dropped. Just another corpse on the ground. One of thousands by now, Henry reckoned. At least this one got to see his killer.

No one noticed that she had just killed one of their own. None of the other soldiers even saw it. One more of them brought down by a stray arrow maybe, that's all any of them would think. Here was a place Henry could murder with impunity, without anyone noticing or caring, yet she didn't want to. All she wanted was to be gone.

Another soldier stepped over the body of the man she had just murdered, and the canopy of shields was complete again. Every now and then another soldier would drop, felled by the constant rain of arrows.

It was almost peaceful. Serene. Henry took a moment to look around, her vision blurred from tears and fear. Thorn was gone. She couldn't hear him, couldn't see him. For all Henry knew Thorn was already dead. For all Henry knew there was no longer any reason for her to be there, lost amidst the crush of nameless soldiers all dying for Rose or the blooded bastards. No reason at all.

Henry turned and started weaving through the crush of soldiers between her and the outer gate. She was small and lithe, always had been, body barely bigger than a girl's, and even with the baggy mail dragging her down, she made good going.

More soldiers were piling in behind the shield wall, a whole new unit of them determined to storm the outer wall now the gate was down. They pushed and shoved to get in, squeezing around the huge frame of the ram. A few of them remarked on Henry threading her way against them, but none pushed too hard. Not many folk were willing to argue with Henry even when she wasn't covered in blood.

Behind her she could still hear folk dying, men and women trying to hold the lines long enough for their comrades to help them from behind. A guttural scream went up. Dozens of voices all crying out, the noise splitting the air so loud and full of pain it made Henry want to vomit.

Henry glanced backwards, over the crush of soldiers, just in time to see a second vat of boiling oil flood down from the inner wall, hitting the raised shields and melting the people below. It dawned on her then that she would have been one of those poor bastards.

There were plenty of soldiers quitting the battle now. Some of those running back were injured, and some were dragging the injured behind them. Henry saw one woman with an arm missing, the ragged end still dripping, wandering about the field, picking up spent arrows. Foolish. Seemed right unlikely she'd ever be using a bow again what with only the one arm.

Folk still jostled Henry as they rushed to get into the fight, their voices so muted that she barely heard them. Idiots, Henry reckoned. People hurrying to die. There was still fighting going on, that much was true, but the front gate hung open now.

Henry looked down at her hands. Both were coated red. The blood had even soaked into her tunic, and that was now looking a dirty brown. She stumbled a step and vomited into the moat, spent a few moments watching the chunks float. Then she struggled back to her feet and started towards the camp, throwing her helmet from her head, and pulling at the chain hauberk.

Rose

"The walls are ours," Rose declared, unable to keep the victorious grin from her face. The baby was moving again, and it was causing no small amount of discomfort. The sooner the battle ended, the better; she needed to sit down.

"We've got a foothold, nothing more," the general replied.

Barely a minute went by without the man waving a new flag in the air, and he was receiving constant replies from the front line. Messengers running to and fro, rotating horses to bring him the latest news. It was especially important now the main gate had been breached as they could no longer see the battle taking place at the centre of the siege.

The soldiers were climbing the ladders as quickly as possible, but the archers on the inner wall were apparently taking their toll. According to the latest report, the number of Crucible defenders stationed on the inner wall nearly doubled those who had been defending the outer wall.

"I'm still not sure we can hold it," the general rumbled. His face was grim, and he had long since leapt down from his horse, letting the beast graze even though they were just a short gallop away from the carnage. He carried the bag full of flags on his shoulder, never far away from his grasp.

Rose frowned and turned her attention back to the siege. The sun had passed its zenith and was just starting to dip. It had been a bloody morning with more death than Rose had ever seen before. She didn't even want to imagine what it was like for the soldiers in the thick of it. For Betrim.

"So many of ours coming back to the camp," Rose said, almost to herself.

"Injured. Those that could escape the fighting and can't fight on. You say it's a lot..." General Verit let out a bitter laugh. "It's nothing compared to the dead."

"Are they pulling back the ram?" Rose asked.

"They are."

"Why?"

"Because we won't be taking the inner wall today." The general reached down and pulled out another flag, a royal blue one, larger than the rest. He turned it over in his hands a few times but didn't raise it. "We've stalled."

"What?" Rose shook her head. "The gate is down. We have the walls. We're winning."

General Verit shook his head right back. "We're losing." He sent a sorry look her way. "We've lost nearly half of our forces in a single morning. Thousands of soldiers dead. Thousands, my lady. If there weren't another wall then maybe we'd have it, push on through... We need to pull back."

"No!" Rose took two plodding steps forward and stared up at the man. "I told you I wanted the city to fall today, General."

He just stared at her for a moment. "And I told you that was fucking madness. That an all-out assault would only break our own forces. I was right, my lady. Look down there. Really look. Your soldiers are tired, they are exhausted, and they are dying. We have a foothold on the outer wall of that city. A foothold we can't keep against the weight of the enemy archers. We still have another gate to break through, one even thicker than the last if your drunkard is right. We can't move the ram up to break that second gate because the enemy is pouring boiling oil onto our troops.

"I don't know if you've ever seen what boiling oil does to a person, my lady, but it would curdle even your stomach."

"You're suggesting a full retreat?" Rose looked towards the city. It seemed to her they were so close to taking it, so close to pouring troops into the city proper. Many of her own soldiers were dead, it was true, their bodies were strewn all over the place, but there were still so many of them able to fight.

"There is no shame in pulling back and reconsidering our options, my lady," General Verit continued. "They will not be fixing that gate any time soon, not well enough that we can't break through it again. Let us pull back, lick our wounds, and consider other methods of attack."

Rose felt dizzy, a wave of vertigo washing over her, and she stumbled a step. The world dimmed, the sun fading for a moment, and all the warmth seemed to flood out of her. She opened her eyes to find herself staring up at the sky. Cotton clouds drifting across the sea. Her mouth tasted coppery, and Lucille's bland face appeared above her, staring down with a look of pure fear.

"Where am I?" Rose said, her voice dreamy.

A horn sounded somewhere close by, loud and echoing as it rolled around the sky. The noise was soon taken up by another horn and then another, somewhere far away.

"Outside of Crucible, my lady."

Rose rolled her eyes and groaned as she struggled to her knees. She could see the walls of Crucible, still tall and proud with little people running all over them like ants agitated by rain. General Verit was just a few feet away from her, waving a royal blue flag in the air. The horns sounded again.

"Why am I on the ground, Lucille?" There was grass beneath her, short and dry. Rose was laid out on it.

"You fainted, my lady," Lucille said, helping Rose to sit and then placing one hand on her forehead and the other on her belly.

Rose winced. She hated showing weakness in front of the man commanding her armies. "This damned child." Rose sighed and struggled to stand. Even with Lucille's help, it took a few moments and a lot of awkward shimmying. "Fainted?"

"It's not uncommon, my lady. Especially when women overexert themselves in this stage."

Rose grimaced and thought above shoving the woman away, so she could stand on her own. "Our troops are pulling back," Rose said, squinting towards the city.

"That is the order I'm giving." General Verit was still waving the blue flag in the air. "Too late to stop me now, lady Rose. See. We're already retreating."

Rose spat and lowered a glare at the man. She wanted to shout and berate him, but she had a feeling he was right. They couldn't sustain the losses they were taking. Her all-out assault had failed. She could already imagine Niles Brekovich and Alistair D'roan gloating over a glass of wine and a feast while their soldiers, the ones who had done the fighting and the dying, ate rations and scant ones at that.

"You acted without my orders, General," Rose hissed. It may have been the right thing to do, but it was also an act of betrayal.

General Verit turned towards her, still waving the flag in the air. He nodded once and for a moment looked truly abashed under his bushy beard. "I'm sorry, my lady. I made the call while you were incapacitated. I honestly believed it was the decision you would have made if you could have."

Rose smiled. The general was not as stupid as he looked, and there were times when she forgot that. He had neatly side-stepped the issue of betrayal in a way that lost neither of them any face.

"I think I may need to rest, General. Are you capable of handling the withdrawal of our troops without me?"

Rose was leaning more heavily than she liked on Lucille and even so the strain of remaining upright was agony. Her ankles felt like they were about to buckle, and she could feel her legs wobbling. Some women went through the entire process of carrying a child and giving birth without so much as a missed step. Rose decided then and there she envied those women.

"Yes, my lady. I'll bring you a report as soon as we have accurate details on losses." The general bowed low then straightened and turned back to stare out towards the city and the soldiers retreating back across the killing fields.

Rose took one last look at the walls that had thwarted her, but the discomfort was more than she could bear, and she turned towards the camp, Lucille supporting her every step. She hoped Betrim was down there somewhere, retreating with the others.

The Black Thorn

Turned out that carrying a big, two-handed axe more suitable for chopping wood than folk was pretty damned useful when there was a wooden door in the way. They were through the first gate and up against the door that led inside the outer wall and up towards the battlements. Betrim had a few dozen soldiers at his back, and most of them belonged to Lost. They were shielding him with their shields and with their lives, and Betrim took a good few swings at the door before his axe bit through.

He half expected an arrow to come shooting out as soon as the first hole was opened, but there wasn't a peep from the other side. Seemed the Crucible soldiers manning the outer wall were far too concerned with the folk coming up the ladders and not paying a drop of attention to those who had busted through the gate. Bit of an oversight, Betrim reckoned, but he wasn't about to bemoan a bit of good luck.

Another couple of meaty swings and he reckoned there was hole enough in the door to stick an arm through and get it unlocked, not that he was about to volunteer a limb. Captain Lost pulled Betrim out of the way and shoved one of his men towards the doorway. The soldier didn't hesitate in thrusting his hand through and felt around a bit before grunting and straining. A loud *thump* sounded from the other side, and the door swung open.

There were still arrows raining down on them. Betrim reckoned he'd seen more arrows in the past day than most fletchers saw in a lifetime. A few of Lost's boys barged through the doorway, and Betrim pulled away from the Captain, inserting himself into the line of folk disappearing up the hefty staircase towards the battlements way at the top.

He reckoned he'd cut a right heroic figure being the one to lead the charge and take the outer wall for good and all. Tales like that were what turned into legend, and Betrim already had more than a few legends to his name. They'd see him not just fighting along beside them but leading them from the front lines. Of course, the front lines were proving to be more than a little dangerous, and Betrim reckoned he might be dead a handful of times over if not for Lost looking out for him, determined to keep him alive.

The light was so dim Betrim could barely make out the man in front of him. He thundered up the winding staircase, big axe in one hand and wanting to take a break and a rest. It seemed to take them an age to get up the steps and all of them were panting by the time they did, but they burst out of another door that led right onto the battlements.

Didn't take long to see the fight hadn't ended during their little run up some stairs. Along the wall in front of them, Betrim could see scores of Crucible defenders all trying to hack at the little wall of attackers as they protected the nearby ladder. All the while there were more arrows raining in on them from the inner wall, just on their right side and higher up, looking down on them.

Betrim wasted no time clearing the doorway and even less time charging forwards to get stuck in as more and more soldiers piled out behind him.

The first defender went down with his back turned and a big axe head planted between his shoulder blades, separating the rings of his mail and giving his spine a similar treatment. The other bastards turned just in time to see a dozen of Lost's troops crash into them, swords biting down over and over again. That first line of defenders was dead before they even realised the fight was on them.

Betrim snarled and brought his axe down again. The blade was deflected just before it took a chunk out of one of the defenders, but it landed on the man's shoulder, and Betrim gave it a sharp tug. The poor bastard stumbled forwards out of his line and was quickly cut down with a sword in the eye. Betrim glanced over to find Captain Lost attached to the other end of the sword, sticking close by as always.

There wasn't really enough room to use a big axe properly. They were shoulder to shoulder, snarling and snapping at the defenders who were doing their very best to back away only to find themselves trapped between Betrim's group and those still pouring up the ladder.

Men and women on both sides were dying now as the defenders

trapped between a ladder and sharp place realised they had little to lose. They threw themselves at Betrim's soldiers even as the bastard archers on the inner wall realised what was happening and started putting arrows over the gap.

Betrim heard shouts behind him as folk went down and he ignored them, slamming down his axe repeatedly, letting the soldier in front of him to do the shielding. This was the biggest problem with battles as opposed to a good fight; battles always came down to folk with shields and other folk with spears. Betrim preferred a fair fight, one that came down to skill and the odd bit of cheating, rather than the threat of a spear or arrow he couldn't see until it was too late. Actually, Betrim preferred not to fight at all; it was better to leave a knife in the other bastard's neck long before they even knew a fight was coming.

If anything, the melee up on the wall was even more bloody and ferocious than the one down by the gate, but with reinforcements pouring in for Betrim's side they were sure to win. He just had to hope he survived long enough to see it all through.

"DOWN!" Lost shouted, and Betrim felt a strong hand on his shoulder pulling him into a crouch behind the first line of defence.

THURKUNK!

Betrim felt the impact behind him, a rush of air and bodies trailing behind it. The screams started up a moment later, and Betrim glanced back to find three bodies skewered by a Scorpion bolt the size of a small tree. For a couple of moments, all he could do was stare at the three corpses, pinned together like a giant human kebab. He reckoned it was fairly likely the bastards on the inner wall were loading another bolt up right away.

"Get in amongst them!" Betrim shouted. "Don't give the fuckers a target."

Didn't take long for that suggestion to turn into an order and everyone had a fair incentive to follow it. Betrim's line of soldiers pushed hard against the defenders, no longer caring about space enough to swing an axe or sword, it was far more important to be out of easy sight of the war machines atop the inner wall. No shield would protect them against a Scorpion bolt hitting its target.

Betrim slipped in spilt blood and dropped his axe. He pulled one of his little daggers from his belt. He had about a dozen more of the little bits of steel hidden about him, enough that it would take a real invasive search to find them all. He pushed against the line of defenders, using his height and weight to get in amongst them, and stabbed up beneath the bastards' armour wherever he could.

It was a close battle full of snarling faces and pitiful cries of mercy. Betrim caught a slash across his ribs, though he couldn't say where it had come from, and was fairly certain he dealt out a whole lot worse.

Another bolt crashed through some of the reinforcements coming in from behind and then another after it. Betrim's group was cutting a swathe through the defenders, and over their heads, he could see the soldiers coming up the ladders. They were having just as shitty a time of it, Betrim reckoned, and it dawned on him then that the Crucible defenders had only just started using the Scorpions. They'd been waiting for the outer gate to fall, waiting for the wall to start swarming with enemy. It wasn't quite a trap, but it was damned close, and it put them in a bad spot. He wasn't the only one to see it either. They were trapped in a melee with artillery pinning them in and the only protection they had, the defenders' own allies, was quickly disappearing.

"Shit!" Betrim cursed as he grabbed hold of a sword arm and stabbed his own dagger down into the bicep attached. A woman screamed in his face, pain and fear all in one, and Betrim hunkered down, lifted her up a bit and pushed her off the edge of the battlements. She plummeted away from him, and her scream was lost to the sounds of battle.

THURKUNK!

Another bolt hit home, but this one wasn't behind Betrim, it crashed through the poor bastards from the ladder assault. The bolt took a man in the stomach, going right through him and taking the corpse with it as it crashed into the parapets and dislodged a fair chunk of stonework.

"What do we do?" someone shouted, a man's voice, but Betrim couldn't tell who. He'd lost track of just about everyone he knew near the start of the fight. Henry and Pug were both gone, hopefully not to the grave, and only Captain Lost had stayed close.

Betrim parried a sword stab, and the blade slipped away into a nearby leg, Betrim reckoned that leg belonged to one of his own men, but he wasn't about to stop and apologise. He brought his left hand down in a hammer blow on the attacker's helmet before stabbing up under his chin, then tried to shake the pain out of his left hand. Hitting a man in the helmet was never a good idea.

"What should we do, sir?" This time it was Captain Lost asking. The man was spotted with blood, and his eyes were fever-bright in the afternoon sun.

They were almost out of defenders and had caught up to the soldiers storming up the first of the ladders. Another bolt ripped home just a dozen feet ahead, and a few more attackers were reduced to meat and bones and shit and blood. He glanced up towards the inner wall. It was hard to tell how far away it was with only the one eye, but he didn't reckon it was far. They had all the time and all the ammunition.

"Archers," Betrim said, quietly at first. "Archers. We need ta start shootin' back!"

The sound of a horn drifted across the sky and it was soon joined by another. All the soldiers nearby, those no longer involved in the fight, stopped for a moment to listen. Betrim cocked his head and waited.

THURKUNK!

Just a couple of feet away one of Lost's soldiers, another man stopped to listen to the horn, found himself impaled and pinned to the stone wall. He gagged on blood and reached out towards Betrim a moment before his hand dropped and his eyes went blank.

"Fuck me," Betrim breathed, unable to take his eyes off the poor bastard stuck to the wall and bleeding all over it. Between the Scorpion bolts and the hail of arrows still raining in on them, they were nothing more than target practice up on the outer wall.

"That was the order to retreat?" said one soldier.

Betrim looked to Captain Lost, and the man nodded to him once. He was keeping both eyes on the inner wall, clearly trying to predict where the next Scorpion bolt would come from.

"Aye. RETREAT!" Betrim screamed just about as loud as his voice could go. "Back down the ladders and back out the stairs. RETREAT!"

Didn't really seem right him being in charge of a battle, but the

Black Thorn knew a thing or two about retreating seeing as how it was just a different word for running the fuck away.

THURKUNK!

Betrim winced, expecting the bolt to go right through him. After a second, he realised he was probably safe from being skewered this time and turned to head towards the ladder. He felt a sharp pain in the back of his head and reached up to check it only his hands wouldn't move, and the stony floor was rushing up to meet him.

Rose

Lucille helped her down into the padded chair, and Rose instantly set about trying to find a comfortable spot. It was a fruitless endeavour. After a fair bit of wriggling around, she settled for mild discomfort. The worst bit of it was that she needed to piss again.

"You shouldn't push yourself so," Lucille said as she busied herself picking up a few things and tidying the tent. The woman had already placed a cup of fruit wine on the nearby table, and Rose had to admit she was damned useful. "Too much stress could bring on the birth before the child is ready."

"Good," Rose said with a sigh. "I'm ready for it. If it doesn't pop out soon, I'll cut it out myself."

Lucille laughed as she picked up a knife dropped on the Acanthian rug. It was one of Betrim's. Probably one of the little blades he liked to keep hidden about himself. It was a trait they all shared. Just about anyone who had ever had a hand in the game carried weapons where it was unlikely anyone would find them.

"You should try not to leave these around, my lady," Lucille continued, placing the knife on the table with the map of Crucible. "Once the child is crawling they will pick up anything, and anything it picks up will go in its mouth."

Rose shrugged. "That's one way to learn about pointy objects."

Lucille sent her a chiding look, and Rose laughed. "What am I paying you for if not to pick up after me and stop the child from getting into too much trouble? I do have a kingdom to run, you know?"

Rose wriggled some more and reached for the cup of wine. "Thank you, Lucille. I do appreciate all that you do." It was true for the most part. She wasn't pleased when the woman questioned her or ordered her about in public, but those times were few and far between and were a small price to pay for everything else Lucille did for her.

The tent flap moved, and Henry walked in. The little woman was covered in dried blood, her face and arms crimson with it, and her eyes looked dead. It was one of the few times Rose had seen Henry without her cavalier hat and, underneath the blood, she could see all the scars the demons of Absolution had left on her face, livid and white and made clearer by the red.

Henry looked up and glanced about the tent, her gaze passing over Lucille and Rose as if they weren't even there, and then focusing on a cabinet at the back of the tent. Without a word Henry started towards the cabinet, her feet leaving muddy prints on the rugs below.

Lucille looked at Rose, something approaching panic on her face, but Rose just shook her head slowly. They were in no danger, or at least Rose certainly wasn't in any danger. She had no doubt that Henry had no love for her, but as long as she was carrying Betrim's child, Henry was as safe as the most loyal of dogs.

Rose watched as Henry stopped in front of the cabinet, pulled the door open and reached inside. She pulled a bottle out, quite a rare bottle of whiskey if Rose wasn't mistaken. Henry then collapsed down beside the cabinet, pushing herself into the small crevice between that and the cot next to it. The little murderess wedged herself in, pulled her knees up to her chest and hugged the bottle close without even taking a sip.

For a long time, Henry just stared straight ahead, barely blinking, the bottle held tight to her chest. Rose watched, and Lucille continued to tidy, cleaning up the muddy boot prints trailed in by Henry.

Rose leaned forward and plucked her cup from the nearby table, holding it up and towards Henry. "Drink to the fallen."

Henry didn't move, didn't raise the bottle to her lips, didn't shift her blank stare. "We'll be joinin' 'em soon." There was no sadness in her voice. No anger or fear. There was nothing. The words sounded dead on her lips.

Rose sipped at her wine and put the cup back down. She levered herself back to her feet and waddled over to the catatonic women.

"Henry," Rose said.

She waved Lucille over and used the woman to help her onto her knees. Now she was face to face with Henry, only a short space between them, she appeared mostly unharmed. The blood belonging to someone else. Probably quite a few someone elses. It seemed strange. Rose knew enough about Henry to know her as Henry the Red for good reason. She had murdered hundreds of people if the stories were true - some for as little as no reason at all.

"Henry," Rose said again, this time waving a hand in front of her face.

Henry looked up, and for a moment Rose saw something else in her eyes; fear and pain mingled together. Hopelessness and despair. Something inside went tight, and Rose felt a lump blocking her throat. It took a lot to force the next words out.

"Henry, where is my husband?"

Henry shook her head. "Don't know. Lost sight of Thorn early on. I... Don't know."

There were tears in the woman's eyes. Rose reached out and took hold of Henry's hands, holding them in her own heedless of the dried blood staining them.

There was a time, not so long ago, that Rose had wondered if things might come to blows between her and Henry. The woman was loyal to Betrim, that much was obvious and true, but she clearly did not extend that same loyalty to Rose, no matter her relationship with the Black Thorn. They had clashed with words a couple of times, once even shouting at each other, but it had never come to sharp objects between them.

Now, looking down at Henry as fat tears started to roll down her blood-stained face, Rose was doubly glad they had never taken their arguments further than words. Henry made no sound as she cried, no sobs or sniffs. She barely moved, just let the tears fall onto their hands.

After a while, Rose simply couldn't remain in her position. The discomfort grew to such a level she was close to screaming. She pulled her hands back from Henry and the woman instantly curled back into her protective ball, hugging the bottle. Rose used the nearby cot to get back to her feet and winced at the pain.

"Shall I send for Suzku, dear?"

Henry looked up at that. Her eyes, ringed red from crying, had a measure of steel in them again. She shook her head furiously.

Rose nodded. "As you wish. I understand. Take as long as you need, Henry."

She couldn't quite contain the worry that was gnawing away at her gut. Betrim had not returned. It was possible he was seeing to some duty with the troops, maybe commiserating with them over comrades lost. It was also entirely possible he was one of the lost. Rose needed to know more; she needed to know what had happened out there, how many soldiers were dead.

"Where is Pug when you need him?" Rose started towards the tent flap, determined to find General Verit on her own if need be, when the big Five Kingdomer ducked in through the tent flap.

General Verit bowed his head, then raised it and made his way to the table with the map on it. His cheeks were ruddy despite the chill in the air. The sun was setting outside the tent, and it wouldn't be long before the only light was the moon and the campfires. So far north and at such a time of year, the nights got very cold.

"Is she OK?" the general asked, waving towards Henry.

Rose moved beside General Verit and leaned quite heavily on the table. "Henry is uninjured."

"The Black Thorn?"

Rose suppressed an urge to scream. "I was hoping you might be able to shed some light on that, General. I'm waiting for a report."

General Verit shook his head. "Would you prefer the bad news or the worse?"

"Both are coming one way or another, General, and stalling does nothing to ease their impact."

His face looked long, drawn out and exhausted. For the first time since she'd met the man his shoulders slumped, and the weight of his armour seemed to be dragging him down.

"We've lost close to nine thousand men, almost half our forces. I estimate we'll have lost another thousand before the sun rises again."

Rose swallowed hard and was glad of the table to steady herself. They had only just made the first wall and had lost so many. Nine thousand. In bits, cold hard coin, she could imagine it, she had seen it before. But in people...

"Another thousand? Injured?" Rose asked.

"Some. We'll lose a few more to wounds, it's true. But most of those we'll lose to desertion."

"What?"

"Any encamped army will lose soldiers to desertion. Some get bored; some want to go back to their families, plant crops or sew other new seeds. Any loss is bound to increase the numbers trying their luck elsewhere." He sighed. "And we suffered quite a loss, my lady.

"I've ordered unit commanders to keep a strict eye on their men, but..." He shook his head. "If people are determined to leave, they will leave."

Rose rubbed at her temples. "We still outnumber them more than two to one."

The general nodded. "We think they lost between five hundred and one thousand soldiers."

"Twenty to one," Rose mused. "By the gods."

General Verit nodded. "Maybe. We can't afford another assault like that, my lady. We either find a way to breach their walls, or we settle in for the long wait."

"How?" Rose asked. "How did it go so badly?"

"It was a trap," Henry said, still wedged in between the cabinet and Rose's cot.

Rose glanced at her and then at the general. He nodded.

"They wanted us to breach the outer wall. They let us pour in, let us climb the ladders." He exhaled a bitter laugh. "I've got to give it to this Niles Brekovich - he's a good commander. It was an excellent plan." The general shook his head. "I should have seen it coming."

Rose frowned. "I'm not sure I understand. How was letting us breach their outer most defences a good plan? How was it a trap?"

General Verit pointed at the map. "The whole city is built like a trap. The inner walls are more defensible; they need to be taken first. The outer walls are a death trap to any attacking soldiers as long as men are stationed on the inner walls. But you can't leave the outer walls alone or the soldiers atop them will continue to rain arrows down on you.

"Brekovich purposefully stationed fewer soldiers atop the outer wall. He wanted us to breach it, wanted us to get our troops up there. At the same time, he wanted us to break through the outer gate. He knew the moment we did we'd have to commit a more sizeable force to push through and take the outer walls. If any assault were to be successful, we'd need to take and hold those walls while we also pushed through against the inner walls."

The general tapped the map where it depicted the inner walls. "Here they had vats full of boiling oil and Scorpions capable of delivering bolts to anyone stationed atop the outer wall. Not to mention more and more archers with better defences. The outer wall has no defences against an assault from within.

"The moment we committed a larger force, he snapped the trap shut and used the inner walls to their full effect. It was a hell of a trap, and we stepped right into the noose. I stepped us into the noose."

Rose drew in a shuddering breath and stared down at the map. "So taking the outer wall without first securing the inner is death and we can't leave the soldiers atop the outer wall at our backs. How many men do they have left?"

"Maybe four thousand. More than enough to hold our ten."

"I don't see it, General," Rose said. "I don't see a path to victory."

"Neither do I. Yesterday I suggested a proper siege. No one in, no one out. Wait until their supplies run dry. Today I suggest it again, but more firmly. We cannot assault this city, my lady. It is unbreakable."

"Even if we could get through again, we couldn't use ladders to gain the inner wall," Rose mused to herself. "We would have to push the gate."

"And I'm told it's so full of murders holes we'd likely just clog up the passage with bodies of our dead." General Verit placed both hands on the table and hung his head. "Order the siege, my lady. We'll settle in before winter hits us. Find the resources to support the troops."

"There are no more resources," Rose said with a sorry shake of her head.

General Verit shrugged, the exhaustion showing proud on his face.

Rose slammed a fist down on the table. The knife Lucille had left there jumped and came to rest again. After a few moments, Rose nodded. She couldn't see any other way around it. She would leave the siege in

General Verit's hands and return to Chade beaten by the blooded bastards. Perhaps she could drum up some support from the Guild in Acanthia, or the free city of Larkos. Word would soon get out that the blooded had won the battle, it might create sympathy for them, might convince their hidden supporters to rise up. This was what Rose was truly afraid of, why she needed to crush the blooded. She might have killed all but three of the families, but their influence was far from gone. The wound of Crucible was already festering, and all the Wilds would suffer.

The tent flapped moved again, and Pug's face appeared. He looked to have aged a decade, was spotted with dried blood, and had a bandage wrapped around his head, completely covering his left eye. His clothing was torn in places and muddied in others, and his right arm was in a sling.

"My lady," Pug sketched an awkward, painful bow.

"Where is my husband?" Rose asked before she could bring herself to calm.

"I don't know, my lady. We were separated when the gate breached. I believe Captain Lost was with him along with his bodyguards. There's a messenger here to see you, my lady. From the city. He has a box with him."

"Let him in," Rose said.

She straightened her back and plastered a regal look to her face. General Verit stepped next to the tent flap, and Pug disappeared out to fetch the messenger. At the last moment, Rose stepped to the side to position herself between the entrance and Henry. The little woman was still collapsed in the corner, catatonic. She didn't need people seeing her that way.

Pug let the messenger in, and General Verit stopped the young man before he could get very far. He was carrying a small wooden box, maybe half a foot by another half and ornately decorated. It was a fine piece of furniture and no mistake. The man had short dark hair and a thin moustache. He didn't look like he had a drop of blood in him. Clearly, Niles Brekovich was not willing to risk sending one of the blooded to treat with her.

Without a word, the general took the box from the man, opened the lid a little and looked inside. His face went from confusion to stony rage, and he closed the lid, placed the box on the table, and put a big hand on the young man's shoulder. It was not a subtle gesture, and the man looked as though he were ready to shit himself there and then.

"I'm... um. I'm told to deliver that and the message directly to..." He closed his eyes for a moment and looked as though he were on the verge of tears. "Directly to the whore."

Rose cocked an eyebrow at that. Clearly, the blooded did not mind wasting this poor boy's life. She plucked the little box from the table and flipped open the lid.

Inside the box was a hand. A left hand lopped off just above the wrist. The hand had just three fingers; a little finger, an index finger, and a thumb. The middle finger was cut off at the first knuckle, barely more than a stump. The wounds were long since healed; years, maybe even a decade for some. It was scarred and calloused and muddy and sitting on a bed of green silk. Blood had leaked out of the severed end, but that had dried up.

"What is it?" Henry asked. The little woman hadn't moved, but her eyes were on Rose now. Red from crying and a pleading look in them.

Rose snapped the lid shut and threw the box onto the table. "It's my husband's left hand."

Henry didn't say anything, but her head slumped down on her shoulders.

"Tell me, young man," Rose said, closing on him. "What message are you to deliver to the whore?"

The man visibly quivered as General Verit squeezed his shoulder harder and harder. "Ow. He, um... Lord Brekovich said that every day your army is here he'll... uh... send you another part of your husband."

DAY 4 – THE BETRAYAL

The Black Thorn

There was a strange feeling that accompanied waking up after a heavy night's drinking; Betrim had long ago realised that it caused him to ache everywhere, almost as though he had taken a rough beating. That's how he recognised the feeling. Without even opening his eye he knew it had been a hefty night and that explained the hole in his memory too. He wanted nothing so much as to keep his eye closed and drift off back to oblivion. Betrim knew full well the best way to beat a hangover was to sleep it off.

It didn't take long for the pressure to start up. Nothing like needing to piss to get a man up. Not that Betrim hadn't pissed himself before, but he was some sort of lord now; important and looked up to, he couldn't be seen pissing himself in a drunken stupor. Besides, his mouth tasted like rotten arse, and that was something that needed fixing.

Betrim reached up to scratch at his burned face. It was strange how he could barely feel a touch on the twisted, melted skin, but it still managed to itch. Instead of scratching, he just sort of poked at his face with a painful hand. More than pain really. Closer to blinding agony, and he was already half blind. He let out a groan and forced his eye to open.

Above him lay a dark, stone ceiling. He tried to reason out where he might be. Last thing he remembered was being in a battle; his army camped outside the city walls. Seemed he should be in some sort of tent and tents didn't tend to be made of stone.

With something approaching apprehension, Betrim rolled his head to the side to see a sturdy-looking set of iron bars between him and the far wall. He knew the sight of a gaol all too well, and it was fair to assume that he was in one now. He let out another groan and attempted to sit up.

"Fuck." Betrim's mouth felt stiff and slow, but it was nothing compared to the searing pain shooting up his left arm.

"Finally awake, I see."

Betrim squinted into the darkness. There was definitely someone sitting beyond the bars. A couple of folk, now he thought about it, silhouettes in the dim light and nothing more. Voice sure seemed familiar though, and Betrim tried to think of how he knew it. He tried to shake his head, clear the cobwebs, but that just brought on a whole new mess of pain and a wave of nausea to make things that little bit worse.

"Wake up, Thorn."

Betrim sniffed and tried to spit, only his mouth was dryer than sun-baked sand. "Lost? That you?" he croaked. Always seemed weird how a man could both be dying of thirst and need to piss at the same time.

"Aye," Lost said from somewhere in the gloom beyond the bars. "Sorry about this."

Betrim nodded.

"You should look at ya hand."

Betrim had been purposefully not looking at his hand, truth be told. It was hurting like he was gripping hold of the sun, and he knew that feeling well. Reckoned the bastards had taken another finger and he didn't have an awful lot left to spare. Even so, it would need looking at eventually, and there was no sense putting it off any further.

Betrim held his left hand up in front of him. Only there wasn't a hand. His arm ended in a bloody, bandaged stump just shy of where his wrist should have been. He stared at it for a few moments, fighting the urge to wince at the pain, fighting the urge to poke at the bloody end. Fighting the urge to scream and rage; fighting the urge to vomit in revulsion. He'd been maimed before and more than once. Two fingers from his left hand, and two toes from his left foot, his left eye plucked from his head and squashed upon the streets of Sarth, the left side of his face burned into a scarred mess. Seemed everything happened to his left side, and Betrim reckoned there had to be a reason for that. But somehow this maiming seemed worse than all the others. This wasn't just a lost finger or two; his whole hand was gone.

Never again would he swing that big axe of his in both hands.

Never again would he hold two tankards of ale at the same time, one for then and one for after. Never again would he hold both of Rose's tits at the same time. So many things that became never again. So many experiences lost. Seemed he'd taken those experiences for granted.

After a few moments, Betrim looked away and rolled onto his knees before pushing to his feet. "Probably did me a favour, I reckon," he said as he looked about his little cell with its dank walls and creeping moss. "Weren't much use with only the three fingers anyway. Reckon now I can get somethin' else there. Knew a lad with only the one hand once. Name of Hook-Hand Rolf."

"I remember him," said Lost.

"Had a hook for a hand," Betrim continued. He found what he was looking for and took a couple of faltering steps towards the bucket in the corner of the cell. "Strangest thing I ever saw him do with the damned thing was gut one of them little rat things that scurry about in the plains. Never seen a man gut anythin' quite that fast. 'Course then he took ta stickin' the skin on his other hand and paradin' it about like some sort of puppet. Was a weird fucker was Rolf." Betrim shook his head and set about trying to pull his cock out of his trousers with only the one hand.

"Look, Thorn," Lost started. "I just wanted to say..."

Betrim drowned out the traitorous bastard with a steady stream of urine blasted into the metal bucket.

"What's that, Lost?" he shouted. "Can't hear ya."

"I never wanted to..."

Betrim pushed a little harder. Wasn't the most comfortable way to piss, and he was splashing a bit over his own boots, but the noise did a good job of drowning out Lost's voice.

Eventually, Betrim ran dry and exhaled loudly, shaking his cock a few times before tucking it back into his trousers. With his back turned to Lost he found he was wincing at the pain lancing through his left arm and cursing at the fact that it almost felt as though he could still feel his fingers. He made sure to school his face back into an emotionless mess before he turned back to the captain.

"So, ya a traitorous fuck piece then?" Betrim said, crossing over to the bars and gripping hold of one with his right hand. At least he still had all the fingers on that one. He gave the bar a bit of a tug, but it held fast. He reckoned they all would, and the door would be fairly secure too. Didn't seem like he'd have much chance of breaking out of this shitty situation.

He could see Lost more clearly now. The bastard was sitting on a wooden chair, a table next to him with a couple of cups and a deck of cards strewn about it. Another soldier, one Betrim didn't recognise, sat on the other side of the table.

Lost shook his head. "I'm not a traitor, Thorn. I was never working for you. Lord Brekovich hired me and my lot on about six months back. Told us to join up with your lot and wait for the right time."

"Right time ta smack me in the head an' chop my fuckin' hand off?" Betrim snorted. He reached up to the back of his head with his right hand and found it damned painful, just like the rest of him.

"Wasn't really the plan," Lost sighed and picked up a cup, leaned forwards and handed it through the bars. Betrim took the little mug and drained it in one. He didn't reckon they were likely to poison him considering he was already well and truly at their mercy. "Just seemed like a good opportunity really.

"Truth is I respect you, Thorn. What you done, getting out of the game like that and making something of yaself. Something to look up to that is. But... Well, Lord Brekovich pays better than you and Rose. A lot better."

"Oh, right? Is this the bit where ya expect me ta offer ya more? Beat that blooded fuck's offer? Well I reckon I fuckin' will if ya get me out of here."

Lost laughed and shook his head. "Even if you let me off, I doubt your wife would."

Betrim nodded at that. "Too right, mate. She'd feed ya ya own fingers for the world ta watch. Still, worth a try, eh? How long was I out?" Betrim looked up and down, left and right, studying the bars. If no one else came for him, he might be able to make a grab for Lost's sword when they pulled him out of his cage. Of course, even once he was free, he was still locked up tight in the middle of Crucible with no way out of the damned city.

"Half a day," Lost said with a wince. "Sorry about the knock to the head."

"Oh aye? What about the hand?" Betrim grinned and waved a bloody stump at the man. "Ya sorry about that too?" He laughed, a rasping noise that echoed about the stone walls of his little cell.

Lost nodded, his face grave. "I am actually."

Betrim snorted. "They do a good job at least?" He wasn't about to take the bandages off to check. "Seal the wound right?"

Again, Lost nodded. "Lord Brekovich wants you alive. Wants you to see what's coming."

"Aye," Betrim fought the wave of nausea that washed over him and won. "And what's comin'?"

Lost shook his head this time. "He'd probably kill me if I ruined the surprise. He'll be coming for you soon. Night set in a while back and it's almost time."

Betrim hated how vague Lost was being, but he had a good feeling that no amount of badgering was likely to shake loose the bastard's tongue. Sometimes there wasn't much to do but sit and wait for whatever was coming. Betrim knew he was already dead; there wasn't a chance the blooded were letting him go, he just had to bide his time and see if he couldn't take one of them with him.

Lost wasn't wrong, and it didn't take too long before the door to the gaol opened, and two more folk stepped in, one of which Betrim recognised. He was big and broad and carried a battleaxe on his back. His hair was shaved at the sides and left to grow long on top, tied into a braid that ran a fair way down his back. Betrim had met the man once before the last time he'd been captured and awaiting execution in Crucible. Seemed to remember his name was Torival.

There was a crazed look in Torival's eyes, a touch of madness. Betrim had seen it before. Folk like him liked to hurt people as much as they liked to kill. No doubt in working for Niles Brekovich he had found a way to embrace his hobbies without running afoul of any laws.

"Get him out," ordered Torival and Lost quickly jumped to it.

Betrim rasped out a laugh. "A whipped dog is still whipped even with a few bits paid for the privilege."

Lost said nothing as he shoved a key into the door and pulled the iron bars open. Torival stepped in and squared up to Betrim, he was an inch or two shorter and a little less broad, but the bastard still had both hands, and that put him at a distinct advantage. He also had a bunch of backup and Betrim was well and truly alone.

"Out," growled Torival and Betrim saw no reason to resist. All it was likely to earn him was a beating and that would serve no one.

"Seem ta remember ya've both blindsided me now," Betrim said as he plodded along through the door to his gaol and out into the cold night. He shivered. "Might be I'm rememberin' it wrong, but I reckon Lost hits harder." He looked over his shoulder and grinned at Torival. "Maybe ya was just pullin' ya blow, eh?"

Torival gave Betrim a shove, and he stumbled a couple of steps but kept his feet beneath him. The chill in the air was already starting to make his bandaged stump hurt a little less, and it was also doing wonders to clear away the remaining fuzzy edges that often accompanied being smacked hard in the head. Unfortunately, the sight that lay before Betrim was anything but comforting.

The gaol appeared to be located near the very outskirts of Crucible's buildings, in front of them now lay a good fifty feet of killing ground with nothing but short grass and space to die. There were plenty of lit torches, giving the night a gloomy feel. What was worst though was the number of horses milling about between the buildings and the inner wall. Betrim had no word for that number of beasts, but he knew a lot when he saw it, and this had passed that a long time ago.

Another shove in his back set Betrim stumbling forwards again. Torival was pushing him right towards the mass of horses, and it was only then that Betrim saw the riders. For every beast, there was a man or woman dressed in leathers or chain and looking ready for a spot of killing like they hadn't already got their fill of it earlier in the day.

Before long they were in amongst the horses and riders. Torival kept a hand on the back of Betrim's collar, making sure he couldn't slip away into the milling mass. Betrim kept his left hand shielded against his body. Last thing he wanted was to have some errant bump making him cry out in pain.

Folk watched them pass and sent dirty looks Betrim's way. It wasn't surprising. He was the leader of the force encamped outside their city. They probably counted him as responsible for every death they had suffered so far. Many of them would have lost friends or family already. Some of them stamped their feet towards him as he passed, shouting and trying to make him flinch. Others spat at him, and some of that spittle hit. Betrim ignored them all. No sense in getting angry over a bit of insult when he was likely to be dead in a couple of hours.

It took a long time to pass the fifty feet to the inner wall. They had to thread through the mass of horse flesh and rider, and more than once they stopped so some burly Crucible warrior could step in front of Betrim and try to scare him with an angry glare and some vicious insults. More than once Betrim had to resist the urge to headbutt someone so hard it left them both bloody.

Once they were done parading him through the troops, they came to the inner wall, with the horses and riders at their back. Betrim found himself staring at the open gate and the raised portcullis. Along with the gathering of cavalry, he was starting to get fairly nervous.

Torival barely gave him a moment to stare up at the giant wall before pushing him onwards, out through the gate and underneath all the murder holes. Betrim glanced up at them and winced. It was probably a good job their ill-fated assault hadn't made it this far; they would have died in the hundreds here, clogging up the passage with their bodies.

There was an odd smell as they left the cover of the inner wall and started the short trek to the outer. Betrim knew the smell as burning, melted flesh. It was horrible stench that stained both the ground and the very air around it, and it would take a few rains to wash it clear. The bodies were gone, pulled away and dumped outside the city limits no doubt, but the ground was stained red by the spilled blood of so many. Betrim sniffed and kept quiet. A part of him wanted to spit, as he often did when confronted with something distasteful, but he wouldn't offer up that sort of insult to all those who had died for Rose's cause. For his cause, too, when he thought about it.

The outer gate hung cracked and open, and there was no effort underway to fix it. The ram was nowhere in sight, and Betrim wondered whether it had been destroyed by the defenders or withdrawn by the attackers.

Torival led them to the doorway that ran up into the outer wall. The wooden door hung there with a gaping hole in it, and Betrim grinned, knowing full well how horrific that made him look.

"Turns out ya don't need a key when ya got an axe," he rasped.

Torival just sneered at him. "Your axe swinging days are over, Black Thorn. Up. Start walking."

One of Torival's soldiers, a bland man with a forgettable face, started up the stairs through the doorway and another shove convinced Betrim it was his turn next. He plodded along, thankful they'd chopped off a hand and not a foot. He still wasn't sure why they'd lopped his hand off, maybe just to show they had some power over him, maybe because it was the most noticeable thing about him after his scarred face. It didn't really matter either way; the hand was gone, and it certainly wasn't coming back.

Betrim considered making a grab for a sword. He still had one good hand, and if he could get it on a sword hilt, he might be able to take a couple of bastards with him. Seemed a fool way to go though, when he thought about it. The Black Thorn wasn't the sort of man to be killed by a couple of no-name soldiers, huffing and puffing as he realised for the second time in as many days just how much he hated stairs.

The wall was said to be a good one hundred feet high, and Betrim could well believe it by the time he had climbed to the top. He was red-faced and out of breath, and his bloody stump was throbbing. He'd liked to have taken a minute at the top of the stairs to catch his breath and maybe to let loose a few choice curses, but Torival pushed him onwards relentlessly. It didn't take long to see why.

Up on the top of the wall, staring out towards the encampment of soldiers laying siege to them, was a collection of blooded faces. Betrim had seen a few of those faces before once or twice, but even those he didn't recognise were obvious. They were a pretty folk, if truth be told, the blooded, with strong features, bright eyes, and a love of fancy clothing. All except for Niles Brekovich. The lord of the Brekovich family stood there in armour that wouldn't look amiss on any foot soldier, and the sword that hung by his side had a hand resting on the hilt. Battered scabbard, Betrim noticed, cleaned and maintained, but it had a few notches in it and had seen some action.

While he might not admit it to anyone else, and especially not Rose, Betrim held more than a little respect for Niles Brekovich. Blooded bastard the man might be, but he was also a world-renowned tactician and just about the only blooded lord in the last four generations who wasn't above getting his own hands a bit dirty. Of course he was also a murderous, evil bastard, but then some of Betrim's closest friends fit the same description.

That was why Betrim had no love for the blooded; they thought themselves better than the rest of the Wilds. Paraded around in luxury while folk like Betrim played the game, lived and died in it, all so the blooded could say their hands weren't covered in shit like those hired to do their dirty deeds.

Aye, Betrim admitted, at least to himself, that he had some measure of respect for Niles Brekovich. He'd also admit he had some respect for Willem Jogaren, and that hadn't stopped him luring the Hammer out of his city and filling him with arrows.

With one hand still on Betrim's collar, Torival pushed him along to meet with the last of the blooded. There weren't many folk in the history of the Wilds responsible for killing quite so many of the bastards. Betrim reckoned he'd earned himself a personal meeting with those he had left alive.

There was plenty of blood up here on the wall as well. Seemed getting rid of the bodies was one thing, but they didn't have the manpower to wash down the walls. Made the footing treacherous and the smell grim as an abattoir.

Betrim glanced out towards the encampment. So many torches and fires he couldn't count them, though it still seemed a whole lot less than just one night ago. He wondered how many folk they'd lost. Made him wonder if they had enough left to survive the shit storm that was likely coming their way.

Betrim was pulled to a halt by the hand still on his collar. He let out a curse as his missing hand set to throbbing all anew. He was sweaty from the recent climb and breathless and wished he looked a bit more menacing to the collection of blooded folk now watching him.

There was a long moment of silence as they all stared at each other. Betrim recognised the unblinking face of Niles Brekovich, and he knew the tall man with a scarred lip would be Alistair D'roan. The third man, standing behind the others, was probably Tanith Fanklin, but they'd never been able to get any accurate reports on what the recluse looked like. Apparently, it took a full-blown war to shake the bastard out of hiding. He was a short man, blooded for sure, but pudgy and wild-eyed.

"I'd bow," Betrim said, "but I don't really recognise ya authority."

"Easily rectified," D'roan said and nodded.

Torival kicked Betrim in the back of the legs, forcing him to kneel in front of those that considered themselves his betters.

Betrim shrugged. He hated being knelt in front of them, and he hated having nothing but a mean, armed thug at his back, but he wasn't about to let them know that. They could take his hand, and they could threaten to kill him, but he'd show them nothing but contempt or mild indifference at a stretch.

"Your insurrection is over, Black Thorn," this from D'roan. The man stood tall and proud with a victorious look on his face like he'd already won the war. Chances were he'd done little but stand there beside Brekovich and look regal. The reports Betrim had heard said that D'roan was a fair military commander in his own right, but much more of a people manager.

Betrim fixed D'roan with a stare from his one eye. He'd always found that only having the one of them seemed to make him more intense, folk quickly backed away from his stares these days.

"Jezzet Vel'urn was a friend of mine," Betrim said, not taking his eye from Alistair D'roan.

The smile dropped from D'roan's face, and he looked nervous for a moment before he remembered that he was surrounded by folk who would protect him, and Betrim was knelt before him with one arm ending in a bloody stump. The bastard might not have been responsible for Jez's death, but he sure as all the hells wasn't kind to her when he had her in chains.

Niles Brekovich turned away towards the army camped outside his gates. He still hadn't said a word, nor blinked as far as Betrim could tell. Anders certainly wasn't wrong about his father having scary eyes.

"We should just kill him," D'roan hissed, secure behind Niles Brekovich and half a dozen soldiers. The bastard might know how to command folk, even won a battle or two in his time, but he was no warrior. Even with only one hand and no weapon, Betrim was certain he could take the blooded lord.

"He's not wrong," Betrim rasped. He wondered if he struggled back to his feet whether Torival would put him right back on his knees.

"Not yet." Niles Brekovich's first words drifted out into the air on a quiet voice that carried well.

"He's a threat!" D'roan insisted.

"No. He's a far larger threat dead than alive right now."

Now Betrim understood. Brekovich feared turning him into a martyr. The Black Thorn was a face and name the whole Wilds knew. Killing him now might only serve to unite the people further and drive the army outside into a frenzy. Much safer to keep him alive and then kill him once it was all done and over.

D'roan glanced at Betrim. Betrim smiled at D'roan.

Tanith Fanklin stood silent towards the rear of the group, not saying a word. Betrim wondered if the man and his family were guests at Crucible or prisoners. The blooded had little love for each other, and Fanklin seemed a timid, weak man at best.

"You've done us a favour of sorts, Black Thorn," Niles Brekovich said without turning away from the torches and campfires in the distance. "The blooded families have long had an agreement. We squabble over land rights, fight army to army, champion to champion when required, but we are all sworn to protect each other also. For one of us to truly wipe another out would be not only unheard of, but it would likely galvanise the others into action against them."

Betrim couldn't say he knew what galvanise meant, yet he could see where Brekovich was going. Nine blooded families down to three thanks to Rose and the Black Thorn. If they didn't die in this city, the remaining blooded would each have three times as much territory as before.

"Gregor H'ost meant to change that," D'roan said, finally braving stepping out from behind his guards and joining Brekovich at the parapet. "He wanted to raise an army large enough to truly challenge us all."

"He did raise that army," Brekovich countered. "Luckily for us, he never had a chance to use it."

"Your handiwork, I believe," D'roan said with a sneer, his eyes dropping to the stump of Betrim's left arm.

"Had a hand in it, sure," Betrim said.

"By all accounts, Gregor was found pinned to his dining table with his own cutlery." D'roan laughed, a savage, ugly cackling. "Exactly the sort of thing you're famous for."

Betrim thought about arguing, thought about telling them he'd never tortured anyone in his life and that the actual killing of Gregor H'ost was done by an Arbiter of the Inquisition. Seemed a pointless waste of hot air though. He'd been trying to convince folk he was innocent of H'ost's death for years, but folk kept pinning it on him regardless.

"Seems a lot of that army is camped right outside ya gates now," Betrim rasped. "Reckon I didn't do much but delay it comin' ta ya doors."

Niles Brekovich turned his head to stare at Betrim with goggling eyes. "A delay is all I needed." Some men might have smiled at the apparent victory, but not Niles Brekovich. The man's face could have been carved from stone for all the emotion he showed.

"You've also killed all of our competition, Black Thorn," D'roan continued. "Six families gone. The H'osts, Jogarens, Ferins, Turns, Y'landers, and the Kairns. All dead. All their lands up for the taking."

"Aye," Betrim nodded. "I know. We took their lands. Even if ya do kill us all, I don't reckon the good folk will just accept you lot back."

"They'll accept anyone waving a sword over their heads," Niles Brekovich hissed. "The good folk are nothing but meek slaves with the illusion of freedom. We'll see how far the support of the people goes when I show them your head, Black Thorn."

Betrim had had quite enough of kneeling before a couple of blooded pricks. He struggled back to his feet with a grunt, more than a little glad that Torival didn't shove him right back down.

"Everythin' ya've said so far depends on ya gettin' out of here alive an' that ain't happenin'. Don't matter that ya've got me. Kill me or keep me breathin', Rose'll bring down these walls either way. She won't care that ya've got me up here with ya."

D'roan laughed. "You're an idiot, Thorn."

Brekovich nodded towards Torival, and the crazy bastard shoved Betrim up towards the parapet, pointed towards the army camped outside.

"I didn't bring you up here to trade jabs, nor threaten your life, Black Thorn," Brekovich said in a cold voice. "I brought you here to watch your whore die."

Betrim bristled, but no amount of shoving would free him from Torival's grip and he was fairly certain the man would beat him to a pulp for little to no reason at all.

"Ya reckon that cavalry down there will do the job, do ya?" Betrim forced a laugh out of his cracked lips. "We still outnumber ya. We got defences..."

"What you have, Black Thorn, is a traitor in your midst."

Anders

The night was dark, Anders was merrily drunk, and the camp was alive with the sounds of soldiers drinking to the fallen. There was nothing quite like a crushing defeat to get folk in the mood for a bit of a knees up. Of course, the mood was a little less raucous and little more sombre than he'd like, but that didn't mean the booze wasn't flowing.

The good thing about losing roughly half their numbers, Anders had to admit, was that they now had a lot more beer than was strictly needed to support the troops. He was already merrily into his fourth cup of the night and wishing it was more like his eighth. Killing people was thirsty work and, though Anders hadn't taken part with the battle himself, he was more than a little thirsty after watching the slaughter. He was quite worried for the boss' life. By now it was common knowledge that Anders' father had captured the Black Thorn, and Anders always found that being right royally toasted was a good way to stave off niggling worries that an old friend was being chopped into pieces.

It was times like this that Anders missed Ben. Six-Cities Ben had never been one to shy away from a night of heavy drinking whenever there was drinking to be had. He had, in fact, on occasion even matched Anders drink for drink though it never ended well for the poor fellow. There was no sense in dredging up the past though; Ben was well and truly dead and rotting now, hanged from the walls of Reingarde. A sorry end to one of the last big names of the Wilds.

Anders missed Rilly even more when he was honest with himself, though that was as rarely as he could get away with. The little vixen was an excellent drinking partner and more than a little savage in the naked frolicking that often followed, and Anders had quite a weakness for such strong women. Unfortunately, Rilly was also a sailor born and bred, and Rose had sent her away with the fleet to help out Elaina Black and the other pirates. It was a good opportunity for Rilly - command of her own ship and crew - but it was also one more friend Anders might never see again, and his selfish side wished she had never gone.

The problem with drinking with the soldiers was, as Anders had come to understand, that they fostered no real respect for him or his many accomplishments. A halfway decent swordsman, Anders might be, but he had never taken part in a real battle and had no desire to. Most soldiers tended to think him cowardly, which in truth they were right; and unseasoned, to which they were quite wrong.

Anders had stood shoulder to shoulder with the Black Thorn and Henry against a small army of demons, and he had killed at least one of them himself. Unfortunately, that was an accomplishment most of the soldiers didn't tend to believe as the idea of demons possessing people was a little beyond the common folk's understanding. As such they often called him a liar and their company quickly became uncomfortable.

So, Anders moved from campfire to campfire, group to group, making sure never to outstay his welcome. This had the unfortunate side effect of seeing him move along quite often when all he really wanted was to collapse down next to a fire and get so drunk he could no longer remember his own parentage.

Occasionally that traitorous part of Anders' mind that liked to mock him, pointed out that he was actually running away, and that he could never run far enough to lose the guilt that followed. He was, after all, here at the heart of his family home, ready to bring the walls crashing down and see what was left of the family brought to Wilds' justice. And it was all because he had accidentally killed his little sister. Oh, he'd killed Alistair D'roan's son as well, and he was happy enough that little shit was dead, but Anders had never wanted his sister involved in any of it. And if it wasn't for her death, then he might still be a Brekovich. He might be holed up there with the rest of the blooded, staring down at the war camp instead of up at the walls.

Anders sniffed away the sombre thread of his rambling mind and considered the possibility of finding his bearings and heading towards the boss' tent, but with the Black Thorn gone Anders expected the welcome he would receive from Rose would be stony with a possibility of ice and daggers.

It dawned on Anders that he really didn't know very many people these days. His circle of friends seemed to be rapidly shrinking.

A friendly face caught Anders' eye. Suzku was collapsed down against a log, staring into the flames of a nearby campfire. The Honin was looking more than a little worse for recent wear and also appeared to have a bottle of something in his hand. Anders had known Suzku for quite some time now, and the man had never once touched a drop of alcohol, preferring to abstain even while Anders was drinking to excess.

"Pern, you old dog," Anders slurred as he stumbled over to the campfire, barely missing careening into a nearby tent. "Why, if only you'd discovered the wonders of alcohol a little sooner. I could have shown you such a time at Fortune's Rest."

Suzku grunted and held out the bottle. Anders rushed forward to intercept it before one of the nearby soldiers could whisk it away. He had no idea what was in the bottle, but he was more than a little certain it would help in his current, dangerously-near-sober state.

"Tastes awful and makes me feel worse," Suzku said with a grimace as Anders snatched the bottle. "You are looking green."

"What's that?" Anders asked as he flipped the cork from the bottle and took a deep swig of the contents. A burning sensation rushed down his throat, slightly spiced. "Mmmm. Rum. I'm entirely not sure why I'd be looking green. I certainly haven't had nearly enough to drink."

"It is not your complexion," Suzku said, narrowing his eyes and staring at Anders. "It is your aura."

"Oh, that." Anders wasn't sure whether Pern could actually see the things he called auras or whether he was just making the whole thing up. He wasn't even sure if such a thing existed, and if it did, he certainly didn't like the idea of a colourful sign hanging around his neck telling anyone, even a semi-trusted friend, how he was feeling. "What does green mean?"

"It means you are nervous."

"Well we are camped outside my father's city, and he did just give our army a sound killing."

"It can also mean you are hiding something." Suzku looked grim, almost like he was considering beating Anders' secrets out of him.

"Well, there's the usual drunken debasement and debauchery. Why just now I'm coming from a rendezvous with a vicious little soldier who felt the need to prove that she was still alive by riding me so hard she needed a saddle."

Suzku pushed to his feet and took a step toward Anders who looked about for backup and found none. The nearby soldiers decided the fire and the cups in their hands were far more interesting than the blooded drunkard about to get beaten up.

"Oh dear." Anders backed up a step, and Suzku followed. He quickly took another swig of the bottle he was still holding, hoping it wouldn't be his last.

"What are you hiding, Anders?" Suzku growled. Now that Anders looked more closely he could see Pern was looking tired, his eyes dark and sunken and a weary slump about his shoulders. Along with the revelation that the Honin had taken to drinking, it was fairly obvious the man was suffering from something.

"The only thing I'm hiding, my good Honin, is an overwhelming desire to run as far away from Crucible and the man in charge of it as possible. The question I might ask, though, it what you are hiding? I've known you for a few years now, Pern, and though we haven't always been the best of friends, I consider us something of comrades in arms these days. Certainly, at the very least, I would say we share a bond over the love a certain little murderess.

"Now, in all this time of knowing you I have never once seen you drink, never once seen you look quite so exhausted, and never once seen you threaten a man half your size over the supposed colour of his aura.

"So..." Anders took a deep breath and let it out as a sigh. "Why don't you tell me all about it? Over a drink or ten if necessary."

"My clan is dead."

"Well, yes, but wasn't that kind of the point? I mean, you've been killing the Haarin sent to, um, kill you for a couple of years now. You knew they'd keep on coming until there was no one left, no?"

"If I had killed them they would have joined the next generation of Haarin. Their souls accepted into one of the other clans. They were robbed of that. Slaughtered, their bodies turned into monsters. Their souls are adrift, forced to wander the world. You know what happens to those souls."

Anders nodded. He really didn't like to think about it, but he knew better than most that there were places in the world where lost souls gathered, coalesced into monsters formed of raw emotion, usually pain and malice. In the Wilds there was the Fade, an area of dense fog that homed all manner of creatures including wraiths. Out on the open oceans sailed the wraith ship, *Cold Fire*. Many thought it to be a myth, but Anders knew better. It stalked him whenever he boarded a ship, and he had seen it dozens of times. Always hunting those who ought to be dead already.

"I never thought I'd say this, Pern..." Anders took a deep breath and readied himself. "I'm appalled at your behaviour."

Suzku frowned for a moment, then looked down at himself.

"Now a man like myself, often given to self-indulgence and, well, self-pity. I'd expect this sort of behaviour from a man like me. Actually, I'd be more worried if, in your situation, I didn't attempt to wallow and drink myself into a grave. But you... this isn't you. You're stoic." He slapped Suzku in the chest and nodded at the man.

"You're a rock. You turned Honin and didn't even flinch. You joined up with us and... Well, I think you'll agree we've both seen and done some things that are likely better left forgotten. This certainly isn't our first brush with necromancers, is it? Remember the Drurr, back in Fortune's Rest?

"You know, I think I'm rambling a little. I may have, um, lost the point somewhat. Please say something. Stop me from making an even bigger fool of myself."

Suzku let out a chuckle. Anders had long ago discovered it took a lot to make the man laugh. "You are right. This isn't me." Pern nodded and took a deep breath, finally raising his eyes to look right at Anders. "Have you seen Henry?

"No. Why?"

"She was down at the main gate with Thorn," Suzku said. "I haven't been to look for her since the battle ended. I was..."

"Scared?" Anders asked. He grinned and slapped Suzku on the arm. "Believe me, my good fellow; it will take more than certain death to rid us of Henry the Red. We'll go find her together, hmm?"

As they turned to head off in search of the little murderess, Anders saw something out of the corner of his eye, a face he recognised. He stopped and stared off towards a man walking purposefully towards a campfire populated by a number of the mercenaries Anders had brought with him from Solantis.

"Anders?" Suzku asked.

"Have you ever had a feeling that you know a man, but you just can't quite place the face?" Anders asked. He was still staring, still trying to rack his drunken mind for the answer.

The man stopped by the campfire and squatted on his haunches. He didn't sit, didn't look like he was staying long. Neither did he have a drink in hand. Now Anders looked more closely none of the mercenaries did. There were a few things Anders thought were madness and not accepting free booze when it was offered was one of them.

"Tell me, Pern," Anders started. "What colour are those men?" He pointed and glanced at Suzku as the Honin squinted.

"Green."

"Nervous, are they? Hiding something perhaps?"

Suzku nodded. "It would appear so. Who are they?"

Anders shrugged. "Mercenaries from Solantis, or well, from the Southern Wilds via Solantis. But the man..."

They were all still dressed in their armour, and all had weapons nearby. It was not uncommon in an army camp, but something about the entire situation seemed off to Anders, and he'd made a habit of surviving things he shouldn't by listening to his instincts.

Anders sighed and turned away. "It's probably nothing. I..." He stopped. "Cousin Nevin. Of course. Oh, fuck!"

"What?" Suzku asked. He still looked tired, and more than a little confused, but the Honin also looked ready for action.

"I, um..." Anders let out a guilty little laugh. "I may have killed us all this time, Pern."

"What are you talking about, Anders?"

"I, um, might have, uh, brought a hostile force into the camp. Um, perhaps you should go and find Rose, hmm? I'm sure you remember how to Haarin. Best bodyguards in the world, yes?"

"I should kill them before they do any damage."

"Well, maybe, but I'd wager that's one group of many. You go protect Rose. I'll, um, find the general and hope it's, uh, not too late."

Anders felt a hand grab hold of his shoulder and turned to find Suzku staring down at him looking very intense. The big Honin pointed a finger.

"The general frequents a camp follower by the name of Honey. That way."

Anders didn't say another word. He knew where the camp followers kept their tents, and he knew of the very lady Suzku was speaking of - she was one of the few whores that followed the camp of whom Anders could well believe was clean.

It was true they could have rallied a few soldiers, killed the mercenaries around the campfire, and taken cousin Nevin into custody, but Anders knew it was likely one of many such groups, and he deemed it a far more important task to inform the general before the insurrection took place. Anders didn't have the firmest grasp of military tactics, but it seemed a sound premise to attempt to get the drop on their band of traitors before the band of traitors got the drop on them.

He started off at a brisk walk, not wanting to alarm any of the brigands who might be looking his way– before long that brisk walk turned into a headlong run complete with shouting at folk to move out of his way and at least one drunken stumble over a tent peg driven into the ground. Anders was fairly certain he broke a toe on the offensive shard of wood, it certainly hurt enough to be broken, but he picked himself up and continued his mad dash without so much as single second of self-indulgent whining. He was actually quite proud of himself for that.

The night was dark, but Anders knew the way well enough, and before long he burst through Honey's flap and into her tent, panting and red-faced and wishing he had time to appreciate the view of the woman as she crouched on all fours as a large man thrust away behind her.

"Anders?" the whore asked, turning her head and looking more than a little irritated at the intrusion.

"Honey," Anders said with a forced grin. He doubted it was her real name, but then Honey the whore sounded a lot more appealing than

Gertrude the whore, and the woman needed an appealing name to go along with her appealing body and appealing line of work.

"I'm busy!" Honey snapped as though Anders couldn't tell. The big man behind her didn't stop thrusting, but he did send an annoyed glance Anders' way.

"You're not General Verit," Anders said, pointing at the man. "Fuck! Any chance you've seen the general, Honey?"

She was still frowning, though whether at Anders' intrusion or the man still thrusting away inside of her, he couldn't tell. "Last customer. Couldn't have been more than a few minutes ago. This one's quick."

As if on cue the man behind her groaned, tensed, and then slumped away, collapsing onto the little cot. Honey rolled away from him and stood, crossing the distance between them. Anders tried desperately not to stare at the woman's breasts or the seed crawling down her leg.

"Any idea where he might have gone?" Anders asked. Honey had an exceptionally round pair of breasts that just begged to be squeezed.

"You stare any longer and I'll charge you, Anders," Honey said, and when he looked up, he found a hard stare on her face. "Think he said he was off to see the queen."

"Right. Thank you. I, uh, have to go." Anders lingered for moment.

"Well go on then. Fuck off."

Anders almost ran right past the general. The big Five Kingdomer was on the way to see Rose, but he'd stopped to share a cup with some of his soldiers. They were crouched around a campfire and one of them, a man with a worryingly thin nose, was plucking away at an instrument and singing *The Ballad of Ches and Elize*.

"General... Verit..." Anders managed between panting breaths.

"Anders," the general said in a tone that left no one nearby under any confusion that he was not best pleased to see the drunkard.

"Right. Fuck the usual hostility, my good man," Anders got control of his breathing and ploughed on before he could be ignored. "We have traitors in the camp."

"What?" General Verit was on his feet in a moment, and the group of soldiers weren't far behind. It dawned on Anders then that if the men nearby were some of the traitors, both he and the general wouldn't likely make it to the end of the conversation.

"Um, well, it appears some of the mercenaries I brought from Solantis may well be working for my father. And, uh, one of my cousins is also here, I guess. Nevin, I think. I seem to remember he's quite the expert when it comes to punching things."

"You brought enemies into the camp?" the general asked. He was looking furious, and Anders really hoped that anger would be vented elsewhere.

"Yes," Anders said slowly after a pause. "But not intentionally."

"Brown," the general growled, and a man in half plate stepped out of nearby tent. With the speed at which the man appeared, Anders could only assume he had been lurking nearby for just such a summons. "Sound the alarm. Have a messenger sent to each unit. The mercenaries from Solantis are to be contained."

"Um," Anders said, raising a hand to interject. "Is it wise to sound the alarm? Wouldn't that, you know, tip them off?"

General Verit rounded on Anders, and the look in his eyes made him back a step. "We have enemies in our camp. They could be working their way through it right now, killing the sleeping and wounded. We need to protect Rose."

"Ah, I've already thought of that. I sent Suzku, a more dedicated bodyg..."

"Good. We need to set up lines watching the city."

"What's that now?"

The general sighed. "This isn't just some mischief the enemy is causing. They mean to attack."

Suzku

Pug and another soldier were standing by the flap to Rose's tent. Pug waved with his left hand, the right nestled in a sling. The squire was still very much a boy, young and innocent just as Pern had been the first time he had left his clan. Swift had quickly scoured him of that innocence. He had made Pern a party to murder, torture, and things even worse. One more reason the man should walk the afterlife alone.

"Do not let anyone inside unless you know them by name," Pern said firmly as he strode past Pug. He pulled the tent flap open without waiting for a reply.

It took only a moment for Pern to assess the situation. Rose was asleep on a sofa near the far edge of the tent. Lucille was gnawing on a strip of dried beef, eyes wide as though she had been caught in some suspect act. Henry was curled up into a ball between the cot and a cabinet. Her face was stained brown with dried blood, and her eyes were closed, but her aura was a swirling mass of changing colours. It was clear, even at only a glance, that Henry was suffering some sort of turmoil. Despite that, Pern found he was simply glad she was alive.

"They're sleeping," Lucille announced in a hushed voice.

Pern nodded and coughed loudly. Henry stirred but did not open her eyes. Pern thought that was strange considering she was usually such a light sleeper after spending so many years on the great plains where death was only a whisper away. Rose cracked open an eye and then frowned. She groaned as she shifted herself into a sitting position.

Usually, Pern would have waited for permission to speak, but he did not feel there was time for such formalities. "We have enemies in the camp. Possibly a great deal of them. Anders sent me here to protect you." Pern finished with a bow of his head.

Rose was an intimidating woman. It wasn't that he really thought of Rose as a queen, though she was close enough as the difference didn't matter. It was that Pern had never truly been able to decipher the woman. She kept such a close rein on her emotions that her aura was often small and almost translucent. Pern simply didn't know how to deal with a person so tightly controlled.

Henry looked up at the sound of Pern's voice, opening her eyes and blinking rapidly. She wriggled and slowly pulled herself to her feet, favouring her right leg quite heavily.

"Are you alright?" Pern asked.

Henry just stared at him a moment before both shaking and nodding her head at the same time. He was about to enquire further when Rose found her voice.

"Who, Pern? Who is attacking us?"

"They aren't attacking yet, my lady. But it appears the mercenaries Anders brought from Solantis may be working for our enemies."

"Idiot," Rose said with a shake of her head.

The tent flap stirred and Pern's sword was in his hand before Pug's face appeared. The boy looked more than a little shocked and just as scared.

"Uh, something's going on out here. Sounds like fighting." His eyes were fixed on the blade in Pern's hand, but now there was no immediate threat he sheathed it once more.

Pern was the first out of the tent, into the crisp night air. There was smoke on the breeze, not the normal wood smoke smell from campfires, but something different, sharper.

"They're setting fire to tents," Rose announced as she stepped in front of Pern. "Why wouldn't they just come for me directly?"

"Perhaps that isn't the point, my lady," said Pug. The boy awkwardly drew his sword into his left hand, but the tip kept dipping, and it looked far from steady. The young squire was not used to fighting with his off hand and would be almost useless in any sort of battle.

"Back inside," Pern said, stepping in front of Rose and trying to guide her backwards with an outstretched hand. The woman did not move an inch. "I can protect you better in there, and you'll be safer out of sight."

"Protect me?" Rose snorted. "I don't remember hiring a Haarin."

"I am Honin."

"And I don't cower from my enemies." There was orange in Rose's aura now, a flaring brilliance, then it was gone. "But I will protect my child. Suzku, you are one of the best warriors we have. I don't need you to protect me. I need you to go out there and kill my enemies."

"I am..."

"If you say *I am Honin* once more I will gut you myself." Rose sighed. "I will go back inside the tent. I have Henry and Pug and," she glanced at the other soldier standing to attention nearby, "this fine fellow to protect me. And just because I barely fit inside the tent does not mean I can't throw a knife. I will be fine, Suzku. So, go out there and kill these fuckers."

Pern hesitated. If Rose were to die here then the entire siege would be for nothing, the last two years of fighting the blooded would be for nothing. But there was no denying that Rose was more than capable of looking after herself and Pern had rarely seen a more dangerous person than Henry. Eventually, he shook his head.

"I..." Pern turned to shepherd Rose back into the tent and stopped when something sharp tapped against his thigh. He looked down to see a paper-thin knife in Rose's hand. She didn't look at it; she kept her eyes locked on his the entire time.

"Go," Rose said slowly and clearly.

Pern took another breath and then stepped backwards. Rose's aura was almost translucent with a hint of blue in it.

The smell of burning was stronger now, and Pern could hear clashes of metal as fighting broke out. The enemy were hidden in groups, strung out between the other soldiers. Every one of those groups they could eliminate was one less that could sow the seeds of chaos.

"Do not let her leave the tent unless it is on fire," Pern said to Pug before he turned away.

Rose snorted as she turned back towards the tent. "If I want to leave, the gods themselves won't stop me."

It was impossible to tell where the sounds of fighting were coming from. One moment Pern would hear the metal song of clashing blades in front of him, and the next it would drift over the night from somewhere behind.

Soldiers were everywhere, some in states of disarray, milling about with no orders and no idea of where to go or what to do, while others grouped together and charged off in seemingly random directions. It probably didn't help that so many of the troops were either drunk or still half asleep.

Pern spotted two soldiers, arguing with a third. The accosted man was one of the black skins from the southern Wilds, and he was shaking his head and pointing towards Crucible. Pern recognised none of the men, but the black skin had the mark of a sergeant stamped upon his breast.

As he drew closer Pern could hear the sergeant appeared to be ordering the two men to the front lines, while they were adamant most of the fighting was going on towards the rear of the camp. Pern was no leader, and he held no rank in Rose's army or any other, but he also knew that discipline was important and now more than ever.

"... can't you hear it, sir?" said one of the men. "The fighting is that way! You need to start ordering the rest of the fuckers over there." He pointed a chubby finger towards the rear of the camp, away from Crucible.

The sergeant shook his head. "Follow your orders, soldier. We need to defend the front lines from possible attack."

"We're already being attacked, you dumb night skin. Back there!" The soldier, a man with a fat head that barely fit inside his helmet, pointed again. "Those bastards snuggled up tight in the city ain't coming for us."

The soldiers were right now that Pern thought about it, most of the noise did appear to be coming from the rear of the camp, and that was the way most of the soldiers were flowing. Armoured shapes clunked past in the dim light, all headed away from the city.

All three men glanced at Pern as he approached. Pern looked down, and he saw blood on one of the soldier's swords, fresh and still dripping. There were no bodies nearby, but one of the tents was on fire.

Pern looked up and met the chubby soldier's eyes and drew his own sword just in time to stop the oncoming thrust. He turned the strike aside and stepped closed, bringing his own blade fully out of its scabbard and slicing the man's arm in one fluid motion.

"He's one of them," the chubby soldier shouted as he fell away, clutching at his bleeding arm.

The sergeant looked confused. The second soldier, a bald man with a twitching eye, leapt at Pern with a dagger.

Pern grabbed hold of the arm with the dagger and twisted the attack away, wrenching the man to a stop as he drew close. Then he reversed his grip on the sword and thrust the butt into the soldier's face hard. The bald man dropped to the ground unconscious.

The sergeant had his sword drawn now, but he looked confused. The chubby soldier rolled onto his front and attempted to scrabble back to his feet. Pern closed the distance between them quickly and thrust the tip of his sword into the soldier's left calf. The man collapsed back to the ground, squealing.

"Stop!" ordered the sergeant in an unsteady voice. "What is..."

Pern ignored the sergeant and instead kicked the chubby soldier onto his back. "You arrived at this camp with Anders Brekovich."

The chubby soldier shook his head. Pern pressed his sword gently into the man's belly, eliciting another scream.

"You arrived at this camp with Anders Brekovich."

The soldier nodded furiously.

"What is your task?"

"Burn tents, kill people where we can; send everyone to the back of the camp."

"What's at the back of the camp?" asked the sergeant.

The chubby soldier was either crying or sweating so hard it looked no different. "It's where most of the men are. Trying to draw attention."

"You were right to send men towards Crucible," Pern said with a nod towards the sergeant.

"What should we do with them?" the sergeant asked.

There was a time, not too long ago, that Pern had seen a man tortured. He had stood by and watched as the man was brutalised and disfigured to get information out of him. Back then he had decided it was something he never wanted to see again, but now here he was and what he had done to the chubby soldier was not so very different. Thorn liked to say that the game changed people, got inside them and once you were a part of the great game, it was a part of you. There was no going back. Pern wasn't even certain the game existed, not really. It was thinly veiled excuse for outlaws to visit violence upon people, commit crimes and blame others for the consequences.

With a casual flick of his sword, Pern laid open the chubby soldier's throat and let him bleed to death on the ground, alone amidst the dust.

"I leave that one to you." The words tasted bitter and heavy in Pern's mouth.

He thought he should feel guilt for the murder of an injured, unarmed man. He didn't. He thought maybe he should feel sadness for the piece of him lost forever, or for the piece of him that was now always a part of the game. He didn't. Pern was no longer sure what he felt and was even less sure that it mattered.

"Where are you going?" the sergeant asked.

Pern pointed with his sword. "The front lines. You should send as many people there as you can. I believe we'll need them."

Anders

"Oh bollocks!" Anders cursed, narrowly avoiding being run through by a spear.

He was deep in the thick of it now with people dying all around him and at least one of them by his own hands. Just yesterday he had cunningly managed to avoid the battle completely by being nowhere near it and so drunk he'd have been a liability; as likely to stab his own troops as anyone else. But now Anders was feeling dangerously sober and dangerously near the front lines.

He felt more than a little useless with his bastard sword when half the enemy, those who had managed to group together before being slaughtered, were stabbing long spears at them. It was just about all Anders could manage to keep the attention of the spearmen without getting a few new holes in him. Of course, General Verit was far from useless and far from Anders. He could just about see the big Five Kingdomer waging into the battle once again with his big mace-weapon-thing swinging all about him. Anders would have stopped to gawk, but it would have likely meant his untimely demise.

A large man with hair almost as red as the nearby fires rushed past the small forest of spears and straight towards Anders. Knowing full well he was unlikely to win in a fair fight, Anders began giving ground as the large redhead levelled blow after blow at him with a sword that looked almost comically small in his ape-like hands.

Anders backed away again and glanced around for something that might constitute help. He decided then he was unlikely to receive any. They might outnumber their traitorous attackers ten to one on the whole, but here on the camp's front lines they were evenly matched at best, if not a little outnumbered. The nearby tents were burning, the nearby soldiers were fighting, or dying depending on how the fighting was going for them, and Anders could just about see some of the traitorous curs doing something beyond the line of stakes between the camp and the city.

The redheaded sword-wielding warrior tripped on a body and

stumbled a step. Anders decided he was unlikely to ever get a better chance and leapt forward with his sword out in front of him. The problem, he knew all too well, was that bastard swords weren't really his thing. They were too heavy and ungainly for Anders' liking, he much preferred a good rapier. Or better yet, someone who actually knew how to fight to do the killing for him.

With his feet in completely the wrong place, the redheaded bastard was just about able to get his sword up in time and knocked Anders' attack wide. Unfortunately, his momentum wouldn't allow him to follow the sword and Anders crashed into the man, sending them both sprawling on the dusty, bloody ground.

With a snarling red moustache just inches away from his own face, Anders grimaced and struggled to turn his sword around to stab at the man. Bastard swords were not really made for such close combat, and before long Anders found himself rolled over onto his back with the redheaded man straddling him.

The first punch knocked some sense into Anders and the second very nearly knocked all of it right back out of him. With a growl and the taste of blood on his lips, Anders managed to bring his legs up and kicked the man simultaneously in the stones and in the gut. He fell away with a shout of pain and Anders turned, scrambled to his feet and reached for the nearest weapon he could find, a small hatchet buried in a log of forgotten firewood.

He turned and leapt at the redheaded soldier even as the man regained his feet and leapt right back. They met with a clash of heads that dazed Anders and then both were on the ground again.

Anders struggled in the dirt, finally getting his feet underneath him and staggered back to standing to find the redheaded soldier lying lifeless with the hatchet buried in his sternum.

"Hah!" Anders shouted. "Got ya, you fucker. Thought you could kill me, huh? Well, fuck you!" Anders spat on the corpse for good measure then decided it was probably time to get a hold of himself as there was still very much a battle going on around him.

In a brief moment of insanity, Anders considered throwing himself back into the fray and getting himself killed. He decided he was better served by jogging off to the back of the fighting and seeing why a couple of soldiers were dragging the general out of the battle.

"We need more men," the general growled. He collapsed onto one knee and grimaced as one of the soldiers peeled away the leather around his gut and sucked a breath through his teeth.

"We need to get you to a medic, sir."

"Ain't got time for that. We need to break through."

The fighting was still quite fierce, and Anders was still quite adamant that he didn't want to rejoin it.

"What are they doing?"

"Destroying our defences," the general winced and got back to his feet, waving the soldier away and using his big mace for a crutch.

Anders sighed. "Yes, but why? And does anyone else hear thunder?"

General Verit and the nearby soldiers stopped and listened. The general somehow managed to pale even in the dark of the night. "Cavalry. CAVALRY!"

Now the general mentioned it, Anders could see that the traitorous soldiers had cleared away a section of the stakes around the perimeter and were now falling back beyond the stakes they had left in place. The thunder was getting louder by the moment, and Anders watched as the first wave of horses crashed through the lines of soldiers chasing after the traitors.

They didn't all make it. The soldiers hadn't managed to clear away all the stakes, and there was still the little ditch to contend with. A large number of horses went down, screaming and bleeding and crushing their riders. Some impaled themselves on the stakes; others pushed past them picking up gashes or broken legs. Unfortunately, those who didn't make it were largely outnumbered by those that did, and Anders saw the Crucible calvary charge through the gap and smash into the soldiers on the other side.

Some bodies went flying, others were knocked to the ground and trampled. The cavalry didn't stop, just pushed on through, widening the gap to allow others to charge in behind them. It took only moments for the entire first line of defence to crumble, most dying to the charge, others turning and fleeing.

"What do we do?" cried the soldier General Verit was using as a crutch.

They were far enough away from the line of cleared stakes, so the first charge didn't hit them, but the Crucible cavalry were already turning their way. Three men on horseback, each with a cavalry sword perfect for cutting through unmounted troops, turned and spurred the horses into a gallop.

The general pushed away from his crutch and stepped into the path of one horse. Anders found another of the beasts coming straight for him and also found himself quite rooted to the spot. He was fair hand at riding a horse, but never had he been charged by one and never had he fought a man on horseback. The unfortunate truth of it was he had no idea how to overcome the challenge, and he was far too sober to die.

The first horse to reach them was the one trying to ride down General Verit. The big man calmly stepped to the side as the beast and rider came near, flowing away from the sword stroke in a manner that belied both his injury and his size. He swung his big mace as he stepped, and it cracked against the horse's back leg, snapping the ankle in two, and the poor beast took one more step before crashing to the ground with a terrified scream.

There was something about a panicked horse scream, a noise that could shatter even the calmest of minds. It was, at least to Anders' ears, even worse than a baby's wail. The only noise he had ever heard that came close to being as mind-crackingly offensive was that of a frog being tormented by a cat. He honestly couldn't see how such a loud, jarring noise could come out of something so small and green and warty. It was an odd thought to go careening through his mind as death rode towards him.

Anders was well and truly out of time and still had no idea of how to fight a man on horseback. At the last moment, he flung his sword forwards and dove to the ground, curling into a ball and covering his head with his hands.

From his protective ball and the sight of nothing but dust and packed earth below him, Anders could feel the vibrations of the charging horses. He heard another scream, definitely a horse, and then it was cut suddenly short. A man started screaming somewhere close by.

Anders unwound from his ball and looked up. The battle was still taking place all around him. Tents were on fire, men on foot were fighting against mounted foes, and bodies littered the ground - turning into little more than bloody lumps into the dim light of the night. He craned his head the other way and saw the horse that had been charging towards him collapsed on the ground, it's neck at a very awkward angle, and a bastard sword lodged in its eye. The soldier was trapped underneath, struggling to free his leg to no avail.

"Up," ordered the general, stooping down to grab Anders under his arm and hauling him to his feet.

Anders considered letting his legs collapse and sitting right back down, but he wagered the general would be happy to leave him there, and more cavalry were pouring through the gap in the camp's defences.

"Get your sword," General Verit growled as he moved around the downed horse and casually brought his mace down on the trapped soldier's face.

Anders tried not to look at the bloody, bony mess as he skirted the horse and pulled his blade from its eye with a sickening squelch. He considered himself to have a fairly high constitution, but he could also taste bile rising in his throat.

The traitorous soldiers were starting to re-emerge from behind the stakes now, emboldened by the overwhelming reinforcements they had just received. They came towards Anders and his little group, twenty men and women all armed and screaming for blood. The first wave went down hard as arrows sprouted from their chests and heads. Anders just stared for a few moments as the bodies hit the floor.

"Fall back!" the general roared and dragged Anders by the collar away from the front lines.

Cavalry were charging into the camp now, units of them chasing down fleeing soldiers and cutting down those who thought to stand in their way. Even more horses were still arriving, bolstering the ranks even as they charged off to kill anyone not dressed in Crucible blacks.

"Fall back!" General Verit roared again. Just how he was so mobile, all while dragging Anders along and bleeding from a fairly nasty gut wound was quite beyond Anders, but he wasn't about to argue with the man saving his life at least once a minute.

More foot soldiers were pouring from in between the stakes now, and another wave went down to the archers who had taken up position behind their general.

"No. Not the foot troops. Aim for the horses!" General Verit shouted. "The cavalry!" He grunted and doubled over.

"Are you alright?" Anders asked. A stupid question really, but it was the only one he could think of.

The general shoved Anders away and struggled back to his feet. "We need to fall back, find reinforcements. Form up." The big man's eyes were darting about the battle playing out in front of them.

The archers turned their attention to the horses, raining in shaft after shaft. Anders couldn't even tell if they were picking targets or just loosing into the throng. More foot soldiers were coming now as well, and a group of the general's troops broke off to meet them. Despite his better judgement, Anders joined them, swinging his sword in a figure eight around him as though he knew how to use it.

Susku

Four bodies lay at Pern's feet as the fifth dropped down to join them. Mercenaries from the far south brought up by of way of Solantis. The sixth, a young man with spittle on his lips and fear in his eyes, turned and ran. Pern did not give chase. He stopped only to wipe his blade on the fallen before continuing on towards the front lines.

A riderless horse charged past him, its tail on fire. The beast was panicked and rightly so, likely there would be no calming the poor animal. Pern watched it for a moment and turned back in time to see a man charging at him with sword raised high. He turned the strike and the man aside with an easy parry. His first reply cut through the soldier's left ankle and the second opened up a gash along his back. The man dropped to the ground mewling in pain and Pern continued on. He would not usually leave an enemy alive, but all the man could look forward to now was a quick death and Pern would not grant him it.

Pern stopped by a burning tent and lifted the flap aside with the tip of his sword. A bloody body smouldered within, and the smell of charred flesh assaulted his nose. Pern let the tent flap fall back into place just as a shout warned him of incoming cavalry.

Two men ran along, threading their way between the tents, chased by three mounted soldiers. As Pern watched one of the men leapt aside, crashing into a tent and thrashing amidst the canvas. The second man was cut down as the first of the horses reached him, not even breaking stride as the rider smashed his sword down on the man's head.

Three horses now came at Pern, one after another. The first man had excellent positioning, and it was all Pern could do to parry his strike as he passed. The second horse came on and Pern side-stepped. He stopped his own sword before striking the horse, not wanting to harm the poor beast. It was innocent of its rider's intent, and its aura was the sky blue of most animals, though yellow fear snaked its way throughout it.

The third horse came on, and Pern stepped into it, flowing out of the way at the final moment and blocking the rider's strike, grabbing hold of his arm and wrenching the soldier from his mount. The horse charged on, free of its burden and desperate to be away from so much fire. The soldier writhed on the ground, his shoulder clearly dislocated. Pern finished the man with a stab to the heart before turning back to the two riders who had passed him. They were gone from sight now, not even stopping to make sure of the kill or to see if their comrade had survived.

"They didn't stop," said the soldier who had dived into the wreckage of a tent. He was struggling to free himself from the canvas and Pern extended a hand, pulling him onto the beaten path next to the trampled body of his comrade.

"They are not meaning to hunt down every one of us, only cause as much carnage as possible before we regroup. We outnumber them, but we are scattered and disorganised. Surprise is on their side, but it will not be for long."

The soldier nodded and scratched at his bleeding nose. It looked broken, but the man didn't complain.

"Where to?" the soldier asked.

Others started drifting towards them, some on their own, others in twos or threes. In only a few moments Pern found himself surrounded by ten soldiers, all wanting to know what they should do. He had never considered himself a leader of men. As a Haarin he had done as he was told. Serve the clan, serve the client. As a Honin he had followed the Black Thorn, trusting to the man's decisions. He had rarely made a single choice for himself, let alone for others.

"To the front," Pern said. "That is where we will find General Verit, and he will need all the support we can give him."

Just those orders, as simple as they were, seemed to bolster the courage of the nearby soldiers. No longer were they lost amidst a battlefield, ambushed and alone and unsure of what to do. Pern had given them purpose and direction.

With his new troops in tow, Pern set off towards the front lines. They checked in tents, and picked up more and more, steadily increasing their numbers. They even found a captain, fighting tooth and nail with four of her troops against two men on horseback. Pern leapt at the first man, dragging him down off his horse, and the second was speared before he realised there were enemies behind him. Afterwards, the captain gave her thanks and command of her troops to Pern. Before long Pern found himself commanding over a hundred soldiers and leading them to the front lines, tackling cavalry and traitorous mercenaries alike on their way.

The closer they got, the more enemies they encountered and the fewer tents were left standing. Bodies littered the ground everywhere - some cut up, and others trampled. The only consolation was that a large number of the bodies were wearing Crucible blacks and there were more than a few horses milling about, unsure of what to do with their riders lost. Some of the soldiers were brave enough to commandeer the horses, but Pern felt safer on the ground, and he hated the idea of putting an innocent creature in danger.

They were fighting for every step now, lines of soldiers holding their ground with shields while others stabbed from behind with spears. Pern walked behind the lines, directing reinforcements as they came, and more were arriving all the time. He wasn't sure how, but he had gone from bodyguard to military officer in the space of a few dead bodies.

When so many people grouped together, it was impossible to pick out individual auras. Pern could only see a mass of orange rising from the group, fear and anger in equal measure.

"Over there, on the left," Pern ordered a group who jogged up from behind. Soldiers were pushing forwards and dying, and the left had just received a cavalry charge. They almost buckled but held strong. It appeared the Crucible cavalry was spread thin now their harrying tactics had failed.

The thunder of hooves alerted Pern a moment before five horses tore past him from behind. He barely managed a shout before the horses crashed through the back of the soldiers' line, crushing bodies and sending the soldiers into chaos. The Crucible riders in front didn't waste their chance, they pushed into the hole and split the line in two, using the horses to bend the walls in on themselves.

"Shit!" Pern swore and charged forwards, crossing the distance in just a few seconds. He leapt at the first rider, pulling the man down from his horse and stamped a heavy boot into his face.

Turning the horse towards the Crucible riders, Pern whispered an apology before stabbing the beast in the backside. The horse reared and kicked and started pushing forwards against the crush of cavalry.

It was chaos in amongst the panic and Pern narrowly avoided being crushed again and again as he stabbed up at the riders. Gone were his practised strokes and disciplined stances. Here, in amidst the insanity and death of a pitched battle, all he could do was stab, block, and hope.

There was screaming in his ears, a man nearby roaring with all he was worth. Bodies pushed against his back and horses pushed in from the front. One of the beasts snapped at him, trying to bite at his face, but was slashed by a sword that came from behind Pern. The horse reared up, blood pouring from its snout, wilds eyes rolling in its head. The poor beast kicked out, but its back legs buckled, and the creature collapsed. Pern and his soldiers surged over it, trampling it to death and the guilt that washed over him almost unmanned him. He pushed it down. Guilt could wait. It had to wait. Guilt is the luxury of the living, and Pern was swamped in it. He deserved it, deserved to feel it, and that meant he had to live.

They pushed back the horses and the men and reformed the line. Pern backed out of the fight, breathing heavily and feeling a dozen new hurts and aches. To his surprise he found they had pushed further forwards and, rather than dwindling, their numbers had grown as more and more soldiers appeared to reinforce them.

Another charge hit the right side of the line, the Crucible troops at the front wheeling their mounts away just before the charge hit, so the defenders had no time to react. The line buckled, bodies flying or crushed into the earth.

"Archers!" Pern pointed at the right-hand side even as the Crucible cavalry who had broken through started to turn their horses around to attack from behind.

They didn't have many soldiers with bows, only a dozen, but they all loosed their arrows at once. Most found horseflesh and the beasts crashed down or turned and ran in a panic. Pern was already sprinting forwards even before the first Crucible soldier struggled to rise.

This was combat he knew. No horses or shield walls, just a string of duels where one shall stand, and one shall fall. Pern didn't relish the killing, but he did relish the fight.

The first of the fallen soldiers struggled to get his sword up in time as he rose from his dead horse. Pern brushed aside the sword and stepped close, using his weight to push his blade through the man's chest and out the other side. It was not a strike Pern would normally use, he preferred slashing strikes as it was far too easy to get a sword lodged inside a body, but sometimes the dangerous attacks were also the most advisable.

Pern pulled his sword out as the soldier's body fell away. It slid free coated red and shining in the light of the nearby fires. Pern wasted no time moving onto the next soldier, not even waiting to see if he had any backup.

The next soldier was up and armed and made an attack as Pern drew near. He sidestepped the wild swipe and brought his own sword up in a deadly arc, severing the man's arm at the elbow. The lifeless limb dropped to the ground, and for a moment the soldier just stared at it, uncomprehending. Pern did not give him the chance to voice the scream that was obviously building up inside; he slashed again, this time opening up half the man's neck with a precision strike.

A horse cantered out of nowhere, a terrified look in its eyes. Pern watched it go, realising his mistake only at the last. A soldier pulled herself up from the other side of the horse, leaping over the saddle and crashing into Pern. They both went down heavy; Pern felt his right elbow hit something hard and felt the numbing tingle spread throughout his arm.

They wrestled on the ground, rolling over and over each other, fighting for control. Pern caught a couple of punches to the face and tasted blood, but he gave almost as good as he got, desperately struggling to mount an offensive with his numb arm as he defended with his left.

Suddenly he found his right arm pinned underneath the woman's knee as she straddled him. Her face was muddy and young, too young for the hatred Pern saw there. Her aura blazed red, and she snarled at Pern, knocking away his left hand and punching him again in the face. The world went bright for a moment, clearing just in time for Pern to see something small and metallic plunging down towards his chest.

It was instinct that got his left arm back up in time. Pure instinct that allowed him to ignore the pain of the knife biting into his forearm. The woman wrenched the knife free and tried again. This time Pern grabbed her hand, and they wrestled there some more, a sharp edge of death between them, already glistening with Pern's blood.

The woman pressed down on the knife, trying to use her weight to overcome him. Pern soon realised he would lose the struggle. The woman was stronger than she looked and the pain lancing through his left arm was like fire. Luckily the woman lifted off his right hand as she bore down on him. Pern twisted the knife in her grip, reached up with his right hand and grabbed her around the collar, pulling her down on top of him.

They lay for a while, Pern panting and wincing at the pain while the woman gurgled and moaned out her last breath. Eventually, he felt his chest grow hot and wet and shoved the woman's corpse off, sitting up and cradling his left arm against his chest.

Pern would have liked to sit there for a while longer, but he didn't have the luxury of wasting time. He was feeling nauseous and dizzy from the pain in his arm, and there was still a battle going on around him, even if it had left him behind.

He cut a strip of cloth from the dead woman's tunic and held it in his teeth as he wrapped it tight around the wound in his arm, tying it off and gritting his teeth against the pain.

Someone clapped him on the shoulder and Pern spun about, his sword held ready to strike, but it was only one of his men.

"We thought we'd lost you, sir."

Pern shook his head and drew in a deep breath. "Where are we?" he growled, setting off towards the line of soldiers now three ranks deep. It seemed they had both grown in number and pushed further forwards despite the regular cavalry charges hitting them.

"The line is holding," the soldier said as they walked. "More troops are joining us all the time. The cavalry is struggling. They don't have the space to get a real charge up, and we've got an armoury worth of spears coming to us. There's a lot of fighting off to the north side, can't see who but some folk are saying it's the general with a larger force. We're also getting reports of fighting further back in the camp, lots of these bastards have broken through and are trying to cut off our reinforcements."

Pern glanced back towards the camp. All he could see in the darkness was smoke and shapes moving against the backdrop of burning tents.

"We need to join up with the general," he said with conviction. "Start pushing north and trust those behind us will deal with any who slip by. We can't let them have any space. Trap them between us and the camp's defences."

The soldier nodded, and Pern had to wonder if he had just given out sound orders or whether the man was just happy to have any. He quickly ran off to relay Pern's instructions, and Pern took the opportunity to inspect his left hand.

He could still move all his fingers and was more than a little glad for that, but any movement sent waves of pain through him, and the makeshift bandage was already soaked with blood.

More soldiers were still arriving, and Pern directed them to where the line looked thinnest. Archers dropped back, remaining close by and only loosing arrows when cavalry managed to break through. They were holding the enemy back for now, but they'd stopped making progress, and the general was still out there somewhere.

Anders

"Where to now?"

"What's that?" Anders asked the woman. She was a sergeant apparently, not that it meant a thing to Anders; he could never quite figure out military command structure. Everybody seemed to answer to somebody, and he answered to none of them, and that was about as deep as Anders was willing to investigate.

"Which way, sir?" She might be quite pretty under the helmet and all the armour, Anders considered for a moment, but with it all on she was fairly difficult to distinguish from any other soldier– which he thought might be half the point. "Sir?"

Anders shook his head. His mind had a horrible habit of wandering off when he was sobering up, and he could already feel the distant pulsing of a hangover. He needed to find some booze and quickly. The last thing he wanted was to be in charge of a small unit of twenty soldiers tasked with hunting down any Crucible troops that might be lurking farther in towards the centre of the camp.

"Oh, no." Anders shook his head quite firmly, ignoring the slight ache it caused. "You don't want me in charge, my dear. I'm not much of a leader of men, or, um, women... Or both... Or any. I'm fairly good at leading my way to the nearest tavern, but I'll wager that would be located behind some fairly high and hostile walls. Much better you lead, hmm? Call it your chance to shine in this darkness. So, uh... Where to?"

The sergeant stood there looking shocked. "The general put you in charge."

It seemed an odd conversation to be having amidst the battlefield with tents ablaze, soldiers dying all around, enemies in their midst, and the occasional flaming horse charging by, but if it got Anders out of the responsibility of leading, then it was a conversation he was willing to have.

"True. He did," Anders admitted. "It's fair to say the man had no idea what he was doing at that point. Perhaps it was the blood loss, I've heard it can affect people in some strange ways. Regardless, I can't be in charge of people. Especially not a small band of highly trained soldiers like yourselves.

"Why, just look at you all. A meaner bunch of rapscallions I've never come across. This man here," Anders pointed at a large man with a hair-lip and a cleft nose, "I'll wager he's a titan in combat, a true legend of the Wilds, hmm? What do they call you, lad? What's your name?"

The man looked confused and a little alarmed at being singled out. "Harren."

"Awe inspiring. And you," Anders continued, waving at the sergeant. "You look like a veteran of more action than I've even heard of. Those youthful looks don't fool me for a moment. Who here thinks the sergeant should lead our merry little band?"

There were a few murmurs of endorsement for the woman. Anders nodded along to them all with a smile.

"This isn't a vote," the sergeant snapped. "The general put you in charge." She poked a hard finger into Anders' chest. "So where to, sir?"

With a sigh, Anders pointed in a direction he vaguely considered to be south. It would likely lead farther into the camp, and he was fairly certain there was a cart loaded with ale kegs along the way. Some people liked to keep a clear head in a crisis, but Anders always found he dealt with a crisis a lot better with a rather fuzzy head.

"Stay close," the sergeant ordered. "Our job is to clean up Crucible soldiers. NOT loot the dead." She sent a scathing glare towards another woman who was wearing a very attractive grin.

"What if it doesn't slow me down?" the grin asked.

"I'll slow you down," the sergeant hissed. There was a definite threat in her voice, and the grin soon slipped from the other woman's face.

Anders waited for a moment while the two women stared at each other. "Well this is very tense," he said after a while. "Usually I'd be happy to watch you two kill each other, or whatever it is you soldier types do, but, um..." He pointed again, and the sergeant turned to see a small group of soldiers wearing Crucible blacks trying to sneak up on them.

Despite being outnumbered, the Crucible soldiers broke into a charge the moment they realised they had been spotted. Differences seemed well and truly put aside as both the sergeant and the woman with the grin leapt into battle together. Anders thought it only right he do his own bit and leapt up right beside them, flashing a winning smile at the women every chance he got.

It didn't take long for numbers to become telling and soon the last of the Crucible soldiers turned and ran. The sergeant shouted at her own men to hold, but blood was up, and a rout was an easy chance at a spot of sanctioned murder, so they all soon found themselves giving chase, Anders included.

It was pointless. The Crucible soldiers were either faster or just simply better rested and before long Anders couldn't even see their quarry any more. The sergeant shouted for a halt and Anders was more than a little grateful for it.

"See," he wheezed, doubling over and struggling for breath. "I told you we'd all be better with you in charge, my dear. It's a matter of authority really. I simply don't have any, but you..." He trailed off as spotted the trampled remains of a campfire and just a few paces away a large keg with a tap already knocked in.

"You're still in charge," the sergeant was also quite out of breath. They all were, but Anders didn't really care.

He stumbled a few steps towards the abandoned campfire, placating his aching head with the promise of the sweetest nectar, or at the very least, something vaguely alcoholic. Anders plucked a discarded mug from the dusty ground and placed it under the tap and turned the little handle to the sweet trickle of beer.

"What are you doing?" the sergeant asked.

"Sir." Anders grinned up at the woman as the mug started to fill. "You say I'm in charge and you military lot always refer to those in charge as *sir*, hmm?"

He could see her gritting her teeth even in the dark. "What are you doing, sir?"

"Keeping hydrated." Anders pulled the mug to his lips and drank deep. The ale had a dusty taste to it, though it didn't overpower the sour tang, yet he finished the mug in one and placed it under the tap for a second go. "Very important in these sorts of situations."

A few of the other troops were drifting over towards him now. Didn't take much to convince folk of the need for a good drink, especially after a brisk run in a blood-soaked battlefield.

"No!" the sergeant hissed and started towards Anders. He quickly raised the mug to his lips again and managed a few good gulps before it was slapped out of his hands. The woman grabbed him by his collar and hauled him to his feet. Her face was just a few inches from his and was twisted into an angry frown.

"You were right. The general should never have put you in charge, sir. You are a worthless..." the sergeant stopped mid-rant and gasped. Her hands let go of his collar, and she stumbled a couple of steps, reaching behind her. The woman with the grin was there, grinning again and holding a bloody knife.

"Oh dear," Anders said as the sergeant collapsed to the ground. The woman with the grin stepped over the dying sergeant and picked up the mug. It was empty, so she knelt down near the keg and started filling it.

The sergeant was staring up at him, still struggling to breathe and clinging on to life. It dawned on Anders that this was entirely the sort of thing a man in his position, a man in charge, should know how to deal with. But he didn't. He had absolutely no idea what to do.

The other soldiers didn't seem like the types to argue; they were sheep, followers who would simply do whatever the strongest of them commanded and right now the woman with the grin was clearly the strongest. It was the way of the Wilds.

Anders knelt down by the sergeant. She was shaking somewhat, maybe convulsing or shivering in the cold. Her eyes locked onto his.

"I'm very sorry," Anders said. "I think this may be my fault... In some way. I must admit, I feel a little guilty."

The sergeant's eyelids were starting to droop.

"Hmm," Anders said and bit at his lip. He glanced over at the group of soldiers now led by the woman with the grin. They were helping themselves to the booze and helping themselves to the loot from nearby dead comrades. "I wonder if I can't do something about that wound."

He reached out and rolled the sergeant onto her stomach. She didn't resist. She didn't look like she had any resistance left in her. Anders poked around at the wound a little. He was no surgeon, but he had quite some experience in both dying and the prevention of it. The woman let out a gasp and went still. Too late to save.

It was fair to say the woman with the grin did not expect her comeuppance so soon. One moment she was digging through a fallen soldier's trousers for a few bits and the next moment she had the sergeant's sword buried in her neck. It was fair to say it was a surprise for most of them actually and the other soldiers fell back in line about as quickly as it took for the woman with the grin to hit the floor, no longer grinning.

Anders looked down at the corpse leaking fresh blood into the dirt. Some lives were well beyond saving, and she was one of them.

The sergeant winced as she ripped her sword free from the woman's neck. "We have a job to do," she growled. "To hunt down Crucible soldiers, not loot our own dead."

The other soldiers emitted a round of solid agreement, and the sergeant stalked away. They all followed, Anders quickly volunteering to be the first among them.

"I feel I should probably know your name," Anders said as they walked. There were sounds of fighting up ahead, the odd whinny from a horse, but the sergeant didn't seem in a hurry. There was a new grim set to her mouth that hadn't been there before. It was always the way when people came back like she had.

"Harriet."

"Sergeant Once-Stabbed Harriet," Anders announced. "Has an odd ring to it, don't you think?"

Harriet turned a haunted gaze on him and her mouth opened as if to say something, probably had some questions about the things she'd seen while she was dead, but she shook her head, turned away, and continued walking.

Up ahead they found a group of cavalry finishing off what was left of some of Rose's soldiers. They had one man still alive, and they seemed to be questioning the poor fellow in between rounds of cutting away at him.

"No doubt they want to find Rose," Anders said.

Sergeant Once-Stabbed waved them all down, and they approached at a crouch, trying to keep low and silent for as long as possible. If they could get close enough, they could start pulling the bastards from their horses before they could respond.

"Oh bugger!" Anders hissed, making sure to keep his voice at a whisper.

"What?" asked the sergeant.

"Well," Anders took a deep breath and let it out as a sigh. "See the brutish one with the black horse and overhanging brow? That's my brother, Francis."

Rose

Pacing, Lucille informed Rose for the fourth time, was not good for the baby. Of course, if Lucille got her way about everything, then Rose would be bed bound and drinking nothing but pure spring water collected from the mountains and eating nothing but fruit.

They could hear the fighting outside. The sounds of steel on steel, men crying, and horses screaming all drifted into the tent along with the smell of burning. They received no reports, and that just made everything worse. Trapped in the tent with only a nagging Lucille and a catatonic Henry, Rose had nothing to do but imagine how badly the battle was going outside.

She imagined soldiers would burst through the tent flap any minute to inform her that her army was destroyed. She imagined them dragging her out to be executed right in front of Niles Brekovich and Alistair D'roan. Her imagination was only serving to shatter her calm and drive her into a rage.

"Are those shouts getting louder?" Lucille asked. The woman was sitting on a chair, nervously tapping her foot on the rug.

Rose cocked her head towards the tent flap. She wasn't sure why. Sound travelled just as well through the walls as it did the entrance. Lucille wasn't wrong. Not just the sounds of shouting coming closer, but also the sounds of combat.

"Henry!" Rose hissed as she checked a couple of her hidden pockets for the knives she always kept close by. Lucille hated Rose carrying knives when she was also carrying a child, but she might not be as quick to mention it after those knives saved all their lives.

Henry didn't move. She'd collapsed back down into her spot wedged between the cot and cupboard almost as soon as Suzku had left.

"Henry," Rose said again, ambling closer and shaking the woman's arm. "We might be having company quite soon, and I wouldn't mind some of that old fire of yours to help greet them."

The little murderess looked up at that, meeting Rose's eyes. There was pain there, pain and sadness, and a weariness Rose understood all too well. For the first time since Rose had met Henry, her scarred little face didn't look savage or feral, but instead looked innocent. Innocence was the first thing the Wilds took from people. The land those blooded bastards had created turned everyone into one sort of monster or another.

Rose reached out and slapped Henry. Well aware the sounds were still coming closer, she didn't have time for Henry to wake from her shock naturally.

"Listen to me, you little bitch," Rose said, lowering herself to her knees in front of Henry and taking her hands. "I know what you've seen. You might not think it, but I know all too well the horrors and the pain of this world, and that sometimes all this shit feels like it's just too much. But you don't just get to stop. You're stronger than that, we both are.

"Both of us were born into nothing and shit, and both of us have dragged ourselves out of the Hells ta be what we are today. We ain't innocent, nothing even approaching it. We're soaked in blood and pain, and some of that we didn't even cause. But we're strong enough to shoulder the burdens of others as well as ourselves."

It took a fair bit of effort for Rose to push back to her feet, stand up and pull Henry up with her. The little woman was looking caught between buying into Rose's speech and wanting to slump back down in the corner.

Henry shook her head slowly. "I was born a princess."

It was possibly the last thing she expected Henry to say, and Rose found it fairly hard to hide the shock from her face. "Huh?"

Henry blinked a couple of times, and her face changed. In just a moment the confusion and innocence were gone, replaced by hard lines and a cold light in her eyes. The pain was still there though, nothing physical, but instead a tormented agony that went far deeper than flesh. "Nothin'."

Rose was still holding her hands and gave them a squeeze. "Doesn't really matter what you were. Matters what you are, and you're Henry the Red, strongest little bitch I know."

Henry sniffed and nodded, not meeting Rose's eyes. "There's fightin' goin' on."

Rose nodded. "Coming our way and I'm not exactly feeling graceful enough to fight right now." She rubbed at her belly. The idea of losing her child to murderous soldiers so close to the end was a fear Rose wasn't willing to entertain.

"I've lost my daggers," Henry said, patting her empty belt.

Rose just pointed over towards a small chest. "Take your pick."

Henry walked quietly over to the chest, threw open the lid, and selected a couple of long knives. The fighting was still coming closer, louder, and Pug ducked in through the tent flap, his sword held clumsily in his left hand.

"Visitors, Pug?" Rose asked in a light tone she certainly didn't feel.

The look the young squire turned on her was enough to freeze her blood, but Rose just smiled at him. "Any details might help. Numbers and such?"

"At least half a dozen left, my lady. Spears and swords." Pug backed further into the tent without taking his eyes from the tent flap. He bumped into the table and edged around it. "Get behind me."

"Oh, how heroic of you," Rose purred. "The very definition of chivalry. Well, I'd say between the four of us we count for at least one fighter in our current states. Perhaps we should cut a hole in the back of the tent and run. I can't move particularly fast right now, but our chances are probably better than fighting."

Pug glanced over his shoulder at her for a moment, his face a mask of fear and determination. He nodded quickly. "That's a good idea, my lady."

"Well go on then."

Pug nodded again and skirted around Rose, moving to the rear of the tent. He'd just about shoved his sword into the fabric when a grunt sounded from outside, and the tent flap moved open. Four soldiers wearing Crucible blacks entered slowly. Pug quit his cutting and ran back to Rose's side.

The first of the soldiers, a tall man with veins that stood out on his forehead, grinned as he stepped forward to allow the others in behind him.

"Well, aren't we the lucky ones. We found the queen bitch whore of them all." His voice sounded like rocks falling down a mountain, dangerous and quite final.

Rose backed up a step and glanced sideways. Henry was frozen to the spot. Far from the little berserker Rose had hoped to inspire. The soldier's eyes flicked sideways too, and he pointed at Henry.

"Lever, Tubs deal with that one. Be careful; she's Henry the Red. Don't let her close."

The soldier took another step, tall and menacing, and Pug charged. The boy took a wild swing, and the blow was blocked, a moment later and a hard fist connected with his face and Pug went down hard, bouncing off the table and collapsing in a heap. He didn't get up.

Again, the soldier advanced, sword held ready and caution in every step. Out of the corner of her eye, Rose saw Lever and Tubs advance on Henry, but she decided she needed to concentrate on her own dire situation.

Tears came easily to Rose's eyes, and she let them well up and fall, running down her cheeks and dripping from her chin.

"Please," she begged, backing up another step and feeling the cupboard at her back. "Please don't. Can't you see I'm with child?"

The soldier's eyes flicked down to her belly and then back up again. He sucked at his teeth. "You come quiet and I won't harm you, nor the child. Can't say what Lord Brekovich'll do, but then you did attack his city. We all lost a few friends in that attack yesterday, so I'll be happy to gut you if you fight back, child or no."

Rose wrapped two protective hands against her belly, drew in a ragged breath, and let it out again. She was shaking, crying, and pinned up against a wooden cupboard. The soldier advanced another step, almost close enough to touch, and Rose let out a racking sob.

Rose could hear Henry finally fighting nearby, but she was outnumbered and in shock and would be no help. Lucille was frozen near the bed, not moving. And Pug was still either unconscious or dead with little matter of the difference.

"Enough of that!" the soldier hissed, taking another step and grabbing Rose's right arm.

Her left hand plucked the knife she had hidden near her belly, and she stabbed it into the man's neck. His eyes went wide, and he tensed. Rose pulled hard, ripping the knife out of his neck and taking his throat with it.

Rose stared into the shock on the man's face for a few moments. His hand was still locked around her right arm, but his other was clutching at his neck, trying in vain to stop the blood pumping out of it. It washed over both of them.

She heard a manic shout just as the soldier in front of her dropped to his knees. The soldier behind, a fat man with an ill-fitting tunic was charging forwards with a spear levelled.

On a normal day, Rose would have gracefully flowed away from the attack, but she was currently anything but graceful and just about managed a hasty fall to her knees. The soldier put his full weight into the spear charge, and the steel tip pushed all the way through the dying soldier still clutching at his neck.

Rose felt a stabbing pain and couldn't help but cry out as the spear caught her flailing left hand, pierced through the palm and then stuck in the wood of the cupboard behind, pinning her there.

The soldier in front of her finally died and slumped forward towards her. His left hand was still locked in a death grip around Rose's right, and his body was pinned to the cupboard along with her left hand. She was helpless to move and helpless to fight back and the fat soldier, breathing hard and looking enraged, advanced.

Rose grunted as she tried to shake her right hand free and only managed to make her left hand blaze in agony. She could feel hot blood trickling down on her chest from the dead soldier's open neck, and his head was resting on her shoulder as though they were locked in some loving embrace rather than a death grip.

She growled in frustration, still struggling to free herself. The fat soldier was looking down nervously, clearly not wanting to get too close even though Rose was obviously incapacitated. He looked around for another weapon. As he turned away, Lucille flew out of the darkness from beside the cot, leaping onto the fat soldier's back and holding on tight while she clawed at his face and wrenched his hair.

The soldier cried out, cursing as he stumbled away and into the table. He was flailing at the woman clawing at him and doing very little to dislodge her. Still, Rose wasn't about to rely on her midwife clawing to death a man easily twice her weight. She struggled again against the death grip of the soldier clasping her right hand, gritting her teeth against the pain in her left.

Rose screamed as she finally tore her hand free of the soldier and, with her left arm still pinned to the cupboard, reached for her last knife and launched it at the fat soldier as he finally dragged Lucille off his back and hurled her across the table. The knife hit him in the groin, and he cried out in pain, but it didn't go deep, and he pulled it free and charged towards Rose, reaching out with fat fingers to close around her neck.

With one last burst of energy, Rose reached down and grabbed the dead soldier's sword, raising it just in time for the fat soldier to impale himself. He cried out, and his hands found her neck, closing around them and squeezing even as Rose twisted the sword in his guts.

She felt the fat soldier die, felt the life fade from him as his grasp around her neck settled into an iron grip. With her left hand still pinned to the cupboard, her right hand slick with blood, and two soldiers' weight bearing down on her, Rose reached up and clawed at the fat soldier's hands, pulling them apart finger by finger until she could suck down a lungful of air.

Rose found herself crying, and this time the tears were real. She was caught between sobbing and laughing and wasn't certain if it was out of pain, fear, or relief.

Over the sounds of her own sobbing, Rose could still hear fighting and close by. She couldn't see over the two dead soldiers bearing down on her, but she could hear Henry growling and the clash of metal.

"My lady?" Lucille's voice, urgent and tinged with pain. No doubt that was the first time she had ever been thrown bodily across a room before. "My lady Rose?"

"I'm alive," Rose managed in a voice that sounded husky with tears.

"And the child?" Lucille's face appeared over the body of the fat soldier and began tugging on his arm ineffectually.

"Kicking like she wanted to take part in the fight." Rose pushed with her right hand as Lucille tugged, but the fat soldier was too heavy for them. It always amazed Rose just how much a body seemed to weigh. To make matters worse her left hand felt as though it were on fire.

"Lucille, the fight. Help Henry," Rose growled. There was no way the two women were digging her free alone.

Lucille's face disappeared from view. "I don't think she needs me."

Now Rose listened and thought about it, she couldn't hear the sounds of battle any more, just the sound of heavy breathing, Henry panting from somewhere nearby.

"Grab there an' pull when I pull." It was Henry's voice, but Rose couldn't see her face. "If ya can push from under there, I reckon it might help."

With a great deal of grunting, ragging, and pain, the three women managed to shift the corpse off Rose. Henry eventually pushed the fat body aside and looked down at her. The little murderess' face was still coated in dried blood, making her scars stand out even more. She looked a frightful thing now there was fire in her eyes again. Rose doubted she had truly dealt with whatever turmoil it was she was struggling with, but at least she had woken from her catatonia, and none too soon.

"Fuck me. That shit weighed more than a horse." Henry spat on the fat soldier's body. "Ya pinned ta this one or somethin'?"

Rose managed to nod. She was feeling a little faint from either the pain or the blood loss or maybe the exertion of having to fight two soldiers in her condition.

"And the cupboard. You'll need to pull the spear free."

"Alright," Henry growled as she grabbed hold of the spear shaft.

The anticipation gnawed at Rose. She could see Henry clearly now, see her getting ready to pull the spear free. Rose almost decided to close her eyes, but she wouldn't show that weakness. She gave Henry a nod and gritted her teeth.

Henry pulled hard, twisted the spear a little as she did, and Rose couldn't help the scream that tore from her throat as the pain in her hand blazed hot and turned to agony. Then it was free, and her hand fell to her side. A moment later the dead soldier finished his collapse, and again Rose found herself trapped underneath a corpse.

Rose was crying again. The pain and the helplessness and the weight of the soldier coupled with the weight of everything she was trying to achieve. It was not the first time she had felt crushed by it all, but usually, only Betrim was around to see it. Now she was watched by both her midwife and a woman who had all but admitted to hating her.

The body of the second soldier was pulled aside, and Lucille was there, kneeling by Rose's side and gently helping her sit up. Henry stood nearby, glancing her way, but then turning towards the tent flap.

"That it, ya reckon?" Henry asked. "Don't hear anythin' else too close."

Rose struggled to her knees and wiped at her face. Both hands were bloody, the red both hers and not hers. "I believe this is far from over," she managed to say, though even talking felt like too much effort. "Pug?"

"Breathin'," Henry said with a sniff. "Usually a good sign."

With help from Lucille, Rose managed to get back to her feet. She plucked one of her fallen daggers from the floor along the way and ambled over to stand next to Henry. The little murderess glanced at her and nodded, and they both turned back to the tent flap.

Anders

They had a plan. Rather a good plan actually. Of course, if anyone involved in the plan didn't perform their job to perfection, or if the plan simply failed, then Anders was unlikely to survive the result. In truth, he was starting to wish he had never suggested the plan.

With something approaching unparalleled courage, Anders leapt up from his hiding place and gave a wave.

"Oh, Francis. Hello, brother." Anders expected a short exchange of insults before the charge, but he found himself quite mistaken as Francis put heels to his horse and within moments hooves were churning up dust in his wake. "Oh shit."

Anders took a couple of hurried steps backwards and then held his ground, wincing and cringing all at the same time as his younger brother thundered towards him with a drawn sword and gleeful grin.

At just a dozen feet away, the sergeant and her partner rose and pulled hard on the rope they were holding, across from them another couple of soldiers did the same. Anders had to admit their timing was impeccable and neither Francis nor his horse had time to react. The horse pitched forward with a panicked scream and crashed to the ground. Francis found himself thrown from his saddle and hit the ground rolling in the dust, his sword lost.

Before the other cavalry could react and charge to the rescue of their fallen commander, the rest of the soldiers popped up from their hidden positions amongst the wreckage of tents and campfires, and the battle was quickly joined.

Anders ignored the new battle and sauntered over to his younger brother who was struggling to stand and seemed more than a little punch drunk from his fall. Anders drew his sword and skipped forwards.

He'd never really had the same malice that his brother revelled in, but then Anders had never needed it. He had been everywhere and done everything his brother had ever done, but he had done it first. Anders was born first, and he was father's favourite first, at least until he had fallen from that favour. He had even been first inside Francis' own wife.

"What a sorry state you look now, little brother," Anders purred as he drew close.

Francis rose in a flurry of dust and Anders had no time to dodge the punch levelled at his face. He took the blow rather well, he thought and stumbled away spitting blood and wincing at the pain. Francis had always been bigger and stronger, even when they were children.

"Shit!" Anders cursed, spitting out some more blood and running a tongue around his teeth to check they were all still there. They were, though at least one felt a little loose.

Francis was breathing heavily and swaying on his feet. His hair had pulled loose from its braid and hung down around his head. With the fire of a burning tent behind him and the flames of hatred in his barely focused eyes, Francis suddenly looked a real terror, and Anders realised he was unlikely to get any backup as the sergeant and her men were busy dealing with the remaining cavalry. To make matters worse, Francis was now holding a sword, and Anders was not.

"Oh dear," Anders breathed, taking a step back. "This was not how I intended things to happen. Can I have my sword back, brother?"

Francis took a lurching step forwards and stopped, closing his eyes for a moment and cracking his neck first to the right and then to the left. Anders could see blood running down from a cut somewhere on his brother's head, and it made a trail down his face like red tears.

When Francis opened his eyes again, he seemed clearer, standing a little straighter. Anders cast around quickly for some sort of weapon and rushed the two steps to pick Francis' fallen sword from the dust just a few feet away from the horse whose neck looked quite broken.

"HA!" Anders shouted, turning back to his brother and holding the cavalry sword in a one-handed grip. "A little more even now, eh, brother? Think you have the stones to fight me like a man?"

Francis took another few steps, his head lowered and a truly menacing look in his eyes. Anders had hoped they might finally engage in some verbal sparring first. He had hoped to buy some time for reinforcements to help him out. For the second time in as many minutes, he realised just how badly his little brother wanted him dead.

Anders took another step backwards and his foot hit something, he glanced down to see a body wearing Crucible blacks below. Francis charged, crossing the last few feet between them and swinging Anders' own sword at him.

The first strike Anders ducked, and then he lunged for his own attack which Francis parried with ease bringing the sword down over his head. Anders blocked and felt the impact travel up through his arms and set his bones rattling in his skin. But his brother didn't let up there, blow after blow rained in and it was all Anders could do to protect himself and back away from his barbaric brother.

They were both trained by the same arms master, an ancient man who'd lived in Crucible since before their father was born. They both knew the same moves, the same stances, and their weapons were almost of a like. The fight was coming down to skill, practice, and conditioning. Anders was fairly certain he was losing out on all three accounts.

Anders parried aside another stab that would have put a sizeable hole in his chest, and dove to the right, hitting the ground in a roll and coming up on his feet a couple of paces away. Francis didn't follow straight away; he was savvy enough to know Anders wanted the gap closed. He knew all of his brother's tricks, and that was making things awkward. Anders decided he needed a new strategy and if there was one thing he had always been good at it was pissing off his younger brothers.

"You've always hated me, little brother," Anders said with a grin, swishing his sword about in the air as he talked. "Though I must admit I've never quite figured out why? Is it simply a case of being born first or..."

Francis rushed in, and Anders stopped talking to concentrate on parrying the next few blows. Their swords clashed again and again, and each time Anders found himself giving ground and struggling while Francis seemed to be getting stronger with each attack. Suddenly Anders found Francis inside his guard, and a hard shoulder sent the older brother stumbling away and swinging wildly to keep the younger at bay.

"Or maybe it's something else?" Anders continued, wincing at the pain and struggling to keep his breath. "I'll wager it's because I've always been father's favourite, hmm? Don't take it too personally, Francis. I inherited his mind, you only got his brawn, and we both know which he puts more stock in."

Francis was struggling to keep his left eye open, with the blood trickling down from his forehead he kept having to wipe it away. With his hair loose and drifting in the breeze and his leathers dusty and well-used, he looked every bit a warrior from the Wilds. Anders, however, with his faded green suit of comfortable cloth, short hair, and the fear no doubt sweating from every pour, looked fairly out of place. It was quite ironic given that Anders had spent almost half his life dragging his sorry arse from one end of the Wilds to the other while his brother had spent almost all of his safe and sound within the walls of very city they were fighting outside.

"You were always his favourite," Francis said, slowly starting to circle Anders.

"As I said."

"Despite always being the fuck up. Even after you killed our sister."

The jab hit home and not just because it was true. Anders might not have done the actual killing, but he was as responsible as anyone else, and they all knew it. It was one of his many sins he knew he would bear for the rest of his life. And it had been the final nail in the coffin that had driven him away from their home.

"Our sister had a name, Francis. Chero. At least I remember it."

Francis ignored him. "Not just father's favourite either; you were always mother's favourite too. More than me or Noen or Chero or Nat. Always the favourite just because you were first."

Anders snorted at that. "Mother never loved any of us as much as she loved the next bottle, Francis. It's a sentiment I share to be brutally honest."

With a roar Francis came on again, slashing first left then right. Anders blocked and parried and decided it was time for a bit of his own offensive. He sent a hasty stab, followed by another and another, and then darted forward and to the left, trying to force Francis to trip over his own feet. Unfortunately, his little brother wasn't so foolish, and all Anders earned for his trouble was a shallow cut along his left arm, blood dripping down onto the earth to mingle with all the rest.

"Even when we were kids, Lisha was always sniffing after you," Francis spat.

Anders knew his brother wouldn't be able to leave that one alone. He'd been in love with the woman since they were five years old and, though they were married now, Francis had to live with the knowledge that Anders had been the one to take Lisha's virginity. Of course, all that really meant was that Anders was the first to have the bloody, awkward sex that most first times comprise of.

"Even our brothers and sisters always liked you more, Anders. Everyone has always liked you more, and you never deserved ANY OF IT!" Francis roared the last and followed with a flurry of heavy attacks that had Anders struggling to keep up and struggling to survive.

Blocking and parrying for all he was worth, Anders started to circle. One step after another he turned, forcing his little brother to turn with him. He wasn't really sure what he was going for, but Francis was well and truly angry now, and Anders figured he should capitalise on it in some way at least.

"Father won't even name me his successor because he still hopes you'll wake up, come back, and beg to be his son again." Francis paused his savage attack, panting and wincing at some pain. Anders thought about rallying the strength to push his own attack but decided there was little in the way of point. He was simply no match for Francis in a straight fight.

"Is that what we're really fighting over, little brother?" Anders asked. "The last two sons of Niles Brekovich fighting over who gets to be the big lord in the big city." He laughed. "You can have it, brother. I never wanted to inherit a damned thing. Father might not have accepted it, but that doesn't change the truth we both know. You, Francis Brekovich, are his heir."

Francis' brow creased in confusion, and he stood up straighter, holding his side with one hand, while his other still kept firmly to his sword hilt.

"You really don't care?" Francis asked as though he simply couldn't understand why Anders wouldn't want to be a blooded lord.

Anders smiled at his little brother. "Not a drop. It's all yours. I mean, not that it matters a damn now seeing as we're about to tear the walls of father's precious city down around him."

"FUCK Y..." Francis never got to finish his curse as sergeant Once-Stabbed and another soldier hit him from behind, bearing him down into the blood-soaked ground and twisting his arms behind him while another soldier brought rope.

Anders squatted down onto his haunches and stared at Francis as he struggled to no avail. "Well," Anders said with a sigh. "I guess now we have a way to get the Black Thorn back, hmm?"

Suzku

The battle had turned. Despite being caught unaware and facing an army of mounted foes, the soldiers of Rose's army had banded together and pushed back. Now the remaining cavalry was trapped between rank upon rank of soldier and the defences of the camp they had sought to circumvent.

Crucible's counter-attack had failed and what was left now was for Rose's army to make them pay as dearly as possible for the attempt. The more men and horses they killed now, the less they would have to face when next they assaulted the city.

"Are we done?" Pern asked the field medic.

"Needs stitches," the man growled.

"Then I will come to you when this is over. Are we done?"

"Aye. Cleaned and wrapped up best I can given the circumstances."

"Good." Pern thanked the man and strode away, back to the lines where he could command reinforcements as they arrived.

The sun was just starting to rise in the far east. Pern couldn't see it yet, nor see any rays of light, but the sky was starting to lighten and reveal the night's work in full and rarely had Pern seen such a massacre.

Bodies, both of horses and men, lay strewn about behind them. Their defensive lines had started a long way back, and the field was full of crushed tents, burned out campfires, and corpses. The battle wasn't even finished yet, and already Carron birds were circling high up above. Some had even dropped down to feed, digging into flesh and tearing it away with razor-sharp beaks. Pern had seen the giant birds before, but never so close, and he wondered at the size of them, each one almost as big as a full-grown man.

More horses fell and the riders with them. Just beyond the banks of shields and spears it was a killing field with bodies falling and being trampled. On their side, if a soldier went down in the wall, they were dragged back into safety to be treated by the dozens of field medics running about, trying to save as many lives as possible.

212

Pern had a new respect for the men and women of the healing arts. Their arms were slick with other's blood and their brows wet with sweat. They worked at a pace that left Pern dizzy and took no breaks between patients. Pern had seen thousands of men die in the past two days and he had fought both trolls and necromancers, but the healers were the real heroes. For them, war was about saving lives, not taking them.

The lines were starting to merge as they pushed forwards, both Pern's and the general's. The soldiers climbed over bodies and drove onwards, pushing the surviving Crucible soldiers back and back. Pern couldn't see it, but he was informed that their spirit was well and truly broken and many of the enemy were fleeing back towards the safety of their city.

Pern started down his line of soldiers. Two officers kept pace with him, ready to relay his commands should he give any. It was strange that it no longer felt strange. Pern had started the day as just another drunken fool looking to forget the things he'd seen, now he was commanding near a thousand men, and they were jumping to his orders as if he'd been born to the position.

The lines joined, the soldiers of Rose's army forming a giant semi-circle, containing the Crucible troops and slaughtering them on mass as they pushed ever inwards, tightening the noose. Pern trusted his troops and their officers to the job now, and he could see the general up ahead. He doubled his pace.

The general was surrounded by his men. He was stripped down to his chest, and two medics worked at sewing up a nasty-looking wound in his side. Some of the soldiers made to stop Pern, but soon moved aside when they realised who he was.

"Glad to see you're alive," Pern said, and he meant it. Not too long ago he had received a report that the general had fallen in battle and it had very nearly taken the fight out of him.

"So, you're the one who's been commanding my men over there?" General Verit asked with a wince as one of the medics poked a needle into his side. He was covered in sweat, and his face, usually fleshy and full of colour, was pale and drawn out.

Pern shrugged. "It was an accident."

The general barked out a laugh that quickly turned into a grimace. "Accident or not, my people tell me you've been doing a fine job of it. Banding folk together and securing the lines. I'll make a captain out of you yet, Honin."

A slim man with a long bow slung over his shoulder trotted up and stopped in front of the general, and for a moment Pern was forgotten.

"Move around the line," the general said. "Get a sight on them as they flee and kill as many as you can. Dead horses are good too, makes for good obstacles. The more we can trap here the less make it back to fight another day."

The slim man with the bow simply nodded and moved away towards a unit of archers waiting nearby.

Pern turned his attention back to the ongoing battle. The general had taken position on a slight rise, and it gave a commanding view. The Crucible forces were done for now. That much was clear. They were a churning mass of death and most of them would never find the way out of the camp. Even those that did were just as likely to lose their horses to the trenches.

"I have a task for you Honin, though I doubt you will like it," General Verit rumbled. He was leaning heavily on his mace and looked to be in more than a little discomfort.

"I have liked very little since this war began," Pern said with a sad smile. "If your task can help to further its end then I am willing."

The general snorted and shook his head. "If only more were like you, Honin." His face went grave. "I need you to select a dozen soldiers, those you believe you can trust. Then I need you to collect a number of Crucible's dead and strip them."

ᴏhe ᴮlack ᴏhorn

"Looks like ya attack failed," Betrim said with a grin.

He was leaning heavily on the parapet, long since given up swaying on his feet. He couldn't remember a time he felt so weak and so tired. It almost felt like his left hand had contained all of his energy and willpower, and now that it was gone he was good for nothing but hot air and wishing he was asleep.

The sky was brightening fast now, and the light revealed the full scope of Crucible's failure. Even from here they could see the battle was lost. They could hear it too. Black smoke curled up into the sky from a hundred different places in Rose's camp, merging into a dark smudge against the brightening blue, but the army had survived, and Betrim had to hope that Rose had as well.

The loss wasn't total though. Crucible's troops, those who had survived, were trickling back towards the city now. Some came in ones and two, others came in large groups. Some came back with their horses wild-eyed and frothing, others walked on their own feet, dragging them along on tired legs. Some even dragged wounded comrades behind them. It didn't matter. Niles Brekovich claimed they had sent nearly two thousand soldiers to route the besieging army and they had been decimated.

The blooded lord remained silent for the entire battle and, now his army had lost, seemed even quieter. He stared down at the survivors with barely a drop of emotion and not a single blink.

Alistair D'roan was not so sombre. He cursed and paced and paced and cursed. More than once his temper got the better of him, and he ordered the nearby soldiers to throw Betrim over the wall, but none of them jumped to his orders. They were all waiting for the real man in charge to make a decision, and Brekovich wasn't nearly so rash as D'roan. They might be seasoned commanders both, but one ruled with his head while the other ruled with emotions, and Betrim knew which of the two was more dangerous.

More than once Betrim glanced around for a weapon, wondering if he could make a grab for a sword and kill Brekovich before his guards could intervene. With the man in charge dead, Rose and her army would stand a much better chance when next they attacked. Of course, Betrim was certain he wouldn't survive the attempt, but he was already dead and just waiting for the axe to fall.

"This is madness," D'roan hissed.

The blooded lord was leaning out over the parapet at the returning troops. Betrim grinned at the thought of taking just a few steps to his left and shoving the bastard out into thin air. He wondered how long it would take for a body to fall and hit the ground.

"You have thrown away the largest part of our forces, Niles," D'roan continued. "We have barely a thousand soldiers left. And I do not see your son returning to us."

The cold stillness that lay behind Niles Brekovich's stare was chilling, but D'roan didn't see it. He was too busy shitting himself at the thought of Rose's next attack.

"Ya could surrender?" Betrim suggested.

"You could die," D'roan replied without looking. Then he turned an evil grin on the Black Thorn. "You will die. And I will be there to watch it. A front row seat to the end of the Black Thorn."

A thick glob of spittle hit Betrim in the face, and D'roan turned away again. He had to admit he didn't really like being spat on. Didn't like the feeling of someone's else spittle sliding down his face. Didn't really seem like he had any sort of choice about it right now though so Betrim kept his peace.

"Evacuate the outer wall," Niles Brekovich's voice was quiet but pitched to carry, and everyone nearby fell silent to hear his orders. "If she comes at us again we will hold her at the inner wall where our defences are strongest."

"We're just giving up the wall?" D'roan demanded.

Brekovich turned a patient stare on his peer. "We are. We no longer have the soldiers to hold it, and the inner wall is far more defensible. A hundred men could hold back a thousand. The gate is thicker, stronger. The portcullis is cast iron. There is no space for ladders. And on the inner wall, we have machines of war."

D'roan looked like he was about to argue, but Brekovich cut him off with more orders. "See to the survivors. Patch them up and get them back into their units as soon as possible."

Already there were men hurrying away to do their lord's bidding. Betrim watched them go, waiting for the numbers to thin out so he could make a real try for a sword and put it in Brekovich's gut. A chest wound would likely end him faster, but not all ends wanted to be fast, and he reckoned Brekovich could do with taking a few good painful days to die.

"Put the Black Thorn back in his cell," Brekovich commanded.

"No!" D'roan snapped. "He dies. Now! Get some rope and hang him from the wall. Leave his body dangling so that whore and her army can see what will happen to them if they attack us. If we can kill their greatest hero, we can kill any of them."

Betrim laughed at anyone calling him a hero. Just a short time ago they'd all have been clamouring over themselves to call him a criminal and the biggest one in the Wilds at that.

Brekovich turned towards his blooded peer and crossed the few feet between them, standing close enough to stab each other. Betrim grinned and pushed back from the parapet. Just a few steps and he could charge into them, taking them both with him on the last fall they'd ever take. A hand appeared on his left shoulder and gripped tightly. Betrim glanced over his right shoulder to find Torival standing behind him, a knowing grin on his face.

"Worth a try, eh?" Betrim rumbled.

"My son has not returned," Brekovich said slowly to D'roan. With that, he turned and stalked away towards the doorway.

D'roan looked speechless for a few moments, then hissed something Betrim couldn't hear and started off after Brekovich. Just a couple of seconds later, Betrim felt a heavy push on his back as Torival directed him back to his cell.

Rose

With the sun rising fast it was looking to be a bright day despite the dark night that it followed. There was a chill in the air that Rose was feeling no matter how many extra layers she shoved on. She soon had to admit to herself that it wasn't just the temperature. Exhaustion and the remnants of fear and anger from the night before had left her chilled to the bone, and she wasn't the only one.

The light revealed the full devastation of their camp and the number of bodies Crucible's attack had left behind.

Rose toured through her camp for the second time in just four days and this time it almost seemed empty. General Verit assured her they still had five thousand men, but that was only a quarter of the number they had arrived with, and the losses showed. Gone was the nervous joviality, the rough and friendly squabbles, and the wild boasting of the younger soldiers. Now the camp was full of men and women labouring to move the dead and salvage what was left of their shelter and supplies.

"Fuck me," Henry swore as they approached the front lines of the camp where the defences were meant to keep the enemy out. Rose didn't need to ask what the little woman cursed at.

Bodies, both of horses and of soldiers, were piled taller than either of the two women stood. The wall of dead was being dismantled slowly as soldiers arrived to carry bodies away, and carts were loaded with the dead. They were being moved just a mile down the road and there they were being burned. Some folk preferred burying, it was true, but they didn't have time to bury anyone right now so giant pyres would have to do.

"I ain't meant for this," Henry breathed as they stared at the mountain of corpses. Much of the venom had gone out of her, and she seemed somewhat diminished for it. She might have snapped out of her catatonic state, but Henry had not yet dealt with whatever afflicted her.

"No one is meant for this," Rose replied.

"Ain't what I meant. Battles an' the like. I ain't... Can't deal with 'em. Last night, me an' you in a tent, back ta back against a few fuckers at a time. Sneakin' into a place an' killin' 'em quiet. That's me. This... I love the sight of red more than most. Blood has a... I like it. Like the way it looks an' smells an' runs an' sometimes don't. But all of this is too much. Makes ya wonder..."

"Wonder what?" Rose asked. She wasn't really sure if she wanted to know, but she wanted the distraction.

"Down there," Henry pointed towards the city. "Down in the crush, the thick of it. I saw folk snarlin' like beasts. Stabbin', clawin', bitin'. Anythin' folk could do just ta stay alive, kill the fucker in front of 'em. Makes ya wonder if that ain't the real face, an' the one they show ya most of the time is just a mask. Makes ya wonder what we're all made of once ya take away the clothes an' the words. Blood an' bone an' shit, an' a desperate need ta take from others ta survive even if just for one more moment."

Rose found herself staring at the little woman, unsure of what to say. With her face and arms washed of blood, Henry almost looked like any other woman except for the scars on her face and the fact that she was missing an ear. It was sometimes hard to fathom that she was one of the last big names of the Wilds.

"Sorry," Henry said in a quiet voice. "Findin' myself a little fff... filo... um... thoughtful of late."

"Philosophical, my dear," came Anders' voice and from close by. Close enough to startle Rose despite herself.

Henry glanced over her shoulder and nodded. "Aye, sounds 'bout right. Still alive then, Anders?"

"Much to my brother's chagrin." Anders winked at Henry and then turned that same wink on Rose. "It takes a lot more than certain death to kill me."

"Did you actually participate this time?" Rose asked, her voice painful and croaky from the bruises the soldier had left around her throat. "Or merely watch from the sidelines?"

Anders laughed. "Oh, my lovely lady Rose, how you wound me. I was in the thick of it all night. I sent up the alarm, and I both swashed and buckled my way through a score of enemies, including my aforementioned brother, who apparently led the attack."

Rose had to think about that for a moment. Not counting the toddler Niles Brekovich got off Emin D'roan, there was only one other son Anders could be talking about.

"Francis?"

"The very same," Anders said, beaming a grin. "We fought an epic duel backlit by fires and bloody slaughter. I was... Well, I was heroic. I led him this way and that, chopped down half a dozen... Nay. An easy dozen of his troops before finally rendering the bastard unconscious."

"You captured Francis Brekovich?" Henry asked. "That the big one who wanted ya dead last we were here?"

"Indeed. The very same. And yes, yes I did."

"All on ya own?"

Anders paused for a moment, frowning. "Sure. Let's say that."

Rose smiled, and for the first time since yesterday's battle, she started to feel a little hopeful again. "Good work, Anders. You see, Henry, he's not entirely useless."

"You called me useless?" Anders asked in a dramatically affronted tone.

Henry shrugged at Rose, and together they turned away from the blooded drunk. "Pretty fuckin' close though."

"Oh yes," Rose agreed. "Very close."

"Oh dear," Anders said. "I believe my worst nightmares may have come true, Pug. These two are actually getting along."

"I... I... Uh..." Pug stammered and stuttered. The poor lad had taken quite a knock to the head in the fight last night, and he had been struggling to form words all morning. He seemed to understand well enough though, and when Rose had tried to send him away, he shook his head quite firmly.

"Yes," Anders agreed. "Well said and quite right. He agrees with me, clearly." Anders stepped up beside Rose and joined her in watching the mountain of bodies being cleared away. "Well that is quite the fucking ghastly sight, isn't it?"

Rose nodded. Here the bodies were piled up in a confined space and it made it somehow worse. So much flesh just dumped on top of more. So much death where a few hours ago there had been life. It had been easy to ignore when she had thought in terms of numbers alone, but seeing so many dead so close made it more real somehow. Rose wondered how many of the corpses were leaving behind loved ones? How many had husbands or wives or children? How many would be missed? Even worse, how many of them wouldn't be missed? Maybe the blooded were right about one thing - life was cheap in the Wilds.

"Have you seen Suzku?" Henry asked.

Anders shook his head, and for once he didn't seem to have a witty retort. "I sent him to you."

"I sent him out to fight," Rose said. She didn't even want to think of how Henry might react if Pern was found among the dead.

"I'm sure he'll be fine. A more capable fellow I've rarely met, and I'll wager Pern is far too Haarin to die."

"He's Honin," Henry said in a dangerously quiet voice.

"Yes, well..." Anders drew in a deep breath and let it out as a sigh. "Perhaps we should ask the general, hmm? He's just over there, and I'll take any excuse to not be looking at this pile of bodies. Oh, General." Anders started waving, heedless of the attention he was attracting. "General. Over here."

General Verit glanced their way, said a few more words to the soldier he was talking to, and then limped towards them. He was quite heavily favouring his left side and winced with every step. Rose had to wonder just how badly her general was hurt.

"My lady," General Verit said, stopping in front of her and attempting a bow. His face was pale and drawn, and he was clearly in more pain than he wanted others to know.

"General Verit," Rose said with a smile. "How goes the clean up?"

"Well. Or as well as can be. We'll be at this for a day at least. I've positioned scouts out around the city. If anyone tries to get in or tries to leave, we'll know about it. The siege continues."

"Have ya seen Suzku?" Henry asked. The little woman hadn't taken her eyes from the mountain of bodies, but there was something in her voice that sounded a lot like worry.

General Verit didn't look at Henry; his eyes were fixed on Rose.

"We should talk. Away from the troops."

"Ooooh, intriguing," Anders said with cheer.

The general shot Anders a stern look, but the blooded drunk just grinned back at him. There was very little, Rose had quickly discovered, that could truly dim Anders' cheer, though being sober was definitely one of them.

Rose let the general lead the way, and she hobbled along behind him with the help of Pug at her side. The boy seemed almost unharmed except for the arm in the sling and the inability to form much in the way of words. She didn't like relying on other people to help her along, but the truth was she was exhausted, and the child in her belly was feeling twice as heavy as it had yesterday. Never before had she felt quite so much like a lumbering beast.

Before long they were back inside Rose's tent and out of the chilly air. This area of the camp had been far enough back that it remained intact, for the most part at least. Tents still stood, and campfires were burning away with food simmering in pots above. There was plenty of work to be done around the sprawling camp and those doing it would need feeding.

The bodies of the Crucible soldiers who had attacked the night before were still lying near the cot. Rose grimaced at them and looked away. She had changed her clothes and washed herself as best as possible, but she could still feel the bruises the soldier had left around her neck, could still feel the hole in her left hand from the spear.

"What in the hells happened here?" Anders asked. He looked at each of the four bodies in turn and then promptly ignored them all as he made his way towards the cupboard that held the alcohol. The same cupboard Rose had been pinned to. He had to shove one of the corpses aside to get to it; there wasn't much that could keep Anders from a bottle.

Lucille was asleep on a sofa in the corner of the tent. The poor woman wasn't cut out for this. She wasn't a player of the game. She was a midwife. She was used to blood, maybe, but not battle, not being thrown across a room. Rose wasn't entirely sure how Lucille could sleep in the tent with the dead bodies lying around, but neither was she about to deny the woman a few hours of much deserved rest.

"We had some uninvited guests," Rose croaked as she removed her overcoat.

"Are you alright, my lady?" General Verit asked as he saw the bruising around Rose's neck. "I can summon a medic."

Rose smiled at him. "They've already been." She waved her bandaged left hand at him. "The hole in my hand... Well, they did what they could. As for the neck, they say time heals all."

She perched on the edge of the cot, ignoring the blood spatters. Half the tent was dotted with blood stains, and there wasn't a person in the room who wasn't drowning in red.

"You have something to tell us, General?" Rose asked.

Henry took to leaning against the tent wall near the entrance while Pug fetched Rose a glass of wine. The general stood as straight as his wounds would allow and glanced at the table.

"The map's gone."

"It'll be around somewhere. Lucille probably knocked it off as she was thrown across it last night."

"I assume you're still set on storming the city?" General Verit asked as he began hunting for the map of Crucible. "Despite our losses."

"What are our losses, General?" Rose asked.

He snorted as he straightened and slapped the map down on the table. "We have roughly a quarter of our army left. I don't have an exact count yet, but..."

"And their losses? How many men do Brekovich and D'roan have left?"

"Hard to say. Maybe a thousand. They lost fewer men than us last night. A lot fewer. But they also had less to lose. Numbers, as you said, can be quite telling."

Rose nodded and sipped at her wine, grateful for the fluid. "The argument does seem more valid than yesterday." She paused and felt the weight of so many dead upon her. "And also less so. Do they have enough left to defend the city."

General Verit laughed and nodded. "A thousand men could defend that inner wall against ten thousand."

"But the outer wall..."

"Appears to be evacuated," General Verit finished. "But it's also a trap and a damned good one. Any men we send up on that wall will be slaughtered by the archers and war machines atop the inner wall. If we don't send men up on the wall, those same archers and war machines will rain down upon anyone attempting to breach the inner gate."

Rose nodded along. "So, we're still at an impasse. Only both sides have far fewer numbers."

"Not exactly," the general said with a weary smile. "Do you remember the caves I told you about?"

"The ones infested with trolls and Drurr necromancers?"

"Just the one Drurr actually," General Verit conceded. "I've had scouts exploring those caves for the past two days. They believe the Drurr was trying to undermine Crucible, find a way inside to raise himself an army of dead."

"Why? The Drurr live underground." The last thing Rose needed on the eve of consolidating her kingdom once and for all was to find the Drurr also had eyes to stop her.

The general shook his head. "Not by choice. The Five Kingdoms have already thrown back two assaults by Drurr forces in the past five years. And this Drurr was a necromancer; I think it likely he was an outcast. Regardless of the why, he failed - for now at least - but my scouts think they may have found a way into the city, though it will require some heavy digging."

"How long will that take?"

"Normally I'd say a week or two..."

"Unacceptable. We have to end this before the Sarth and the Five Kingdoms can reinforce our enemies. We may be reeling, but so are they. We should capitalise on it. Preferably before they send me any more parts of my husband."

"Oh!" Anders said cheerfully from the bottle in his hand and in his mouth. "I doubt very much my father will be doing that any more, not now we have good old Francis locked up tight."

"We have a captive?" General Verit asked.

"Yes, quite," Anders said. "My younger brother. We engaged in an epic duel..."

"Yes," Rose said. "We do. And I haven't decided what we're going to do with him yet."

"Do with him?" Anders asked. "I thought we'd trade Francis for the boss. Get Thorn back down here with us where he belongs. No?"

Rose frowned at Anders and then turned back to the general who was smiling again. "Usually I would say it would take us a week or two to dig our way in, but I believe we could do it in a day."

"Then tell your scouts to get started, General. Today we clear the camp, burn the dead, and mourn. And rest. Tomorrow, I intend for us to attack."

"I had a feeling you were going to say that," the general said, rubbing at his neck and grabbing the bottle from Anders' hand.

"You're not going to argue?" Rose asked.

"No. I believe we may have enough pieces in place to actually take the city this time. I'll be sending a small force through the caves. I'm not sure where they will come out, but once inside the city they will head towards the inner wall, attack from behind while our main force distracts those on the inner wall. We'll lose a lot, but if they can open the gate and the portcullis, we can storm the city."

"Why not send all of our forces through the caves?" Anders asked.

General Verit took a hefty swig and winced at the taste before passing the bottle back to Anders. "If they see the majority of our force moving north your father will know something is wrong. I also doubt there will be much room to funnel troops in through the caves. They'll be moving in ones and twos at most. It would take hours to get even a thousand soldiers through, and I doubt we'll be able to keep it quiet."

"I want to send a second force through the caves as well," Rose interrupted. "A smaller one to track down the blooded inside the walls."

"An assassination squad?" General Verit asked.

"Me," Henry said with a bitter laugh that contained no humour.

Rose nodded. "I don't want you to kill them unless things start to go badly, Henry. Just keep them in one place. Make sure none of them escapes the battle."

"Unless things start to go badly?" Henry asked.

Again, Rose nodded. "Yes. And if they do then I want you to kill every last blooded you can find in there."

It would be bloody, gruesome work, Rose knew. There would be children in there, probably young enough not to understand the situation they were in. It was work Henry had done before, work she had sworn never to do again. It was also the work she was suited to.

Henry nodded. "Pick me ya quietist an' we'll do ya dirty work for ya."

"We still have to hope your father doesn't see it coming," General Verit said, grabbing the bottle from Anders once again. "Hope he doesn't have something in place to stop us."

"Oh, I'm sure he will. Quite shrewd, my father."

"Tell me about him," Rose said. "Tell me what Niles Brekovich is like. What he cares about. What drives him."

Anders let out an almost manic laugh. "My father never really cared for anything. Well, apart from his name." Anders paused and wrenched the bottle from General Verit only to find it empty. He glared for a moment as though the emptiness offended him, then moved towards the cupboard for another. No one stopped him.

"I think he cared for me, for a while at least. Back when he thought I might be a dutiful son and take over the family business," Anders laughed as though he made a joke. No one joined him. "He cares for Francis, but only because there's no one else to continue his legacy really. He's long since given up on me."

"Proven ya ain't dutiful?" Henry asked with the ghost of her usual sneer.

"Quite. Many times over, I believe, my dear. No, my father is the very definition of cold-hearted. Indeed, it has been suggested that my mother's death wasn't entirely an accident and my father may have had a hand in it."

"S-s-sug-g-g..." Pug stammered.

"Suggested by whom?" Rose said, and Pug nodded enthusiastically.

"Um... well... by myself. Mostly. But I'm sure others have said it too. I mean, father has always been after more sons, hoping to produce one with my wit and Francis' loyalty. He never really cared for the daughters, just fodder to be married off to the other blooded or foreign people of influence."

"What does that have to do with your mother?" Rose said.

"Well she stopped bearing him children. Lost a few early on and after Francis she only gave him two daughters. It was no real surprise that she died and left father free to hunt down a new wife, one younger and with wider hips and noble birth. Just so happens Emin D'roan got herself captured, and he quickly put a child in her, turned out to be a son, but a bastard one and also a D'roan."

"But ya da is allied with the D'roans," Henry pointed out.

"For now, certainly. Though I very much believe it to be a marriage of convenience. Think about it. Even if my father and Alistair do throw us back, crush us into the dust, and reclaim their former glory as the parasitic rulers of the Untamed Wilds. What then? Hmm?

"Let's tick them off. The H'osts, well they were the first to die and none too soon. The Turns, the Ferins, the Jogarens, the Y'landers, and the Kairns. All dead by your hands. That leaves just three blooded families left.

"The Fanklins are led by a weak man with no ambition and, by all accounts, his brothers, sisters, sons, and daughters aren't much better. They've been steadily losing land to the other families since long before Rose and Thorn turned up to kill them all.

"That leaves our dear friend Alistair D'roan as the head of the only family who could possibly stand in the way of my father claiming the whole of the Wilds all for himself. Now it's entirely possible that my father is quite happy with sharing the Wilds three ways, but I doubt it. And believe me, the last thing my father wants is someone of D'roan blood sitting in his place once he is gone."

"Who was your mother? What family did she belong to?" asked Rose.

"She didn't belong to any. She was Acanthian. Third daughter of, um, some noble merchant or something. Married off when she was just twelve years old, and two years after that she pushed me out squealing and entirely too sober. Which probably explained all the crying. I'd wager most babes would be a lot happier if they were drunk."

"How does any of this help?" General Verit asked.

"It helps," Rose started, a little frustrated that her general couldn't see it, "because the better I know a man, the better I know how to unman him. And if I can unman Niles Brekovich, then he might make a mistake."

"Even if he does. This D'roan apparently knows his stuff too," the general complained.

Rose let out a sigh. "One problem at a time. Anders, tomorrow morning we attack. Before that, I have a job for you, and I don't think you're going to enjoy it."

DAY 5 – THE CITY

Anders

For the second time in just a few days, Anders found himself standing before the walls of Crucible within easy bowshot. Parley seemed a good word for '*putting oneself in harm's way*'. At least he wasn't alone this time. This time he had ten hardy soldiers, each armed and armoured, and of course one very tied up brother.

Francis' hands were manacled, his legs tied, and a dirty gag was shoved rather roughly into his mouth and secured with a belt. It was not a very dignified situation to be in, but he dealt with it well enough, neither struggling, nor shouting; even after Anders informed his brother that the gag was one of his old socks.

Bodies lay all over the trampled field outside the city. There hadn't been time to clear them away and the bodies left inside the city walls after Rose's army pulled out had been unceremoniously dumped outside the limits. Thousands upon thousands of lumps of dead flesh rotting on the battlefield, feeding crows and worms and anything else that feasted on carrion. There were even a few laughing dogs about, dragging bodies away. It was a grisly sight that Anders preferred not to think about.

With the sun already high enough to be shining over the tops of the walls, Anders could see the outer wall was quite empty. No doubt his father had long since given the order for it to be evacuated with only a skeleton crew to keep an eye on the army encamped outside.

"Hello?" Anders shouted quite loudly. "Anders Brekovich here. I have my little brother, Francis Brekovich. We're pretty much the last of Niles Brekovich's sons. Don't worry about the knife at little Francis' throat; we don't really intend to kill him. Just, you know, making sure you parley rather than shoot pointy objects at us, hmm? So, uh, send for my father, please. I'm fairly certain he'll come to the wall for this."

There was movement atop the wall and Anders settled in for what was likely quite a wait. They were safe enough though. While within range of any archers atop the wall, they were also within range of the general's archers behind them. Any attempt at a rescue for Francis would soon result in a lot of death, and it was quite likely both the Brekovich boys would be among the casualties.

"Good boy," Anders said, patting Francis on the head.

"How long do we wait?" asked Sergeant Once-Stabbed. Anders was quite grateful for her presence. He had, in fact, sought her out for exactly the job.

"As long as it takes."

"What if he don't come?"

Anders laughed. "He'll come. The last two Brekovich boys standing side by side just a mere stone's throw away. He'll come."

Francis let out a sound, but it was very hard to determine what it was underneath the gag shoved into his mouth.

"I don't reckon ya could throw a stone here all the way from there," said one of the soldiers, a burly monstrosity with no hair on his eyebrows. "Too far."

"But you'd have the height from up on the wall," said another, this one a shorter man with arms as thick as Anders' thighs. "Looks pretty high up."

"It would depend on the stone and the thrower," said No Eyebrows.

"Someone real strong and a small stone?" asked Thick Arms.

"Actually, you would want a largish stone, though not quite bordering into rock or boulder territory," Anders joined in more to take his mind off the wait than anything else. "Needs to be heavy enough, so the wind doesn't slow it too much."

"Mhm." No Eyebrows nodded sagely. "Maybe a run-up too?"

"A run-up would just end with the thrower falling over the edge, like as not," said Sergeant Once-Stabbed. "Throwing stones is about technique. You'd want to lob it from the waist, get some spin on it. My brother and I used to skim stones like that on the Erinlake, back when we was younger. I reckon the technique is pretty similar, just one is over water and the other through the air."

"I never thought of it like that," No Eyebrows said.

"What about a sling?" asked Thick Arms. "Would that count as throwing? Ya can get a stone pretty fucking far with a sling."

Before long they found themselves agreeing that they were definitely within stone throwing distance in one form or another though it very much depended upon the rules of the contest. Before much longer they had hammered out a series of rules for the contest and Thick Arms had named it The Crucible Hammer Throw. No Eyebrows was just about on the verge of going looking for suitable stones when Anders saw movement atop the wall and thanked the gods for it. The conversation had gotten quite out of hand, and he was in no mood for frivolities.

"Father? Is that you up there?" Anders shouted, cupping his hands to his mouth though he was fairly certain it made no difference. He waited a few moments for anything resembling a response.

A face appeared at the parapets, and Anders squinted before letting out a sigh. "Oh, do bugger off, Alistair. I'm here to talk to my father. You know, the one in charge. I don't need another underling. I have my very own right here." He patted Francis on the head again, and his little brother struggled to no avail.

"Save your strength, Francis," Anders said with a sigh and then lowered his voice. "You're going to need it, little brother."

Another face appeared at the parapets, and this one Anders knew very well. It should have brought a smile to his face to see the Black Thorn alive, if not looking too well.

"Hi, boss," Anders shouted with a wave. "Is my father treating you well?"

Anders couldn't be sure, but it certainly looked as though Thorn laughed.

"Better than last time, I reckon!" the boss shouted. "Hasn't tried ta feed me ta the laughin' dogs just yet. How's Rose?"

"Oh, quite well." Anders nodded enthusiastically. "Her and the baby both. Had a bit of a run in with some soldiers last night, but... well... she killed them. I'm told it was a sight to see."

Anders saw the Black Thorn stagger and fall silent - no doubt being manhandled from behind and told in no uncertain terms to be quiet.

Eventually, Niles Brekovich's face appeared at the wall, staring down upon his two sons with stern, unblinking eyes. Anders very nearly lost his nerve as the weight of that stare hit him and he was fairly certain he saw Francis shrink away too. One son a traitor and the other a failure, Anders reckoned their father was not entirely proud of either of them at that point.

"Hello, father!" Anders shouted and took a step backwards, draping an arm over Francis' shoulder. "Look, your two boys together again. Fast friends now, don't let the chains and gag fool you. We worked out our differences and came to the mutual realisation that I really just don't care about Crucible or your inheritance. I think it's fair to say, though I may share your blood, I'm just not really a Brekovich. Hmm?"

Their father just stared down at them both, and Anders swallowed down the lump in his throat before continuing.

"So, we decided once and for all that Francis here is most definitely your heir. It was quite the realisation, and I believe we both grew a bit during the conversation. Francis here even cried." He looked at Francis and nodded. "Better he rules after you're gone, and we all just let me drink myself to death in some shitty tavern out in the middle of nowhere, hmm?"

Niles Brekovich stared down in silence for a while.

"Get on with it, Niles," D'roan hissed, his voice sounding quiet so far below.

After a scathing glare sent D'roan's way, Anders' father turned back to his two sons waiting in the field outside of the city. "A trade then?" he said loudly.

Someone had once told Anders that it was unwise to poke a bear. Unfortunately, Anders had a horrible habit of not listening to good advice.

"What was that, father?" he shouted. "I'm afraid you'll have to speak up. We're quite a way away and..."

"A TRADE THEN!" Niles Brekovich roared.

It was the first time Anders had ever heard his father truly shout. Even after all he had put the family through his father had never shouted at him, or anyone. Anders found himself stunned, shocked into inaction.

For a few moments he just stood there, staring up at his father. He realised his mouth was hanging slightly open and quickly shut it, taking a moment to look down at the ground and collect his thoughts.

Francis made a sound, mumbling something from beneath his gag. Anders ignored him, drew in a deep breath and sucked up every drop of courage he could muster. This was his task; the one Rose had set him. It wasn't pleasant, and saying it wasn't pleasant was an understatement and an insult to all things that weren't pleasant. In fact, it took every drop of courage and will Anders could muster not to damn his orders and make the trade there and then.

"I'm afraid you've made a mistake, father," Anders said loudly, not looking up.

He turned to the soldiers behind him. "Down on the ground. Hold him tight, hands and legs.

"I'm not here to offer a trade," Anders shouted. He pulled a knife from the sheath on his belt, a short thing, curved at the tip and sharper than a razor blade.

He turned away from the walls of Crucible and sighed out a shuddering breath.

"Belt," Anders said, and Sergeant Once-Stabbed undid and pulled Francis' belt free. "And the trousers please." With a bit of effort, the sergeant tore Francis' trousers away.

Anders dropped down to his knees between his brother's splayed legs. The look on Francis' face was pure panic. Terror poured off him, and he was shaking rather violently despite the eight big soldiers holding him down.

Anders pulled a small leather thong from his pocket. He reached down and grabbed his brother's cock and balls, gripping them hard and wrapping the thong around and around, pulling it tight.

Francis was whining through his gag now, tears streamed down his face, and he met Anders' eyes. They were the eyes of his little brother. No matter what the man had become, Francis was Anders' little brother. They had grown up together, known each other all their lives. They were never friends, not really. But surely some bonds were deeper than friendship.

Anders held up the knife and considered it for a moment. He could hear shouting behind him, someone screaming from up on the wall. He ignored it, not even letting the words sink in.

"I'm really quite sorry about this, Francis," Anders said, blinking away tears. "Not really my choice, but we all have our parts to play. Hold still, please. As still as you can anyway." He laughed though there wasn't a drop of humour in it. "I'm afraid I've only done this the once before, and it was very messy. Rose wants you to live, if at all possible. So, um... well... here we go."

The Black Thorn

They looked small from so high up on the wall, but it was easy to see what Anders was doing. Hard not to see the intent when Francis Brekovich was stripped half-naked, held down by eight big folk and a knife waved about between his legs. Hard not to hear the screams even muffled by a gag. Someone else was shouting nearby too. Niles Brekovich leaning out dangerously far over the parapets and hurling obscenities at the son doing the cutting. He quickly fell silent when he realised it would do him no good. Anders wasn't just threatening.

"What are you doing, Niles?" D'roan insisted. "Just fucking shoot them."

Niles Brekovich didn't respond. He stared down at the bloody scene below, his face pale and drawn and his eyes distant. Betrim saw the man blink once, twice. No tears though. Just horror. Raw horror.

"Idiot!" D'roan hissed and turned to the nearby soldiers with their bows strung but by their sides. "Shoot them!" He pointed out over the wall.

"Ain't gonna happen," Betrim rumbled. Torival gave him a shove, but Betrim ignored it. There was nothing he could do if the big captain wanted to deal him some real damage, with his right hand tied to the front of his belt and his left hand missing, though they'd still tied his left arm to the back of his belt, gave him a real helpless sort of feel.

"Throw him over the wall!" D'roan ordered. The nearby soldiers glanced at each other and then to Brekovich who was standing still as a statue watching his oldest son cut the balls off his heir.

"Don't reckon they're listenin'," Betrim growled. "Reckon they know who's in charge."

"Niles. Shoot them!" D'roan shouted.

Betrim laughed, despite the gruesome mood and the murderous captain at his back. He knew he was already dead. There was no way Brekovich was letting him get away now. He'd be lucky if they left him whole, though now he thought about they'd already taken a hand, so he would never be whole again.

"He ain't gonna shoot at his only sons," Betrim said. He turned a bit and leaned against the stone of the parapet, giving the blooded lord a stare with his one eye. "Last thing he wants is ta see his bloodline ended."

D'roan glared at Betrim for a moment before turning to Brekovich. The screaming had died down now. Either it was over, or Francis had passed out.

"You have another son, Niles. My daughter Emin gave you a son."

Betrim laughed again. Torival gave him a shove.

"Fuck off," Betrim rasped before turning his attention back to D'roan. "Ya really think he wants his bloodline relying on a D'roan? Ya must be one deluded cock, mate. That bastard he got with ya daughter was never anythin' but an insult ta you. Ya actually think ya a player in the game, don't ya?" Betrim shook his head slowly. He was slightly amazed Brekovich hadn't ordered him shut up yet, but then he wasn't even sure the blooded lord was listening.

"Ya really think ya here 'cos this fuck wants an alliance? Really reckon ya got a seat at the table? You're a pawn." Again, Betrim laughed. "Only reason ya here at all is 'cos Brekovich needs your pieces ta win the game. Moment me an' Rose are dead, you'll be followin', and ya bet ya stones that Brekovich here ain't gonna name a half-D'roan brat his heir.

"Trust me. I been in this game long enough ta see another player, an' you ain't a player, D'roan. Ya just another piece."

"Well!" Anders shouted. Betrim turned to see his friend staring up at the wall, hands slick with red and holding something small up for all to see. "It's done. Smaller than mine."

Francis was either unconscious or dead, but it was hard to tell from so high up.

"Best we retreat, I think," Anders announced and waved at his escort. The soldiers started dragging Francis' prone form away.

"Good day to you, father. I'll, um, leave this here, shall I?" He placed the little bit of bloody flesh on the ground. "Lisha might want it as a– souvenir or something, I suppose."

With a wave, Anders turned and hurried after the soldiers. He was soon out of bowshot. Niles Brekovich stood there, still and quiet. His shoulders were slumped, and he blinked again.

Betrim found he had a nasty cramp in his shoulder, but with both arms tied tight to his belt there was little he could do to stretch it out, so he just grimaced through the pain.

"They're going to attack, Niles. Can't you see that?" D'roan continued. "That whore hasn't assembled her army on the field again for nothing. We need to retreat. Back to the inner wall and hold it."

Niles Brekovich stood there a while longer, staring down at the bloody stain where one son castrated the other. Eventually, he turned in silence, shoulders still slumped, and walked away towards the stairs that led down to the bottom of the wall. Torival followed, leaving Betrim without a guard for the first time since he'd woken up captured. Only problem was he couldn't really capitalise on it with his arms tied and his left hand not only missing but also throbbing like a touch of rot had got inside.

"Well," Betrim said to break the silence. "Guess ya in charge now after all, mate." He grinned at D'roan, knowing full well it twisted his burned face into a horrific visage.

Alistair D'roan turned hateful eyes on Betrim and then blinked. Betrim reckoned that was when it hit, the realisation that he was in charge of defending a siege against a determined force.

"Aye," Betrim growled with a laugh. "Don't reckon this soggy arse is leadin' owt." He nodded towards Tanith Fanklin.

"Rope and oil," D'roan said quietly. His eyes flicked up to the army camped out beyond the killing field. Though the army wasn't so much camped as it was assembled and shaping up for a second go at the walls. "Now!" He clicked his fingers until two of the nearby soldiers snapped to his orders.

Betrim adjusted his lean a bit. He was finding it fairly hard to get comfy considering his left arm ended in a raw stump and was tied to his trousers. It also didn't help that his arm was feeling a touch warmer than it should and his fight against the shakes was a constant, real struggle. Infection, he decided, was definitely setting in. Not that it would have a chance to wreak its havoc on him. He knew what was coming.

"Evacuate the outer wall," D'roan continued. "Archers and technicians to their posts." Now the initial shock had worn off he was starting to sound a bit like a competent commander. It was a right shame, Betrim reckoned, as he been hoping D'roan would take the opposite approach and collapse into a listless mess.

One of the soldiers came trotting back with a large wineskin. D'roan sniffed at it and grinned. He took two steps toward Betrim and squeezed the skin, spraying sticky liquid all over him.

It was fair to say Betrim hadn't been expecting a dousing and he took to spluttering and a bit of coughing. Had a strange taste in his mouth and it took him a moment to realise what it was. Lamp oil.

"The fuck?" Betrim blinked his right eye rapidly, trying to rid himself of the oil dripping into it. Turned out having his hand tied and not being able to wipe shit away was a real problem in some situations.

"I'm not surprised you can't understand," the blurry form of Alistair D'roan said as he squeezed another spray of lamp oil onto Betrim. "You fucking idiot!"

Betrim stumbled back a step and felt a thrill rush through him as he realised he'd moved from the parapet and, other than a waist-high lip of stone, had nothing but air and a long drop behind him.

"Niles was the only thing keeping you alive, Black Thorn. These men are loyal to him, yes, but they also know to follow orders and right now my orders are that you're dead."

Betrim spat out some more oil and wiped his eye on his shoulder in time to see one of the soldiers handing D'roan a length of rope with one end tied into a noose.

"Tie the other end off," D'roan ordered.

Betrim didn't much like the idea of hanging. He'd been hanged once, and it hurt well enough the time when there wasn't a hundred-foot drop on the safe side. He liked the idea of burning even less and the idea of burning, and hanging wasn't one he even wanted to entertain.

"Goodbye, Black Thorn," D'roan said, stepping forwards with the noose in front of him.

"Aye," Betrim growled. "Fuck that."

Betrim lunged forwards as quick as his shaking body would allow and sank a nearly full set of teeth into D'roan's neck, biting through cloth, collar, and flesh alike. He tasted blood and sweat and fear, and he didn't feel like giving anyone a chance to save the bastard. Betrim flung himself backwards as hard as he could, tumbling out over the parapet into the fatal drop below and dragging Alistair D'roan with him.

ℛose

"NOOOO!" The girlish scream tore from Anders' mouth.

Rose was feeling quite a similar sentiment as she watched her husband drop to the earth. She didn't voice it. Couldn't. She watched the Black Thorn die in silence and felt the world around her dim a little. No one could survive such a fall, not even Betrim.

Rose lost sight of the two bodies plummeting to the earth behind the banks of spears in front of her. She never saw the impact. She felt it though. A horrid feeling in her stomach that refused to let her breathe, a loosening of the bowels as they turned to water. Rose stood in silence, and her army stood with her.

They had all heard so many stories of the Black Thorn and his legendary ability to escape death. Even before Rose had met the man his name was bigger than any other the Wilds had produced in generations. Gone. Rose placed a hand on her belly. But not forgotten. Never that.

"My lady..." Lucille started. She was already at Rose's side, a supportive hand on her arm. Pug was nearby too, his face a picture of shock. General Verit stood with a face like the grave– pale and drawn and all hard lines.

Rose gasped, blinking away tears. "Thank you, Lucille, I'm well aware." She didn't need the midwife telling her what to do, but neither did she pull her arm away from Lucille's support.

"Who was that who fell with my husband?" Rose asked.

"L-l-loo-k-k-k." Pug stopped yammering and took a deep breath. The poor lad appeared to be concentrating quite hard. "D-D-Drron..."

"D'roan?" Rose asked.

Anders was nodding. "Hard to say for sure." He seemed deflated, completely devoid of his usual humour. Rose could understand, but none of them had time to grieve right now, least of all her.

"Then let us hope our plan worked," Rose continued. If Francis' mutilation had the desired effect, and Niles Brekovich had also quit the field, then Crucible was as good as leaderless.

"General Verit, are all your pieces in place?" Rose was feeling quite uncomfortable, and the child moving in her belly was not helping matters, though she supposed it was probably necessary.

The general nodded slowly. He looked at Rose, a frown creasing his brow. "Morale might have just taken a hit though. Not many folk could mistake that for anything but the death of the man in charge."

"I am in charge, General," Rose corrected him. "I was always in charge. That being said, I'm afraid I must leave the battle entirely in your care."

The general had shifted his gaze and was staring down at the ground below Rose. He nodded again. "Aye. That might be best."

"I want this city taken by the time I am finished, General," Rose put every drop of authority she could muster into her tone, and the big man nodded, though he looked far from happy at the order.

"My lady," Lucille said again.

"The pain has not started yet, Lucille," Rose interrupted her midwife. "I am sure I will let you know when it does."

"Are you?" Anders started, then stopped and waved a hand in the air, purposefully looking anywhere but at the rather obvious wet patch on Rose's dress. "Now?"

Rose nodded. "It would appear so. I believe my watching my husband die may have shocked our child into making an appearance. Perhaps she wants to storm the walls herself."

Anders giggled a forced laugh and looked awkward. There was no mirth there.

"I have a task for you too, Anders," Rose said. "I want you to go down there and find my husband."

Anders let out a snort. "He's dead. That fall..."

"Then find his body," Rose interrupted. She was finding her patience worn thin and she'd never had a lot of it for Anders in the first place.

He looked set to argue for a moment then threw his hands up in the air and sighed. "Why do I always get the hard jobs?" he asked as he sulked away.

"I believe I have to go and give birth now," Rose said. "Good luck,

241

General."

The big Five Kingdomer nodded. "You too."

Rose turned and let Lucille and Pug lead her away towards the camp and her tent. Only a dozen paces away she heard the first horn sounding as General Verit began ordering her troops into position.

Henry

The caves were darker than midnight's arsehole without the torchlight, and that made Henry more than a little glad for the flickering flames. She liked night as much as the next blade in the dark, but she liked to be able to see her own nose at least.

The scout led her and her little band farther and farther down into the earth. They twisted back on themselves at least twice, and it didn't take long for Henry to completely lose any sense of direction. How the scout seemed to be able to navigate without even a map was beyond Henry. But then she supposed that was why the scout was the scout and Henry was the assassin. Each of them had their own parts to play, and some were bloodier than others. And some required being able to tell left from right down deep in the dark where one wall looked as much like any other.

"What's ya name?" Henry asked, her voice echoing around the cavernous black. She didn't really care to know the scout's name, just wanted some sort of distraction.

Up on the surface, near the city, outside and inside its walls, folk were dying. They'd been waiting up near the cave entrance, Henry and her scout, for the signal from the general. The moment they'd seen it they knew the army would be marching on the city walls. That meant they had limited time to break into the city, fight their way to the walls, and open the gates. All except Henry's little crew who had to break into the city, fight their way to the blooded, then keep them quiet or slit their throats, depending on how the battle seemed to be going.

"Marline," the scout whispered into the cloying darkness. She didn't turn to look at Henry but kept her eyes in front, watching the black.

Marline was taller than Henry, though most full-grown folk tended to be, and had red hair tied into a tight bun at the back of her head. She looked like she had a wiry strength to her and it was a look Henry knew well. The scout carried no weapons save two little picks hanging from her belt, and the torch lighting their way.

"Ya Five Kingdoms?" Henry asked though she didn't need to. Marline had a Five Kingdoms' accent, and she was one of the soldiers General Verit brought with him. Small talk was not one of Henry's strengths.

"Born and bred," Marline said as she turned to her right and led Henry further into the darkness.

It seemed Marline wasn't the real talkative sort, and usually that would have put Henry in a good mood, but she wanted to talk. She wanted to take her mind off the urgency of their mission, the weight of so much rock and earth above, and the creeping darkness that threatened to engulf them should their torches gutter out.

"Were you down here with Suzku?" Henry asked. She'd barely shared a word with him since the siege started, but she'd heard the stories of trolls in the caves and the massacre they wrought. She'd also seen the look on Pern's face afterwards.

"No," Marline said, and that seemed all the answer Henry was getting.

"He ain't down here then?" Henry kept on, relentless.

Henry wanted to know where Pern was; she needed to find out. No one had seen him since the attack. She'd heard plenty of stories about how he took a force and kept them together, commanding a small army by the end of it. Seemed almost impossible that the Honin Henry knew could be capable of commanding soldiers, but it wouldn't be the first time he'd surprised her. Now he was missing, and she refused to believe he was among the dead they had burned.

"No."

"Fuckin' abrupt, ain't ya?"

"I'm concentrating," Marline hissed. "You want to get lost down here in the dark? No. So shut the fuck up and let me lead us through this."

Henry bristled. Actually, she reached for a knife, halfway to drawing it out and stabbing the woman in the back before she realised just how fucked that would leave her. She had no idea where they were going and even less idea of how to get herself there. The truth of it was that Marline held Henry's life in her hands. Henry hated her life being in other folk's hands.

Weren't much longer before she saw other lights ahead. A general lightening of the gloom and then flickering torches driven into the walls of the cave. Henry could make out the floor, the walls, the ceiling. For the first time since stepping out of the daylight, she could see just how big the cave was and it left her feeling a little bit awed.

Above her, the rocky ceiling was at least twice as high as Henry was tall and it was that again wide. All the walls were slightly rounded and rough and looked to have been clawed right out of the rock. Henry couldn't imagine what sort of creature could gouge away at solid rock. Neither did she have to try for very long.

The cave was fairly heavily populated with soldiers waiting around all over the place. Some were chewing on rations, strips of salted beef, while others sharpened their swords or whispered to each other. Close to a hundred folk, Henry reckoned, and barely a word spoken between them.

There was a nervous apprehension in the air. They all knew how dangerous their task was, and they all knew they weren't likely to survive it. They also all knew just how important that task was and how much of the battle above them hinged upon their success. About as much pressure as the rock above pressing down on them, Henry reckoned.

Henry saw her own little crew. Eight of them and a shadier bunch she hadn't seen since her days on the Boss' crew. General Verit had picked his assassin squad well, and they were all veterans of the game - each with their own name, and each with over a dozen kills to that name.

Burns, a fat man with even more burn scars than Thorn, was the first to spot Henry and he nodded at her through the darkness. Henry split off from Marline and sauntered over to her little crew.

"Don't like the dark," said Urting Uther, his voice a quiet lisp.

"Be up in the light soon enough," Henry said.

"Who're you?" asked a freakishly tall woman with dark hair and darker eyes.

"Henry the Red." Henry stepped towards the woman and stared up at her. "You can call me boss."

The tall woman grinned. She didn't have to tell Henry her name;

everyone knew Long Tall by sight and, though Henry had never met the bitch before, she now knew why.

"Nice ta meet ya," Long Tall said, her voice slow and monotonous. She held out a hand.

Henry looked down at the offered hand for a moment then laughed. "Ya all know the job?"

"Know who's in charge," said Burns with another nod. His face barely moved as he spoke, and Henry would have bet a few bits he didn't have any eyelids.

"We only kill 'em if shit up there looks ta be goin' bad," Henry hissed at her little crew. "Otherwise we just keep the blooded fuckers alive 'til Rose can get her hands on 'em. Don't reckon they'll like the prospect so we might have ta restrain 'em some."

A deep laugh rumbled out from a short man with a bald head and eyeglasses that made his stare goggle at Henry out of the gloom. "I have rope," the man said in a voice as deep as his laugh. He patted at his hip and Henry could see a number of different types and lengths of rope hanging from his belt.

"Right," Henry said and realised the general might have given her the eight people he most wanted rid of from his army. "Anyone else hear that scratchin' noise?"

Burns pointed away towards the largest cluster of soldiers, and Henry sniffed, spat, and strode away from her little crew. They seemed a right murderous group of bastards, and she was already wondering how many of them she'd have to kill to keep the others in line.

Marline was close by, squatting on her haunches and chewing on something. The scout glanced up as Henry approached and looked a little manic in the flickering light of the torches.

"We ready ta go yet?" Henry asked.

Marline shook her head. "Diggers ain't done."

Now Henry was closer to the throng of soldiers she could hear the scratching noise a bit louder and a bit clearer, and it was less scratching, and more scraping. Deciding she wasn't likely to get a sufficient answer from the terse scout, Henry moved off, pushing through the soldiers until she could see what they were all watching.

Beyond the group of armed folk, Henry found ten men with whips and torches acting very menacing to what looked like four giant apes. She'd seen the big monkey things a long time ago down near Chade, come up from the southern Wilds, but these weren't quite the same.

Each of the creatures was slightly larger than a full-grown man, though not as large as some. They had yellow skin that sagged as though there was too much of it for the bones and flesh beneath. The legs were short and stubby, and the arms were long and gangly, each one ending in an oversized paw with four clawed digits. Henry caught sight of one of the monster's faces, and it looked like a chubby child with the features and wrinkled skin of a real elder. Huge nose, huge eyes, cracked lips. To say the beasts were repulsive would have been something of an understatement. Henry had never seen their like before and, judging by the interest of the nearby soldiers, neither had most of those gathered. She found herself wondering what colour they bled.

"You the captain of the other squad?" asked a broad man with a wide nose and a back as straight as a spear.

Henry shrugged, then realised he might be after a real answer and whether she liked it or not she was in charge.

"Aye, looks like. Them trolls?"

The broad soldier nodded. "Young ones. Found them after the general killed the adults. Put them to work digging."

Henry could see they were digging. Powerful claws ripping at the stone, tearing it apart and leaving rubble behind. There were other soldiers nearby using shovels to scoop up the rubble, depositing it at the sides of the steadily narrowing cavern. One of the trollings turned its head to the side and looked back at them, a moment later a whip cracked across the monster's back, and it raised its arms to shield its face. Henry could see then that some of its claws were cracked and its hands were dripping with something dark and viscous. Another crack of the whip and the trolling turned back to the stone wall and started scraping again.

"They can be used, though crudely," the broad soldier said.

Again, Henry smothered the urge to stab someone, though she couldn't really say why, just felt a sudden need to visit violence on folk. "We close?" Something about seeing beasts used in such a way gave her the itch. It was an itch she knew all too well.

"Should be."

"What happens to the trolls after?"

The broad soldier shrugged. "We kill them. Can't allow monsters to outlive their usefulness." That didn't sit right with Henry at all. She wondered how many of the soldiers she could kill before they took her down.

There was a loud crumbling sound followed by one of the trollings letting out a hoot, quickly joined in by the others. Before long they were all hooting and clawing at the crumbling rock in front of them. Henry couldn't see much beyond, but it looked like the cave wall was giving way to some sort of cavern, and she could hear splashes on the other side.

Before the whip-wielding soldiers could stop them one of the trollings squeezed through the widening hole and Henry heard a louder splash from the other side. The other three trollings piled after the first, and soon all of them had disappeared into the black beyond. The splashing intensified for a while, slowly fading to nothing.

"We're through!" called the broad soldier. "I think we lost the trolls."

Henry spat and hoped the beasts could swim, hoped they found some way out of the death the soldiers had planned for them. They didn't deserve to die for it.

"My turn." Marline pushed through the crowd of soldiers behind Henry. She had her little picks in hand and a length of rope tied around her waist. Three lanterns hung from her belt. "I'll shout as soon as I've found a way through."

With that, the scout squeezed through the hole created by the trolls and was gone, her figure and the light from her lanterns disappearing upwards.

"What exactly is through there?" Henry asked, peering into the hole the trolls had created.

"Cavern filled with water," the broad soldier said. "Most wells just collect groundwater, but Crucible has an entire cavern underneath it. Marline finds a well; we climb up it."

"Fuck," Henry swore, looking a little nervous.

"What? You know how to climb a rope?"

"Aye," she sent a glare at the soldier that had him wiping the smile from his face. "Just don't know how ta fuckin' swim 'case I fall."

Suaku

The city bells had been ringing most of the morning, calling the men and women of Crucible to defend their walls. Now they fell silent. Pern could still hear them sounding in his head. It was a memory of the noise, nothing more, yet it would take some time for that memory to fade.

Disguised in their stolen Crucible blacks, Pern and his hand-picked squad had retreated with the very soldiers they had been fighting against, insinuating themselves into those heading back to the city. His dozen was now split up, moved to different sections of the city. Pern had been sent to the infirmary where the physicians spent some time patching him up. His arm was cleaned, stitched, and bandaged. The bandages on his head and midsection had been changed, and several his other little wounds had been looked at and dismissed as minor injuries. One of the physicians made the joke that '*Pern had obviously been in the wars*', and the woman had no idea how right she was.

He hoped the physicians would survive the siege. They had no idea Pern was one of the enemy. No idea he was tasked with opening the gates from the inside. They'd patched him up and he was thankful for it. Unfortunately for them, he was likely going to be the death of them. They didn't deserve it. He didn't warn them.

The problem with Crucible was that it was unlike most cities Pern had seen. The buildings were widely spaced and squat things mostly consisting of just the one floor, though many had quite extensive cellars. This meant that there were very few places to hide and Pern needed to hide until the rest of his dozen found him. If he was spotted, still dressed in the Crucible blacks he had looted from a corpse, he would no doubt be sent to defend the wall and defence was the last thing on his mind. So Pern crouched in the doorway of one of the buildings closest to the gate.

He could hear shouting, raised voices drifting down from the soldiers atop the wall. It appeared General Verit was marching his army forwards and that meant the distraction would soon be well underway.

Once the fighting started Pern and his small group of soldiers would have to work quickly.

A man walked past, not one of Pern's and not a soldier at all. It was sometimes easy to forget that the good folk lived in the city as well. If Rose's army took the walls, they would likely die in the city as well. Even more deaths to lay in front of his conscience. Pern wondered just how many people had to die for Rose's war to end?

The man startled at the sight of Pern and then put a hand over his heart. "Scared the fuck out of me, ya did," the man said and took a deep breath to steady himself. "Shouldn't you be up on the wall?"

Pern shook his head slowly. "This building watches the killing field. If we lose the inner wall, you'll be glad I'm here manning the scorpion inside." It was half a truth at least. There was a scorpion inside, and there had been two men manning it, watching the gate for signs of the attacking army breaking through. Both men were now dead by Pern's own hand. He had positioned himself in the doorway because he neither wanted to see nor smell his handiwork.

"Oh," the man said with a nod. "Well..."

"You should go home," Pern interrupted. "Lock your door and wait for the all clear."

The man snorted. "You must be one of the new ones. Crucible won't fall. Never been breached, our city. Besides, I got work to do. Can't go laying about just 'cos we're under siege." The man wandered away, mumbling something about *know-nothing mercenaries*.

Pern wasn't sure how long passed until his full dozen arrived. It was hard to keep track of time in the shadow of a doorway with nothing but the sounds of fighting drifting over the wall to occupy him. He was well aware folk were dying outside the walls again, and he was well aware that the taking of the city relied on him. The waiting was always the hardest part. The killing was always the easiest. It seemed to Pern they should be the other way around.

It was no accident he had ordered them to meet where they did. They had a number of covert jobs, and the first was to move through the buildings watching the gate. They had to kill the soldiers in the first wave of buildings, or the war machines would wreak havoc on the attacking army even once they breached the inner gate.

Pern moved quickly, utilising the camouflage of wearing Crucible blacks, and went from building to building. It was bloody work and left a bad taste in his mouth. One more detestable thing he had done in service of someone else, and it would not be the last time he wetted his hands in blood this day.

They cleared close to twenty buildings of their inhabitants, moving swiftly in pairs from one to the next, killing those inside with barely a sound. Once they were done they reformed at the building closest to the inner gate. There was fifty feet of killing field between them and the wall, and now there was no one watching it.

From their position, they could see the portcullis behind the gate was guarded by a large unit of soldiers with shields and spears. Should Rose's army break through the gate, they would be trapped there while spearmen did as much damage as possible from the front and archers did as much damage as possible from the murder holes above.

"We can't take on all of 'em. Must be a hundred men," said a thin man with a thick moustache. His name was Olsen, and he was spotted with the blood of those they had already killed.

"They are not our objective," Pern said. He pointed towards a doorway that led into the wall itself. It looked small from so far away, set into such a large barrier of stone. "Our task is inside the walls. We have to find our way to the murder holes within and kill those inside. Then, we need to find the portcullis winch and raise it."

"What about the gate?" asked Olsen.

Pern did not have all the answers. The general had told him as much as he needed to know. It was safer that way in case Pern was captured.

"I was given no orders regarding the gate," Pern replied quietly. "We are to clear the murder holes, raise the portcullis, then remove our stolen uniforms and join up with the rest of the army."

"What if the army fails to break through, Captain?"

Pern paused for a moment. He was no captain. He had no rank whatsoever. He was Honin. Yet he was also in charge of these soldiers

"Then we see if thirteen men can take on one hundred." Pern

pointed at the soldiers guarding the portcullis. His men laughed, a nervous laughter and their auras matched it.

"Slow and steady," Pern said after a moment, "like we belong."

He stood from his position and started forwards, leading his unit towards the door to the inner wall.

Rose

Gritting her teeth did little to help with the pain, though it did wonders to help stop her from screaming. Rose had heard a great many stories of childbirth and even seen a fair number of other women go through the ordeal – pregnancies in a whore house were a simple fact of life. None of the stories or the witnessing prepared her for the pain. It felt as though the damned child was trying to tunnel its way out through her spine. Lucille was at her side, the smaller woman steadying Rose with a hand on her arm and soothing words. Pug stood at the entrance to the tent flap, his back turned so he wouldn't see Rose soil her dignity. Usually, dignity was something Rose took very seriously, but right now she swore she'd do just about anything to get the creature out of her.

Another wave of pain hit, and Rose staggered, catching herself on the table and screaming even through her gritted teeth. A face appeared through the tent flap, one of the soldiers set to guard her. Wide eyes peered at Rose for just a second then the face was gone. She hammered a fist down on the table and cried out again.

"Breathe," Lucille was saying.

Rose realised the little midwife was right, she was forgetting to breathe, and her vision was going a little blurry around the edges. She gasped, sucking down a few mouthfuls of glorious air and revelling in the brief respite from the pain.

Sweat plastered her hair to her head and dripped down her face. Her legs felt wet from the sweat and the blood and everything else, and the pain was just about all Rose could remember.

"How is the battle going, Pug?" Rose asked during a lull in the ordeal. She tried her best to look patient and in control. A quick glance at the mirror in the corner of the room told her she looked manic at best and ghastly at worst.

The squire ducked out of the tent flap leaving Rose alone with Lucille. The midwife was following Rose as she paced from one end to the other, keeping her steady and rattling off instructions.

"Isn't it time yet?" Rose asked. She was already exhausted, and the pushing, which she was assured was the worst part, hadn't even started yet.

"I can check again," Lucille offered.

Rose sighed and climbed onto the bed again, crawling onto her hands and knees and gripping hold of the table in front while Lucille manoeuvred behind and lifted up her dress.

"Almost," Lucille said.

"Really?" Rose couldn't keep the optimism out of her voice.

The tent flap moved, and Pug walked back in, his eyes going wide and his face flushing red. He quickly turned away to stare at the wall.

"The battle, Pug?"

"J-j-j-ust-t-t-t star-star-star..."

"Just started, yes," Rose said and then stopped to scream as another wave of pain hit her. The world went very bright and very painful. She gripped the table so hard her nails dug into the wood, and she could feel herself shaking.

"It's time," Lucille said after the wave of agony had died down. "On the next one, I need you to push as hard as you can."

Rose managed to nod along with the sobbing she couldn't keep down.

"Pug," Lucille continued. "On the table there. No, where I'm pointing. Yes, it's a stick I know. My lady, you may want to bite down on it."

Pug started feeling his way around the table to the bed, trying his best not to look at Rose as he held the stick out for her.

"Like a horse with a bit?" Rose asked, struggling not to collapse.

"Better than biting through your tongue, my lady."

Rose had to admit Lucille was certainly right about that bit. "The gates, Pug," she managed to say. "Are they open?"

The young squire shook his head. "N-no."

"Fuck!" Rose swore.

The next wave of pain started to come on, and Rose shoved the bit into her mouth and pushed, screaming out her pain.

Suzku

Inside the wall was cramped, damp, and dark. It reminded Pern of the cave - only without the possibility of trolls. The giant monsters wouldn't fit inside such close confines. Pern guessed the closeness was another purposeful design to keep the entire city almost impossible to assault. Even should the walls or the gate be taken, it was only possible to move single file up or down. Ten defenders could hold up against a thousand in such a situation. Luckily for Pern and his dozen, the defenders were not expecting an assault from inside the walls just yet, and so they found the winding staircase upwards to be undefended.

They soon found themselves in a maze of corridors and little rooms. The wall was nearly hollowed out in this section with multiple holes in the floor all looking down upon the tunnel that housed both the gate and the portcullis. The rooms were stocked high with arrows and each contained half a dozen soldiers, some resting, others staring down into the holes, ready to release a hail of arrows onto the attacking army.

The first lot of archers were more confused than alarmed as Pern and three of his dozen sauntered into the room. They were all wearing Crucible blacks, and no one expected that a small unit of soldiers had infiltrated those fleeing the slaughter at Rose's camp.

"Who are you?" asked one of the archers lounging by a wall, rubbing a cloth up and down the length of his unstrung bow.

"Sent to protect you," Pern said as he moved farther into the little room, two of his dozen following him in. "In case the wall is breached."

The archer laughed, drawing the attention of the other five in the room. "The wall is never going..." He was interrupted by a scream from somewhere nearby.

Pern's sword cleared his scabbard in an instant and the first of the archers went down with a rent neck and a spray of blood against the far wall. Nine men in a small room made for close fighting and Pern's sword was not the handiest of weapons in such a situation, but it was still far better than attempting to use a bow at such close range.

The second archer died with Pern's sword through his gut and the third charged, dropping his bow and swinging fists at Pern's face.

Pern left his sword in one man's gut and wrestled with the archer, brushing away flailing arms until he could grab hold of the man's head. He crashed the archer against a nearby wall four times until the skull cracked and the body stopped moving. Pern let the corpse fall to the stone floor and retrieved his sword.

The other three archers were dead now as well, and Pern's soldiers were still intact. They had no time to celebrate their little victory; there were other rooms to clear, other people to kill. As they moved from the room, Pern took one last look back. Already there was blood starting to run towards the holes in the floor, dripping down into the tunnel below like crimson rain.

The next rooms went almost as cleanly with the archers providing little resistance despite being ready. Arrows were loosed as Pern and his soldiers rushed through doorways, but some of his troops had brought shields, and once they were in the room the archers stood little chance of fighting back.

Room to room they moved through the warren inside the inner wall of Crucible, slaughtering as they went. Pern lost four of his dozen clearing out the murder holes and took a knock to the head that staggered him, making his ears ring, and his eyes go white. When he recovered, he found the archers dead and one of his own men looking down on him. Pern nodded, ignoring the pain that brought, and struggled back to his feet. He threw up. A wave of vertigo turning his stomach upside down.

He didn't want to admit it, even to himself, but Pern knew he was testing his limits. In the last few days, he'd barely slept, had eaten next to nothing, and had taken enough injuries to put most folk firmly in the ground.

In just a handful of days, he had fought his clan, brought back to un-life by foul magic. He had fought trolls and a necromancer. He had fought an invading army all mounted on horseback. And now he was deep inside the enemy's stronghold, fighting them once again.

Pern wasn't the sort of man to look at the bigger picture. When he looked back at all he had done, looked forward to all he still had to do, he found it exhausted him. It was much better to live in the now, moving from moment to moment, following someone else's plan.

With the murder holes cleared it was time to move onto the next stage of the general's plan. They needed to raise the portcullis. The giant iron grate was raised and lowered by a winch system that Anders assured them was located further up into the wall. It would require four men at the very least to operate, six if they wanted it done quickly.

"Are you alright, sir?" asked one of the soldiers.

Pern nodded slowly. He was leaning against a damp wall, his eyes closed as he fought the waves of nausea and exhaustion that threatened to unman him.

"I am... Honin," Pern replied and pushed away from the wall, opening his eyes and taking only a moment to find his bearings before heading towards the exit, stepping over the bodies of the recently dead–four archers and one of their own.

As nine men they ascended the staircase single file again, Pern leading the way with sword drawn. They were still wearing their stolen Crucible blacks, but that was no guarantee any more. It was quite possible those above had heard the shouts and the brief sounds of battle. It was also quite possible they might spot the fresh blood that speckled the soldiers making their way up the stairs.

Nearly encased in stone as they were, they could hear no sounds of the battle that would be waging outside. It seemed odd to Pern that so many men and women could be dying out there, just a short distance away, and he could neither see nor hear any of it.

Shadows moved up ahead, and Pern heard the soft scuff of leather on stone and hushed voices. He rounded the next bend and stopped just a woman flew at him with daggers drawn.

Pern's sword was next to useless in such close confines and so was his height and weight advantage. He flowed sideways against the outer wall of the staircase, pushing at the woman's arms. One knife found his hip and bright white agony flared to life.

Overbalanced and with no purchase, the woman floundered in mid-air before crashing down face first. The soldiers behind Pern wasted no time in stamping the life out of the attacker.

Another soldier waited a few stairs up, short sword drawn, watching Pern as though he hoped the fight wouldn't come. Even with a fresh wound slowing him down, Pern rushed up the stairs to meet the man, brushing aside the frenzied swipe with his own blade and then barrelling into the man, bearing them both to the ground.

Pern rolled aside and let his own men edge forwards to stab the unfortunate soldier as he lay prostrate. It was not a pleasant way to go, nor a heroic one, but the fool had been foolish enough to attack them on the stairs, and even more foolish not to bring adequate numbers to the defence.

Back on his feet with two fresh corpses behind him, Pern continued on. He was limping now, fresh blood soaking into his trousers, pain with every step. There was no time to rest though, no time to dress his wound and heal. If the portcullis wasn't raised Rose's army couldn't break through, and if they didn't breach the city, Pern and what remained of his dozen were as good as dead.

A doorway opened up to the left, the staircase continuing upwards. Pern stopped and glanced through the opening. An arrow loosed and Pern pulled his head back inside the stairwell. The deadly projectile clattered against the wall nearby and dropped to the ground.

"Narrow corridor," Pern said, his voice a whisper to his remaining eight. "At least twenty feet. Door at the far end blocked by shields. Archers watching."

He let out a sigh. They had a couple of shields between them, but they were small things and wouldn't protect them nearly well enough. There seemed little they could do against twenty feet of killing ground.

Worst of all was that in the flickering light Pern recognised one of the faces at the far end of the corridor. Captain Lost. The very man tasked with protecting the Black Thorn.

Anders

"Go find the boss' body," Anders grumbled in a fairly poor representation of Rose's voice. "Nice easy job." That she might never had said the second part was a sober thought that the majority of Anders' drunken mind rejected.

He kicked at the outstretched hand of a corpse. The man might have been quite handsome in life, but in death, he was just another grotesque in a sea of them. Face frozen in pain or terror, dried blood at the corner of the mouth, rotting wound in the chest. They all looked much the same as any other when they were dead. The living were ever a far more interesting lot to Anders' eyes and most certainly to his nose.

Somewhere around ten thousand people had died outside the city walls just a few days ago and the inhabitants of the city hadn't yet had time to clear the field of bodies. In fact, they had taken those who had died inside and deposited them outside, adding to the mountains of putrid, rotting flesh.

It never failed to amaze Anders how quickly the flesh of men and women turned to rot once the bodies were nothing but that. Between the smell of that flesh, the smell of loosened bowels, and the sight of birds, both great and small, tearing into open wounds to pull out stringy red meat... Well between those things Anders was finding it fairly hard to keep his breakfast down. Only his steadfast refusal to lose the alcohol churning in his stomach was stopping him from bending over and retching.

The sounds of battle drifted over the wall and down towards him as he picked his way in between corpses. He couldn't see the battle, but he was fairly sure there would be men and women dying up there too; some on the outer wall, some at the gates, waiting for General Verit's insurgents to open the way from the inside.

Occasionally an arrow would overshoot its mark and drop down somewhere nearby. Anders was too close to the outer wall for any of them to hit, but it was fairly unnerving all the same. He was not unaware that he had been given the safest job Rose had to offer, but he was also quite aware of just how daunting a task it was.

"Find one body in amongst TEN FUCKING THOUSAND!" Anders shouted as he took another vicious kick at a body, this time aiming for the corpse's face and connecting with solid *thwack* and a blossom of pain in his big toe, the same one he so recently cracked on a tent peg.

"Fuck, fuck, fuck, fuck, fuck, fuck, FUCK!" Anders finished his tirade by glaring at the offending corpse and giving his shoulders a good slump. He had to admit it wasn't the daunting nature of the task that put him in such a foul mood, but the task itself. He didn't want to see his friend's body. In a lifetime of watching those he knew and loved die, Anders simply wasn't sure he could take it any more.

He judged he was near to where Thorn had fallen, but it was quite hard to tell so close up. Not to mention his own memory of the event was rather incomplete as he was far too busy at the time wanting to believe it was all a rather bad dream.

A little flower of hope blossomed inside. There was no guarantee Anders even had a chance of finding Thorn's body. He'd fallen out of the wall at some speed, it was true, but there was ten feet of solid ground at the base of the wall followed by nearly double that as a moat. It was entirely possible Thorn had hit the water and sunk. Given that the moat was murky with mud and blood and bloated bodies already, Anders decided his willingness to take a dip to look for the body of his deceased boss to be somewhere below non-existent.

All in all, his search seemed like quite the fruitless endeavour, and Anders still wasn't even sure he really wanted to find Thorn. Ignoring the idea of finding his friend's dead body being quite disturbing, there was also the slight problem that Rose would likely be angry at Anders for not bringing Thorn back alive, no matter how unfair that might be.

Anders let loose a growl. "I promise you this, boss, if you're dead I will head on down to whatever Hell you're terrorising and drag you back up here to deal with your pregnant, slightly deranged wife."

A worthless threat really given that he was threatening a dead man, and Anders had it on good authority that none of the Hells actually existed anyway. No Hells, only Death's Grey Isle. Which wasn't really all that grey anyway. Nor was it an island, now Anders thought about it.

Anders was just about ready to give up and take to looting the dead when he spotted Alistair D'roan's lifeless corpse half in the moat and half not. It appeared the bastard had survived the fall somehow, but not the fairly grisly wound on his neck. Anders had seen bites before, and this one looked bad. So bad he gave up trying to control his stomach and got rid of his breakfast right there beside the moat. There was something about seeing someone he knew dead. Something that made it more real, even when it was someone he truly hated.

Eventually, Anders got control of his convulsing stomach and knelt down next to D'roan's body. He was soaked through and had the same look of fear and pain on his face that so many of the dead did.

"Couldn't happen to a more deserving bastard," Anders announced.

The corpse of Alistair D'roan did not argue. His ghost gave it a go though, and Anders ignored it.

"What's that? You agree with me that you were a complete cunt in life, and you're glad I had your son murdered? That's very nice of you to say, Alistair. I think this may be the first time we've ever agreed on anything. Now, could you perchance point me in the direction of your murderer? I know you never really got on with Rose during your life, but I think you'll agree that death tends to lend a new perspective to things, no? And she would like to see her husband's body for some reason. I know. I didn't ask, and I wouldn't advise you do either."

Anders let out a chuckle. "What's that? Just over there, you say?" He looked up to find the Black Thorn right where the dead body of Alistair D'roan had told him to look.

Anders stood up with a groan and stepped up onto the lifeless chest of D'roan and down the other side of him. He approached Thorn slowly, wincing and not at all sure of what he was expecting or hoping to find.

The Black Thorn was very much still in the moat with only his head and one arm, ending in a bloody stump, out in the open air. His face looked pale and slack, features tugging to the left slightly from the burn scar.

Anders bent down, grabbed Thorn under the shoulders and heaved backwards, slipping and sliding in the mud as he slowly pulled the man's body up out of the moat and onto dry land. It took a whole lot of dragging and even more grunting and groaning before he had Thorn's body all the way out of the wet, and when he did the damage looked even worse.

Thorn's left hand was missing, no doubt about that, and Anders was a little afraid to look under what was left of the bandages. His face was pale, but bruised, and he had a right leg that was very clearly broken. Worst of all was the fact that the Black Thorn was well and truly dead. There was simply no mistaking it.

"Shit," Anders breathed at last and slumped down onto the ground next to Thorn.

He fumbled at his jacket pocket and realised his hands were shaking and not just a little. Eventually, he reached inside and pulled out his hip flask, worrying at the top and resisting the urge to scream. He took a deep swig once the lid was off and relished the taste. Anders loved a great many different types of alcohol, actually he was fairly certain he'd never met a drink he didn't like, but whiskey was without a doubt his favourite, and it just so happened that Rose and Thorn had a bottle in their tent that was untouched. At least it had been untouched until earlier in the morning, and now it was very close to empty.

Glancing down at the body again, Anders felt the need to look away. He'd seen dead bodies aplenty, and he'd even been dead once or twice himself, not to mention having caused a fair bit of the final condition, but this felt different. This was one of his friends, probably his closest of friends given that Henry swung between comrade and threatening to gut him on a fairly regular basis.

Anders took another swig and swallowed it down quickly. "Drink to the fallen," he said, holding his flask up to the giant wall that loomed up above him, casting him in shadow. He lowered his flask and tipped a healthy swig over the Black Thorn's scarred lips before taking another himself.

"You know, I hate this city, boss." Anders sat cross-legged on the ground surrounded by dead bodies and stared up at the walls. "Always have. Everything bad that has ever happened to me has had something to do with this shit hole. And yes, I do include the very inconvenient mess that was being born.

"When you said Rose was going to tear down the walls." Anders laughed. "I was happy. I actually hoped she would, and she'd also set fire to the whole fucking place while she was at it. Of course, then I realised how hopeful thinking that was. Should have just left it well and truly alone. Should have just left my family to rot away and fade out hiding inside their stone prison.

"I appear to have gone a bit maudlin. I'm very sorry. Probably not at all what you want to hear after just waking up, hmm?"

Thorn let out a groan and coughed, muddy water spilling up out of his mouth and over his face. The coughing turned to retching and was followed by a lot more moat water. His eyelid flickered, and his big body began to move. First his left arm and then Anders realised his right was still tied to his belt.

"Let me get that for you, boss." Anders plucked the knife from his boot, leaned across and sawed through the rope holding Thorn's right hand in place. "Quite disorientating coming back, I know first hand."

"Why's it dark?" Thorn asked in a slow, rasping voice.

"Could be the walls blocking out the sun," Anders suggested. "Could be the shadow of death still looming over you. Could be that you haven't opened your eye yet. Takes a few moments for the body to remember how to be a body."

"Eh?" Thorn opened his eye and raised both arms and stared at them as though for the first time. He struggled to sit up and cried out in pain.

"Easy, boss," Anders cooed. "Pretty sure your leg is broken, and your face has seen better days. Not many of them to be honest."

"Anders?"

"Not the sight most folk want to come back to see, I know. Probably wish I was your wife right about now. Well, maybe not right now. Judging from what I know of the experience, Rose is probably not a particularly welcoming sight right now."

"Rose?"

"Your wife," Anders said with a nod. "Fairly terrifying. Heavily pregnant. Did I mention terrifying? Don't worry, it'll all come back in a few moments."

"What?" Thorn groaned again and grimaced through the pain as he struggled to sit up. "I threw myself over the wall."

"Yes. I was wondering about that, boss. Why?"

Thorn frowned and buried his head in his hand, spitting up even more muddy water. "I... um... I remember tasting oil. Smelled it. There were rope. That fucker D'roan was gonna burn me an' hang the body for good measure. Didn't much fancy it."

"Rightly so. I have it on good authority that burning hurts. Your's, in fact." Anders took another swig from his hip flask to find it running low. He held it out for Thorn to take.

"The battle?" Thorn asked.

"Waging as we speak. The general has a cunning plan, I assure you, though I must admit to having no clue as to how it is going." Anders paused for a moment and cocked his head towards the wall. "It sounds bloody. Can a thing sound bloody?"

"Rose?" Thorn asked after swigging from Anders' flask.

Anders let out a chuckle.

"What?"

Anders shrugged and grinned at Thorn. "I just... I suppose it takes someone of quite extraordinary character to come back from the dead and ask about others before themselves. Trust me; I've been there. First thing out of my mouth was '*Oh shit, how am I still breathing and where's the booze?*'."

"I was dead?" Thorn asked.

Anders shrugged.

"I saw..."

"I know." Anders nodded. "Seen it too, boss. Been dead once or twice. Makes you wonder if those bastards over in the Five Kingdoms have it right, no? His name is Azara, in case you were wondering. Five Kingdomers call him Merlet and the Acanthians just call him death. Many names and many faces, but all roads lead to his kingdom."

Thorn sniffed, and his eye focused on Anders, the intensity right back to normal. "Rose?"

"Last I saw she just starting to pop and still giving everyone orders. Told me to come and find you, in fact. That was a while back though; I suppose she might have pushed the brat out by now. I must admit I'm not sure how long that sort of thing usually takes."

"You really chopped ya brother's cock off?" Thorn asked, frowning as though he were still trying to sort through recent memories. Anders could well understand that. Coming back was a little disorientating no matter how many times you did it. Every damned time one more piece of him left behind in that place.

Anders let out a shuddering sigh and picked at some of the dried blood underneath a fingernail. "It wasn't really my idea. I... your wife is..." He shook his head and then plastered a smile on his face. "Best not to dwell on things, boss."

"You brought me back." The way Thorn said it was more of an accusation than a thanking.

"You've saved my life enough times, boss. It's not really any different."

"It's different, Anders. Ya wanna tell me how?"

"Nope. Don't worry, boss. You're still you. You're just going to have to trust me this time."

"Help me up," Thorn growled.

"Already? Don't you want to sit and contemplate our place in the world a bit more?"

"Anders!"

Thinking better of further arguing, Anders scrambled to his feet and helped pick Thorn up from the ground. There was an awful lot of leaning going on, and most of it was falling quite heavily on Anders' shoulders. He looked up at the distance between them and the camp and let out a sigh.

"Sooner it gets done, the sooner it's done," Thorn growled and started forwards, wincing with every step despite Anders supporting most of his weight.

Henry

Henry was first up the rope right after Marline scuttled up it for the third time. '*Born to climb*', one of the other soldiers called her, and Henry could believe it was true. Henry, on the other hand, was not born to climb. And she thoroughly hoped she wasn't born to fall. There were two others on the rope below her, Long Tall and the Weird One with the lust for tying folk up. Henry doubted she could expect being caught and rescued should gravity assert itself. She shimmied up and up, gripping with her feet and with her hands, looking neither up nor down. It wasn't the first time Henry had been suspended by very little above a watery grave, though she thoroughly hoped it would be the last time.

It came as a bit of a surprise when arms reached down to help her up and sunlight muted by grey clouds bathed her face. Henry climbed up over the lip of the well and stared about with wide eyes, hands going straight to the daggers sheaved at her belt. Marline barely spared her a glance as the climber quickly went back to the well to help the next person up and out.

Now they were here, deep inside the enemy city, Henry realised just how exposed they were. The well opened up into a small square filled with empty stalls and surrounded by low buildings. She was standing in a market and a big one at that.

Long Tall flopped out of the well and rolled to a stop on the dusty ground beneath her, breathing heavy and eyes wide and fearful. Marline went back to the well again.

"Up!" Henry hissed, reaching down and half pulling the freakishly tall woman to her feet. "Gotta be quick an' quiet. Don't like how exposed we are."

Long Tall wasted no time in taking the bow from over her shoulder and knocking an arrow. Biggest bow Henry had ever seen, now she thought about it. Almost as tall as the woman holding it.

"I don't see no one," Long Tall whispered and Henry was glad to discover the woman could lower her booming voice. "Shouldn't there be good folk around or somethin'?"

"Middle of a fuckin' war," Henry replied as the weird one struggled out of the well. "Smart good folk will be hidin' in their homes. 'Sides, they ain't really so much a threat. It's the soldiers I'm worried 'bout avoidin'."

The Weird One struggled to his feet, bulging eyes beneath the glasses whipping one way then the other. He already had a whip coiled in one hand and short, curved sword in the other. Henry didn't like the looks of the Weird One, but then it was often the ones she didn't like the look of who were most useful in a pinch.

The rest of her crew appeared out of the well one by one, and before long all nine of them were ready to go. They waited just long enough for the captain to appear, the one all the soldiers answered to. They didn't need to wait around, but Henry thought it would be best.

"You still here?" the captain asked almost as soon as his head popped out of the stone well.

"Wanted ta say goodbye," Henry said with a sneer that quickly slipped from her face. Truth was she didn't really have anything to say and little reason to wait for the captain. Truth was she was just a little bit nervous about leading her own crew of cut-throats.

"Right. You know your role?" the captain.

"Fuck you!" Henry spat at the man's feet and turned away, not waiting to see if her crew followed after her. The captain and his lot would scurry out of their watery hole and attack the gate. Chances were most of them wouldn't make it back. Probably still better chances than Henry and most of her lot of making it back though. Deep inside the enemy's city, they had to find the bastards who ran the place, probably the most heavily guarded lot, and try not to kill them.

"Ya know where we're goin'?" asked the Weird One as they reached the edge of the market.

Henry turned on the bastard and had him pressed up against a stall with a knife to his throat before he realised she'd even heard him. She grinned up into his face and pressed the knife close to his skin.

"'Course I fuckin' know. Probably the only one of us been here before." She left out the part that last time she was in Crucible it had been in chains and ended in her escaping her own execution.

Henry was aware that the rest of the crew had gathered around and were watching rather intently, though no one looked to be in the mind to interfere. She wondered how Thorn did it, kept folk in check like he did. Maybe it was because people liked to follow a good leader who seemed to know what they were about, and he certainly liked to sound as if he did. Of course, Henry knew that most of the time the bastard was just winging it and making shit up as he went along.

"Alright," the Weird One said, holding up his hands complete with whip and sword. "Just checkin'. Lead the way, boss."

Henry backed up a step and nodded. She glanced around at the others. "Aye. Alright. It's the centre of the city. Big fuckin' buildin' looks like a boat but upside down. Rounded roof."

Henry took another step back. She hated the idea of turning her back on the Weird One after threatening him, but she knew it was something she had to do. Had to show them all she wasn't afraid of them. With one final nod, more to gather her courage than anything else, Henry turned and stalked out of the cluster of stalls towards the buildings waiting nearby.

She waited, jaw clenched and nerves fraying, but she received neither a sword in her back nor a whip coiling around her neck.

They didn't make it to their target without being spotted and nor did they make it without incident. Luckily for Henry, she had just the sort of crew to deal with both.

At first, it was a few of the good folk, people trapped in Crucible with the blooded and their army. The good folk took no part in the game for the most, they just went about their lives working, fucking, keeping their heads down. Unfortunately for them, it was the good folk who tended to get stabbed when those playing the game went at each other.

The first to spot them was a man of middling years and greying hair, opening his window at the wrong time. Burns crashed through the man's door with his shoulder, and Long Tall followed him in. One strangled cry and a few moments later and it was done. Henry didn't stop to watch, nor look in at the aftermath. There was a time she would have, just to see the colour of the man's blood, even already knowing it would be red. Different shades of red though, some lighter or darker. Everybody was slightly different on the outside and slightly different on the inside.

They crept along as quiet as possible after that little spot of murder, Henry hoping they'd draw no more attention. Good folk might get caught up in the game often enough, but that didn't mean they deserved it.

The second time they were spotted things didn't go quite so smoothly. They were passing by a tall building, looked to be at least two stories high, and just up ahead was the main thoroughfare and the very building they were looking for. Built on a rise in the ground, so folk had to go up a bunch of steps to see their betters, it was one of the largest buildings in the city. Didn't look like much when compared to other cities, but here in Crucible, it was the closest thing they'd find to a mansion. No walls around it, but a dozen soldiers stood around outside.

A cry went up. A woman's voice shrill and close by. Henry winced. The Weird One moved fast, and the scream vanished at the same time the whip cracked. He pulled hard on the whip, dragging the woman off her feet and closer. She was a thin slip of a girl, barely looked old enough to bleed. Pretty despite the mud and dust on her face. The Weird One stabbed his curved sword into her belly twice while keeping the whip coiled tight around her neck to stop her from screaming. Henry didn't even have a chance to stop him. It didn't make a drop of difference; the guards had already heard the shout and were on their way to investigate.

"Looks like it's time for a fight," Henry said, grinning and wishing she still had her hat. It did a good job of hiding her scarred face, and folk tended to underestimate her if they couldn't see the scars– something to do with being so small, she reckoned.

They were outnumbered, though not by a lot, and that made things difficult. Henry didn't like to fight fair odds, too much chance of not making it out the other side. It was always so much safer when they had numbers on their side, either that or surprise and right now they were lacking both. A straight-up fight was likely to end in blood on both sides of it, and the soldiers had more bodies to spare and more chance of reinforcements.

The fear poked cold fingers through Henry's chest, and she saw that battle down at the gates once more. Trapped by the press, barely able to move. Stabbing, slashing, stabbing. Luck, both good and bad, the only factor in whether she survived or died one more nameless among thousands.

"We got a plan?" asked Burns as he struck at flint to light the torch he was holding. Henry had never heard of someone purposefully fighting with a flaming torch, but now she thought about it, it seemed a real clever idea.

She forced down the cold fear, desperately blinking away the blurred edges of her vision. This wasn't a battle; this was a fight. This was where Henry the Red excelled. This and knife work in the dark. Wasn't too long ago she had sworn to stop doing this sort of thing. An oath made to herself and for herself. But Thorn wouldn't let it go. He wouldn't let Henry the Red just be Henry. He needed her to be his quiet blade at least one more time.

"Kill the fuckers. Try not ta die," Henry replied and stepped forwards into the street to face the oncoming soldiers. She twirled her little daggers around in her hands, trying to look menacing, trying to hide the fear, and fixed the lead soldier with a baleful glare.

Eleven soldiers had left the safety of the big building and the final one, a big bastard with a big axe, watched for a moment before turning and pushing through the doorway. That left eleven against nine, and those odds were slightly better.

Henry heard a *twang,* and the first soldier died with an arrow sticking out of one eye. She glanced back to find Long Tall already pulling another from her quiver. Ten against nine was even better odds.

The soldiers didn't look like they liked the idea of standing around and waiting for Long Tall to pick them off, so they charged. Moving together at a run. The last thing any of Henry's crew wanted was a crash and the crush of combat, so they spread out around the dusty street, forcing the soldiers to turn and meet them. This was where Henry the Red excelled, in a fight where she could single folk out, kill them up close, and then get stabby from behind.

A whip cracked, and one of the soldiers lost his feet, but Henry didn't have time to take advantage of it as she was being rushed by two men both with short swords and round shields. It was a piss poor match up when she thought about it, but Henry had long ago realised that thinking about it was a good way to end up dead.

She brushed away a sword stroke and kicked the shield as hard as she could. Didn't have much weight to put behind the boot though so it just ended with her taking a few steps back.

The second soldier moved around to Henry's left, trying to flank her. She took a low stance, on the balls of her feet, ready to leap away when one of the bastards came close. Then the first soldier collapsed, screaming. He had an arrow buried deep in his thigh.

Henry leapt at the second soldier, getting in too close for him to use his sword and stabbing around his shield. She took a hard knock to the chest and reckoned she'd have a bruised left tit when all was said and done, but her knife found soft flesh, and she twisted the blade, watching the agony on the soldier's face as she tore up his insides.

The first soldier was already dead by the time Henry finished with the second, one arrow in his thigh and another in his neck. Long Tall wasted no time in selecting another target, and another soldier went down. Burns was down too, his torch lying forgotten in the dust as a young woman wearing Crucible blacks stabbed into his body again and again with her sword. A whip cracked and coiled around the woman's neck, and she came out of her bloodlust just in time to eat a curved sword.

Two soldiers were cornering the big man, Ogre, with the mallet, and he was falling back again and again towards the buildings on the left. Henry charged forwards without a sound and planted both daggers into the back of one of the men, bearing him down to the ground before springing up and back to her feet. She was too late though, the other soldier charged forwards and stuck a sword in Ogre's gut. Two giant hands found the soldier's head and the man screamed as thumbs dug into eye sockets. Both of them died together, locked in a grisly embrace.

Things were not going as Henry had hoped. Her first time in charge of folk and already two were dead. She turned back to the others to find another one, a young man with pretty eyes and an ugly smile, lying face down in the dust. Three out of nine of them dead already.

The final soldier dropped when a second arrow hit him in the chest. Henry wasn't about to check each and every corpse, but it seemed Long Tall had been involved in a good few of the kills.

"Ya pretty fuckin' handy with that thing," Henry said with a sneer as she grouped up with the survivors.

Long Tall shrugged. "They gave me plenty of room," she boomed.

It was almost a shame to find the Weird One had survived. Of all the members of her little crew, Henry would have liked to see that one in the ground most of all. Even more of a shame to see Burns dead. Henry had thought him a reasonable enough man for someone who got his name from setting fire to shit.

"That it?" the Weird One asked as he re-coiled his whip. "I expected more of a fight."

Henry ignored the bastard and started towards the big building, stepping over the bodies in her way. She mounted the steps two at a time, eager to find the blooded within. Two giant elephant skulls watched them from the top of the stairs through empty sockets. Anders had once said that his father had killed them both with his own two hands. It dawned on Henry then that capturing the blooded lord might not be as easy as Rose wanted it to be. Hopefully, Anders was lying as he often did.

The doors were a bit heavier than Henry expected, and it took a bit of help from the Weird One to get them moving, but once they did, they swung open and hit the walls with a loud *boom*. It was fair to say she had just announced their presence.

The others followed her in, and Henry crept along at a slow pace. There were no torches, and the gloom was thick with dust hanging in the air. They were in an antechamber, a good ten foot by that again with a couple of benches and little else of note. Beyond was a single doorway, and Henry knew from experience it led into a large hall the Brekovich's used for banquets and the like. She almost expected to find the bastards sat around eating while folk died for them, but the hall was empty save for a couple of mangy dogs hunting around for scraps. One of the dogs barked at them and ran off, but the other ignored them in favour of a bone it was gnawing on.

Week-old straw covered the floor, and the tables and benches sat empty. Up at the end of the hall sat a small throne on a slightly raised dais. Henry didn't remember the throne from before, but then it had been a few years since she was last in the hall, and Niles Brekovich was just about the only blooded lord still alive. Didn't surprise her that he might want to call himself some sort of king given that they were right in the centre of the City of Kings.

A strangled cry went up from behind, and Henry turned to find Long Tall choking on her own blood with a few feet of steel sticking out of her chest. As she dropped, her eyes already going blank, a broad battleaxe buried itself in Urting Uther.

The twelfth soldier, the big one with a mad glint in his eyes, stood between them and the entrance, or exit depending on how it was looked at. Henry had seen the man before and reckoned his name was Torival. Not that his name really mattered much.

The three remaining members of Henry's little crew backed into the room, away from the battleaxe-wielding madman. Just the Weird One and a tall lad with a lazy eye left to back her up now. Three on one sounded like good odds, but there was something about the madman with the axe. Something that made Henry want to run and hide.

Suzku

Pern could feel his blood boiling. He was Honin, trained as Haarin; his emotions should not be allowed to surface so freely. He fought for control and lost. He was glad he was unable to see his own aura, the red seeping into it would have only disgraced him further.

They were still trapped in the stairwell, unable to enter the corridor beyond the opening. Unable to get to the winch that would raise the portcullis. They were also cut off from the battle outside. Pern had no idea how it was going, whether the army was already at the gate, whether they had broken through and were now relying on Pern's group to raise the portcullis. The entire battle could be lost on their failure to move down a corridor held by a handful of archers.

"Sir?" asked on the men, one of the few left.

They had only three shields, and each one was a small round thing barely more than a wooden buckler. Pern remembered Swift claiming he could pluck arrows out of the air and loose them back at the enemy, it seemed a baseless claim, but then Swift had been a dangerous man. For a brief moment, Pern considered attempting the feat. The madness quickly passed only to be replaced by a different form.

"Shield," Pern growled, and the closest soldier complied immediately. He took a deep breath and let his anger and shame burn bright inside. "Follow me in."

"What?" a couple of the soldiers asked in unison, but Pern had no time for their complaints and no time to wonder what might happen if they didn't follow his order.

The first couple of arrows hit the little shield, sharpened heads punching through the wood and the impact jarring Pern, but not stopping him. He launched into a crouched charge, headlong down the corridor with the shield held up to protect as much of his head and chest as possible.

Pern roared, screaming as he tore away at the distance between him and the winch room. He wasn't sure if he was shouting to scare the enemy soldiers, or to bolster his own courage. He wasn't even sure if it was courage that was driving him onward.

Another arrow thudded into the shield, and something hard punched into his right leg, almost making him fall. Pern stumbled, and the last of his breath ripped out of him in a scream of agony.

His leg hurt like it was on fire, but it held and Pern continued his charge. Another arrow whisked past, and there was a scream from behind. Then Pern was down the length of the corridor. He had just enough time to see the little wall of shields blocking the doorway before he hit it, crashing into the soldiers and collapsing over the top. The world whipped over and over in a blur of movement, dark grey stone, and men shouting at him. The arrow lodged in his leg pulled against something, the shaft snapping but not before it dimmed Pern's vision from the pain.

He heard a second crashing and shouting as the soldiers behind Pern followed him into the winch room. Rolling away and staggering to his feet, Pern shook the shield from his arm and looked up just in time to block a sword stroke. The blow hit him hard, almost breaking through his defence, and the follow-up swing knocked him back to the floor. Pern rolled again, gasping at the pain in his leg, and used the momentum to flow back to his feet. He staggered backwards as the Crucible soldier came at him until something solid hit his back, arresting his momentum with solid stone.

A sword flashed out at Pern, and he brought his own blade up again. Metal clashed against metal, and he launched himself off the wall, shouldering the man in front of him, sending him staggering away.

Between the pain in his leg, that in his arm and in his chest, and the knock he had taken to his head, Pern was certain it was only his rage that was keeping him going. He didn't feel in control and neither could he find the composure that he used to win his fights. He swung his blade at the man in front of him once and then again, wild swings that were blocked with ease. Each time the man backed away a step, and each time Pern stepped in to fill the gap between them.

It was Captain Lost, Pern realised. The Crucible soldier in front of him, the man he was fighting. It was Captain Lost, the man who had sworn to protect the Black Thorn.

"Traitor!" Pern hissed, fixing the man with a glare he thought Thorn would be proud of. "OATHBREAKER!"

Captain Lost looked worried. Even in the dim, flickering light of the torches, Pern could see the fear on the man's face. He held his sword up though, a good defensive stance.

To Pern's left lay the winch, a giant wooden construct in the centre of the room. Beyond it, he could see what was left of his own soldiers fighting with the Crucible men. He was behind them all, facing off against a man who should already have been dead.

Lost feinted right and then twisted, stabbing in from the left. Pern almost fell for it, already halfway to bringing his sword to bear when the real attack came. It was an obvious move and one he should have seen coming. Instead, he just about managed to stumble out of the way of the blade, limping and favouring his right leg heavily.

"You were supposed to protect him," Pern accused, limping forwards and bringing his sword down in a heavy two-handed strike.

Lost brushed the stroke away and stepped backwards, eyes darting about for some way to gain the advantage. He shook his head. "I..."

"YOU SWORE TO PROTECT HIM!" Pern pushed forwards again. Two steps each with a wild swing that connected only with steel. "You betrayed him."

Again, Lost shook his head. "I was never working for him. Can't betray a man if I was always on the other side."

"You lie. You swore an oath to protect him and switched sides when he needed you most. You disgraced yourself and your clan!"

"What?" Lost waved his sword at Pern and then danced back and around the giant winch in the centre of the room, trying to put something between the two of them. Maybe the Captain knew Pern was bleeding, knew he was wounded. If he could draw the fight out long enough, Pern might succumb to his wounds or the other Crucible soldiers might come to his aid.

Pern shook his head, trying to clear the fuzzy edges. Lost was right. He hadn't sworn to protect Thorn, and he had no clan to dishonour. Pern did though.

He was Haarin once. One of the best bodyguards in the world. His clan took the money, and he protected the client. It had been his job to protect Swift in life or follow him into death. Instead, Pern betrayed his vows. He may not have dealt the killing blow, but he gave Henry the sword to do it. Swift was evil, a monster of a man, of that there could be no doubt. Pern believed Thorn to be a better man, more honourable. Now he wasn't so sure.

Lost was moving farther around the winch now, emboldened by the fact that Pern had stopped. He stood there, still as stone, with the winch in front of him and the Crucible soldiers behind, battling against his own troops.

Pern's thoughts were a maelstrom of chaos. He had seen the things the Black Thorn had done or had ordered done. Pern himself had done things in Thorn and Rose's names that he couldn't justify. He was no longer sure he hadn't discarded his honour for nothing. Disgraced his clan for nothing.

Thoughts of his clan only paralysed him further. They were dead because of him. They had come here because of him, and the necromancer had killed them, brought them back and damned their spirits to wander the world, cold and lost. All because of him.

The rage drained away from Pern, but the shame did not. He realised his anger was never directed at Captain Lost but at him himself. And now he understood why.

Lost still watched Pern from the other side of the winch, a look of confusion on his face.

Now the anger was gone, Pern felt the pain wash over him. A dozen different wounds clamoured for his attention, and his sword point dipped. He was struggling to stay standing, and the fight wasn't even done yet.

With a sigh, Pern turned his back to Lost. In front of him, the remaining Crucible soldiers held back his own men. With three practised sword strokes Pern ended the fight and the final five of his men flooded into the room.

Pern heard the clatter of steel hitting stone as Captain Lost dropped his sword and dropped to his knees. The men did not show him the mercy he begged for.

"Turn the winch," Pern said, his voice slow and sluggish to his ears. His sword dropped from his hand, and he staggered into the corner of the room, slumping down against the wall. He needed to rest, if only for a little while.

𝕳enry

"Ain't no sort of sense ta this fight," Henry said from a low crouch. She was ready to spring into movement at a drop, a true pit fighter stance. Didn't mean she wanted the fight.

The Weird One swished his whip about, trailing it across the floor and keeping a good distance. Seemed to know his stuff, the Weird One. The lad with the lazy eye edged sideways, trying to move around and flank the mad-eyed axe wielder.

"Killing you makes sense," the axe-wielder said, his voice a growl. He stared straight at Henry, almost looking like he was paying the others no attention at all. Henry knew better though; he wanted Lazy Eye to attack and was giving him an opening. "Saving my lord makes sense."

"Aye," Henry agreed. "It would if we was here ta kill him. We ain't though. Ain't here ta kill any of 'em. Here ta protect 'em."

The mad-eyed axe wielder squinted, and Henry saw his jaw clench.

"Sounds odd, right? Truth fuckin' does. Usually."

"Why?" the axe-wielder didn't relax a drop.

Truth was Henry didn't really know what she was doing. Stalling for time, maybe? Hoping the man would relax long enough for the Weird One to crack his whip? All she really knew was she didn't want to fight the man because she knew she'd lose.

"'Cos pretty fuckin' soon Rose's army is gonna swarm through this city murderin' folk as soldiers do when their blood is up. Reckon ya know that much. Ain't just me an' my merry few got in. Got a few hundred folk opening the gates. Won't be long now 'til that big wall of yours is lost and once it is... Well, then the city is lost.

"We're here ta find what's left of the blooded. Stand in front of 'em an' stop the rest of Rose's lot from..."

"You're Henry the Red," the axe-wielder said. "I know your reputation."

Henry spat and stared up at the man. She felt anger and defiance blazing in her eyes. "I ain't... I don't do that sort of shit no more." It was a lie. But she wanted it to be a truth. Henry looked down at the floor, at the mouldering straw, at the blood of Long Tall soaking into it. "I ain't the Red no more. Just Henry. Rose sent me ta protect those fucks an' that's what I'm gonna do."

"Why?"

"Ain't ya been listenin'? She don't wanna do things the blooded way no more. She wants a united Wilds, a fair Wilds. Laws an' shit. Wants ta put an end ta the game. Ain't doin' that by fuckin' killin' everyone. Says she wants ta be... merciful and shit." Henry spat again.

"That true?" the Weird One asked. "An end to the game?"

Henry nodded. "Aye. Reckon if anyone can do it, it'd be her."

"What will we do?" asked Lazy Eye. "I ain't nobody without the game."

"Ya ain't nobody now," the Weird One said with a nasty smile.

The axe-wielder was watching them all. Lazy Eye's guard was down; he was looking at Henry. If the axe-wielder wanted a chance to even the odds a drop, he wasn't likely to get a better one. Yet he waited.

"She's offerin' exile rather than death," Henry continued, ignoring the baleful stare Lazy Eye was sending towards the Weird One. "Wants ta show the Wilds, the folk of the Wilds, good folk an' us players both, what mercy looks like."

Still, the axe-wielding madman did not look sold on the idea. Henry decided to take a risk and straightened up out of her crouch. She put her daggers away, back into their sheaths.

"Ain't a reason ta fight us. City is lost already," she said with confidence, though she wagered the outcome was far from certain yet. "All we're gonna do is stand in front of your blooded bastards an' make certain our own folk don't cut 'em down."

Henry nodded at the Weird One and then again at Lazy Eye.

"Ya want us ta put our shit away?" the Weird One asked. "Before that fucker has?"

Henry let out a sigh. "Aye. I do. Show of faith. Just like what Rose is tryin'. A different way ta all the killin'."

The Weird One looked like he was wrestling with the idea for a few moments, but eventually, he sheathed his sword and started to coil his whip. Lazy Eye grumbled a bit then put his own sword away. Henry held up her hands to the axe-wielder.

"So now what?" she asked the man.

He nodded. "Now we see what Lord Brekovich says about your different way."

The axe-wielder started forward, stepping over the body of Long Tall. He was aiming towards a doorway that led off the left of the hall, probably led to some fancy sleeping quarters or the like. He nodded at Henry as he passed and there was respect there, one fighter to another both serving someone better than them.

As soon as the axe-wielder was past Henry, she leapt at him, latching onto his back, a knife slipping into her hand from her sleeve, and stabbing into her neck. She stabbed him three times as she rode him to the ground and then another two times once he was face down on the mouldering straw. Didn't take the bastard long to die from wounds like that. Before long he was nothing but a body and blood soaking into the floor. Henry found she was crying but couldn't say why.

The Weird One and Lazy Eye were standing nearby, shocked looks just about covering it. The remaining dog was already edging closer to the corpse, smelling death and a good meal.

"What happened to doing it a different way?" asked Lazy Eye. He looked like he was trying real hard to keep some distance between himself and Henry, like she might turn on him next.

Henry looked down at the red blood covering her hands and the little knife glinting in the light. "The fuck do ya think this is? Sarth or some shit? This is the Wilds. Ain't no such thing as a different way. Just didn't want that bastard swingin' his axe at me is all."

"Kill or be killed," the Weird One said. Looked like he was keeping a bit of distance too.

"Aye." Henry wiped her eyes on her sleeve. "An' that dumb fuck just got himself killed. Come on. Let's go find the blooded cunts."

"Um." Lazy Eye hesitated. "I'm confused. Are we killing them too?"

Henry shrugged as she wiped the axe-wielder's blood on her tunic. "Probably."

They didn't find any more guards in the building; Henry reckoned the bastards thought they were safe. There were a few servants running to and fro - no doubt seeing to their masters' needs. The Weird One had an unnerving accuracy with his whip, and once it was wrapped around a person's neck, they were good as stabbed. They killed three servants before they finally found the first of the blooded. Needless deaths, but most seemed to be these days.

Henry recognised him. Hard not to. Lord Niles Brekovich was drunk as Anders on a bad day and staring into a crackling fire in what looked to be a study full of books and fine furniture. He didn't rise from his chair when they entered, didn't even look up. Might be he was past being able to see anything anyway. An empty glass bottle dangled from one hand and he was blinking away tears.

Nearby stood another person Henry recognised though this one wasn't blooded. Anders had called her Lisha, and she had cut off one of his fingers just a few years back. Henry had watched, tied to stake and unable to help. The bitch would have chopped up more of Anders if Thorn hadn't intervened. Lisha was armed and armoured and drew steel as soon as they entered the room.

One more woman sat in the room, tending to some young babe barely looked old enough to crawl. She was also armed with a sword and definitely blooded. Henry reckoned she'd seen the bitch before but couldn't dredge up a name. By the way she held the child, it was clearly hers.

Henry stood silent for a moment, taking in the scene as her two remaining crew moved in behind her.

"Don't need that one," Henry said, pointing to Lisha. "Keep the other two nice and safe long as we can."

"Do we kill her?" asked Lazy Eye.

"Aye. 'Less she surrenders. Ain't here ta hurt anyone. Doesn't mean we won't. You," again she pointed at Lisha, "drop the steel, or we'll see how ya bleed. You," she pointed at the other woman, "drop the steel, or we see how the kid bleeds."

The woman with the child weighed her options for a moment and then threw her sword down on the rug at her feet.

"What are you doing, Emin?" Lisha asked. "We can take them."

"Last chance," Henry said. "Put it down."

"I will no..."

The whip cracked and wrapped itself around the woman's neck, and the Weird One tugged, pulled her off balance and into a table. Lisha crashed to the ground and let go of her sword, tugging at the length of leather coiled around her neck.

"Do we kill her?" asked Lazy Eye for the second time.

Henry shrugged. "Makes no difference. We're only after them." She walked forwards, ignoring the woman on the floor struggling to breathe, and closed on the other one, the one with the babe.

"You're the D'roan bitch? The one that bastard put a child in?"

Emin D'roan stood up straight and nodded, defiance in her eyes.

"Ya love that thing all the same?" Henry asked.

"Yes."

"Good. Then sit the fuck down an' keep it an' yaself quiet. Might be ya can both survive this."

Henry turned to find the two remaining members of her crew staring down at Lisha. The woman had pulled the whip from around her neck and was backed up against a nearby table.

Henry shook her head. "Just fuckin' tie her up an' do the same for this bastard while ya at it," she waved towards the semi-conscious Niles Brekovich.

"What about the others?" the Weird One asked as he pulled a length of rope from his belt and bent to tying Lisha's hands behind her. "There's gotta be more blooded around."

"Don't matter," Henry said and spat on a nearby fur rug, looked to be some sort of big cat, lots of stripes and a snarl like it hadn't wanted to die. "We ain't got enough folk no more ta find 'em all. An' these ones are the only ones that matter. Last of the Brekovich line right here. Well, last ones still got their cocks attached."

Anders

They could hear the scream even a dozen paces outside the tent. While Anders had never seen such a thing, he was fairly certain the noise was akin to a cat being gutted alive. Even the Black Thorn slowed to a stop and gave the tent a good eyeballing.

It had taken them some time to limp back to camp with Anders carrying most their weights. Unfortunately, Thorn's leg was very much broken and not able to sustain any pressure, so Anders had to do most of the work. Upon arriving at the camp, and after a brief series of questions mostly concerning the fact that Thorn was still alive, they were led inwards towards Rose's tent and ordeal.

"I, uh, think I'll leave you here, boss," Anders said. "Don't really fancy seeing..." He waved towards the tent. "Whatever is going on in there."

"Birth, I reckon," Thorn said, looking a little pale either from the wounds or the thought of it. "All been through it at least once in our lives, Anders."

"And it was quite traumatic the first and only time. I think it far wiser if I saunter off to find us some booze. To celebrate afterwards, of course. After it's, you know, over."

"An' how am I supposed ta make it inside without you supportin' me, eh?" Thorn tightened his grip on Anders' shoulder to further emphasise how much he was not going anywhere.

"I'm certain one of these strapping lads will help," Anders nodded towards the nearby soldiers guarding Rose's tent. "Or that one there, she's strapping and beautiful. What more could you want from a crutch?"

"We're goin' in, Anders," the Black Thorn said and leaned forwards, forcing Anders to move along with him before they both went down in a sprawling mess.

Another scream ripped the air to pieces from inside the tent. Anders had seen a great many folk die in a fair number of horrific ways, yet none could claim the pain that scream seemed to boast.

"You know, boss, this whole birth affair is– quite messy, I believe. It's not really a place for men."

Another scream, determination giving way to hopeless agony.

"Especially not men like us. There's a difference between death and life, and I'm afraid we just don't belong witnessing the latter."

"Shut up, Anders," Thorn growled.

They were at the tent flap now, and the soldiers outside gave Thorn an incredulous look. The sort of look that was full of awe. The sort of look they no doubt reserved for heroes who had survived something impossible. It was probably better they didn't know the truth.

Thorn lifted up the tent flap. It was dark and hot within, and the smell made Anders wince. It was a smell of piss and shit and something else he couldn't place and didn't want to. Unfortunately, Thorn was already on his way in, and that gave Anders no choice but to step inside the nightmare that lay before him.

It took a moment for Anders' eyes to adjust and then he was fairly certain he wished they hadn't. The tent looked as though a particularly messing storm had recently hit it, and before that it had passed through a slaughterhouse. Blood and bloody cloth seemed to be the fashion of the day, and every bit of furniture he could see was wearing it.

Pug stood to the side of the tent flap, eyes wide and fixed straight on the scene on the bed. Lucille and another woman, this one tall and built like a blacksmith, were gathered around the bed in various states of assisting their mistress.

Rose was on all fours, clutching at the bed and panting. Her face, normally so beautiful and schooled, was a sweaty, pale mask of pain and exhaustion. Even from here, Anders could see her legs were covered in sticky red blood.

Anders stopped and even Thorn's tugging forwards didn't move him from the spot. He watched as Rose panted, drawing shallow breaths and then one bigger one before she screamed again, her face contorting.

"Anders!" Thorn growled, but Anders just stood still, shaking his head rather firmly, unable to take his eyes from the scene in front of him yet wanting nothing so much as to turn away from it.

"No, I don't think so."

Pug noticed them, and he stepped forward and embraced Thorn in what looked to be a very awkward hug, not that Anders paid it too much attention with the screaming woman on the bed.

"B-b-b... T-h-hor-n," Pug stammered.

"Aye. Easy there, Pug."

"Yes," Anders said slowly, not looking. "The boy was quite beside himself when we thought you were dead, boss. Cried like a woman when he saw you fall from the walls."

"T-t-h-a-a-a-t..."

"Yes, I know, Pug. But don't worry, no one thinks any less of you."

"What's wrong with him?" Thorn asked.

"Took a knock to the head defending your wife. Seems he's having some trouble talking now, though he still seems able to think clearly enough."

"Betrim?" Rose's voice was shrill and filled with pain and weariness.

"Aye, love," Betrim leaned forwards, and this time Anders had no choice but to half carry the boss over to the bed.

Up close the scene looked even worse. The bed sheets were stained with all manner of unhealthy colours, and chief among them was bright red. Anders took to looking up at the roof of the tent.

"You need to push again, my lady," said Lucille.

"You're alive," Rose said, and Anders thought he detected real emotion in her voice. Odd that such a thing seemed so alien to him.

"My lady, push!"

The scream that tore through the air had Anders wincing and wishing he could cover his ears. Unfortunately, he was too busy keeping the Black Thorn upright, and the big man's grip on Anders increased to quite painful levels.

Anders' eyes dropped, more by accident than anything else, and he discovered he had quite a good view of Rose's rear end.

"Oh, bloody hells!" he cursed and quickly looked back at the roof. He was fairly certain there were tears in his eyes, and he was just as certain that he never wanted to participate in carnal activities ever again.

"The head is crowning, my lady. Push. Push!"

Anders' eyes slipped again, but he managed to direct them towards Rose's front end. Her face was still pale, something Anders thought a bit wrong given the amount of grunting and teeth gritting that was going on. She scrunched her eyes up tight and tensed.

"What can I do?" Thorn asked, a note of panic in his voice that Anders had never heard before.

It seemed all three women on or around the bed had very little time to spare either Thorn or Anders, so they stood there, watching something that no man had any cause to ever watch. Anders was fairly certain he'd have run screaming from the tent and emptied his stomach, not that there was anything left in it, had Thorn not been leaning so heavily on him.

"One more, my lady. Deep breaths. One. Two. Three. And push!"

Rose screamed. Thorn's grip on Anders tightened. Lucille, standing at Rose's back end, pulled something small, pale, and covered in gore out of her.

"That's it, my lady. She's out," Lucille said though her face was quite grave.

"Um," Anders said. "Don't they usually cry a bit more than that?"

"Is she alright?" Rose asked, still on all fours and shaking from the exertion. Lucille took a knife and cut the odd fleshy rope that attached the baby to the mother. Anders had to look away to keep whatever dignity he had left to him. Rose was staring at Thorn.

"Is she..."

"Alive," Lucille confirmed as she quickly wrapped the babe in tight cloth.

"Good," Rose said just before her eyes rolled back in her head and she collapsed.

"My lady?" Lucille finished wrapping the little child. "My lady? Shit. Here, take the child." She held out the little cloth bundle to Anders.

"Oh, I don't think so," Anders shook his head.

"Pug!" Lucille shoved the baby towards Anders, and he had no choice but the reach out and take it, holding the little thing in one arm while he supported the father with the other. "Go fetch a physician."

"This normal?" Thorn asked, his eyes darting from Rose to the child.

Anders found himself quite frozen and unsure of what to do. The little, wrinkled face within the bundle of cloth squirmed about, its eyes firmly shut.

"Oh, fuck me." Anders breathed.

"Loosen up," Lucille ordered him. "And don't drop her." She turned to Thorn, and there was concern on her face. "There's no such thing as normal in this situation, but she has lost a lot of blood."

The women worked quickly, though Anders couldn't really say what it was they were doing. They flitted about, tending to the unconscious Rose. Thorn leaned in close, starring down into the little bundle in Anders' arms.

"So small," the Black Thorn said, his voice containing more than a little awe. He looked like he wanted to hold the child, but with only the one hand, and that being used to hold onto Anders, there wasn't much chance.

The physician didn't take long, especially with Pug pushing the man through the tent flap. Within a few moments, the activity around Rose increased, and Anders saw a number of sharp objects, those often used in the magical art of surgery.

Pug approached, and Anders handed off the duties of being a crutch while the Black Thorn was supported over to a nearby chair. Sitting appeared to be quite the problem considering his leg was still broken, but the big man managed it. Once he was settled, Anders slowly and carefully handed the child to Thorn's one good arm. It was strange to see the Black Thorn smiling down at such a small life. It also wasn't the most pleasant of sights given the scars that tugged and pulled on his face.

The whole thing was all a bit much for Anders, and he was feeling the dangerous fingers of sobriety tugging at him. Thorn didn't even look up from the little form of his child as Anders turned and walked towards the tent flap, stoically ignoring the frenzied activity by the bed. He couldn't do anything there; Rose's life was well and truly in the hands of the physician.

Outside the smell of slightly fresher air did wonders to steady Anders. The afternoon was shaping up to be quite a crisp affair, and the nearby clouds even hinted at rain. With so much blood to wash away,

Anders hoped it would be a downpour.

He found himself swaying on his feet and not from the booze for once. Anders was exhausted. Probably not the same level of exhaustion Rose was feeling, if she was able to feel anything at all, but then Anders had not just pushed a living creature out of himself. He had to admit he probably wasn't as tired as Thorn either; Anders knew first hand just how wearying it could be to come back from the dead. Still, he was exhausted all the same. Weary down to his very bones and in need of a warm bed, a warm body to share it with, and a few bottles of whiskey all to his very own.

With a glance back towards the bloody tent, Anders realised there was a cupboard back inside full of booze. Normally there would be no lengths he wouldn't go to to secure himself a drink, but he couldn't face it.

The guards outside the tent watched Anders, one with a sympathetic look, and the other sporting something harder and woefully unforgiving. Then their eyes moved as one, and they were suddenly standing straighter and staring at something else, something behind Anders' slumping form. He turned to see General Verit limping towards them, his face long and drawn. There was something about the way the general was walking, something lighter in his step.

"How goes the battle, General?" Anders asked.

"Won. How goes the birth?"

"Also won, though we're still waiting to hear about possible casualties."

"The baby?"

Anders grinned. "Alive and healthy, as far as I could tell. Smells a bit strange and is a touch quieter than I thought a babe would be."

"Lady Rose?" The general glanced past Anders towards the tent.

"Reports aren't in just yet. Lots of blood. Birthing appears to be a rather messy affair. Certainly not for the likes of us men, hmm?"

The general nodded, still staring towards the tent. Anders took a deep breath and steeled himself for an awkward line of questioning.

"So, um, we won?"

"Yes," General Verit said with a curt nod.

"Right. City is ours then? Gates open and troops inside and all that?"

Again, the general nodded. "Yes."

"An epic battle, I'm sure." Anders swallowed hard. "And, um, my family? Father and the like?"

General Verit tore his eyes away from the tent and focused on Anders. It was one of the many times in life where Anders really wanted to find a nearby hole to crawl into. Or better yet, a tavern.

"Reports are still coming in," General Verit said slowly. "The gates have fallen, and the last of the defenders have surrendered. Casualties haven't been counted yet. I thought Rose might like to know we've won."

"Right," Anders said with a nod. "Last I saw she wasn't entirely conscious and the physician didn't look like he wanted help. At least not from the likes of us. We're far better at killing than... well, saving."

"Did you find Thorn?"

"Oh, yes," Anders said with cheer. "He's quite alive now, though not in the best of, um, health. Some broken bones, missing hand to match his missing eye. Still, handling it rather well all things considered. More concerned about his new daughter, I think."

"Alive now?"

Anders shrugged. "He was less so when I found him."

Again, the general nodded, his eyes narrowing. "Folk don't come back like that."

"Not usually. Special circumstances though. He's still him. Alive, not dead. You'll just have to trust me on this one."

The general looked unconvinced.

"Have you heard from Henry?" Anders asked. "Or Suzku?"

This time the general shook his head. "I should report to Thorn."

"No. No," Anders quickly took a step backwards, holding up his hands. "I'll let him know. You should go and see to, um, things. Be in charge and, yes, things. I'll go ease Thorn's mind about the battle."

Once more the general looked past Anders towards the tent, then nodded. The man looked as tired as Anders felt. Everyone did.

"I suppose there'll be some sort of celebration tonight?" Anders asked. "Lots of drinking to the fallen."

The general nodded and turned away. The lightness in his step gone. Anders waited for the general to disappear amid the remaining tents before turning back to the tent and clapping his hands together. Now he had a reason to go back inside and a reason to celebrate, and there was plenty of alcohol inside to do it. But first, he had some good news to spread.

DAY 6 – THE SPOILS

Rose

Sitting in a cushioned chair inside Crucible's biggest building, the same building that had so recently been Niles Brekovich's home, it was easy to forget just how many people had died to get Rose there. It was easy to forget, even if just for a moment, that she would soon be joining them.

Rose glanced down at the child in her arms. Her child. Her daughter. The most important thing she had ever done in her life. And also her murderer. Apparently, it wasn't uncommon for women to die in childbirth, though it was slightly less common for them to have the poor grace to stick around for a few days.

Three fires were blazing away in three separate hearths around the hall, and still Rose felt cold. She was wrapped in furs, almost as tightly as her daughter, and yet the chill crept in. Blood loss, or so the physician said. Internal bleeding that couldn't be fixed. It was a small wonder Rose was still alive at all, but the folk in the know told her it wouldn't last. She would get weaker and weaker and eventually just die.

Lucille hovered nearby, ready to take the baby at a moment's notice, but for now Rose was feeling strong enough to hold her. And watch her. Her little, wrinkled face, soft skin, the wisp of hair on her head, blues eyes the colour of a washed-out sky.

The midwife assured Rose the child was healthy despite the lack of crying. Apparently, some children just didn't cry whereas others never stopped. Rose was happy her little one was of the former.

Pug stood near the entrance to the big hall, waiting for word of the gathering. It wouldn't be long before all was ready and then Rose would need to marshal every bit of strength she had left in her. She couldn't help but show weakness in her weakened state, but she'd damned well show an iron will as well.

"Reckon we're lucky," Betrim said. The rhythmic tapping of his wooden crutch on the straw had long ago announced his approach. The man said he felt like death, but he looked surprisingly healthy for someone who had recently taken a tumble from some very high walls. His left arm was in a sling, the hand long gone, his right leg was in a splint, and his face was swollen and bruised in places. There was some confusion over how he had survived, and neither Betrim nor Anders were willing to make the matter clear.

"Why's that?" Rose said softly. The child wriggled a little, maybe at the sound of her father's voice or maybe her mother's.

"Takes after you. Don't reckon she'll end up with my ugly grin." And he was grinning. Rose had noticed Betrim couldn't help but smile every time he looked down on their child. It was a fairly horrific sight to be greeted with.

"We can but hope," Rose agreed.

"We namin' her yet?" Betrim asked. He shuffled over to the nearby table and sat down on the edge, grimacing at some twinge of pain.

"Yes," Rose said and took a deep breath. "We're calling her Winter."

"Mhm," Betrim grunted and nodded his head. He had a look on his face, a look Rose knew well. It was the look he wore when he had something to say and no idea how to say it. She briefly considered leaving it well alone, but that had never been her way.

"What is it, Betrim?"

The Black Thorn shook his head and stared at her with his one eye. "I ain't got a drop of an idea of how ta raise a kid, love. Don't even know where ta start."

Rose had thought this might be coming. "You will have others to help," she said, her voice barely more than a whisper to stop from waking Winter. "People to advise you at every twist and turn. And it can't be much harder than leading the most cut-throat group of criminals in the entire Wilds."

Betrim scoffed. "Don't know how ta run a fuckin'... well, anythin', let alone a... what are we callin' this? A kingdom? An empire?"

"Again, you will have help. And I have plans for the Wilds, Betrim. Detailed plans that you will follow to the letter."

He smiled at her. "Can't read, love. Never needed ta."

Rose smiled back at her husband. "You will find someone who can. Maybe you can even learn yourself."

Rose saw Pug greet someone and then nod, turning back to the hall.

"T-t-the-e-e-re." The lad stopped, took a deep breath and composed himself. A day ago, Rose might have found the delay in the message as frustrating, but not now. Maybe it was the child bundled in her arms, or maybe it was the looming spectre of death, but Rose found she had more patience. "R-r-red-d-dy."

"Thank you, Pug," Rose said, watching Winter to see if her raised voice woke the child. "We'll be out soon."

"Ya sure ya wanna do this?" Betrim asked. "Ya lookin' pretty..."

Rose fixed her husband with a stare. "Weak?"

He shrugged. "Never that. Tired though."

"That's exactly why I have to do this."

Rose nodded towards Lucille and the woman rushed forwards, picking Winter from her arms. It took quite some effort and a little help from Betrim to get Rose to her feet and even once she was up there were a few moments of dizziness that threatened to put her right back down again.

"Stay close please, Lucille. I want everyone to see my daughter."

Pug rushed across the hall and took up position next to Rose, supporting her with a steady arm. She hated relying on him but was more than grateful for the support. Betrim led the way, his crutch tapping on the ground, and Rose followed, leaning on Pug. It seemed to take forever until they were finally at the doors that led out into Crucible.

"Well?" Betrim said. "Let's go end this fuckin' war."

The door opened to a crisp morning washed clean by the rains the night before. The cold was the first thing to hit Rose, and it struck like a slap in the face. It set a shiver running down her spine, and she pulled her fur cloak tighter about herself.

It was strange to think that the battle had barely touched this part of Crucible. Outside the walls and inside nearly twenty thousand men and women had died over the course of just a few days, but here, deep in the heart of the city, the ground was clean. The buildings stood untouched. The smell of smoke was already a distant memory.

The soldiers had moved in this far, of course, looking for men and women in Crucible blacks to kill, or maybe just for houses to loot. They had found the blooded, holed up inside the great hall, and they had found Henry and what was left of her crew protecting the blooded. By all accounts, it had been a terrifying standoff, but the folk of Rose's army knew Henry well enough to know not to cross her, so the blooded survived.

Rose shook her arm free of Pug as she stepped out onto the steps that led down to the ground. She dreaded the thought of navigating those stairs on her own in her current condition, but she would not show the blooded just how weak she was.

A cheer went up. Hundreds of voices raised in welcoming Rose and her Black Thorn to the city they had promised to bring to heel. It was soldiers for the most, but there were some good folk cheering them on as well. It was entirely possible not everyone who lived in Crucible had supported the Brekovichs, and that was something Rose would have to remember when it came time for punishing those who allied against her.

The cheer went on for far too long for Rose's comfort. She would have loved to bask in the victory and the praise and the attention, but she feared her legs would collapse beneath her if things did not start moving along soon. Even so, she stood there at the top of the stairs with her husband and her daughter, and she smiled down on those who had sacrificed so much to put her where she was.

"Don't know 'bout you, love, but I'm findin' this pretty fuckin' unnervin'," Betrim said in a low voice that almost didn't make it past the noise.

Rose smiled. "Folk have been cheering you for a while now, Betrim."

"Aye, ever since you decided ta start spreadin' rumours I was some sort of hero. Always found it unnervin' ta tell the truth."

Rose turned her head to look at Betrim. "You are a hero. The Guardian of the Wilds."

"Ain't a hero, an' I ain't a guardian of anythin'."

"You are the guardian of our child."

Rose watched as Betrim drew in a deep breath and let out as a sigh with a resigned nod of his head. "Always gotta win, don't ya."

"And you can be the hero," Rose continued, more to herself. "And I will be the villain. One last time."

"Eh?"

The crowd was quieting now, and Rose didn't feel much like answering Betrim, so she raised her hands, marvelling at how much effort that seemed to take, and smiled.

"Thank you," she said, hoping her voice carried because she couldn't find the effort to raise it. "We've all sacrificed so much to get here. We've all lost so many."

A morbid hush settled over the crowd, Rose took the opportunity to point to the small clearing at the bottom of the steps where the last remaining members of the nine blooded houses knelt on the hard ground, hands bound behind them and guards keeping them from running.

"All because of them." Rose was more than happy to lay the blame for the whole thing at the feet of the blooded and soon there would be no one left to argue with her. Nor would she be left to be argued with.

The crowd turned to jeering, and even a few stones were thrown in the general direction of the blooded as they knelt at Rose's feet. The projectiles were soon stopped when more of them hit the guards than the blooded.

Rose started down the steps, slowly at first, measuring each one and making certain her feet were solid and legs didn't wobble too much. She knew she looked frail and weak, but managing the ordeal by herself would look better than being half carried to the ground.

She had a cold sheen of sweat across her forehead by the time she reached the bottom and was fighting the urge to shake and collapse. In front of her knelt the last of the families she had sworn to kill. Sixteen men, women, and children. All blooded. All part of the problem, the disease that infected the Wilds.

Rose knew none of those in front of her was responsible for her sister's death. She knew the man responsible had died long before she started her crusade. She also knew that her sister's death wasn't just the actions of one man but the symptoms of a much larger problem. The blooded were a pox, but not for much longer.

Henry waited at the bottom of the steps. The little murderess was ready to act as executioner, but there was a grim set to her face that Rose didn't recognise. She was an assassin, a knife in the darkness, and no matter how much she might like to believe otherwise, there was no escaping some irresistible truths. Henry was a killer, a murderer. But not today. Perhaps even she could change.

"You keep your knives sharp?" Rose asked, pitching her voice loudly enough for the blooded to hear her.

Henry looked a little shocked. Even beneath her new cavalier hat, Rose could see the woman blush to suddenly find herself centre of attention.

"Aye. As a razor."

"May I borrow one?" Rose asked.

"Ya sure?" Henry asked. She tilted her head just enough to eye Rose from underneath the hat. "Ain't this somethin' ya should be gettin' someone like me ta do for ya?" A waver in her voice betrayed Henry's apprehension.

Rose shook her head slowly and lowered her voice to barely a whisper. "I'm already dead, Henry. Let these fuckers' blood be on my hands."

The little murderess just stared for a few moments, silence stretching between them, before she nodded. She drew one of her knives out of its sheath, flipped it over in her hand, and held it out.

It was a small thing. Half a foot of shining steel, slightly curved towards the tip and with a plain, unadorned hilt. There was some discolouration on the hilt as Rose looked closer, the wood taking on some of the red from those the knife had been used to kill. She reached out and plucked it from Henry's hand.

Turning back to the blooded kneeling before her, Rose could see fear on some faces now. True fear. Terror from those knowing that they were about to die. She ignored the crowd around them and focused in on the line of people bound and awaiting execution.

Sixteen of them. At least a few of them children, some barely able to stand, and weeping. Chances were the brats didn't even understand what was happening, just knew their hands were tied and the soldiers standing behind them had a firm grip to stop them from moving.

Rose started to her left, walked towards the furthest of the blooded and stopped in front of the old man. He had a wrinkled face, tanned and hard lines. Old eyes, just starting to go milky, stared back at Rose as she stopped in front of him and considered the knife in her hands.

"What happened to doing things a different way?" asked Larisa Fanklin. Of all the members of the Fanklin family, she was the only one with a backbone. She would be the fourth to die today.

Rose took a step back from the old man in front of her and looked right, eyeing Larisa for a few moments before sweeping her gaze further until she could see Niles Brekovich at the far end of the line of those awaiting their execution.

"My daughter will do things a different way," Rose said. "Me? I intend to see you all dead before I breathe my last."

Rose stepped forwards, ignoring the slight wobble in her legs, and reached down. The old man couldn't go anywhere with the soldier holding him in place, and Rose saw the fear in his eyes as he finally realised what was happening. She drew the blade quickly across his throat, and his blood leaked out, running down his neck and into his clothing.

Rose had once heard that the older a person got, the more watery their blood became, and it certainly seemed true. The old man gagged and gurgled and spilled blood over the ground and over Rose's furs. Finally, he died, the soldier behind him letting go and the body dropped to the ground with a *thud*.

One down and Rose took a step back. Next in line was Lord Tanith Fanklin himself. He was a pudgy man, soft and weak. He shook his head and fixed his terrified gaze on the crimson knife in Rose's hand.

"P-p-please don't," Tanith begged. "I can be useful. I don't care about power. I have connections. I know things. I know people."

"Oh, do die with some dignity, Tanith," Anders' voice called from somewhere behind. Rose ignored them both. "He was always like this at parties too, begging for approval. Quite unbefitting really."

"Please don't. Please. Please."

Tanith Fanklin, the lord of one of the last remaining blooded houses, was still begging for mercy even as Rose dragged the knife across his throat. His blood spurted out thick and crimson. It coated the knife and stained Rose's hands. It splashed against her furs, soaking in. She should have stepped back, but instead, she let the red wash her feet.

Once Tanith had dropped to the ground and twitched out his last, Rose took another step back. Her legs wobbled, and she stumbled a step, somehow managing not to fall. The exhaustion was catching up with her, her own blood loss. The pain inside felt as though there were something digging around her guts with claws.

"That's enough, love," Betrim said, his crutch tapping as he moved forwards.

Rose held up a hand to stop him. She got control of herself and straightened, fighting through the pain inside. Her face felt sweaty, loose strands of hair plastered to her cheek. It took some effort to shrug out of the fur coat and she let it drop to the ground. Dressed in a white shift that did little to hide her recent pregnancy and was already bloody, some of it her own, Rose took a deep breath and turned back to the line of blooded.

Next in line was a young girl, only seven or eight years at most. Her name was Carlot Fanklin, and her eyes were wide and light blue, almost like the sea. There were tears there, running free and silent down her cheeks. The girl shook, whether from fear or cold or both, Rose couldn't tell, but the soldier behind her had a tight grip on her shoulders.

"Don't," pleaded Larisa from beside her daughter. "She's just a child."

Rose had to stoop a little as she reached down and sliced through the girl's neck. Larisa wailed, a high-pitched scream of pain and fury. Carlot's blood gushed out of the wound on her neck, soaking down into her dress. She tried to breathe and gagged, her eyes wide and uncomprehending. It did not take long for Carlot to die. Rose considered the possibility that it was just because children had less blood to bleed. Either way, she had to die. Any of them who could remember who they were and what they had been to the Wilds *had* to die.

"You monster!" Larisa managed to scream between sobs.

Rose noticed a few of those closest in the crowd turn away, disappearing into the sea of faces. It was a horrible thing she was doing, and that was why *she* was doing it, not someone else. All the blood would be on her hands.

"Monster," Larisa said again, more quietly now. She was staring down at the body of her daughter, leaning towards the dead child but the soldier behind her held fast. "Monster."

"Yes," Rose agreed, her voice flat. "I am. And I will be the last of the monsters."

Larisa lurched upwards to her feet and lunged at Rose. The soldier behind wasn't ready and lost his grip as the blooded lady pushed forwards and crashed into Rose, bearing them both down to the ground.

There was screaming; Rose knew that much. Larisa's voice in her ear, tight with pain physical as well as emotional. Rose understood, she too was in pain and more than she cared to admit. The blooded woman lay on top of her, dying with a knife in her chest, blood leaking out over both of them and Rose couldn't find the strength to push the woman off her.

The soldier moved into view, grabbing Larisa and pulling hard. Rose kept hold of the knife and saw it slide out of the woman's flesh.

She lay for a while. Amid the mud of the street and staring up at the sky. Then Henry was there, reaching down and pulling Rose up, checking her for wounds. She wouldn't find any, at least not on the outside. Something was definitely wounded inside, Rose could feel it.

"Ya alright?" Henry was asking, and she wasn't the only one. There were a few of them around her now.

Rose nodded. "As I can be. Help me up."

Henry pulled Rose to her feet, her wiry strength surprising.

"That's enough, love," Betrim was saying again.

Rose shook her head. She was beyond weary and struggling to keep her feet under her, but she still held the knife. "No. It isn't. It won't be enough until they are all dead."

Betrim sighed. "Then we get someone else ta do the killin'. Don't have ta be a spectacle."

Rose drew in a deep breath and then let it out again. She let anger lend her strength, even if only temporarily. She let the memory of a blooded lord beating her sister to death fuel that anger. Rose drew herself up straight and pushed past Betrim. Larisa hung in the soldier's grasp, moaning in pain and bleeding from the wound in her stomach. Rose stalked up to the woman and dragged the blade across her throat. There was a moment of panic in her eyes. It soon gave way to a blank stare as death settled in.

The soldiers did a much better job of holding their captives after that, making certain Rose was safe from any reprisal. She moved down the line slowly, watching each one of the blooded die in front of her. Three more Fanklins died before Rose came to the first of the D'roans.

Jayson D'roan was a tall, thin man with his brother's sneer. Alistair might have been the head of the family, but his younger brother was well known to be the enforcer. He was handsome, even with a blackened eye and a bloody nose, and looked as cruel as Rose herself.

"You look like shit," the blooded lord spat as Rose approached. It was true; Rose was covered in blood and mud and as dishevelled as she was pale and waxen. She no doubt looked almost as though she was dead already.

"You look like a corpse." Rose lunged forwards and stabbed the knife into the man's neck. His eyes went wide and angry, and Rose twisted the knife and ripped it free. Blood spurted out at her, and she took a step back to stop it hitting her face. Jayson D'roan twitched and spasmed in his guards' grip. He did not go quietly into his grave, and neither did he go quickly.

Rose's hand was slick with blood. So much so she could feel it underneath her grip and all the way up to her elbow. Even so, she wasn't even halfway through the executions yet.

More and more folk had turned and gone now. Some still watched on eagerly, some even cheered and bayed for more blood, but many couldn't stand the sight. Especially not given who was next in the line to die.

Rose shivered in her white shift stained red and brown. With Jayson D'roan dead, the next blooded in line was Orson D'roan, or Orson

Brekovich, Emin D'roan's young son. The child was still a babe. The guard held the boy gingerly, and the lad stared up at his captor, occasionally making a play for the man's beard.

"No," this from Emin D'roan, next in line. "You're a mother now. Surely you can understand. You can't do this."

Rose stared at the child for a moment longer before turning to the mother. "He raped you. You never wanted this child."

Emin argued. "Maybe not by him. Maybe not at all. But I love him. Kill me, if you must, but not him. He... He won't even know he's blooded. Kill us all, but not him."

"ROSE!" Niles Brekovich roared from down the line. "This is..." A solid punch to the face from one of the nearby soldiers shut the man up before he could lay down any threats.

Emin was shaking her head, her eyes pleading. She was a strong woman, a beautiful woman, a warrior as well as a mother and Rose could understand that. She stepped past the child, stopping in front of Emin and held the knife up.

Emin nodded, gratitude in her eyes. Rose placed the knife to Emin D'roan's neck and slowly drew it sideways until the woman was choking on her own blood.

Rose stayed there and watched Emin die. Watched the soldier drop a lifeless body to the ground, the beauty she had in life seemed lost in death. Then she stepped close to the child and the boy went silent.

A ragged breath escaped her lips and Rose looked up at the guard holding the boy. His face was a picture of horror, tears in his eyes.

"Take the body away," Rose said with a weary shake of her head. The guard looked confused for just a moment, then turned and stumbled away from the line before Rose could change her mind.

Rose continued down the line, one after another until all the D'roans were dead. Some pleaded, some threatened, some just accepted their deaths in resigned silence. Two children died, neither as young as Orson. Rose felt sick to her stomach and slick with sweat and blood despite the cold creeping inside of her, making her shiver.

The first of the Brekovichs knelt before her was different, a woman of middling years with muscle that spoke of swinging a sword rather than wearing a dress.

"You're not blooded," Rose said, surprised by how flat her own voice sounded as though all emotion had drained out of her along with the blood trickling down her leg.

The woman raised defiant eyes at Rose and spat, hitting her shift.

"That's Lisha Tenith," Anders said loudly. "She's, um, married to my brother Francis. She also chopped off one of my fingers a few years back so... have at her!"

"Are you pregnant?" Rose asked.

"Eh?"

"Are you pregnant with Francis Brekovich's child?"

The woman shook her head. "Nor likely to be after what you did, Anders, you fuck!"

"Hah!" Anders shouted. He sounded quite far back. "You can't say that tiny little thing satisfied you, Lish. Why mine was at least twice as large on a cold day. You remember."

"Take her away," Rose said wearily. "Keep her locked up for a year. If she starts to show, kill her. If not, let her go."

The woman looked stunned as the soldiers dragged her away to throw into some gaol cell for the next year of her life. Rose stepped sideways to find Francis Brekovich slumped on the ground, mewling. His skin was pale and had a yellow tint, and his eyes were bloodshot and distant. He barely looked alive. It appeared Anders had done a poor job; his brother was dying of infection. The man barely moved as Rose drew the knife across his throat, spilling even more blood on himself. He died with barely a sound.

"Ahhh! Bitch! Whore!" Niles Brekovich screamed, trying to pull free from the soldiers holding him. One of the guards raised a hand to cuff the man to silence, but Rose stayed him with shake of her head. She moved past the next three prisoners to stand in front of the last lord of the Brekovich family.

Niles Brekovich looked almost as dishevelled as Rose herself. He squinted up at her with red eyes and unkempt hair pulled free from its braid. He struggled as she came close, but his hands were bound behind him, and two soldiers held him on his knees.

"I told you I would end your reign and your line," Rose said quietly.

Niles Brekovich struggled again and then stopped, staring up at her, the light of hatred in his eyes. "You don't look well, Rose."

She shook her head. "I'm dying. But I'm taking you all with me. My daughter will grow up safe from you and your kind. Free from the pain and suffering and death you have visited upon the Wilds for generations."

"The daughter of a whore and criminal will never be anything more than that," the blooded lord spat.

Rose just stared down at the man. "I suppose you and I will never find out. At least she'll have a chance. That's more than any of you blooded will have." Rose turned to continue her slaughter.

Niles Brekovich cackled out a laugh. "My line won't end, whore! I have one son who you won't kill."

Rose stopped and turned back to the laughing man. He looked so confident, so secure, even though he was bound and kneeling in mud, awaiting his own death.

A small unit of soldiers waited nearby, next to Betrim and Henry and General Verit. Rose pointed at two of them and then at Anders. "Add him to the end of the line."

"What?" Anders squeaked as the two men moved forwards and grabbed his arms. "Wait. No!"

"Love..." Betrim started, but Rose stopped him with a tired stare.

"Don't," she warned her husband. "Just don't."

"Shit," Betrim cursed and settled back down onto his crutch.

"Wait. What? Boss, you can't let her do this. I've been loyal," Anders whined as the men dragged him forwards and pushed him down next to his father. "I'm not a Brekovich. Disowned. Disinherited. I never wanted to be in the first place."

"Gag him," Rose ordered as she moved back to the next blooded in line, an old woman with a face abundant in skin. Anders' protests quickly became muffled, but they didn't stop.

"I'm ready to die," the old woman announced.

"Good for you," Rose said without a trace of emotion as she slit the wrinkled throat.

Next up was a young woman, pretty and bright-eyed. She died with almost as much dignity as the old lady. Then came another child, a younger girl of just a handful of years. Rose let out a strangled sob as she cut that throat, spilling yet more blood over her hand and clothing. She was sick to her stomach, wearier than she had ever been and felt like collapsing from the pain inside. Worst of all was the numb feeling inside her head, as though she had nothing more left to feel.

Niles Brekovich stared up at Rose with real hatred. He struggled right up until the end. Even as Rose plunged the knife into his neck and ripped it out the other side, the man struggled as though the only victory he had left was to spill as much of his blood as possible over Rose's once-white shift.

Rose stared down at Niles Brekovich's corpse as it leaked out red into the mud. She poked it once with her foot. It didn't move. She stepped to her right to see Anders mumbling something through his gag and shaking his head. He glanced down at his dead father and then up to the knife Rose was holding, slick with blood.

"Enough!" Betrim shouted.

Rose blinked away tears. She was staring down at Anders and brandishing the knife as though she were really about to kill him. Maybe she would have if not for Betrim's interruption. She nodded to the guards holding Anders in place and stepped backwards, dropping the knife and collapsing down onto her knees in a puddle of Niles Brekovich's spreading blood.

Suddenly Betrim was there, lowering himself awkwardly and grimacing at the pain in his broken leg. His one eye searched her face.

"That's enough, love. He ain't one of them. It's over now."

Rose collapsed forwards against her husband's chest and sobbed. The last of her energy fleeing along with the willpower that held her together. She cried there for a while as Betrim shifted uncomfortably. He didn't try to stop or calm her, nor tell her it would be all right. He just sat there and let her cry.

Eventually Rose felt her tears go dry. Still, she sat there collapsed in Betrim's arms. He smelled of sweat, and he smelled of the Black Thorn. It was a comforting smell, and Rose could feel herself drifting off despite the pain in her abdomen.

"No," she said suddenly, pulling away from Betrim a little and staring up into his eyes.

"It's alright, love. It's over."

Rose shook her head. "Not yet. I can't go yet. Anders..."

It took a bit of looking around, but she saw Anders standing near Henry at the edge of the steps leading back to the great hall. He had a bottle in one hand and a smile on his face as though his recent brush with death was already forgotten.

"I need ta talk ta Anders," Rose said. Her voice sounded slow and heavy to her ears.

After a few moments, a couple of soldiers gently hauled Rose to her feet and Pug was there, steadying her and giving her a worried smile that didn't quite cover the concern in his eyes.

Rose glanced at the bodies she had left in her wake. Fourteen corpses lying in the mud. The end of her crusade, and the end of the blooded. The beginning of the new Wilds. The crowd had all but gone, just a few folk stayed nearby, waiting to see if one more person was about to die.

"Clear those away," Rose said, waving a bloody hand towards the bodies.

"Chop the heads off and burn 'em," Betrim said. "Just in case."

"You gave me quite the scare, my lady," Anders said as he sauntered closer. "I honestly believed you were about to kill me. I suppose that was the point though, hmm? Not so convincing next time please."

Rose shook her head, trying to clear the blurred edges. "Inside," she said with effort. "I have plans– for the Wilds. You're going to help Betrim– do them." She took a deep breath. "Carry them out."

"Right," Anders said, nodding his head. "How extensive are these plans?"

Rose felt a bit of clarity coming back, though along with it the pain seemed all the sharper. "Extensive."

"Hmm. We'll need drinks then."

"Lucille," Rose said, casting about for her midwife in something close to a panic. She found the woman nearby, gently rocking the little baby in her arms. Rose breathed a sigh of relief. "You too, Lucille. I want Winter with me from now until..."

"She ain't gonna leave ya side, love," Betrim said. He looked tired and concerned, and there was something else in his one eye, something that looked a lot like grief. "None of us are."

Suzku

Pern stared up at the cloth roof of the tent and watched an insect crawl across the bleached-bone surface. It was a tiny creature, barely as big as a fingernail, and lost, making its way across a world it didn't even understand. Just a few feet away, crouching silent and unseen in the corner of the tent, sat a fat black spider. Pern had already seen the little monster capture at least three similar insects, wrapping them up in a sticky thread and attaching them to the web of its lair.

Up there in the heights of the infirmary tent, that spider was the top predator. King of its little bleached-bone domain, feeding on everything smaller and less well-armed than itself. Yet Pern could reach up with his one uninjured hand and crush the little king if he chose to.

The idea played through Pern's head time and time again. He was certain there was a lesson to be learned there, but he couldn't fathom it. He was far too busy considering his own position.

Pern had woken up in the infirmary after the battle. The physicians said he was lucky to be alive considering how much blood he had lost. They also said he'd be confined to his bed for the next few days at least while he recovered. At first, he argued, but those arguments soon ran dry when he tried to sit up and promptly lost consciousness. The rigours of war had finally caught up with him.

They assured him the battle had been won and in no small part thanks to him and the rest of his little squad. General Verit himself had even been to visit to congratulate Pern and to share a drink.

The general had looked almost as bad as Pern felt. His face held no smiles any more, and not even the fiery rum they shared seemed to take the edge off what looked a lot like grief. They sat in silence for a long time, sharing cups, with the occasional toast. Eventually, Pern asked after the survivors of his squad and the number of casualties taken in storming the city. General Verit shook his head and looked like he was about to launch into a tirade, but stopped, took a deep breath and simply said, *"Shouldn't speak ill of the dead. Especially not those who ain't yet stepped over.*"

It took Pern a bit of prying before the general admitted that Rose was dying. Something had gone wrong in childbirth and she was bleeding on the inside, the physicians unable to do anything about it. Some wounds just couldn't be healed apparently.

Then General Verit went on to describe the end of the blooded. Men, women, and children slaughtered in the mud outside their own homes. He admitted such murder wasn't uncommon during the heat of battle while blood was up, but afterwards that same killing was horrifying at best and unforgivable at worst. The general seemed to be thinking towards the latter.

Eventually, the general made his offer and left, leaving Pern to stare up the roof and the little insect edging ever closer to the spider. Leaving him to ponder his options.

He didn't see Henry arrive, didn't hear her approach. She had cat-like stealth about her, light-footed and silent as a summer breeze. He didn't know she was there until she sniffed about as loudly as a person could. Pern rolled his head to the side to look at her.

Henry had found a new hat, a little larger than her last and red rather than blue, but still cavalier in style. She'd liked hats that served to hide much of her face even before the demon's claws had raked the skin there.

"You look well," Pern said quietly. And she did. Of all of them, Henry seemed to be the only one that had emerged from the siege of Crucible unscathed, at least on the outside.

She grinned at Pern and nodded, pulling a nearby chair over and slumping down into it. She leaned back and put her boots up on his cot.

"You don't. Thought you Haarin were supposed ta be good in a fight or somethin'. Looks ta me like ya got ya arse kicked."

"I am... Ho... Hmm." Pern stopped to think about his situation. As a Haarin he had served his clan and the client they chose for him. As a Honin he had been hunted by his clan, forced to run and to kill. But his clan were dead now. All of them dead. "Can I still be Honin without a clan?"

"Eh?"

"It was the title they gave to me. An indication of my dishonour. They are dead now. Can I be dishonoured without anyone to dishonour?"

"Eh?"

"I believe I am now neither Haarin, nor Honin. Perhaps I am now just Pern."

"Right. Reckon ya've been Pern for as long as ya've been alive. It really taken this long for ya ta figure it out?"

"Yes."

"Well, I reckon they don't go pickin' Haarin based on sense then. Good job ya big as a horse an' easy on the eyes, eh?"

Pern rolled his head back to staring at the roof of the tent. The little insect was close to the spider's web now. All it would take was a single twitch of a strand, and the spider would strike, rushing out of its lair and capturing the poor creature, never to be free again.

"I heard what happened," Pern said as he watched the insect flirt with death. "Outside. I heard what Rose did to the blooded."

"Aye?" Henry said, and Pern could hear the sneer on her scarred face. "Killin' folk like that ain't easy. 'Specially not the way she is right now."

"Not easy," Pern echoed. "Not necessary."

"Had ta," Henry argued. "She couldn't leave none of the fuckers alive ta come back at us. Protectin' Thorn an' the Wilds. An' the kid."

"Maybe," Pern admitted. "Maybe killing children isn't the answer."

Henry's feet disappeared from his cot, and he heard her lean in close. "She ain't the only one done it."

The insect stopping moving, so close to the web. "You've killed children on Thorn's orders," Pern admitted.

"An' on others'. Jogaren brat weren't the first."

"Does that make it right?"

"Right?" Henry snorted. "Ain't such a thing here. How have you not figured that shit out yet? Been with us long enough, eh?"

Pern nodded at that. The insect moved forward, stepping onto a single strand of webbing and the spider erupted from its lair and dragged the little insect back inside its nest of silk.

"General Verit made me an offer," Pern said before his courage could fail him. "To join his personal troop."

"What's that? How's that any different from workin' for Thorn an' Rose?"

"He's leavin'. The war is over. This war is over. There will be others for him to fight."

"An' ya thinkin' of joinin' him ta fight 'em?"

"I did well enough in command of men," Pern said. "The general was impressed."

There was a long silence. Pern resisted the urge to turn his head to look at Henry.

"This 'bout the kids? There ain't gonna be no more killin' kids. That's the whole point, I reckon. Rose did what had ta be done, so it don't have ta be done no more."

Pern drew in a deep breath and released it slowly. He knew an argument was coming and Henry never responded well to arguments.

"I chose you and Thorn over Swift. When I let you kill him. When I helped you kill him, I dishonoured myself and my entire clan."

"Didn't think honour were an issue no more?" Henry said, her voice angry and the red of her aura flaring out so strongly Pern had to close his eyes to stop from seeing it. She hated talking about Swift and with good reason. "Didn't ya just say now they're dead it ain't an issue?"

"They are dead because of me."

"They're dead 'cos some fuckin' death wizard killed them."

Pern shook his head. "They're dead because they came here. They came here because of me."

"Sounds ta me like they're dead 'cos they were fuckin' idiots couldn't let a thing go."

"They are dead because of me," Pern repeated. "All of them. Whether I did the killing or not. They're dead because I made the choice to save you all from Swift."

"Aye?"

"I'm no longer certain I made the right choice."

Again the silence. Pern could see Henry's aura now even through closed eyes. It burned like fire, hotter than any he'd ever seen before.

"Ya made the right choice," Henry said eventually. "Saved me."

"I saved Thorn and Rose as well," Pern argued. "And look at what they've done."

"United the Wilds," Henry said, her voice bordering on shouting. "Killed the fucks been stranglin' it for... Forever."

"Murdered children," Pern countered. "Sent tens of thousands to their deaths. How is that any better than Swift?"

"Well for a start, neither Thorn nor Rose ever cut me up an' left me for dead," Henry hissed, her voice quiet and filled with rage. "Reckon that makes 'em better if nowt else. Don't reckon they've ever sent slaves ta some fuckin' heretic witch hunter ta put demons inside neither. Never set a city on fire just ta have a pissin' contest with a pirate."

Pern couldn't argue with her logic, but neither did it answer the question he had for himself. He no longer knew if Thorn and Rose were worth following. Worth protecting. But he was certain General Verit was. A man who cared for the men and women under his command, a man who chose carefully which causes to fight for. A man who fought with his troops, rather than ordering others to fight for him.

After a while Henry spoke again, her voice calmer and softer. "So ya thinkin' ya wanna take him up on the offer? Start crewin' with the general. Some sort of officer?"

"Yes." He opened his eyes to see Henry shaking her head, her aura still blazing red around her, still the most mystifying aura he had ever seen.

"I can't go," Henry argued. "Rose is dyin'. Can't leave Thorn alone to run the Wilds, look after a kid. I might not know much 'bout raisin' a child, but I know a fuck load more 'bout girls than Thorn ever will."

"I know," Pern said, and the silence that settled between them was painful to bear.

"Ya know?" Henry shook her head. "This weren't you askin' me ta come with ya. This were you sayin' goodbye. Eh?"

"Not right away..."

"Fuck! A goodbye is just that, no matter how much warnin' ya give. Fuck you, Suzku." Henry spat on the floor and launched to her feet, knocking the chair to the ground. She didn't even look back once as she stormed from the infirmary tent. Pern wasn't sure he could blame her.

He turned his attention back to the spider. The little beast had finished wrapping its catch in silk and hung the bundle from its web like some sort of grizzly trophy. King of its bleached-bone little world, but soon the tent would come down, and that little king would need to find a new kingdom.

Henry

Henry kicked open the door to the big hall and stormed through the antechamber. She barely even glanced at the bloody spot where Long Tall had died, and continued on her rampage, giving a nearby chair a thorough flipping over.

"Shhhh!" hissed Lucille.

Henry turned on the midwife, about ready to shout or stab. The protest, whichever form it was likely to take, died when Henry saw the little bundle in the woman's arms. Winter stared out from the cloth wrap, watching Henry with calm blue eyes like a still lake. Took the fight right out of her.

"Sorry," Henry said and then spat onto the straw. Lucille was swaying from side to side, almost like a dance, and she nodded once to Henry then swayed away towards one of the crackling hearths. Rose sat near that hearth, eyes closed and slumped in a cushioned chair.

Henry stalked towards the far end of the hall where Thorn sat in another chair, one leg splinted and stretched out in front of him. He was watching her in silence with that one eye of his. Almost amazed Henry just how intense a stare could be when there was only the one eye to deliver it. She pulled another chair into place and relaxed into it, filling a nearby cup with a jug of something that smelled a lot like mead. Still, Betrim watched in silence, a smile tugging at the corner of his mouth, stretching his burn scar into a horrific visage.

"What happened ta the fancy chair?" Henry asked after a few moments. She sipped at the mead and relished the sweet taste as it ran down her throat.

"Anders," Thorn said, twisting a little to glance back at the wreckage of the throne that had previously stood proud on the raised dais. "Wandered in here with a big hammer an' not a word. Trashed the thing, then wandered out again whistlin' an' skippin'."

Henry nodded. "Meant somethin' ta him I guess. Rose?"

A shadow passed over Thorn's face. "Asleep. Told not ta wake her, just hope she wakes up herself. Ain't a certainty at this point."

Henry had never seen Thorn look so sad. They'd been together for years, longer than most folk in the Wilds had cause to be. They'd crewed together, killed together, fucked together. They'd taken on an army of demons side by side, and faced off against wraiths in the Fade. They'd stormed a hostile city to kill the man in charge, and they had freed slaves in Solantis, starting a revolution that forever changed the city. They'd been through so much together, yet now Henry realised this was the first time she had ever truly seen Thorn sad. She wished she had some sort of comfort to give or fancy words to make it all better. Wasn't really her strength though.

"What's got you on the warpath?" Thorn asked eventually.

"Suzku is leavin'. Fuckin' off with the general when he goes. Some shit 'bout leadin' folk an' you an' me bein' too dishonourable." It wasn't exactly the truth as Pern had said it, but Henry didn't so much care about the truth as having someone to bitch to.

"Ya ain't goin' with him?" Thorn asked.

"No!" Henry snapped, insulted that he would even have to ask.

"Shhh!" Lucille hissed again. Henry sent the woman a glare but decided to keep her voice down all the same. Either for Rose's sake or for Winter's, it didn't really matter. Both were worth a bit of quiet for.

"Wanna hold her?" Thorn asked. "She's quite calmin'."

"Eh?" Henry asked and glanced back towards where Lucille was dancing around with Winter in her arms. "No. I ain't... Don't reckon I should."

"Fair enough." Thorn sipped at his mug. "Ya ain't gonna hurt her. Trust ya enough for that. Even Pug had a go." He thumbed towards where the lad was standing near the entrance. Henry hadn't even seen the lad when she had stormed in. Come to think of it, the boy hadn't left Winter's side since the child was born.

Henry just shook her head and crossed her arms. She did want to hold the child, though not really sure why. Seemed someone like her, someone so stained by blood, shouldn't go too near something so innocent.

"How'd you survive?" Henry asked, deciding to change the subject.

"Saw ya fall over the wall. Seen folk fall like that before. They don't survive."

"Not sure I did." Thorn stabbed a knife into a bit of meat on the nearby table and shoved it into his mouth, chewing. "It's all a bit fuzzy really. Like the mornin' after a real skinful. Remember sinkin' my teeth into D'roan's neck. Throwin' us out over the wall... Reckon we must have hit the water. Can't see it any other way." He shook his head. "Next thing I remember is wakin' up to Anders' voice an' the sounds of battle. Bastard brought me back somehow."

"Anders?" Henry asked. "Anders saved ya life?"

Thorn shook his head. "Told ya. Didn't survive. He brought me back."

Henry had to think about that for a few moments. Eventually, she put her mug down and fingered the hilt of one of her knives. "Folk don't come back like that. Said so yaself enough times."

"Aye," Thorn said with a shrug. "Yet here I am."

"Hmm," Henry stared into Thorn's one eye for a bit longer before letting go of her knife and refilling her mug. They sat in silence for a while, listening to the crackling of the hearth and the gentle sing-song of Lucille's voice as she hummed to Winter. Henry looked back a few times, watching the midwife dance around with the child.

"Ya really reckon I'll be alright ta hold her?" Henry asked eventually.

"Can't think of anyone I'd trust more," Thorn replied quickly. "'Sides, she's gonna have ta get used ta our scarred faces at some point."

Anders

Rose didn't make it back to Chade. She never made it out of Crucible. Two days after she killed the rest of the blooded, Anders wandered into his father's old hall to find Thorn looking as grim as a stormy morning. Winter was crying. For the very first time, the girl was crying.

"Ah," Anders said. He felt as though he was intruding on a tender moment he had no right to see.

Rose was sitting in a chair by the fire. She'd been there for days, but now there was something different about her. Her skin looked thin and whiter than normal, and she slumped in a strange, boneless fashion. She no longer had that indefinable spark of life.

Thorn looked up at Anders. There might have been tears in his eye, but they certainly didn't fall. He was gently rocking Winter back and forth in his right arm, but still, the child let out shrill cries.

Anders gave Rose's corpse a wide berth and tried his very best not to look at it. It wasn't that he disliked corpses in general, just he'd seen enough of them recently to last quite a while. Especially when they were corpses of folk he knew.

"Ya reckon..." Thorn started, letting the question hang.

Anders shook his head. "I'm something of an expert on dying, B.T. Got a few under my belt. Some deaths you just don't come back from. She's gone. Sorry, boss."

Thorn nodded. "Not entirely gone." He looked down at the crying babe swaddled in his arm. "Reckon she left me somethin' behind ta remember her. Eh?" A forced sentiment if ever Anders heard one.

"Indeed," Anders said and forced a smile. "Born in blood and battle. Something tells me that one is going to be quite the terror. Can't you stop her crying?"

Thorn let out a weary sigh. "Tryin'. She ain't stopped since Rose stopped breathin'. Some sort of connection or somethin', I reckon. Bloody Lucille should be around somewhere. I sent Pug lookin' for her."

Anders glanced around the hall for something alcoholic to drink and spied a half-full mug that smelled like wine left out in the air too long. He downed the mug in one, wincing at the bitterness, and washed it down with a swig of brandy from his flask. Some people liked to call booze liquid courage, and Anders was very much one of them. Why, all of his greatest heroics had been done under the influence, though the same could be said about his most cowardly acts. Actually, Anders was fairly certain most of the acts he had perpetrated since the age of ten were under the influence of one alcohol or another.

"Boss, I need to leave," Anders said before he could think himself out of it.

"What's that?" Thorn looked up at him, frowning and wincing as Winter let out a particularly vocal admittance of some discomfort.

"I, uh, I need to go," Anders pointed towards the door.

"Right. Off ya go then." Thorn shook his head.

Anders rolled his eyes and resigned to having to explain himself. "I mean, I need to leave the Wilds... For a while."

"No," Thorn said, staring down into the face of his child. "Can't go, Anders. I need ya here... Or down in Chade. Ya the only other one who knows Rose's plans for the Wilds. Need ya ta help an' read shit for me."

"Other folk can read things to you, boss."

"Other folk might not be trusted. 'Sides Henry ya about the only fucker I do trust these days."

Anders couldn't fight the smile that erupted onto his face. Of course, one look at the corpse in the room wiped that smile right back off.

"I'll be back, boss. Soon. I hope. It's just..."

"Drake?" Thorn asked.

"Quite. Dual loyalties and all that. The Pirate Isles are in a fairly crucial time and... I'm needed. I think."

Thorn let out a sigh and shook his head. "Can't stop ya. Well I could, but I ain't going ta."

"Thanks, boss. I'll be back to help just as soon as I can." Anders started towards the doorway and stopped, turning back. "It's important."

"Eh?"

"Rose's plans for the Wilds. They're important. It's not the sort of thing that will happen overnight - changing the game - but all this was the first step." Anders let slip a bitter laugh. "First step is always the hardest, and... well, bloodiest I suppose. It'll work, boss. We'll make it work."

"I fuckin' hope so," Thorn said, glancing over his shoulder at Anders. "I ain't ever gonna call myself king. Don't reckon the Wilds needs it, nor wants it. Certainly don't reckon they deserve a bastard like me on any sort of throne. This one though," he nodded towards Winter crying in his arms. "She's gonna be queen, and things'll be different. Just gotta hold everything together 'til she's old enough, eh?"

"Quite. Better than all of us. Shall I..." Anders paused for a moment, glancing at Rose, "get someone to remove the body?"

Thorn shook his head. "Nah. Not yet."

Books by Rob J. Hayes

First Earth Saga

<u>The Ties that Bind</u>
The Heresy Within
The Colour of Vengeance
The Price of Faith

<u>Best Laid Plans</u>
Where Loyalties Lie
The Fifth Empire of Man

City of Kings

Other books

<u>It Takes a Thief...</u>
It Takes a Thief to Catch a Sunrise
It Takes a Thief to Start a Fire

Drones

Coming soon

Never Die

www.ingramcontent.com/pod-product-compliance
Lightning Source LLC
Chambersburg PA
CBHW021404110726
47901CB00008B/2056